A VASSAL OF SHADOW

A VASSAL OF SHADOW

TALES *of* ATHEARIA

BOOK 1

J. C. ROBINS

Podium

Cover design by Cover Kitchen

ISBN: 978-1-0394-8598-3

Published in 2025 by Podium Publishing
www.podiumentertainment.com

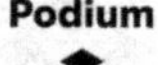

To my family.
Thank you for feeding me.
I might be a broke artist,
but at least I'm not a starving one.

THE ATHEARIAN GODS

Scias - Goddess of Wisdom and Hunting. Sacred animal: the stag.
Essian - God of Prophecy and Sight. Sacred animal: the eagle.
Ashearan - God of Death. Sacred animal: the crow.
Sheara - Goddess of Healing, Fertility, and Childbirth. Sacred animal: the lizard.
Celdric - God of Mischief, Thieves, and Shadows. Sacred animal: the snake.

THE KALTAN GODS

Brazial - God of War. Sacred animal: the wolf.
Lios - God of the Sun and Fire. Sacred animal: the dragon.
Tammearia - Goddess of the Moon and Water. Sacred animal: the horse.
Pasaphae - Goddess of Love. Sacred animal: the black widow spider.
Amari - Goddess of Fate. Sacred animal: the blue-eyed cat.

PROLOGUE

Everyone in Ravenrook had gathered to see the boy born of a miracle and destined for greatness. Enforcers lined the roads, their arms splayed wide as they attempted to create a barrier between the procession and the crowd. After several unsuccessful attempts to push my way to the front, I turned back and scaled up the cracked stone of the local courthouse, grateful that the enforcers were too busy to take notice of a ragged child making his way toward one of the high window ledges.

Craning my neck, I stared out over the sea of heads, trying to spot the carriage among all the dancing performers and armored guards. The procession was the most exciting thing to ever come across this worthless town. My gaze lingered on the large, lacquered boxes intended for the Sacred City—gilded and gleaming. The litter bearers struggled under its weight, their faces pinched and sweating as they marched to the slow beat of drums. My mind conjured up images of all the treasures that could be hidden inside, from mountains of gold coins to goblets filled to the brim with rubies instead of wine.

The people began to cheer as Lord Bastian Hardcastle rode around the corner with his son, Emrys, by his side. They sat atop dapple-gray horses with bridles draped in sapphires. The pair of them were just as embellished as their steeds, adorned in matching cobalt vests stitched with silver and gold flowers. The spectators surged forward, just barely held back by the wall of enforcers as they tossed fans of palm leaves and stalks of lavender onto the cobbled road while they passed. I held my hand up against the sun, squinting to get a better look at the fabled seer with his bone-white hair. The people liked to say that his hair was a sign—one that showed he'd been touched by divinity long before he had ever taken his first breath.

It was no secret that Lord Bastian and his wife had tried for years to conceive, but it was only when the goddess Sheara laid her hands upon Lady Kaliah that their destiny was rewritten, for nine months later the couple had their heir. At his birth, his father foretold that the boy would be the greatest seer of his generation. The first step of the prophecy was fulfilled during the celebration of Emrys's tenth birthday, when he was visited by the god of foresight, who gifted him with power. Not long had passed before Emrys had spoken a grand prophecy of his own. No one knew of what it predicted, though many had spun wild tales about the fate of the world. Whatever it was, it must've been important, because they were traveling to the Sacred City to deliver the prophecy to the gods in person.

From the stories I'd heard, I imagined Emrys to be inhuman. Not only was he a miracle, but he had also been marked by a god and chosen as a vassal. Those blessed with divine blood could heal wounds with a touch of their hands. They could read a hundred books and recite every word. They could whisper corpses back to life and summon fire to their fingertips. Emrys would be graceful, ethereal, dazzling. I half expected him to glitter in the sunlight like a diamond that had fallen from the sky.

I was sorely mistaken.

Emrys was tall for his age, but his frame was thin and willowy. His pale skin and placid gray-blue eyes made him look as though the very life had been leached out of him. He did not resemble the great and magnificent seer that the songs sang of. Truth be told, he appeared rather weak and sickly. He looked like what he actually was—not a hero of yet-untold legends but someone who was never meant to be born.

His gaze frantically searched the crowd, as though he was trying to find someone amid the sea of faces. He must not have found whoever it was he was looking for, because his lips tilted downward in a disappointed frown. Lord Bastian held out a hand to his people, and their cries of adoration transformed into a roar of excitement. He glanced over at his son, who proceeded to give a small wave of his own. That's when I saw it—an emerald ring cast in silver. The stone glinted in the sunlight as if to wink at me in challenge. I stared at it, transfixed and unable to look away.

On impulse, I swung myself off the ledge and trailed after the procession, elbowing my way through the crowd until a set of sturdy gates forced me to stop outside a large manor with a red terra-cotta roof. It belonged to the minor noble family that was hosting House Hardcastle for the night before they continued their pilgrimage to the Sacred City. The garden surrounding the manor was so large that it had a gravel road leading all the way up to the entrance. I cast a nervous glance toward the guards and then back at the estate. Between the disbanding procession and flurry of footmen, I had lost sight of Emrys.

Common sense dictated that I turn around and go home. I had no idea why I was even standing there in the first place, gazing into a world that wasn't mine like a fish in a pond that dreamed of walking into the forest. It was ridiculous . . . and yet when a cart laden with barrels of wine approached the gate, I rolled underneath it, clinging desperately to the underbelly as the guards inspected the authenticity of the trader's documents before granting him entry to the premises.

I hadn't expected it to be so easy, but as soon as I was in I blended into the frantic chaos of servants. I'd realized a long time ago that the world had decided I was not worth their attention, and I used that to my advantage. Scooping up a forgotten basket, I pretended to be one of the dozen errand boys. Not once did anyone question my presence.

When darkness fell, I snuck into one of the unused bedchambers. I suspected that the young lord's door would be guarded, and so I came in through the outside, leaping from balcony to balcony until I got to the one that I was looking for. It was a beautiful room; inside was more wealth than I could hope to accumulate in my entire lifetime. Instead of moth-eaten tablecloths, the drapes on the window were woven from silk and dyed an expensive shade of purple. Not only were the floors polished to perfection, they were also softened with plush rugs. I ran my fingers over the decorative carvings of the bed frame, so different from the bug-infested mattress that I was used to.

A log shifted in the hearth, making me jump, but when I looked around the room, the only thing keeping me company was my own shadow. I began my search for the ring, unsure if it would even be in here, but it seemed that fate was on my side that night, because the ring was resting on the bedside table as though waiting for me to take it. Slipping it into my pocket, I disappeared into the darkness.

I was halfway back to the orphanage before I finally dared a glance over my shoulder. When the only thing I discovered was a drunk man stumbling out of a nearby tavern, a giddiness took over me. Unable to stop myself, I slipped into an alley and held the ring up to the moonlight.

"And what is it you've got there?" The voice startled me, making me fumble and almost drop my prize. I clamped my fingers around it, clutching it protectively to my chest as I tried and failed to locate the person who had spoken. Cautiously, I started to retreat toward the main road.

"Are you going to make me chase you, boy? I would advise against it. It won't do you any good." His tone wasn't threatening, just matter-of-fact, and that made me hesitate for a second. Then my instincts took over and I bolted down the road. This wasn't the first time I'd had to run from pursuers, and since it was night, I had the advantage. It would be easy to disappear, to slip into one of a dozen hiding places and let the darkness take care of the rest. I had almost made it to one of my favorite spots when my foot caught on something, my momentum causing me to scrape the skin off both my forearms as I fell.

"You really should watch your step," the voice taunted. I scrambled back to my feet, my breathing ragged and my heart thundering, but the stranger still hadn't shown himself. I fled again. This time I took a trickier route, taking a turn in the direction of the slums and using my knowledge of the terrain to guide me through the night. I scrambled up the discarded crates that were piled up on the side of the old bakery and collapsed atop the tabletop roof, my lungs begging for air. I allowed myself a brief moment of recovery before crawling toward the edge and peering down the street. Finding it empty of everything except long stretches of shadow, I let out a small sigh of relief.

"You're fast. I'll give you that." I swiveled around to find my pursuer standing directly behind me, basking in the soft light of the moon. He was perhaps the most unremarkable man I had ever laid eyes upon. He had the sort of face that was difficult to remember, in the sense that it was neither particularly beautiful nor particularly ugly. He wasn't particularly tall nor particularly short. There was no cause for my eyes to linger on him longer than a fraction of a second, and yet I dared not look away from him. Not only had this man managed to follow me in near complete darkness, but he also didn't appear to be out of breath. He crouched down next to me, and though I was sure my mind was playing tricks on me, the night seemed to physically sway in his presence.

"What's your name, kid?" he asked, his voice taking on a strange quality, like a soft touch against my skin that coaxed my darkest secrets to the surface. My name almost slipped past my lips, but I caught myself just in time.

"My mother always told me not to talk to strangers," I retorted.

One side of his mouth lifted up in the barest hint of a smile. "If I were a gambling man, which I am, I would guess that your mother is six feet under."

At his words, a familiar flame of indignation sparked inside my chest. "How much you willing to put on that?" I challenged.

He cocked an eyebrow, but after a moment of thought, he produced a small leather pouch and gave it a jingle. "How say you to six silvers and a dozen coppers?"

A smug sense of satisfaction spread through me as I extended my hand. "The joke's on you. She died during the last plague, which means she's ash in the wind, not six feet under."

The man barked out a humorless laugh. "That's fair enough," he said, his eyes shimmering with something akin to approval. He moved to drop the pouch into my palms but then wrenched it back at the last second. "First, your name."

"That wasn't part of the deal," I objected.

"And life isn't fair—what's your point, kid?"

I huffed out a breath of annoyance before answering. "It's Leon."

The man pulled open the drawstrings and removed one of my coins.

"What are you doing?" I demanded.

"Taking a piece of silver every time you lie to me."

"I'm not lying!"

He confiscated another coin, his grin growing as though this were a game. "Let's try this again. What's your name, kid?"

"Fine," I relented. "It's Avery."

Another coin disappeared.

"That wasn't a—" My protest stopped short when his fingers reached in for yet another piece of silver.

The man brandished the coin between his thumb and his forefinger. "You still have three left if you want to give it another try," he said, his tone half teasing and half daring.

Whatever game this was, I didn't want to play it. "Koven. My name is Koven."

He stared at me for a long moment before dropping the coin back into the pouch and handing it over. "Well, *Koven*, it's a pleasure to make your acquaintance. Now, if you would be so kind, will you show me what you stole from the young lord tonight?"

My eyes went wide. He couldn't possibly have known about that. I had been careful—at least, I thought I had. Was he a guard from the manor? Or worse, someone who spied for the church? He certainly had a face that could easily get lost in a crowd. Perhaps he'd been following me the whole day and I had simply paid him no mind. My throat constricted, the sensation choking me, as though my body were already practicing for the noose that would be slipped around my neck.

"The ring, Koven," he said with a hint of impatience.

I probably should've denied it. Instead, what came out of my mouth was a defiant "No."

"Ah, well, if you put it that way," he said with a heavy sigh, "then I guess there really is nothing more I can do. I suppose I'll just be on my merry way." He stood up, brushing at his trousers as though there was dirt on them, and then he casually held the ring up to the moonlight so that he could better inspect it.

Confused, I unfurled my palm only to find that I was now clutching a small stone. The man turned the ring over in his hand, carefully appraising the fine silverwork that whirled around the rectangular emerald.

"Were you planning to sell it?" he asked. I blinked at him, my mind still trying to figure out how he had snatched it from me without my noticing. He repeated the question, though with less curiosity this time, and I got the distinct impression that his attention was a fickle thing—intense one moment and completely devoid of it the next.

"I'm not stupid," I said, somewhat defensively. "Any jeweler that could afford even half its worth would know exactly which family it belonged to. I don't have a death wish."

"Why did you steal it if not for wealth?"

"Because I could," I answered.

He smiled at that. "If you got caught, you could've been whipped, or had your hands cut off, or worse. You could've been hanging from the gallows right this minute. It seems like an awful lot of risk for no payoff."

It was my turn to smile, and my face split into a grin worthy of my triumph. "But I didn't get caught."

The man tutted his tongue. "Oh, Koven, Koven, Koven. That's not entirely true, is it? After all, I caught you." With a flash of his fingers, the ring became a dull-gray coin. Realization dawned on me, and I yanked open the drawstrings of the coin purse to find that only two silver pieces remained.

"Impossible," I muttered under my breath, half wondering if this entire day had just been one long fever dream. Then I blinked and there was only one silver piece left, the lonely-looking coin nestled atop a handful of rusty coppers.

"I assure you, this is most definitely possible." He stepped in closer, his body moving with the quiet repose of a seasoned thief. "I saw what you did today, Koven. You're daring—not fearless, but daring. It's an important distinction. Only fools are fearless. We who are daring understand fear. It's a survival instinct. It keeps us alive. It makes us cautious without dulling our intrepid nature. We know the risks and we take them anyway. We don't let fear cripple us. Instead, we use it as fuel for our fire. There is nothing that we wouldn't dare." Placing a finger under my chin, he tilted my face upward so he could examine me more closely. "I know those eyes," he mused. "Green and murky, like a river that hides the monsters lurking within."

His brown eyes melted away into liquid gold, and I sucked in a sharp breath at the realization of just who it was that stood before me. It all made sense—the way he was able to hide in the darkness as though he were a part of it, watching me from the shadows while he remained completely hidden from mortal eyes. The man who stood before me was not a man at all. It was Celdric, the god of deception and trickery, of shapeshifting and illusions, of travelers and thieves, of shadows and lies.

"You want power," Celdric said, amusement curving at his lips. "I can see the hunger of it inside you . . . You can have it, you know. All you need to do is ask."

He was right. I did want it. Vassals of the gods were heroes woven into legend. They were the upper echelon of society. They were strong, and they were respected, and they were feared. They were everything that I was not. "I want it," I said, and Celdric's smile widened.

"It will be dangerous," he warned me. "Many who walk this path end up dead."

But death was no stranger in Ravenrook. It knocked on the door of every household, claiming the young as well as the old. The idea of dying didn't frighten me so much as the idea of dying unremarked, trapped in a life of such little consequence that fate hadn't seen fit to even give me a family name. I wanted to be a person who mattered. "Still sounds like a bargain," I retorted, and Celdric chuckled.

"Then you will worship me as your patron god, and when you draw your last breath in this mortal realm, the blood in your veins will be mine to claim." Celdric placed a thumb to his canine, splitting open the skin. Golden ichor welled up, and I stood frozen as he smeared his divine blood across my lips. My tongue snaked out to taste it. It didn't taste of salt and iron. It tasted of the night, seedy with sin and sweet with secrets. It hummed on my tongue with the promise of power as I licked my lips clean.

Without another word, Celdric turned to leave. "My ring?" I called after him, and then immediately regretted it. Celdric was a *god*. Who was I to demand anything from him? I prepared myself for the wrath that would surely follow, but he only flashed me an impish grin. He reached into the pocket where he had slipped it.

"Sorry," he said. "Sometimes I just can't help myself." He studied the ring one last time and then tossed it high into the air. I caught it reflexively. When I looked up again, Celdric was gone.

It was the early hours of the morning by the time I crept back into the orphanage, half dazed as I tiptoed around the creaking panels so as not to wake the matron. As quietly as I could, I crawled atop my straw-stuffed mattress and pulled the musty blankets all the way up to my chin. I cradled the ring against me, certain that I couldn't possibly fall asleep after such an eventful night, but then a fever began to spread through my body, burning through my blood until it felt as though my very soul was on fire. Tossing and turning, I was dragged into unconsciousness.

My eyes opened into a world of utter darkness, but it didn't alarm me nearly as much as it should have. Here the darkness felt like it belonged to me and me alone. As I wandered deeper into it, doors started to appear around me. They were different shapes and colors, some engraved with strange symbols, while others glittered with gemstones. They whispered to me, urging me to open them and see the treasure that was hidden within.

My attention was drawn to a large golden door that shined brighter than all the others. The frame was carved like long, twisted snakes. Its voice was the most alluring, radiating with the promise of power. I reached out for it, but then my eyes snagged on a black door just a few feet away. It was so dark that it was barely noticeable against the background. It didn't whisper to me like the rest. It was completely silent, and that silence pulled me in. I walked toward it and took hold of the handle. As soon as I touched it, all the other voices went dead quiet. I cracked the door open and wisps of shadow crept out.

The darkness was slow at first as it climbed up my limbs, but it quickly turned violent as it tried to envelop me. My mouth opened in a scream, but one of the shadows clawed down my throat like smoke before I could make a sound, heavy and suffocating. Just when I thought I was going to die, my lungs expanded and I breathed it in. The darkness surged through me and a smile spread across my face as power seeped into my blood.

The gods were known to favor royal and noble lineages, bloodlines that had suckled on golden blood for generations, their positions in society already deeming them worthy of divine power until such time as their strength failed and they fell from grace in the eyes of their patrons. However, the gods marked others as well. We were all their children, and we all had the chance to prove ourselves in their eyes, especially Celdric, who was known to mark vassals while he was frequenting taverns and gambling dens. Yet the possibility of being chosen as a nameless child in an entire kingdom full of nameless children was like being a single drop of water plucked from the ocean. It was hardly surprising that the matron didn't believe my story of Celdric marking me with his blood, but she was required by law to summon an enforcer to substantiate my claim, her irritated expression promising a world of punishment if this turned out to be nothing more than a waste of her time.

The enforcer arrived at the orphanage a few days later, her face hidden behind a gilded mask as she ordered me to hold out my hand. She proceeded to press a Rasalan coin into my palm, and while the metal was harmless to mortals, it burned those with divine blood. I bit down on my lip, swallowing the scream that rose up in my throat as the metal seared into my skin like hot iron and my power was leached from my veins. When she finally removed the coin, my hand was left raw and blistered. Satisfied that I had passed the test, she gave a nod to the stunned matron and then took me away. I left with nothing but the threadbare clothes on my back and the emerald ring hidden in my pocket.

I had never ventured outside of Ravenrook before, and my stomach twisted with a mixture of excitement and apprehension as the enforcer guided me into a carriage. The journey to the Cenobium passed in long hours of silence. However, the meals at the inns were some of the best I'd ever had in my life, with grilled meat and an assortment of steamed vegetables instead of the bland gruel I was used to eating twice a day. I was provided with multiple sets of clothes that actually fit me as well as warm baths in the evenings. It was a life of absolute luxury. At least, I thought it was, until the Cenobium came into view from the window of the carriage.

I'd heard stories about far-off places that were too marvelous to put into words, but never before had I experienced such a sight myself. The towers of the school seemed to pierce through the sky, their spires decorated with stained glass windows and polished rosewood frames. The carriage came to a stop outside the golden gates, which bore the crests of the five Athearian gods. The stag of Scias, the goddess of wisdom. The eagle of Essian, the god of foresight. The lizard of Sheara, the goddess of healing. The crow of Ashearan, the god of death. And the snake of Celdric, the god of mischief.

"Wait inside," the enforcer instructed as she clambered out of the carriage to speak to the guards at the gate. However, patience had never been my strong suit and I was eager to stretch my legs after the long journey. I quietly snuck out the carriage. Unfortunately, the moss-covered walls prevented me from seeing anything that lay beyond.

"You're finally here!" someone exclaimed. My head twisted in the direction of a tree that was partially hanging over the garden wall. Although I had only ever seen him once before, his bone-white hair made him impossible to forget. Emrys of House Hardcastle was perched atop one of the branches like a bird about to take flight. He jumped down, his black-and-gold cassock fluttering in the wind as he sailed through the air. I expected his feeble legs to crack on impact, but he landed smoothly, as though he was well practiced in the art of escaping.

He smiled as he stuck out his hand for me to shake. "I'm Emrys."

I hesitated before finally gliding my hand into his. "Koven."

"I had a feeling that you'd like the ring," he said, sounding immensely pleased with himself. "It brings out the color in your eyes."

My heart stammered at the accusation. I was all too aware of the punishments that could be doled out for stealing from someone like him. It was a conscious effort to keep the panic from showing on my face and instead morph my expression into one of feigned confusion. "I have no idea what you're talking about."

It was obvious he didn't believe my lie, but rather than responding with anger or outrage, his smile only widened. "Don't worry, I won't report you. The ring is yours to keep. Consider it a gift." He made it sound like we were friends—like we had been friends for a long, long time. "I'm so excited to finally meet you. When I was in Ravenrook, I tried to look for you in the crowd, but there were so many people there that it was impossible to find you."

My confusion became genuine as his words slowly sank in. He'd known that I was there in Ravenrook, that I would be watching him as he rode through the streets of my hometown, and when I arrived at the Cenobium, he'd been waiting to greet me . . . as though he'd been expecting me . . . as though he possessed the ability to peer into the future and know exactly what was going to happen. My mouth fell open at the realization that he had set me up. "You wanted me to steal that ring!"

His eyes glittered as he stared back at me, a treasure trove of secrets hidden in their depths, and I got the feeling that this was not the first time we were having this conversation.

"Welcome to the Cenobium, Koven."

CHAPTER 1

Dusk was my favorite time of day. It was a beautiful thing to watch the sun slip from its perch in the sky, forced to yield to the darkness as the moon and stars rose up to take its place. Night would soon descend upon the world, and its approach was like a whisper in my ear, sending a pleasant shiver down my spine with its promise of power. Dressed in a fresh set of academic robes and armed with more than a dozen daggers, I stood in front of the bell tower along with the rest of my cohort from the House of Shadows. Master Moore surveyed his students with cold, calculating eyes. It was difficult to guess what he was thinking, because his mouth was always downturned in a sneer, as though permanently displeased with everyone and everything.

Celdric was the god of many things: thieves, secrets, mischief, shadows. All useful attributes for spies and assassins. Master Moore had spent the last seven years preparing many of us to take on such roles after graduation. Unlike the other gods, Celdric had a disproportionally high number of vassals from the basest parts of society, vagrants and scoundrels who were forced to lie and steal in order to scrape a living, but such skills could be honed and harnessed for the good of the kingdom. As a vassal of Celdric, I could choose to serve one of the great noble houses, or if the Cenobium gave me a high enough recommendation, I could even join the king's shadow court. There were also other, less appealing options available. Those marked by Celdric were favored among houses of inquiry, which was gruesome work but at least it paid well, and then there was the Sacred City, which was always in need of more informants to send north to Kalta. It had been nearly three centuries since the last Holy War, and Brazial had long since grown bored in this era of peace. If he decided to start another one, the Athearian gods wanted to be prepared, and students from the House of Shadows were well trained when it came to slipping into places unseen.

While there were many different paths my future could take, there was only one future that I wanted. My fingers curled around the emerald ring that hung on a chain around my neck. The familiar weight of it served to comfort me as Master Moore began to pace the stone dais. His steps were careful, measured, and impossibly quiet, as though he were nothing more than an apparition. He might actually have been one. His talents lay with illusions. He could create a dozen perfect replicas of himself and conjure beasts of fiction with fierce claws and a growl that made the ground quake, but it was merely a trick of the senses.

"I have a riddle for you," he said slowly, his voice a low drawl. "What is the minimum number of grains needed to make a pile of sand?" He paused, allowing his students to ponder on it for a moment. "Split yourself into pairs and find me an answer. You have until dawn."

The spymaster flickered out of existence. It seemed he had been an illusion after all. The assignment sounded simple enough, just a straightforward information-gathering exercise. I had completed hundreds of them during my time at the Cenobium. A flash of blond curls moving through the crowd caught my attention. I quickly made my way toward Rita, and from the wry smile she gave me when we finally found each other, it seemed she'd had the same idea that I did. She was also a former Ravenrook resident, and she liked to show it. Her ears were decorated with metal studs, her upper lip had been split open from a recent fight, and beneath the sleeve of her cassock, her left arm was inked with tattoos.

"Would you like to partner up for the assignment?" I asked her, but before she managed to get a word out, my roommate slung an arm over my shoulder.

"I'm a little offended that you didn't ask me first," Faelan said. He shifted his amber eyes to Rita, his voice turning as sweet as treacle as he said, "You don't mind if I steal him from you, do you, Rita?"

He proceeded to use the sharpest weapon in his arsenal, which never failed to miss its target: He flashed her a disarming smile. Whereas Celdric used his power to look ordinary and forgettable, Faelan was the complete opposite. He had skin like river clay, brown and smooth, with eyes framed by thick lashes and hair that fell around his face in tightly coiled copper curls. However, Rita was not one of the swooning ladies of his cousin's court. She had been born and raised in the Dregs, the most derelict district in Ravenrook, which meant she was never one to pass up an opportunity to strike a bargain.

She folded her arms across her chest. "And what if I did mind?"

"Then I'll owe you one," Faelan countered.

Her expression turned pensive as she contemplated the offer. A favor from a prince was no small boon, and a favor from Faelan in particular was probably too tempting an offer for any girl to resist.

"Do I not get a say in this?" I asked.

"Evidently not," Faelan said. He focused his gaze back on Rita, his voice oozing with charm as he said, "For what it's worth, I pay back my favors with *exorbitant* interest."

Her azure eyes brightened. "I do like the sound of that . . . Very well, I'll find myself someone else to partner up with."

"You're the best," he replied before dragging me away. "So, where shall we start? The library, perhaps? Maybe a philosopher of old has divined the answer in one of those dusty scrolls."

"I don't think that's the purpose of this assignment," I told him, earning me a curious look. "Research is a task better suited to vassals of Scias. This can't just be about finding the answer. It has to be about *stealing* it."

He gave a slow nod of understanding. "You think Master Moore has hidden the answer somewhere?"

"I do."

Faelan spun around in a slow circle, and I didn't need to be a seer to divine what he was thinking. The Cenobium was massive. The gardens alone stretched farther than the eye could see, encompassing everything from the mausoleum on the southern boundary all the way to the forest that claimed everything north of the combat fields. The buildings were numerous, including the academic towers, the chapel, the armory, and the five boarding houses. It was too much to investigate in a single night. However, knowing Master Moore, there would be hints scattered throughout the campus that would help narrow down the search.

As night finally claimed the sky, flaming torches flickered to life across the Cenobium, illuminating it with hundreds of small glowing lights, as though the gods had pulled all the stars down from Celestrial. The darkness was like a caress against my skin, a lover's touch reminding me that it was just a whisper away, but this assignment was one of stealth, not strength, so I left the power of the night untouched while Faelan and I headed to the academic towers. That seemed the most obvious place to begin our search. He started with the divine history wing, while I headed for the theology lecture halls. Firelight flickered across the old stone walls, and my eyes strained against it, yearning for complete darkness. At my command, my shadow extended out from me to snuff the flames as I walked past. My eyes took a few seconds to adjust. Then the world around me snapped back into focus with such clarity that I could make out the individual brushstrokes on one of the portraits of Scias, a set of antlers curling out from her head with eyes of shining gold and a stern expression that gave her the appearance of a disappointed parent.

The portrait must've been commissioned more than three decades ago, because now her hair would be turning silver and the skin around her eyes would be starting to wrinkle. I had never seen a portrait of the gods after they had aged. Any painter that dared to capture that mortal flaw would probably have both their hands cut clean off so they could never repeat such a sin. When the gods took a new host—someone young and beautiful and powerful—that was how they wished to be portrayed until time caused their human vessel to wither and they were forced to wear the skin of another.

Portraits of the other Athearian deities were also readily available to be admired. Even though I walked past Celdric's likeness every single day, I always struggled to remember what he actually looked like, his bland features slipping from my mind like water rolling off a roof. Then there were the twin gods, who more often than not appeared in the same painting. They formed a startling contrast of colors. Ashearan preferred black robes, a pair of artificial wings protruding from his shoulder blades. His sister, on the other hand, was everything he was not. Sheara was the light to his dark. The compassion to his cruelty. The life to his death. She wore a bright-orange dress, flowers sprouting beneath her feet, whereas the ground withered a few inches away where her brother stood.

I paused briefly in front of the visage of Essian, who had favored House Hardcastle for many generations, his gift of foresight allowing them to become one of the wealthiest families in the country, second only to the king. Although he was depicted as a man in the prime of his youth, no more than twenty years of age, there were dark crescents beneath his eyes. His skin possessed a sallow complexion, his expression both distant and haunted, as though he were trapped inside a nightmare. Even the eagle that sat atop his shoulder had a sorrowful air about it, like it no longer had the strength to conquer the sky. It was a morose illustration of the god. And what was even more unsettling was how much it reminded me of Emrys every time I looked at it. With each passing year, the enthusiasm that had consumed him as a child had gradually faded into a constant state of exhaustion.

I peeled my gaze away from the portraits, forcing myself to focus on the task at hand. I pushed open the door to the lecture hall. After a cursory glance, I wasn't hopeful that I would find anything advantageous inside. I wandered through the room anyway, because sometimes appearances were deceiving. Sometimes what you were looking for was hidden in plain sight.

This was not one of those times. Stepping back out into the corridor, I was about to search the neighboring room when a flicker of movement caught my eye. Creeping down the passageway, I turned my head around the corner to find Master Moore slinking toward the divination tower.

I called upon the shadows to cloak me, allowing me to blend into the darkness, completely unseen, as I followed the spymaster through the twisting set of passageways. He proceeded to split himself in two, one version of him heading up the spiral staircase of the divination tower, while the other turned left, in the direction of the courtyard. It was impossible for me to tell which was real and which was the illusion. However, Master Moore held open contempt for students from the House of Sight. He considered seers to be notoriously unreliable sources of information, their visions often too confusing or vague to make sense of events until after they had come to pass. After a heartbeat of indecision, I turned left into the courtyard.

I continued to follow him past the trickling fountain, where he split himself into three this time, each one splintering off in a different direction. I thought perhaps I had given myself away until I realized that I was no longer the only vassal watching him. The sound of flapping wings overhead drew my attention to the sky. While a bird might not have been suspicious in and of itself, the fact that it circled overhead like a vulture in search of a carcass gave the student away. Such a ruse might work outside the Cenobium, but Master Moore knew all our tricks. After all, he was the one who'd taught them to us.

I hurried after one of the replicas, only for him to flicker out of existence. Muttering a curse, I raced back into the courtyard in an attempt to find him again, but he was no longer there. Frustration was the enemy of patience, so I tried to push the emotion aside as I leaned against one of the pillars, contemplating my next move. Perhaps this was why Master Moore had tasked us with working in pairs—trying to tail someone like him was an impossible feat to manage alone. This could be one of his rare lessons in teamwork—a lesson that no one in the House of Shadows enjoyed. I pushed myself off the pillar, intent on finding Faelan, only to have him drop down from the roof, landing in a crouch as soundlessly as a cat.

"I saw Master Moore putting something into a drawer," he informed me, but I didn't allow myself to get my hopes up just yet. The spymaster was not a careless man. He was more slippery than a snake, with his tricks extending far beyond his ability to cast illusions and warp reality.

"I've seen several different Master Moores around campus. Are you sure that was actually him?" I asked.

Faelan shrugged. "There's only one way to find out for certain."

It was the best lead we had at the moment. Faelan led me back into the main building, my brow furrowing as he started up the spiral staircase of the divination tower. Had I been wrong when I chose to follow the spymaster out into the courtyard? One could never be too certain when it came to him. It wouldn't surprise me if he'd deliberately taken the path that would throw trailing shadows off his scent.

The top of the staircase opened up into the divination room, which was where the seers spent most hours of their day. An assortment of cushions spanned out over intricately woven rugs, the faint scent of incense still tainting the air. The floor was a chaos of divination cards and bronze ritual bowls. Various star charts plastered the walls. Faelan ushered me over to a set of storage drawers that were tucked into the corner of the room, which must've been used to store the more potent incense, because each one possessed a shiny set of metal locks.

"Master Moore placed something in this drawer," Faelan said, pointing to one in the middle. "You know that lockpicking has never been my forte, but do you think you can get into it?"

I arched my eyebrows at him as I produced a set of lockpicks from my pocket. "Don't insult me," I said, inserting the picks. Faelan gave me an encouraging pat on the back.

"You should be careful. You know what Master Moore is like. If there was ever going to be a twist, it would be here and now."

He wasn't wrong. The divination tower could be a ruse to throw us off track, or it could be a trap. Back when I was still a third year, one student had dared to rummage through Master Moore's writing desk in search of his book of secrets and ended up getting bitten by a viper that was hidden inside. The student didn't make it to the remedial house in time.

Slowly and with great caution, I shifted the picks until I heard a soft click. I let my shadow reach out to open the drawer in my stead just in case there was a nasty surprise waiting for me. When no snake slithered out, I peered inside. A folded piece of paper lay atop an assortment of glass vials. I hesitated. This whole process had gone too smoothly, and dawn was still many hours away. Deception and scheming were an inherent part of Master Moore's lessons. It couldn't be this easy. Yet there was no sign of a trap.

Steeling my nerves, I reached for the paper and unfolded it. Long cursive letters were sprawled across the page.

If the prince gets your ring before you get this piece of paper, then you've failed.

My heart sank like a stone in my chest, my hand darting for my necklace, only to discover that it was missing. A sudden cold gust of wind rippled my hair, and my gaze snapped to Faelan. He was balanced on the window ledge, the shutters having been flung wide-open. My chain dangled from his fingers, the emerald ring glowing softly in the moonlight.

The test had never been to find the answer to the riddle. Faelan's test had been to steal my ring, and my test had been to see through his deception to his true objective. When had he managed to take the necklace from me? I knew Faelan had light fingers—the man could lift jewelry from a mark as easily as a priest could absolve sins—but I was also a vassal of Celdric, not so easily fooled by common tricks. However, as the last few moments played out in my mind, I realized my mistake. Faelan had patted my back while I was preoccupied with the lock. That was when he stole it from me and I'd been too distracted to notice.

Faelan flashed me a playful smile and winked. "You can't say I didn't warn you."

I lurched forward, but it was too late. He leaped out the window, the long folds of his cassock wrapping around him, distorting his appearance as he somersaulted through the air. Then he extended his feathered wings, my necklace clutched in his talons as he flew far out of my reach. I slammed my hand against the window in frustration. I had a gift for hearing when a lie rolled off someone's tongue, but Faelan knew how to play the game of half-truths and misdirection better than anyone. He was right; I couldn't say that he hadn't warned me. I had no one but myself to blame.

I dragged myself back to the bell tower as it struck six o'clock, exhaustion seeping into my bones as the first light of dawn broke through the trees. Rita was standing off to the side with her arms folded across her chest. From the murderous glint in her eyes, I suspected that her night hadn't gone any better than mine.

Master Moore materialized in front of the bell tower, his raven-black hair slicked back as he scrutinized his students with an intensity that made it difficult not to squirm beneath his gaze. "Trust," he said, his voice low and unhurried, "is just as lethal as poison. Everyone has their own secrets, their own motivations and goals. You should always be on your guard. A friend could be an enemy and an enemy could be a friend . . . you'll never know who is who if you willfully close your eyes. Remember this lesson. One day, it might very well save your life."

My eyes flicked toward Faelan, who twirled my necklace carelessly around one of his fingers.

"Dawn has now fallen upon us," Master Moore continued. "Go conduct your morning prayers and get some rest. This afternoon there will be combat classes held for all the seventh years in preparation for your trials. I would recommend that you pay particular attention to Master Snyder's lesson today. The final exams are brutal. They are designed to separate the worthy from the unworthy. The weak will fall, but the strong will survive. Heed your training and trust your instincts, and perhaps you will emerge intact on the other side." He regarded his class with cold indifference as he said, "May the gods have mercy on your souls."

They wouldn't, and from the somber expressions of those around me, I wasn't the only one who knew it. In less than two weeks, half of us would likely be dead.

CHAPTER 2

Despite the long hours of the night, Faelan had a spring to his step as he made his way toward me. Rita smoothed out the kinks in her strawberry blond hair. Then she scowled at herself for the self-conscious gesture and deliberately messed it up again. "I need a drink," she muttered under her breath before stalking off in the direction of the chapel, no doubt intending to raid the reverend's wine collection. Even after all these years at the Cenobium, she remained a Ravenrook resident down to her blade-dented bones.

Faelan was wise enough to return my ring without protest. Once I slipped the chain back over my neck, the emerald ring safely hidden beneath the collar of my cassock, my resentment over the assignment dissipated but didn't disappear entirely. "I promise I had every intention of returning it," Faelan said, placing a hand over his heart in a dramatic display of sincerity. "No hard feelings?"

Break his fingers, whispered the voice at the back of my mind. *See if he ever steals from you again after that.*

I pretended not to hear it.

"No hard feelings," I replied, conjuring a smile onto my face. "Like you said, I can't say you didn't warn me."

Faelan swung an arm over my shoulders. "I don't know about you, but I'm more than ready for bed." He flashed me a playful smile as he said, "Victory sure is exhausting work."

The House of Shadows stood black and gleaming against the rising sun, the building carved from blocks of obsidian. The pillars along its terrace were shaped to resemble snakes with dark scales and topaz eyes; their necks were arched and their fangs bared as though they were about to strike. It wasn't as dramatic as the House of Death, which was constructed almost entirely of bone, but it still made an impression.

The House of Shadows had become somewhat of a trophy room for the god of thieves. The building was filled with priceless paintings and tapestries. An assortment of crystal chandeliers hung from the ceiling. The walls were lined with shelves upon shelves of golden chalices and porcelain vases. There were some objects that I didn't even know the function of, but they sparkled in the light, which was probably what had caught Celdric's attention when he decided to take them. While my fingers itched to pocket some of the smaller trinkets, I knew better than to steal from Celdric. He was an unpredictable god; he would either pat me on my back for my bravery or flail me alive for my impudence, and I wasn't eager to find out which one it would be.

The prayer room consisted of several shrines. Each one was already occupied with a student who knelt before the altar, their heads bowed and their lips moving with silent words of worship. Although it was still the early hours of the morning, offerings of gold and jewels were piled high on the stone slabs. They always were this close to the end of the academic year. I watched as one student took a stick of charcoal and wrote a secret down on a narrow slip of parchment, which she proceeded to burn in the candle flame. As she rose back to her feet, I moved to take her place before the altar.

Carefully, I cleared my mind of thought before bowing my head in prayer. Asking anything from the god of mischief seemed like an awfully dangerous game to play. However, forgoing the ritual completely was just as perilous as taking part in it; the gods did not enjoy being ignored. As I had no wealth to offer Celdric, nor any tantalizing secrets to share, I held my hand over a bronze bowl, a golden snake coiled around its rim. With one of my daggers, I traced the familiar scar along my palm and allowed my blood to drip into the dish.

Celdric, I offer you my blood, blessed as it is with the power you gifted me. I ask for nothing in return. My prayer was careful and rehearsed, sating his need for worship without inviting unwanted attention to myself. The gods were not in the habit of granting wishes. A favor given demanded a favor in return, and the gods had long memories. It was safer to ask for nothing, to hide my prayers beneath all the others that demanded riches, or protection, or the heads of their enemies. Besides, I was of the opinion that if I wanted anything, Celdric would expect me to be crafty enough to get it myself.

Clenching my hand into a fist, I returned the dagger to its sheath. Drops of my blood slipped between my fingers to drip onto the floor as I exited the prayer room, exhaustion robbing me of the concentration needed to keep my steps silent. The sleeping quarters were located at the end of a long corridor, which was lined with suits of armor, their metal polished to a shine and their swords crested with precious stones. Celdric had been stealing ceremonial armor and weaponry from the Kaltan rulers for centuries. There were even pieces that had been taken prior to the Rift, before Tammearia commanded the ocean to rise up and split the continent in two.

Faelan shoved open the door to our room. In three long strides, he collapsed atop his bed, not even bothering to unlace his boots as he sprawled across the silk pillows. He attempted to close his eyes but quickly pouted when the morning light fell over his face. "Koven, could you—" His voice was cut short when I pulled the drapes across the windows, plunging the room into darkness. "You're the best."

It was a white lie he told so often to so many people that it was nearly imperceptible to my ears. The traces of deceit woven into his words were subtle, but they were there. However, the sound wasn't unpleasant, like it would be if the lie held malice or ill intent. This one was harmless, tinted at the edges with warmth. "I mean it," Faelan continued, his voice already dreary with sleep. "You're the best roommate I've ever had."

At least that much was true.

"That's because I'm the only one who hasn't tried to sleep with you," I muttered.

A good-humored grin spread across his face. "That's a good point. Upon further contemplation, I would like to amend my statement. You're officially the worst roommate I've ever had."

I rolled my eyes at him. It was probably fortunate that Faelan hadn't been born into the direct line of the crown. Scias took the divine right to rule quite seriously and had developed a penchant for killing off the heirs she didn't like. Faelan's sense of humor might very well have earned him a death sentence in her eyes.

Pulling off my cassock, I folded it and placed it inside the cupboard. The day was too warm to crawl beneath the blankets, so I lay on top of them. It wasn't long before Faelan started to snore softly from across the room, his ability to fall asleep on command an enviable thing, while my mind decided to torture me with thoughts of the upcoming trials. The gods did not share their blood with the weak. Those that survived the final exams would be considered worthy of the power in their veins and graduate from the Cenobium. However, those that failed would meet their death, either at the hands of other students or at the hands of our patron gods if they deemed our performance unsatisfactory.

The trials were notoriously brutal. Even the king had lost both of his older siblings to the exams. But for those who passed, who proved themselves in the eyes of the gods, graduating from the Cenobium was the golden key to unlocking a life of power and influence. For vassals already born to wealth and title, it allowed them to continue their family's legacy. For vassals born to nothing, it allowed them access to some of the highest positions in service of the army, or the church, or some of the greatest noble houses in the kingdom.

With graduation less than two weeks away, I couldn't help but feel an equal mixture of anticipation and apprehension. I'd heard many different stories about the final exams. Stories about how vassals of Ashearan would snap their fingers and half a dozen students would drop dead, their veins dark with poison and their skin withering to an ashen shade of gray. Stories about the rancid scent of burning flesh as those marked by Lios set their opponents on fire. Stories about how the gods would watch their vassals tear each other apart and laugh as though it was the most amusing thing in the world.

In my weaker moments, I sometimes tried to envision what my life would be like if Emrys had chosen not to wear the emerald ring that day, but my imagination never managed to get far. A life without power was no life at all. Ever since Celdric marked me with his blood, I could feel the unmistakable thrum of his divinity coursing through my veins, filling all the hollow parts of my once-empty existence. Power always came with a price, but at least in this it was worth it. There was no fate so terrible as that of obscurity, and though a vassal's life might be short, possessing the power of a god was far from insignificant.

The grass that carpeted the combat fields was a lush, vibrant green, having been watered for generations with the blood and sweat of those blessed by the gods. Akira of House Marcaida was already there when I arrived, her long black hair tied back in a neat braid and her combat uniform free of any wrinkles. The stag of Scias was stitched into the back of her tunic, a majestic set of horns curling from its head. Although she was more than a head shorter than me, she was just as terrifying as the rest of her bloodline, with a jagged scar that tore across her throat and sharp eyes that could slice a person in half with a single look. She was destined to be the future queen of Athearia, so long as she survived graduation. I didn't doubt that she would. The girl was just as lethal as she was clever.

Her gaze slowly shifted toward me. The intensity of it never failed to unnerve me, and when her eyes issued a silent order summoning me to her side, I quickly obeyed. "Have you spoken to Emrys yet?" she said, and though her face remained a smooth mask of calm, her voice carried a slight note of impatience. "The trials are just around the corner and he still hasn't told me anything about them."

"What makes you think I would know any more than you would?" I replied, careful to keep my tone neutral.

"Because he tells you everything."

That wasn't entirely true. Admittedly, he did tell me a little more than he told most others, but that was only because he was preparing me to join his shadow court after graduation. And even then, he still hoarded his secrets like a dragon hoarded its gold.

When I informed Akira that he had not, in fact, told me anything, she pressed her lips into a thin line. She didn't like not knowing things. Information was just as vital to survival as strategic alliances. It was another advantage afforded to those of noble houses, who had their allegiances forged long before they ever set foot inside the Cenobium. House Hardcastle and House Marcaida had protected each other since the institution's creation, and that friendship persisted to this day, with Emrys offering Akira insights from his visions and her granting him the protection that came with an alliance to a warrior bloodline. My friendship with Emrys had naturally meant a friendship with Akira by association—a fact that she was not at all pleased with in the beginning, but I liked to think my presence had grown on her over the seven years we'd spent together at the Cenobium.

"To be forewarned is to be forearmed." Akira looked as though she was about to say more, but she hesitated as she surveyed the growing number of students gathering on the field. She lowered her voice to a whisper when she said, "The trials are fast approaching. If there are preparations we need to make beforehand, we don't have much time left. You should remind him of that. He listens to you."

The only counsel Emrys kept was his own, but I gave a small nod to placate her right before the combat instructor hobbled onto the field. All the students fell into a respectful silence upon his arrival. Master Snyder was an ancient man with a silver beard that traveled halfway down his chest. He carried a walking cane flecked with old crimson stains that he had yet to clean. He gave a wave of his hand, and at his signal, the healers surged forward, their saffron dresses swaying around them as they began to dole out sticky balls of candle wax to the class.

Master Snyder handed his walking stick to a healer, who held it dutifully as he used his hands to sign. *Place the wax in your ears.*

I did as he ordered, shifting uncomfortably as the world went silent around me, cutting me off from the one sense that I relied on the most to warn me of incoming danger.

Why do you think we teach you the hunting language of Scias? the combat instructor asked.

The silent dialect was incredibly convenient for communication between vassals of Celdric during an infiltration exercise, but the House of Shadows was not the only one required to learn it. The entire school was. Someone must have attempted to answer Master Snyder's question, because he gave a slow nod.

Yes, the ability is useful in a variety of combat and stealth scenarios, he signed. *But I'm not looking for the obvious answer . . . Who do you believe to be the most formidable vassal to face in battle? Is it those marked by the god of war, one man possessing the strength of ten? Or is it those favored by Lios, who can conjure flames to their fingertips?*

Neither, Akira signed in response. *Vassals of Brazial and Lios are strong, but they are predictable. In the last Holy War, it was a vixen who nearly crippled our military when she persuaded one of the commanders to slaughter the entire war council. Athearia lost most of its leadership in a single night.*

Correct, Master Snyder signed. *There is no power more insidious than that of a charm-speaker. While I cannot divulge the nature of the trials, I can inform you that this year's exams have been set by Ashearan and Pasaphae and will be located on the island of Spire. Surviving death is as simple as outrunning it, but resisting the lure of a vixen is another challenge altogether.*

That was the reason for the wax; a vixen's power resided in her voice. If one couldn't hear her speak, then she was essentially rendered powerless. However, trying to survive the rest of the trials without being able to rely on sound would not be an easy feat.

I tried to locate the wisps of white hair that made Emrys stand out in a crowd. He was too tall to hide himself completely, and I eventually found him lingering in the back. The shadows beneath his eyes were dark enough to resemble bruises, his cheekbones sharp against his sunken features. He didn't seem surprised by the information. As though he could feel me staring at him, his gray-blue eyes met mine over the sea of students. *After the lesson*, he signed, already guessing my desire to speak with him. After a moment of hesitation, he added, *Watch your back.*

Instinctively, I glanced over my shoulder. The only person behind me was Rita, who wore the irritable expression of someone who drank too much and slept too little. She arched a questioning eyebrow at me. I quickly turned my attention back to Master Snyder, but I must've missed some part of his lecture, because he was looking directly at me, his gaze narrowed with obvious disapproval.

As you will be deprived of one of your senses, he continued to sign, *it's of utmost importance that you maintain your focus at all times. Even the slightest slip in concentration can result in death . . . . Wickwire will give us a demonstration.*

The Cenobium had required me to give a family name upon my enrollment. As I didn't have one, I'd scrambled for something to say and blurted out the first one that popped into my mind, which just so happened to be the name of the local madman who had lived on the street corner outside my orphanage. It seemed as good a name as any at the time. In hindsight, I might've picked something a bit more regal, but it wouldn't have helped me much. Everyone could see that I lacked nobility just by looking at me. I didn't walk like them, or talk like them, or eat like them. Not back then, anyway. I had since learned to mimic their mannerisms—blending in was a vital skill for a student from the House of Shadows—but a part of me would always be that orphaned boy from Ravenrook, the one who had so little he even had to steal someone else's name. But it was good to have a reminder of what this was all for. While those born of noble houses had everything to lose, people like me had everything to gain.

I stepped forward to take my place in one of the circular fighting pits, the ground beneath my feet softening with sand. Master Snyder's gaze scanned over the crowd to select my opponent. *Honora will be the challenger,* he declared, and it was all I could do not to sigh as Faelan took the place opposite me.

Best two out of three? he signed, his lips curving into a roguish grin. It wouldn't matter how many bouts we did. While the sun still brightened the sky, I would lose every single time. Faelan was the top student in the House of Shadows for a reason.

Master Snyder lifted his walking cane and slammed it against the ground, signaling the start of the battle. I didn't hesitate. With my mind, I reached out toward Faelan's shadow, commanding it to rise up and wrap around him like chains. He must've anticipated my opening move, because he leaped off the ground, his arms extending into wings as he took on the shape of a falcon. With a frantic beat of his wings, he soared up into the air and then came spiraling back down with a cry, his feathers morphing into fur and his beak splitting open into a fierce snarl as he shifted into a wolf. I rolled out of the way as his claws slashed into the ground, sending a spray of sand into the air upon impact.

I flung a dagger at him, but it bounced harmlessly off his pelt. His bulky frame and gold-tinged fur were a far cry from the common mountain wolves of Athearia. Faelan had taken on the form of a wolf of war, one of Brazial's creations, which possessed an almost impenetrable skin. The only thing known to cut through it was Rasalan steel—of which I had none. Once again, I summoned the shadows to bind him, tendrils of darkness wrapping around him. He let out a feral snarl, froth dripping from his jaws in a very unprincely manner. As the thick cords of muscle lining his legs struggled against the restraints, I willed the shadows to tighten their grasp on him. He decided to switch tactics. Instead of fighting the restraints, he shrank himself down, his fur giving way to sleek, black scales. He slithered out from the shadows, easily slipping through its grasp.

I threw several more daggers in quick succession. He nimbly darted around each one, then reared his head back in a strike. My shadows rushed up to form a shield. Faelan's scales shimmered as they changed to mimic the shade of a desert snake, allowing him to blend seamlessly into the sand. I blinked and then he was gone.

My heart thudded against my rib cage as I tried desperately to locate him. Usually, I would rely on my ears to pick up on the subtle sound of him moving through the sand. He also had a habit of hissing before he bared his fangs, but that warning would do me no good with the wax seals blocking my ears.

After another scan across the sand proved futile, I lowered myself into a crouch and burrowed my shadow into the ground around me. Eventually, Faelan was going to have to make a move. I just needed to be quicker than he was. Fortunately, patience was not one of his virtues, so I didn't have to wait long. It was the glint of his amber eyes that gave him away. He lurched forward with frightening speed, and my shadow leaped up, wrapping around him completely like a net that had been sprung upon an unsuspecting trespasser. It was a perfect little prison of darkness, hovering just a few feet above the ground. Had it been another opponent, perhaps it would've been enough, but this was Faelan Honora. He expanded his form again, pushing out against the confines of the cage.

Then something struck me from behind, pain skewering through my skull like a hot poker and causing my vision to fracture with stars. My shadows dissolved and Faelan fell back to the ground in his original form, his expression even more startled than mine. I spun around to discover Master Snyder peering down at me, his walking cane possessing a fresh smear of blood. He had managed to sneak up behind me without me ever noticing his presence, a feat that should've been difficult to do with any vassal of Celdric, much less a seventh year.

If we were in the trials, you would be dead, Master Snyder signed. *All of you have a choice to make: keep your ears and risk falling under a vixen's spell, or shield yourself from the vixen and risk falling prey to everything else that wants to kill you.*

I tentatively touched the wound at the back of my head and instantly regretted it as the pain intensified. My eyes gravitated toward Emrys. He was no longer hovering at the back of the crowd. He stared at me from the front row, his combat uniform loose on his willowy frame. With a slightly sheepish expression, he signed, *I did try to warn you to watch your back.*

Sometimes I wondered if the House of Sight gave their students special lessons in how to make their advice as unhelpful and vague as possible. I shuffled out of the ring, my head throbbing and my hair sticky with blood. Akira stood with her arms folded across her chest, clearly unimpressed with my performance.

Meet me in front of the House of Tribulations tomorrow at dawn, she signed, and I resisted the urge to sigh. It felt like a punishment, but I knew it wasn't. Akira was one of those people who thought the House of Tribulations was actually *fun*. Between the deadly traps designed by Scias and the dusty libraries she spent the rest of her free time in, I questioned whether she understood the definition of the word. Her gaze panned over to Emrys as she added, *You should come as well. You need the practice.*

While seers weren't known for their battle prowess, they were trained in the art of defense, wielding a staff with the same proficiency as a hunter might wield a spear. However, Emrys didn't possess the physical strength needed to do any sort of real damage. Thus far, his preparations for the trials mainly consisted of him drinking potions of shaewood root, crawling into bed, and dreaming of the future. Though, from the dark crescents marring his eyes, I couldn't help but think that whatever future he saw last night, it wasn't a very pleasant one.

Akira watched Emrys as she waited for a response, and the combat instructor must have noticed her distraction from his lesson, because he proceeded to summon her into the ring. Only once she had taken up a fighting position did Emrys shift his gaze onto me. He raised his hands to weave silent words on his fingers, and it was all I could do not to smile as all those hours he spent scouring the future finally paid off.

I know what is going to happen in the trials.

CHAPTER 3

The House of Sight was a startling shade of white. Even its interior was devoid of any color, the floors and furniture all carved from the same pale-silver wood. Essian was cautious with the number of mortals he chose to share his gift of foresight with, so the House of Sight had an abundance of empty rooms. Unlike vassals of Celdric, who were forced to share their space between two or three students, Emrys's sleeping quarters only possessed a single bed. The small table next to it was overflowing with a staggering pile of books. A messy assortment of empty vials was balanced precariously on the edge, the pungent scent of shaewood root still lingering in the air.

Emrys perched himself on the windowsill. He no longer fit as easily as he did when he was a boy—his legs were much too long now—but he pulled them up to his chest as he peered out at the winding gravel paths and twisting spires that made up the Cenobium. I moved to stand next to him, one shoulder leaning against the wall.

"I have seen the trials," he said as he stared out the window. "The gods will throw us into a maze. The vixens of Pasaphae will know how to navigate it, so they can serve as a guide, but they are a double-edged sword. They need protectors. However, they won't guide more people than they have the power to control, and many vixens are spiteful by nature. Much like their patron goddess, they enjoy twisting friends into foes for their own amusement."

The information caused me to frown. "So the only way to get through the trials is to be put under a vixen's spell and just hope that they are in a benevolent mood?"

"There are ways to navigate the maze if one has the patience and the persistence to figure it out." Emrys turned his head to look at me, those gray-blue eyes of his shimmering like a veil that obscured a world of secrets.

He had likely lived through the trials a dozen times over in his dreams, trying on the different possible futures like another person might try on clothes, picking a different route each time until he found the one that guided him out safely on the other side. The extent of his foresight was a terrifying thing, far surpassing anything a vassal should be capable of, but his very existence was a miracle brought about by the goddess of life. He had always been unnaturally gifted, even back when he was a boy with a fledgling power he didn't yet fully understand.

"You know the way through," I said.

"I've mapped the passageways in my dreams," he confirmed. "I can guide us, but I need you to make sure we're grouped together for the trials. Reverend Richards finalized the list today. It's in his office. He will send it to the Sacred City first thing next week, so you need to sneak in before then and rewrite it, placing the two of us together with Akira. That way I can get both of you through the maze."

The reverend's office was located at the back of the chapel. However, he had long since grown wise to the antics of those marked by Celdric—the lock on his office door was next to impossible to pick. Fortunately for me, I happened to know someone who had made a copy of his key so she could have regular access to his wine cupboard. Sneaking in and out shouldn't be too difficult. The gods wouldn't even classify it as cheating. They didn't believe such a thing existed; there were only those who survived and those who didn't.

"I have one last favor to ask." Emrys made an attempt at a smile, but it didn't quite reach his eyes, weighed down as it was with exhaustion. "Would you stay with me? Just until I fall asleep."

The combat class had consumed most of the afternoon and now the sun was beginning to set, inviting the moon to rise up and take its place in the sky. I loved that blurred line between light and dark, the tug it had on my soul as the world slowly gave itself completely to the shadows. Emrys, however, dreaded the coming of night. Where there would always be a small part of me that remained a nameless orphan from Ravenrook, there would always be a small part of Emrys that remained a boy who was scared of the dark and the relentless nightmares that plagued him upon its arrival.

"My class tonight doesn't start until the eleventh hour," I told him. "I can wait with you until then."

He climbed off the windowsill, practically dragging his feet toward the bedside table. He pulled the top drawer open with too much force, causing the empty vials to topple over, some falling to the floor while others rolled into the spines of his books. He didn't even seem to notice as he pulled out a fresh vial, the liquid inside tinged with a green hue. Flipping open the lid, he poured the contents down his throat and then crawled beneath the white blankets.

I gathered up the empty vials and stuffed them into my pockets. It was nearly the week's end, which meant that his supply was almost depleted. I would need to go to the remedial house in the morning to get them refilled. Emrys peered up at me through half-lidded eyes. "I will not be up at dawn to run the House of Tribulations with Akira." His voice was already thick with sleep as the shaewood root took effect. "I'm already tired enough as it is."

"I'll tell her. Should I inform her about the trials as well? She'll want to know."

"No, I'll have that conversation with her." With a heavy sigh, his eyes finally fluttered closed. "The less detail she knows, the better. Her fate is such a fickle thing, susceptible to change with the slightest nudge. Pull at the thread too much and it will begin to fray . . . we don't want . . . we don't want to . . ." His voice petered out as he fell asleep.

He had once tried to explain to me how the future worked, because, contrary to popular belief, not all things were destined to come to pass. Fate was crafted from thread, not carved into stone, but the technicalities of it went well beyond my understanding. What I did know was that there were very few seers throughout history who possessed the sort of power needed to see the various possible futures and then steer events toward the desirable outcome the way Emrys could. That sort of power was often too much for a mortal mind to bear. A vassal would likely be driven to madness or melancholy long before they ever reached that point, dragged away by enforcers to live out the rest of their days in the cold, barren recesses of Ismadore.

As Emrys tossed and turned in a restless fit of sleep, I wondered if madness was a fate that could be circumvented, or if it was inevitable, just like death.

My existence isn't a sign of madness, the voice whispered, *but your denial of it is.*

I studiously ignored it. Having a voice in my head was one thing, but I refused to go so far as to have an actual conversation with it. From the window, I watched as the night claimed the sky and the campus flickered to life with hundreds of flaming torches. Before leaving for my evening classes, I lit one of the oil lamps in the corner of the room. Emrys rarely slept through the night, even with the help of the shaewood root, and waking up to complete darkness never failed to send him into a panic. With soundless steps, I crept out the door and disappeared into the night.

Classes ended just before dawn, the silhouette of the academic towers just barely visible against the purple-blue sky. My eyes strained as they adjusted to the incoming light, fatigue setting into my limbs as the night finally drew to an end. While the rest of Celdric's vassals slunk back to the House of Shadows, I dragged my feet toward the other side of campus. Birds chirped cheerfully from the treetops as the world began to wake up, a joyous tune that seemed displaced at this ungodly hour. A falcon glided overhead, circling the air above me several times before swooping down. Faelan landed gracefully on his feet, his feathers morphing into flesh as he reverted to his original form.

"Where are you going?" he asked. "The House of Shadows is in the opposite direction and I'm tired."

I arched my eyebrows at him. "Then go to sleep. I'm not stopping you."

"The last time I went back to the House of Shadows without you, a line of girls formed outside our room that stretched all the way down the corridor."

"What a travesty."

"It was exhausting."

"You do realize that you can just tell them to go away, don't you?"

He looked at me as though the suggestion was nothing short of absurd. "Simply blowing out the candle doesn't stop the moth from seeking the flame."

"Your humility is truly something to be admired," I said, skirting around him and continuing down the path, my boots crunching loudly against the gravel, because I was too tired to keep my steps silent. He jogged to catch up to me.

"Don't tell me you're running the House of Tribulations," he said, sounding horrified by the prospect. "It's *dawn*. That's a terrible idea for a shadow-walker."

He wasn't wrong. My abilities were at their peak during the night and at their weakest first thing in the morning when all the strength the darkness lent me was sapped away, leaving me completely drained in its wake. The House of Tribulations had been designed by Scias specifically for the purpose of training for the trials. It provided countless scenarios and puzzles that tested one's strength, intellect, cunning, and adaptability. It was the best way for a student to prepare for whatever horrors the gods had planned for the final exams. Unfortunately, the goddess of wisdom took that preparation a little too seriously, and not every student that went into it was fortunate enough to walk back out. Training in the house while I was at my weakest certainly had its dangers, but only training when I was at my strongest wouldn't serve to benefit me, either.

"It wasn't my idea," I told him. "It was Akira's. But the trials can happen at any time. Night or day. Dawn or dusk. I need to be prepared for any scenario."

Faelan fell quiet for a moment before asking, "Is Akira running the House of Tribulations with you then?" His tone was casual, nonchalant, as though he didn't care either way. He wasn't fooling me. I did the polite thing and pretended not to notice.

"She is."

"You know, a bit of training would do me some good," he said, stretching out his arms. "And it's not like I would be getting any sleep if I went back to the House of Shadows. Might as well do something useful with my time."

Akira was already waiting at the House of Tribulations with a fully stocked quiver slung over her shoulder and a newly strung bow clutched in her hand. The house behind her was a foreboding sight, still half cast in shadows in the early hour of the morning. The twisted roots from the surrounding trees crawled up the wooden walls as though they were trying to reclaim their fallen brethren. It made the structure look abandoned—a place that common sense dictated no one should enter—and yet here I was at the crack of dawn to do just that.

Akira's gaze scanned over the horizon before piercing into me. "Where is Emrys?" she asked.

"He sends his regrets, but he will not be able to join us this morning," I informed her.

"I, however, will be," Faelan added with a grin. "I *love* early-morning training."

The declaration rang false in my ears. Akira didn't look like she believed him, either. "Faelan, you hate getting out of bed before noon," she said. "You've been that way since we were children."

"Things change. I seem to recall you hiding beneath your father's writing desk during storm season, and now you barely bat an eye when the thunder rolls in from the east."

It was hard to imagine Akira cowering before anything, even as a child, but Faelan wasn't lying this time. "There is no dishonor in having fear, only in the failure to overcome it," she said. Yet despite her dignified words, she still glowered at Faelan like she didn't appreciate the reminder.

Holding true to her intrepid nature, she led the way into the House of Tribulations. Faelan and I followed her down a long corridor. It seemed that the house was eager to split us up, because three archways appeared at the end of it: one to the left, one to the front, and one to the right. Hanging from a hook were three keys. We each took one.

"I'll find you both inside," Akira said, which would've been a ridiculous assertion coming from anyone else, but she did seem to have a knack for navigating the house that most others did not. She walked through the archway directly in front of her. The wood groaned as soon as she passed through it, the archway shifting closed until it was a solid piece of wall, preventing anyone from trying to follow her.

"Try not to die," Faelan told me before stepping through the entrance on the right.

I attempted to rub the fatigue from my eyes. I didn't have a good feeling about this, but there wasn't anything that could be done at this point. The only way to get out of the house was to go through it. I walked through the remaining archway and emerged into a room that was modeled after the royal palace. The floors were carved from marble and polished to a shine. Thick columns supported an upper terrace, which appeared to be empty. My gaze flicked from the key in my hand to the various doors located throughout the room. My heart sank in my chest when I noticed a lone figure lounging against one of the pillars and realized that the House of Tribulations was forcing me into a duel. There was only one key, and the house would only allow one of us to leave. At least, that was what the challenge appeared to be. There were always creative solutions to be found in the House of Tribulations. Unfortunately, my opponent was Cahal Blackwood, and as a vassal of war, he was *always* looking for a fight.

I spat a silent curse at the rising sun. Had it still been nighttime, I could've slipped through the darkness and escaped into the shadow domain. However, while the sun still brightened the sky, I was trapped in this realm, which also meant that I was trapped inside a room with one of the most bloodthirsty warriors on campus.

His dark gaze met mine across the room and he took slow strides toward me, swinging his broadsword up to rest against his shoulder. The seams of his combat uniform strained against the thick cords of his muscles, the back of his tunic bearing the wolf of Brazial. Ever since the Rift was created, splitting the continent in two, the Kaltan gods and the

Athearian gods were only supposed to mark vassals within their own territories. As a son of House Blackwood, Cahal had been earmarked for the god of death, but Brazial trespassed into Athearia to claim him anyway, and that one act had nearly started another Holy War. Ashearan had been furious, and though his sister managed to keep the peace between the two kingdoms, that peace was growing increasingly tenuous. The Cenobium was left with only two options: either surrender Cahal to Kalta, or make an exception and allow him to be admitted. The school chose to do the latter, giving him a room in the House of Wisdom, but he didn't belong here, and he certainly acted like it, growling at anyone who so much as dared to glance in his direction.

Cahal's upper lip curled with contempt as he came to a stop a few paces away from me. "I have been stuck in this room for nearly half an hour. I thought when the house eventually gave me a challenger, it would be worth the wait. But this"—he gestured at me with his sword—"is just insulting."

One of the most vital lessons I learned as a first year was that some fights were not worth my life. I tossed him the key.

Coward, the voice hissed at me, but it wasn't cowardice. It was survival.

Cahal caught the key but didn't make any attempt to leave. Every instinct in my body screamed at me to flee, but without the night to call upon, there would be no escaping into the shadows. "I'm not going to prove much of a challenge for you," I said in a futile attempt at diplomacy. "I wouldn't want to waste any more of your time."

"No, not a challenge," he agreed, "but you could certainly be a form of entertainment."

He moved faster than the eye could blink, the tip of his sword slicing into me before I had the chance to react. My chest. My arms. A slash across my cheekbone. I stumbled back, flinging several daggers at him in response, but he simply used his sword to swat them away with all the fervor one might show a fly. I commanded my shadow to rise up in some semblance of a shield, but the tendrils of darkness flickered and spluttered like a flame caught in the wind. He kicked through it with ease, his boot connecting with my abdomen and sending me flying backward. Before I even managed to land, Cahal was already waiting for me on the other side. He slammed me down to the ground, knocking the breath out of me and cracking my ribs in the process.

With gritted teeth, I grasped for my power, dredging it up from the depths it had retreated to. The darkness slipped through my fingers. Frustration welled up within me. Master Snyder often cautioned against relying on emotions for power. Emotions were fickle things, notoriously unreliable and difficult to control. I, however, had always found anger to be a steadfast friend during desperate times. I let it spread through me like wildfire.

I am your master, I growled at the shadows. *Obey.*

This time when I reached for the darkness, the darkness reached back. My shadow wrapped around Cahal. The restraints were nowhere near as stable as what I would like, but they locked him in place just long enough for me to drive a dagger toward his ribs. He twisted away at the last second, my conjured chains evaporating like smoke, and the edge of my blade only just managed to graze his side. He pressed a hand to his ribs, his expression turning as cold as stone when his fingers came back slick with blood.

It was a small victory, but I didn't have much of a chance to relish it as Cahal brought his sword down on me again and again, shallow cuts piercing my limbs like a dozen snakebites. I quickly realized that he was toying with me much like a cat did with a mouse, battering his prey over and over again simply for the joy of it. He proceeded to press the tip of the sword against my chest, his head canting to the side like he was contemplating whether or not he should just ram it through me and be done with it.

My heartbeat was hammering so loudly in my ears that I almost didn't hear the soft creak of a door opening, nor the quiet footsteps that followed. I glanced at the upper terrace, where Akira plucked an arrow from her quiver and let it fly with a twang of her hunting bow. In a blur of movement, Cahal effortlessly snatched the arrow from the air. He clenched his hand into a tight fist and the shaft snapped in half.

"Cahal, you know that he's under my protection," she said, sounding annoyed. I would've preferred outrage, but her tone still held a definitive edge of warning to it. "Do not make me turn this into a political matter."

"Out of deference for House Marcaida, he's still breathing." Cahal slid his sword back into its sheath. "Though why you would ever extend your protection to this guttersnipe is beyond me. It's unbecoming of someone of your station."

"I don't recall asking for your opinion."

The two of them held each other's gaze in a long stretch of silence until Cahal broke the tension by shifting his attention to the key in his hand. After a close inspection of it, he strode toward one of the doors on the far side of the room and unlocked it without any difficulty. He peered back at Akira. "We're scheduled for a game of skirmish this afternoon. I expect that you will still be in attendance."

His tone was devoid of any inflection, making the statement sound like more of a demand than a question. Akira's mouth curved into a sharp smile. "Cahal, when have I ever missed the chance to kick your ass?"

"Bold words for someone who retreated last week."

While her expression remained a mask of indifference, I didn't miss the way her hands tightened on the railing. "A tactical withdrawal is preferable to defeat," she countered, "and my name is still at the top of the leaderboard."

His lips curved into a sharp smile of his own. "For now," he said. Then he disappeared into the next room, the door automatically slamming shut behind him.

As soon as he was gone, I sagged against one of the pillars for support, my blood soaking into the granite. A quick inspection of the cuts showed that they weren't deep enough to cause any real concern. My ribs, however, ached with each lungful of air.

Akira hooked her hunting bow onto her back before vaulting over the railing and landing in a graceful crouch. "How extensive are your injuries?" she asked.

"Just a couple of scratches," I retorted with a dismissive wave of my hand.

"You look like you're about to faint."

"That's because I've spent too much time with Faelan. His penchant for the dramatic has rubbed off on me."

"Speaking of Faelan, we should probably find him before he changes rooms." She unlocked one of the doors with her key. A pensive expression flickered across her features as she considered one of my daggers that lay discarded on the ground. She picked it up and proceeded to jam the blade into its hinges for good measure. "That should stop it from swinging shut of its own accord."

I regarded the door with a healthy dose of skepticism. A single dagger seemed like a minor obstacle for this house to overcome. "How do we know if it will work?" I asked. No sooner than the words left my lips, Akira gave my back a firm shove. I stumbled through into the next room. She stared back at me from the other side.

"I think it works," she said, crossing over the threshold to join me. A second later, her eyebrows shot all the way up to her hairline. I turned around to see what had caught her attention. Faelan was missing most of his clothing—as was the girl who was in the middle of searching for his key with an unnecessary level of thoroughness and enthusiasm.

Akira cleared her throat. Neither of them seemed to notice. The girl rolled on top of Faelan, pinning both his hands to the floor. He could've easily slithered out of the position if he so desired, but from the shameless grin on his face, it would appear that he was rather enjoying himself. Akira cleared her throat again, louder this time. The two of them froze to glance in our direction.

"Akira, Koven, thank the gods!" Faelan exclaimed. "It would seem that I've found myself in an utterly hopeless situation and am in dire need of rescuing."

The girl had the good sense to bolt for the exit while she could with Faelan's key in her hand. "Ah, I'm finally free of my captor," he said, his voice thick with false relief as she disappeared into the next room. While he moved to grab his rumpled cassock from the floor, Akira stepped back into the previous room.

"Koven, are you coming?" she said.

I looked between her and Faelan, but Akira would one day be my queen, and she possessed a commanding presence that made it difficult to do anything other than to follow. As I moved to stand by her side, Faelan stared at the two of us, his brows knitting together in confusion.

"Where are you two going?" he asked.

"We're going to continue through the House of Tribulations," Akira replied flatly. "You just allowed your opponent to take your key. If these were the trials, such a lapse in judgment could cost you your life. Perhaps you should reminisce on that while you're stuck here."

"But these aren't the trials," Faelan pointed out, flashing her a roguish smile that could thaw the iciest of hearts. Her heart wasn't made of ice, however; it was made of pure steel. "Come on, Akira. I know you're not going to leave me stranded here. You're far too honorable for that."

She proceeded to prove him wrong by yanking out the dagger that was jammed into the door's hinges and slamming it shut. She slid the blade back into one of the empty sheaths at my waist. "I assume you have a pair of lockpicks on you?" she said, and I nodded in confirmation. "Good. Then let's keep going."

CHAPTER 4

I staggered into the remedial house, exhausted and bleeding, with one hand clutching uselessly at my throbbing ribs. I forced my feet to keep moving, certain that I would collapse the moment I stopped. The healers were marked by their bright-orange robes, the fabric pinned at their shoulders with a pair of brooches that resembled a lizard curling round in a circle to swallow its own tail. Several of them let out exasperated sighs at the sight of me, but I liked to think they would miss me once I graduated—or died, whichever option came first. Serenity stood on the far side of the hall, grinding herbs into fine powders at one of the apothecary tables. Her long brown braid was decorated with purple aster flowers, the long hours she spent in the garden marking her skin with a golden complexion. The soft song she was humming to herself came to an abrupt end when she saw me, her dark eyes widening with concern.

She abandoned the pestle and mortar on the workstation and quickly wiped her hands on the hem of her dress before rushing forward to grab me. I sagged against her as she guided me into a nearby seat. The House of Tribulations had left me in a dismal state. Her gaze darted from the smoldering sleeve of my cassock to the dozens of shallow cuts littering my skin. When the examination showed nothing life-threatening, she huffed out a breath of relief. She knelt in front of me, and taking hold of my hands, she said, "If you keep this up, I might start thinking you're getting yourself injured on purpose just to have an excuse to speak with me."

I had, actually. On at least four separate occasions. However, ever since Emrys declared that he wanted her to be the one to brew his sleeping draughts, I no longer needed to fabricate a reason to come and see her. "Not this time," I replied.

I thought that maybe her eyes sparkled slightly at the comment, but they fluttered closed before I could be sure. I swallowed the groan that tried to escape my throat as her power poured into me, the sensation accompanied by that of a thousand needles piercing in and out of my skin until my body was once again made whole. I slumped forward in my seat without intending to, my face hovering close to hers, and when her eyes finally fluttered back open, she seemed startled by our proximity. However, she didn't move away, not even when I dared to brush my thumb over the ridges of her knuckles.

"I'll miss these visits after graduation," I said, voicing my thoughts aloud. "I suppose you'll return to your fishing village to open up your own remedial house like you've always wanted."

She exhaled out a long breath, disappointment darkening her eyes. "I wrote to the church, but unfortunately, they don't have unlimited resources. The funds for the remedial houses are directed to the cities, where the population and demand are the highest. If I want to build a remedial house in my village, then I will have to come up with the money myself."

Neither of us voiced the obvious solution to her problem: House Blackwood would give her the necessary funds out of obligation if she asked them for it. After all, her sister had nearly married into their wretched family. She would have been the next Lady Blackwood if the wedding hadn't ended in absolute disaster. After what happened, House Blackwood pledged to take care of any and all of Serenity's financial needs, as though gold could replace what was taken from her, but she would never accept a handout from them. She would view it as blood money. "I actually wanted to ask if you knew whether House Hardcastle was in need of another healer?" she said tentatively. "I know that I'll be a new graduate, but I've been making Emrys's sleeping draughts since fifth year. I'm well versed in botany and have an in-depth understanding of not only medicinal herbs but poisons and remedies as well. I'm a hard worker and—"

I placed my hands on her shoulders, stopping the torrent of words that was tumbling out her mouth. "There's no need for you to list your accolades with me. I'm living proof that you're a gifted healer. House Hardcastle would be lucky to have you, but unfortunately, I'm not House Hardcastle. This is probably a conversation you should have directly with Emrys."

I wanted to assure her that he would say yes, but the truth of the matter was that no one could possibly fathom what went on inside Emrys's mind, not even me. He definitely seemed to favor Serenity over other healers. He was quite adamant that she be the only one to prepare his sleeping draughts, so it would stand to reason that he would be happy to offer her employment after graduation. While I knew that his family already had a god-gifted healer in their service, they could certainly afford to hire another one if they so wished.

"I can talk to him first if you would like," I offered, and Serenity's eyes lit up like stars in the night. "It's the least I can do after all the broken bones you've mended for me."

She reached out to give my arm a grateful squeeze. "Thank you, Koven. I would appreciate it. I know that Lord Emrys holds your counsel in high regard, but of course, I would understand it if he has no need for my services after graduation."

"No need to thank me. This is purely for selfish intentions. After all, who else would have the patience to keep putting me back together every time I break?"

The comment elicited a warm smile from her lips, and just like sunshine, it made me feel a little bit weak in the knees. Clearing my throat, I gathered up the empty vials from my pockets and placed them on the edge of the apothecary table. "Speaking of Emrys, he needs his sleeping draughts prepared for next week. I'll make sure to remind him that you've had hundreds of opportunities to poison him and not once have you ever taken it. He should think long and hard about that before denying you a position in his house."

"I would never!" she exclaimed, and I couldn't help but laugh at the look of absolute horror on her face.

"I'm only jesting. Don't worry, I'll discuss it with him the first opportunity I get. No threats. I promise."

Emrys, however, was nowhere to be found. He wasn't in the mess hall, or the library, or his room in the House of Sight. I collapsed atop his empty bed while I waited for him, but no sooner than my head hit the pillows, sleep rose up to sink its teeth into me. When I finally awoke with disheveled hair and bleary eyes, Emrys was tucked into the corner of the bed with a half-finished book in his hands, as though manifested by a dream. His skin was so deathly pale that I was certain my hand would simply pass through him like a ghost, but when I reached out to touch him, I found him to be made of sturdy flesh and bone rather than wisps of smoke.

He peered up from the pages. "Ah, you're awake. I trust that you're well rested." I groaned in response, and his lips curved in a slight smile. "You wake up with about as much enthusiasm as I do."

I didn't wake up screaming from night terrors, but I decided not to point out that particular distinction. "There's something I wanted to ask you," I muttered, my voice still thick and rough from sleep.

"Yes, Serenity is more than welcome to serve in my house. Anything else?"

It was eerie when he did that, predicting what I was about to say before I even said it, as though he'd already had this conversation with me before. "No, that was it."

Emrys closed his book and set it aside. Nostalgia flickered across his face as his gaze caught on the emerald ring that had slipped free from beneath the collar of my cassock. "Do you ever regret taking it?" he asked, his voice wistful, like he was no longer here but back in Ravenrook, riding atop his dapple-gray horse as he waved at the adoring crowd, knowing that I was watching him from somewhere in that sea of faces.

"How could I regret it? My life would have amounted to nothing had I stayed in Ravenrook."

I wasn't sure he had even heard me. His gray-blue eyes had taken on a peculiar sheen as his fingers skimmed the surface of the emerald. He was probably peering into some distant part of the object's history. Every gift that a seer was known to possess, Emrys had inherited them all. He could walk through the future while he slept, a mere hour stretching to last a lifetime in the world of dreams and nightmares. He could touch an object and read its past like a book from its very first chapter all the way to its last. He could speak prophecies and read a person's fate in the palm of their hand. Yet he always refused to do the latter. He liked to say that knowing one's destiny was a dangerous thing. The way he looked at me sometimes made me too nervous to ask what mine had in store for me.

"It wasn't even stealing," Emrys murmured. "Not really. The ring was yours by birthright. It belonged to one of your ancestors many, many years ago."

That was the first I had ever heard of it. As I shifted into a sitting position, the ring slipped from his grasp and he blinked several times, as though he was the one who had just awoken from a deep slumber. I studied the ring with renewed curiosity. It had always felt like it was supposed to be mine, but I was also born with light fingers and a heart filled with desire, so it was difficult to know for certain.

"I don't suppose this mysterious ancestor of mine has any more treasures waiting for me to reclaim?" I said, and though my tone was flippant, the small glimmer of hope that sparked to life inside my chest was very real.

"All lost to time, I'm afraid."

I heaved a disappointed sigh.

"He traded his heart for everything, only to find out that everything was nothing without his heart."

It was cryptic, just like most things Emrys said when he dared to speak about his visions. He reached out as though to brush some of the disheveled hair away from my forehead but then seemed to think better of it. His hand dropped back down to his lap.

"I could tell you about him if you would like. I could tell you a lot about your family, but it's not the most pleasant history."

It was a rare opportunity, one that Emrys didn't afford to most others. Perhaps there was a time that I might've accepted it, but the past held no interest to me. My mother was dead and I'd never met my father, which had probably been a blessing. The stories I'd heard about him indicated he was a man that spent more time in harlot houses than he did at home, swindling a living from the gambling dens and abandoning my mother like a shade in the night when he fell into a debt that he couldn't afford to pay back. Although my mother was beginning to fade in my memories, I could still recall times when she would sit me on her lap and gently stroke my cheek, reminiscing on how I looked just like him. She didn't make it sound like a compliment; she made it sound like a tragedy.

I didn't want to know about him, nor any of the men that came before him. That was not my history. My history was here and now. "Sometimes the past is better left buried," I said.

"And sometimes the past comes back to haunt you in the most insidious of ways."

"You speak more and more like a seer with each passing day. Soon, you'll be incapable of holding an intelligible conversation altogether." My tone was teasing, but Emrys didn't react. Instead, he fell quiet, like he was deliberating whether or not to tell me something.

"Obscurity was never going to be your fate, Koven," he said eventually, his voice laden with yet-untold secrets, giving the statement an air of prophecy. He paused for a moment, absentmindedly picking at the skin around his nails, which were already little more than bloody stumps. I placed a steady hand atop his to prevent him from ruining his fingers any further. Some of the tension in his shoulders eased at the touch, like ocean waves calming to still waters. Yet there was an undeniable sadness in his eyes when he looked up again. "It's a heavy thing to see what I see and know what I know . . . sometimes, I wish Essian never marked me."

A thread of unease wound its way through me. What he was saying was dangerously close to blasphemy. "Sometimes," he continued, his voice so soft it was practically a whisper, "I think the blood of the gods is more of a curse than a blessing."

My grip on him tightened in anger, not because he had such thoughts, but because he was foolish enough to voice them out loud. No one was safe from the inquisitors, not even the nobility. "You shouldn't say such things," I chastised. My tone was harsher than I intended, but it was nowhere near as harsh as what would happen to him if the church suspected him of dissent.

He offered me a small, almost apologetic smile. "You're right, of course. Forgive me. I'm just tired. And it's not like there aren't many benefits that come with being able to look into the future." He opened one of the drawers of his bedside table and searched through the contents before producing an ancient blade, the handle crafted from polished rosewood and the bronze pommel shaped into the head of an eagle. He slid the curved knife partially out its sheath, revealing the symbol of a winged shield etched into the metal. It was the crest of House Hardcastle, which meant that this wasn't just any dagger. It was a retainer's relic.

"Although you can't formally be my retainer until after graduation, this was always going to be yours. I have seen more futures than I care to remember, and the one thing I know with absolute certainty is that I cannot walk through this world without you by my side."

I accepted the blade, the metal cold to the touch and surprisingly heavy in my hands. It was not a knife intended for throwing or fighting; it was one of status and recognition. Such moments probably should've been followed by solemn oaths and respectful bows. Etiquette, however, had never been my strong suit. I shook my head as though dissatisfied with the gift. "One of the richest families on the continent and there's not even a single fleck of gold."

The edges of his eyes crinkled with amusement. "If it's not to your liking, you can give it back."

I clutched the blade protectively to my chest. "Absolutely not. It's mine now. You're stuck with me."

He grinned. It was his first genuine smile in a long time, one that reminded me of the day he leaped over the campus wall to greet me, before his nightmares began to erode it away. "Always?" he asked. Being the greatest seer of his generation, he must've already known the answer. I gave it to him anyway.

"Always," I promised.

CHAPTER 5

As the bell tower chimed in the distance, students began to filter into the mess hall for their evening meal, the room quickly becoming lively with laughter and chatter. Statues of the gods were molded into the walls of the building, their hulking presence staring down at their vassals from above, and the gilded chandeliers hosted a collection of glowing candles to light the hall. Each of the long tables contained a feast of its own that filled the air with a range of fragrances, from the sweet scent of citrus to the smoky aroma of seared meat.

Akira was already seated at one of the tables, her expression pensive as she wrote something down on the piece of parchment. As I moved to take one of the empty seats next to her, I cast a curious glance over her shoulder to see what she was writing. I bit back a teasing smile when I found that it was a letter addressed to the king, which contained numerous revisions where she had scratched out sentences and agonized over her word choice. Knowing her, this was only one of many drafts. It was an unnecessary amount of effort. Zyair adored her, and she always seemed to soften in his presence. Even though he was fairly young for a king, having been crowned only a few years ago after he graduated from the Cenobium, he was a natural-born leader, blessed with a calm head and wisdom that went well beyond his years. He and Akira would make a formidable pair. The goddess Scias had made a good match with them.

When Akira shot a look of warning in my direction, I quickly averted my gaze and slid into the neighboring seat. Emrys claimed the position on the opposite side of the table and immediately turned his attention to the selection of desserts that stretched out before him. He added a slice of carrot cake topped with crushed walnuts to his plate. With the trials drawing ever closer, I decided that a little bit of indulgence was in order and helped myself to one of the strawberry tarts that were dusted in a fine coating of sugar.

"You should eat a balanced meal," Akira chastised. "The trials will soon be upon us, and it's important for you to keep your strength up."

"Or maybe I'll die anyway and regret not enjoying the finer things in life while I still had the chance," I countered before taking a generous bite out of the pastry.

"It wouldn't be possible for you to regret anything if you're dead," she replied flatly as she dipped her quill into the inkpot.

"That's really poetic. You should put that in your letter to the king."

She shot another look in my direction that let me know she wasn't amused by the suggestion. As she shifted her focus back onto the letter, I quickly finished off the rest of the tart, enjoying the way the crunch of the shell blended with the sweetness of the strawberries. I was just about to grab a second one when a series of raised voices drew my interest to the table that was designated for the first years. I lifted my head a little higher, wondering what was happening, but then a small huddle of students from the House of Sight rushed over toward Emrys. One of the boys carried a stack of divination cards with him, his face round and his eyes full of panic.

Emrys turned in his seat to face the boy, offering him a friendly smile. "Is something the matter?"

"A war is coming!" the boy declared. "We were consulting the cards, and they foretell a great battle."

The young seer placed three of the divination cards on the edge of the table. The first displayed two crossing swords, a card associated with conflict and battles. The second card held the painted visage of Ashearan, his face shadowed beneath the hood of his long robes and a pair of dark wings unfurling from his back. The card served as a premonition of death. The final one depicted Maylore, the bringer of calamity: the monster that had once sought to consume the world before the gods descended into the mortal realm to protect it from his corruption. He was portrayed to be more beast than man, with fierce red eyes and horns that curled out his head like that of an ibex. The card signified impending disaster. When the three of them were together, they combined to create an omen of war.

Emrys didn't appear worried by the formation, nor did anyone else at the table. I had seen it six times before and now it had come back around, just like the gray clouds and fierce winds that signaled the start of storm season. "The final trials always mimic the omens of war," Emrys informed the younger seers. "Battle, death, and calamity. All these elements come together at the end of every academic year."

The boy let out a breath of relief, and the edges of his lips tugged upward into an abashed smile. "Oh, I didn't know that. I'm sorry for bothering you."

"Not at all," Emrys said as he returned the cards to the rest of the pack. He lifted his fork back up, intent on resuming his meal, but the younger seers continued to linger behind him. They exchanged heated whispers with each other until he cast them a sideways glance. "Was there something else?" he asked.

The boy at the front of the group fidgeted nervously with the cards. "Yes, there was." His voice was caught somewhere between shy and hopeful. "We were wondering if you would allow us to read your fortune for the upcoming trials?"

I could tell from Emrys's expression that he wasn't enthusiastic about the idea. However, Faelan made an appearance before he could find a way to politely refuse the boy's request. "A fortune reading, count me in," Faelan proclaimed, and the younger students all grinned with excitement at having earned the attention of the king's cousin. The boy quickly shuffled the deck and then fanned them out. Faelan picked one, but he didn't look at it just yet. Instead, he placed a hand on Emrys's shoulder. "You're next. This is a good learning opportunity for them, and should we not be trying to foster the talent of the upcoming generation?"

Emrys shifted uncomfortably before plucking out a card of his own. Faelan set his sights on me next, but I was already reaching over the table to take a card. I could still remember what it was like to be a first year—the awe that I felt when I looked at the seventh years, who seemed to have all the power and confidence in the world. I had idolized them, and now I was one of them. I let my fingers hover above the deck, the seers watching with growing anticipation as I almost drew out one card, but then changed my mind at the last second and picked another.

The boy extended his arms as he held the cards out for Akira, who eyed them with obvious skepticism. "The accuracy of divination cards has long been a contentious debate among scholars," she said.

"Oh, come on," Faelan goaded, flashing her a smile oozing with charm. "You don't need to take everything so seriously all the time. Take one. It'll be fun."

She must have reached the conclusion that it would be quicker to do as he suggested than it would be to argue with him, because she heaved a sigh and selected one of the cards from the center of the deck. Faelan flipped over his card. His smile slipped as it revealed a bleeding lamb upon a stone altar, otherwise known as The Sacrifice. "Okay, maybe it's not so fun," he muttered under his breath.

"I wouldn't worry about it," Akira told him. "Each card has multiple meanings and interpretations, all of which are so broad and vague that they hardly have any real insight to them." She flipped over her own card, which showed The Weeping Widow, a woman dressed in black with her face buried in her hands.

"That card is associated with loss, grief, and sorrow," said one of the seers. He looked like he wanted to say more, but then Akira returned the card to the pack.

"Yes, I'm well aware," she replied. "It's hardly a surprising prediction for a daughter of House Marcaida. Sorrow and grief are the whetstones on which we sharpen our swords."

That was certainly a positive spin on the long line of tragedies and misfortune that had plagued her bloodline. Her family had been favored by the god of death for nearly a thousand years, and as a reward for that unyielding loyalty, his blood had cursed their lineage with madness. It was what had ended the lives of her parents, and her grandfather, and her great-grandfather before that. Akira was easily the sanest one in her family, though it was hardly much of a competition when the rest of her relatives were prone to fits of murderous rage.

I glanced down at my card, which depicted a snake coiled around a grinning man. "The Trickster is all about cunning and guile," the boy explained, and I tried to keep a straight face as he attempted to replicate the mystical tone of a seasoned seer. "It's a good card for a vassal of Celdric to draw. These virtues will earn you the favor of your patron god. Heed them and they will stand you in good stead for the trials to come."

I lowered my head in a somber bow. "Thank you for your guidance, wise soothsayer."

His grin widened. Then one of his friends elbowed him and he quickly rearranged his features into something more solemn and regal. "May fate see fit to favor you, child of the gods, and may you walk a path paved with the stones of faith, strength, and . . ." His voice trailed off as he struggled to remember the rest of the words. The boy closest to him leaned forward to whisper into his ear. "May you walk a path paved with the stones of faith, strength, courage, and conviction," he finished, drawing an invisible star with his hand to complete the performance.

The boys proceeded to turn toward Emrys with expectant eyes. When he hesitated, it made me very curious to know just what card he had drawn.

I commanded his shadow to slither up behind him. He blinked in surprise as it stole the card from his hand. He attempted to snatch it back, and I flashed him a mischievous grin as the shadow danced away from him. I was just about to grab the card when the tablecloth was yanked to the side, causing food to topple over and plates to shatter as they crashed to the floor. Akira muttered a curse when the inkpot tipped over and ruined the letter she was in the process of writing. My concentration fractured and the shadow evaporated into smoke, the card fluttering to the ground as I glanced farther down the table, trying to ascertain what the commotion was all about. Cahal had keeled over, one hand fisted in the tablecloth while the other clawed at his throat. His face was red as he spluttered and gasped for air. He had been poisoned again.

The students from the House of Death sniggered as he frantically dug through his pockets for his medicinal vials. They contained the various remedies for the different poisons that grew in the gardens on campus. He couldn't be sure which one of them he needed, so he took them all, his hands shaking as he tipped them into his mouth. His skin was slick with sweat as he finally managed to stagger back to his feet, his breathing growing steadier with each breath. He glared at the vassals of Ashearan with a look that promised retribution. In another life, he would've been one of them, but ever since he'd walked into the Cenobium with the wrong god's blood in his veins, they had made frequent and persistent attempts on his life in the hopes that killing him would earn them the favor of their patron god. Unfortunately, Cahal had proven to be a resilient adversary, and now I suspected that they tormented him for no other reason than the sheer pleasure of it.

His expression was one of barely contained rage as he stalked toward the exit. Faelan attempted to give him a conciliatory pat on the shoulder as he walked past, which was an objectively terrible idea. Cahal responded by shoving him into the table, his hand clenching tightly around Faelan's throat. Faelan held up his hands in a placating gesture, but there wasn't much point in reasoning with a vassal of war while they were angry. Every shadow in the mess hall flickered in warning, and Cahal's gaze met mine from across the table. It wasn't dawn anymore. This time if he wanted to fight, I could summon the darkness of the night to splatter him against the floor as though he were nothing more than an insect caught beneath the heel of a boot. However, it was only when Akira rose to her feet, her features set in a disapproving scowl, that he finally released his hold on Faelan.

The group of young seers stood frozen in place, wearing matching expressions of fear. Cahal glanced down at the cards and, slowly, he drew one out. His gaze hardened as he glanced back at the students from the House of Death, who were all toasting in celebration at his near demise. He tossed the card aside as he walked away. It landed next to a serving jug that had fallen over in the commotion, and the card quickly grew damp inside the puddle of spilled water. The boy rushed to retrieve it. He shook it out in a futile attempt to dispel some of the liquid, and as he did so, I caught a glimpse of a hooded man wielding an ax. While I didn't put much faith in divination cards, I couldn't help but feel a hint of unease snake its way through me. Out of all the cards in the deck, Cahal had picked The Executioner.

CHAPTER 6

The common room in the House of Shadows came to life as soon as the sun went down. Students crowded around makeshift dice and card tables, gambling away favors as well as coins. The room itself was draped with priceless tapestries and oil paintings, the cabinets all overflowing with gold figurines and lacquered jewelry boxes. Having run out of space to display his impressive collection, Celdric had even taken to hanging necklaces and bracelets from the chandeliers, the assortment of colorful gemstones causing a rainbow of light to dance across the obsidian floor.

Rita lounged across one of the seats next to the hearth, the dagger in her hand flicking in and out of view as she listened to Faelan recount one of his stories. She was not the only one crowded around the fire. The prince had a whole audience hanging on his every word. Rita turned her head toward me as I approached. A purple bruise was blossoming under her left eye, the wound too minor to warrant a healer's touch. That was not the only injury she had sustained courtesy of Master Snyder's combat lesson. The knuckles on both her hands were dusted with a collection of cuts and scabs, and she wore them like a set of matching trophies.

Leaning in close to her ear, I dropped my voice to a low whisper. "I need to get into the reverend's office."

She flashed me a mischievous smile. "Is this your way of saying you want to get drunk? Because if so, I am in."

I hesitated for a moment, wondering how much I should tell her. Faelan briefly cast a curious look in our direction before continuing with the valiant tale of how he'd wrestled a wolf of war with his bare hands. He unbuttoned his cassock to show off the claw marks that raked across his chest, earning him a bout of high-pitched giggles from his audience.

I gestured for Rita to follow me as I exited the common room. She must've thought that raiding the reverend's wine stock was exactly what

I had in mind, because her excitement was palpable as she trailed behind me. I exited the house and stepped onto the empty veranda outside. The snake-shaped pillars surrounding it glimmered softly in the moonlight like shadows caught between the night and a distant flame. Their topaz eyes gave me the eerie feeling of being watched, so I called upon the darkness to cloak me and Rita, allowing the two of us to blend seamlessly into night. She blinked in surprise, staring up at the murky veil that hung over her head like a shroud.

"What if I told you we could choose who we get to partner up with for the trials?" I said, careful to keep my voice low. "But we need access to the reverend's office in order to rearrange the groups."

Her sea-blue eyes sparkled with intrigue. "I would say that's *very* interesting . . . But what if I told you that picking our partners and getting drunk are not mutually exclusive?" With a grin, she tugged off her necklace to reveal a copy of the reverend's key dangling from the chain. "You should live a little, Koven. Remember your roots. Let's make our worthless ancestors proud."

Drinking was a terrible idea, but so was attempting to argue with Rita when asking her for a favor. "Very well," I relented. "*One* drink, so long as Reverend Richards doesn't know anyone has been rummaging through his office."

Rita scoffed as though insulted. "What am I? A first year? I have a foolproof system. I'll even show it to you, seeing as you're the classmate I hate the least."

"Please, stop. All that affection will thaw my cold, black heart."

"The trick is not to have one in the first place." Although she said it in jest, there was an undeniable truth to the statement. While alliances were essential, attachments were easily exploited. There was a subtle yet distinct difference between the two, which made friendships at the Cenobium both a precious and a precarious thing. The thought caused me to glance down at the retainer's relic that was tucked into the gilded sash around my waist. I liked to think that on a balance of scales, it tipped in favor of the former.

Candelabras lined the sandstone walls of the chapel, thick streaks of wax running down the length of the metal stems like wet paint. The pillars were carved with the ten-pointed star that represented the different gods: the five patron gods of Athearia and the five patron gods of Kalta, a symbol the church still used even after the pantheon fractured and divided itself in two.

Although the chapel appeared to be vacant, one could never be too careful. I didn't drop the cloak of darkness that concealed Rita and me as we crept past the reverend's lectern and ornate altar to his personal office, which was located in the back. Rita jammed her key into the lock and it gave way with a twist. It took my eyes a few seconds to adjust to the dark before the room came into focus. There was a shelf stacked with rare editions of the Holy Book, a wine cupboard in the corner, and a writing desk with a chair constructed from antlers, an homage to Scias's wisdom in guiding the students of the school toward greatness. Though it might've been more accurate to have the seat built from the bones of those who fell short of that standard.

As a fellow vassal of Celdric, Rita didn't have a problem seeing in the dark, either, as she began searching through the reverend's desk. It was a useful ability, and one of the many reasons why those marked by Celdric were trained to be spies. Most of the students in the House of Shadows possessed gifts that made it easy for them to slip into places unnoticed. A good portion of them were shapeshifters with the power to change species, like Faelan, or wear the face of another, like Rita. My ability to command the shadows also lent itself nicely to missions of stealth, allowing me to use the darkness like a cloak and hide from prying eyes, but there weren't many shadow-wielders like me. The only other one at the Cenobium had been reckless enough to get romantically entangled with a student from the House of Death. It hadn't ended well for her, leaving me the sole shadow-wielder on campus.

Joining Rita at the desk, I riffled through the opposite set of drawers. My eyes caught on a letter sealed with golden wax, the crest of the Cenobium stamped into it. With the tip of my dagger, I carefully peeled the wax away from the page, my lips curving into a triumphant grin as the page revealed a list of names. It looked as though the students had been split into groups of five. None of the healers were listed, because their final exam always consisted of putting the rest of us back together after we made it out on the other side. It must've been nice to be marked by a merciful goddess like Sheara, who abhorred the bloodshed and violence the rest of her brethren reveled in.

"Found it," I whispered to Rita, who quickly peered over my shoulder. Pulling the reverend's seat forward, I sat down and produced a fresh piece of paper. I dipped the quill into a pot of ink. "Who do you want to undergo the trials with?"

"That depends . . . What do the trials consist of?" she asked.

I fell quiet as I contemplated my answer. Emrys hadn't told me much. I knew that the trials would consist of navigating our way through a maze, but not much more beyond that. Emrys hadn't explicitly told me *not* to share the information he gave me, but he hadn't given his explicit permission, either. Information was a powerful thing, but it was dangerous as well. If too many people knew what the future held, it could risk changing it altogether, and rarely for the better. "I would recommend you join my team," I said. "Along with Emrys and Akira."

Rita held my gaze, and I thought she might try pressing me for more information, but then her eyes dropped back down to study the names. "Who should we have as our fifth?"

"Faelan?" I suggested.

"I'm not so sure about that," she said slowly, her expression growing serious. "He's a prince, and you know what vassals of war are like. They will narrow in on him like wolves on a deer carcass. Having him with us will put a target on our backs. There's no need for us to make the trials any more difficult than we need to."

"And here I thought you found him pretty to look at."

"He is pretty to look at," she admitted. "But this decision needs to be strategic."

"I think vassals of war will try to kill us anyway, whether Faelan is with us or not," I countered. "And there's no denying his skills as a combatant. He's the best the House of Shadows has to offer."

He was also a friend, but Rita wouldn't appreciate an argument based on sentiment.

"And doesn't he still owe you a favor?" I reminded her. "He can't pay you back if he's dead, and how nice would it be to have a prince in your debt?"

"Fine," she relented. "Faelan can be on our team."

I began rewriting the list, grateful for the forgery classes that formed part of the fourth-year curriculum for students from the House of Shadows. The quill looped across the page, mimicking the reverend's handwriting as I shuffled the names around. I paused when I came across Cahal's name, remembering the way he had sneered as he sliced into me again and again inside the House of Tribulations.

He deserves it, the voice purred from the back of my mind, and I was inclined to agree with it.

The corners of my mouth twitched upward as I grouped him together with several students from the House of Death. While it would be awfully inconvenient for him to be partnered up with vassals who wanted him dead, I doubted it would do him any real harm. He might have been an asshole, but he was a tenacious one. Still, I felt a thrill of satisfaction roll through me as I penned his name. I finally signed off the document with the reverend's signature and sprinkled on some of the pounce powder to help dry the ink.

Lighting one of the candles on the desk, I placed a golden wax capsule in a smelting spoon and held it over the flame. Once the wax had melted into a shimmering puddle, I carefully poured it over the folded page and used the sealing stamp that was located in one of the drawers to embed the school's crest into it. I held up the letter for closer inspection, and with a satisfied smile, I slipped it into the desk drawer and tidied up the supplies.

"Now, time for a celebratory drink," Rita declared as she flung open the liquor cabinet. The shelves were lined with dozens of bottles. Her fingers skidded down four rows before she started counting off the bottles. She finally plucked one out.

"I don't know why you even bother stealing this stuff," I said, collecting two of the bejeweled chalices that were used for communion during chapel services. "Communion wine is awful."

Rita pulled out the cork and poured two generous helpings, the yellow hue of it symbolic of the golden ichor of the gods. "It would be," she said with a smirk. "I drink half of it and fill the rest up with water, so Reverend Richards doesn't notice his inventory has diminished. The original vintage is actually pretty good."

I arched my eyebrows at her, more than a little impressed with such a petty use of her deviousness. Celdric would be proud.

I raised up my chalice. "To our worthless ancestors."

"To our worthless ancestors," she repeated, clinking her chalice against mine.

I took a sip. My eyes widened with pleasant surprise at the subtly sweet flavor that coated my tongue. Rita was right; the wine was pretty good.

"Drink up, Koven. You've got to enjoy every damn second of this life before you're dead, which could be sooner rather than later."

"You know what your best quality is, Rita? You have the most charming sense of optimism."

She snorted in a very unladylike manner and drained her chalice. The liquor was already starting to color her cheeks, a jovial smile tugging at her lips. "You and me, Koven, we're going to make it. You know why? We're survivors. We have been since the day we were born, fighting for every scrap this world has to offer us. Even if you're going to sell out and serve in a shadow court."

"What's wrong with joining a shadow court?" I protested.

"I haven't bled all these years just to bend my knee to the nobility. No, not me. I'm going to join the House of Inquiry, and they'll send me to the four corners of the world. I'll get to visit every major city on the continent."

"You'll still be bending your knee; it will just be to the high inquisitor."

She raised one shoulder in a shrug as she proceeded to uncork another bottle of wine. "The church already owns us. At least this way they'll be forced to pay me."

The simplicity with which she said those words was almost as unnerving as the words themselves. While the gods had blessed us with their power, that hadn't come without a price. We lived at their mercy and died at their pleasure. We even allowed them to wear our skin, offering ourselves up as cages of flesh and bone in which they could anchor themselves to the mortal realm. The gods demanded utter devotion, especially from those they had venerated with their blood, and they had little tolerance for those who disobeyed their laws. The scars carved into my back began to ache as though to remind me of that.

I forced a smile onto my face as Rita refilled my chalice. "Like I said, Rita, you have the most charming sense of optimism."

CHAPTER 7

The chapel was beautiful when the daylight filtered in through the windows, the stained glass depicting passages from the Holy Book, many of which took place back when the gods had been in one pantheon instead of two. The ten gods descending from the celestial realm to live among us. Sheara healing a blind man who had proven his faith by gouging out his own eyes. Tammearia calling down rain to lands of drought so that crops could grow. Lios bringing down fire on the twin cities, burning them for their heathen ways. Ashearan raising an army of the dead to vanquish the heathen uprising. Each window depicted the power of the gods displayed throughout history in all their wrath and all their mercy.

Reverend Richards took his position at the podium, dressed in long golden robes that signified his holiness and piety. His hair was only just starting to gray at the temples, and his mouth was etched with laugh lines, as though he spent most of his time smiling. From where I was seated in the back, I couldn't see him very well, which I was grateful for as I pressed the side of my face against the cold stone blocks of the wall. My head was throbbing with a vengeance, a constant pain that stabbed at the inside of my skull like a blunt knife.

My worthless ancestors were probably sneering at me from their graves, downright appalled at my inability to hold my liquor. I couldn't help but wonder if my father was among them. The only people in Ravenrook who lamented his absence were the tavern owners, because what little coin he did have, he had spent on their not-so-fine establishments. I might've had his eyes, but at least that was one trait I hadn't inherited from the man. Though it didn't feel like much of a victory as I tried not to throw up on the hymnbooks lining the pew in front of me. That level of desecration in this sanctified building would definitely earn me a long and painful punishment in the penance room.

Next to me, Faelan leaned in closer to whisper in my ear. "I'm a little offended that neither you nor Rita invited me to join your little escapade last night. You look truly awful, which means it must've been a fun time."

I didn't trust myself to speak, so I simply grunted in response. His lips twitched as though he was fighting the urge to laugh. I slumped back in my seat, tugging at the collar of my cassock in a futile attempt to dispel some of the heat radiating off my body as the reverend began his sermon.

"Glory be to the gods!" he exclaimed, so full of energy despite the early hour.

"Glory be to the gods," the students echoed back.

"Hallowed be their names!"

"Hallowed be their names," the students repeated.

"With the seventh years now coming to the end of their studies at the Cenobium, they will soon earn their place in this world." The reverend's voice shone with pride as he stared out at the sea of faces filling the chapel. "Blessed as you are by the gods, you have been earmarked for greatness. You will be the head of your house, leading it with strength and faith into the next generation. You will be officers in the Divine Army, protecting our borders from Brazial's wrath in the north. You will be intelligence gatherers for the church, ensuring the stability of our realm. You will be historians, healers, advisers, and preachers. You will be loved, you will be feared, and above all, you will be revered. Praise be to the gods!"

"Praise be to the gods," the students echoed.

"However," the reverend continued, his voice grave, "first you will need to pass the trials, where you will be judged before the gods themselves. They will determine whether you have proven yourself worthy of the blood in your veins. The final exams are set by one god of Athearia and one god of Kalta, bringing the two pantheons together in a show of unity and cooperation. But make no mistake, this is first and foremost a test of strength. A test of will, and fortitude, and resilience. The vassals of Kalta will test you, just as you will test them in return. They are war, and fire, and ice, and seduction. Whereas we are death, and wisdom, and prophecy, and cunning, and mercy. Regardless of which pantheon you kneel before, the power of the gods is something to be respected as well as feared. That is why such power cannot be held by the weak. These trials are designed to push you to your breaking point. Only the strong will survive."

Reverend Richards stepped to the side of the podium, his expression solemn. He peered up at one of the stained glass windows. This one depicted Scias as she sat atop a throne, a set of antlers curling out from her head, her expression cold and observing as vassals died at her feet like a sacrifice laid at the base of an altar.

"I always think it prudent to reflect on the past when looking toward the future. Many years ago, the gods went to war with one another and the ensuing conflict tore the continent apart, leaving scars upon this land that will never fully heal. That is what happens when two powerful forces collide. So, I encourage you all to let these trials serve as not only a reminder of your strength but also a reminder of the strength of others."

The reverend paused to give his audience a chance to contemplate his words before he said, "Vassals of Essian, may your foresight guide you safely through any tribulations you might encounter. Vassals of Ashearan, may your strength see you overcome any obstacle. Vassals of Scias, may your wisdom be your compass and your arrow strike true. Vassals of Celdric, may your cunning serve as your sharpest blade. And vassals of Sheara, may you take mercy on all the souls that have the courage and the fortitude to survive."

The air grew heavy with his words, and I exchanged a nervous glance with Faelan. He had lost two of his cousins to the trials, but the one who had survived to become king would've told him of some of the harrowing experiences he was forced to endure.

The reverend returned to the podium. "As you prepare for graduation and claim your place in society, I thought it pertinent to discuss the importance of *duty*. Please turn your books to chapter one, verses three to fourteen."

I reached for one of the Holy Books tucked in the pew, my tired eyes struggling to locate the appropriate passage amid the tiny script. The reverend cleared his throat loudly before he began reading the passage aloud.

"Maylore in his endless jealousy sought to consume the world, but the gods in their wisdom and compassion stepped out of the celestial realm to live among us, their presence shining a divine light on the evil that had corrupted our souls. Through their love we are rescued; through their mercy we are healed; through their guidance we are saved; through their wrath we are cleansed. It is by their grace we are able to live free of Maylore's tyranny.

"With divinity comes great power, and through their mercy, they shared that power with some of us. These chosen few are there to heal us, to protect us, to lead us; they are the vassals of the gods and through them the gods' will is done. Humans are weak, but with the blood of the gods, we are made strong; humans are corruptible, but with the forgiveness of the gods, we are made pure; humans are foolish, but with the knowledge of the gods, we are made wise.

"*We must show gratitude for the gifts bestowed upon us by the gods. We must be humble and obedient; we must be reverent and faithful. All we do, we do to serve and exalt them. This is our one and only duty.* Hallowed be their names."

"Hallowed be their names," the students chanted.

The reverend closed his Holy Book and stepped back toward the ornate altar to bless and prepare the wine for communion. When he returned with a golden chalice clutched between his hands, my stomach churned in revolt as last night's memories clawed their way through the blurry haze of my mind. The reverend summoned the students forth to receive his blessing.

Before I joined the long line that stretched down the center aisle, I attempted to smooth down my hair and neaten my cassock. The last thing I wanted was to give him a reason to admonish me. When it was my turn to stand in front of him, he lifted a clammy hand to caress my cheek as though in fondness.

Everything inside me recoiled at the touch.

"It has been a while since you were last required to give penance, my boy. It seems you have taken my lessons to heart."

If the lesson was to get better at not getting caught, then I had practically mastered it by my final year at the Cenobium. "Yes, Reverend," I said, lining my voice with the required level of humility. "I thank you for your unwavering guidance and for the eternal grace of the gods."

He smiled, so friendly, so welcoming, so deceiving. "Grace be to the gods," he agreed. "Let us hope that you do not falter again before graduation. I take no pleasure in punishing those that have strayed"—that was a lie—"but such is the burden of a shepherd so that the sheep do not fall prey to the wolf."

"And such is the burden of the sheep to know pain so that they are spared the dangers of the wolf," I added, unable to help myself.

The reverend's smile took on a subtle edge. "Indeed."

I knelt before him, and he raised the chalice to my lips. "With their blood, may the gods bless you and provide you with strength," he said, tilting the cup until the yellow wine slid down my throat. The liquid was warm and insipid, and I tried not to gag as soon as it hit my tongue. "Always remember your duty to uphold the one true faith. May the gods have mercy on your soul. Hallowed be their names."

"Hallowed be their names," I repeated.

CHAPTER 8

The auditorium in the main academic tower was large enough to host an entire cohort of students. As history was one of the core subjects required to be studied by all five houses, the staggered rows of pews were packed full of seventh years, from the eager vassals of Scias in the front of the class to the disengaged vassals of Ashearan seated quietly in the back. A crate had been placed atop a table near the entrance to collect the final assignment given by Master Alden. I added my essay on Athearia's golden era of arts and culture to the growing pile of scrolls. It was one of my finer pieces of plagiarism. The trick was to steal small pieces of information from multiple students rather than just one and then dumb it all down to make it less suspicious. While Rita had her tricks with siphoning off communion wine, I had my tricks with conquering boring academic assignments.

Emrys lingered halfway up the stairs, his wisps of white hair sticking up at odd angles as though he had forgotten to brush it that morning. He was speaking with Serenity, who was beaming and nodding with enthusiasm until Cahal intercepted their conversation. Grabbing her by the elbow, he yanked her toward him. She attempted to wrestle herself out of his grip, but she would have better luck trying to pry open the steel bars on a prison cell. I hurried up the stairs, his voice cutting through the noise to reach my ears as I drew closer.

"—gave my brother my word."

"I appreciate your concern, Cahal, but I'm perfectly capable of looking after myself." Serenity's voice had risen to match his, and she drew in a deep breath as though trying to calm herself. When she spoke again, her voice was softer, filled with compassion and understanding that he didn't deserve. "I don't blame your brother for what happened. I know it was an accident, and I know that my heart was not the only one that broke because of it. He owes me nothing, which means you owe me nothing. But if you truly feel like you need to do right by me, then you should allow me to live a life of my choosing."

"The position in my house will be well compensated and relatively safe," said Emrys.

"Relatively?" Cahal repeated incredulously.

"Safety can never be guaranteed," Emrys replied, keeping his tone diplomatic, "but I'm sure you would agree that it's safer than a position with a warrior household close to the border."

Cahal made a noncommittal sound at the back of his throat as he contemplated Emrys's words. However, his bout of indecision melted away as tendrils of shadow twisted down the length of his arm to wrench his fingers apart, freeing Serenity from his grip. His expression hardened as she stepped toward me. "This was your idea, wasn't it?" he snarled, the edges of his mouth curling downward in disdain as he regarded me. "You think if she's indebted to you, she'll finally let you between her legs. You vassals of Celdric are so fucking predictable."

Rip that insolent tongue from his mouth, the voice demanded, a red-hot anger seeping into my lungs like air.

Serenity stared at Cahal, her expression wounded and her eyes full of hurt. Maybe it was about time I started listening to my instincts.

I slipped a dagger into the palm of my hand. Emrys gave a small shake of his head as though he knew exactly what I was thinking. He held my gaze, a silent warning in his eyes. No, I probably wouldn't emerge victorious in a direct confrontation with Cahal, but just because some wars were destined to be lost didn't mean that they weren't worth fighting . . . yet not all battles needed to take the form of clashing swords.

I tucked the dagger back up my sleeve.

"Serenity's mind is her own," I replied. "If anything, I'm the one indebted to her for all the broken bones she has mended for me over the years. She's a brilliant healer, and any house would be lucky to have her as a retainer. It's not my fault that Emrys can see that."

"Thank you, Koven," she said pointedly.

"Serenity—" Cahal started to move toward her but stopped when she took a deliberate step back and held up a hand in warning.

"No, Cahal. Unless the next words out of your mouth are an apology, I don't want to hear them."

The muscles along his bottom jaw flexed like he was testing how an apology might taste on his tongue and finding it to be bitter. Without another word, he stalked down the stairs to take a seat in the front of the auditorium.

Serenity exhaled a long breath and brushed some of the loose strands of hair away from her face. "I'm sorry about that," she said softly.

"Oh no, absolutely not," I said. "You do not apologize for that asshole."

A trace of a smile found its way to her face. "He can be a bit of an ass sometimes," she agreed.

A student from the House of Death was slinking her way up the stairs when she stopped to stare at Cahal. He gave her a wary glance as he passed her, but as soon as his back was turned, a cruel smile tugged at her lips. She extended her hand and a scythe appeared in a haze of smoke, the curved blade hooking threateningly around his neck. I arched an eyebrow at the scene. The vassals of death were growing bolder and bolder as the day of the final exams approached. The entire auditorium fell silent as they watched the exchange.

"Did you know that Ashearan has placed a price on your head for the trials?" she said, her singsong voice at odds with the malice shining in her eyes. "Your weight in gold and a position as first lieutenant in the army."

It wasn't uncommon for gods to offer rewards for prized kills that they deemed would prove the strength and valor of their vassals, but typically they were offered for defeating a powerful opponent on the opposite side of the border. However, Cahal was technically a vassal of war, and Ashearan wanting him dead wasn't a revelation. Still, the declaration made the air grow thick with tension.

"Because killing me has gone so well for everyone who has tried over the past seven years," Cahal retorted. Then in a flash of speed, he was standing behind her with a knife pressed against her throat. He pressed his lips to her ear. "I welcome you to try."

The auditorium doors swung open and Master Alden walked in, her hair tied up in a neat bun atop her head and her arms laden with a stack of books. The scythe dissolved and Cahal quickly lowered his blade. The two of them glared at each other before he continued down the stairs.

"You should start packing on the pounds," the girl called after him with a grin. "I want to be rich."

He ignored her.

Concern darkened Serenity's eyes as she watched him go. Despite his horrid personality, the two of them were bound by the same tragedy, and because of that shared history, a part of her would always care for him. It brought up an ugly emotion inside me, an emotion that I had no right to, and just like the voice in the back of my head, I decided that my best course of action was to ignore it. "Do you think he'll be okay?" she asked me.

In hindsight, it probably wasn't the best idea to place Cahal and that girl on the same team for the trials. I offered Serenity a reassuring smile. "He'll be fine," I said, which could've been the truth. Who made it through the trials alive was something to be decided by fate. Perhaps she would favor him. Then again, perhaps she wouldn't.

"I hope you have all put in the necessary time to paint a vivid picture of the golden era of arts and culture," Master Alden said, her loud voice echoing through the auditorium.

Serenity quickly shifted into one of the empty pews. Emrys and I slid into the seat next to her as the historian began her lecture.

"The decades leading up to the Rift were a truly marvelous time for both Athearia and Kalta," Master Alden said, depositing the stack of books on her desk before taking up her position behind the lectern. "The free exchange of thought and knowledge in cities such as Xyllon was unprecedented. Not only did it house more than a dozen amphitheaters, but it was also home to one of the largest libraries on the continent before it was consumed by dragon fire. The loss of life was a tragedy, of course, but so was the loss of one of the greatest periods of our history. That level of intellectual collaboration has never managed to be achieved again."

Master Alden peered out at the class, hoping to find the same fervor she had for history reflected in the eyes of her students. I must not have been the only one with a bored expression, because she heaved a long-suffering sigh. "Why don't we put the lecture aside for now and have a discussion about why we even bother to study the past at all. Would anyone care to hazard an answer?"

"To understand how we came to be, we must first look to the past," Akira said from the front row. "The gods descending to the mortal realm completely altered civilization, establishing the one true faith and shifting power to the church. Even the creation of vassals changed the way we approached daily life. Healers had the power to combat plagues. Rainbearers could put an end to drought. Vassals of Scias allowed for the rapid advancement of infrastructure. Everything in this world can be traced back to monumental moments throughout history."

Master Alden gave an encouraging nod. "An excellent point. Anyone else?"

"If we learned from our past mistakes, we might be less inclined to repeat them," Emrys added, taking me by surprise. Like me, he was usually content to leave the class discussions to the students from the House of Wisdom. "Take the city of Xyllon, for example. It stands as a beacon of what can be achieved in this world if we work together, but it also doubles as a cautionary tale of what we stand to lose if another Holy War were to break out. An entire city burned to the ground over the course of a single night. The resulting loss of life was massive, the likes of which the world had never seen before, and Xyllon was only one of a dozen major cities to fall in war. The gods quite literally split the continent in two because of it. It's not something that we should be eager to repeat."

"Quite right," Master Alden said solemnly. "Having the ability to look back and reflect on the past will help equip you with the wisdom you need in order to pave the way for a better future."

"And yet history still has a habit of repeating itself," Emrys muttered to himself, which caused me to frown.

I leaned toward him. "What did you mean by that?" I murmured, careful to keep my voice low.

He cast an apprehensive glance in my direction before quickly averting his gaze again. "Nothing," he told me, and all the hairs on the back of my neck bristled.

He was lying.

CHAPTER 9

With the trials looming ever closer, I forced myself to train in the House of Tribulations every single day. The house seemed to recognize my need to push myself, and the rooms increased with difficulty each time I entered it. I eventually found myself back inside the room that was modeled after the royal palace, but this time the walls were splattered with blood. I wasn't sure if those crimson stains belonged to other students, or if the house was just getting more creative with its decorations. A row of armored knights crouched on the upper terrace, staring down at me like an audience that had gathered for a show. One of the mechanical knights stood in the middle of the marble floor, a key dangling from its neck.

The gears and cogs of its body whirred as it lifted its spiked mace. I sprinted forward, daggers flying from my hand only to bounce off the metal plates without leaving so much as a graze. The knight brought down its mace in a mighty swing. I managed to roll out of the way just as it cracked into the marble floor. Before it could prepare itself for another attack, my shadow rose up from the ground to wrap around the creature, holding it in place as I rammed one of my daggers into a chink in the armor where the neck connected with the rest of the body. A triumphant smile curled at my lips as the terrible screech of metal echoed through the room. Then the dagger was ripped from my fingers as the cogs ground the weapon to dust.

The knight strained against the ropes of shadow and sweat beaded down my forehead as I tried to keep it locked in place. I commanded the shadows to tighten their grip until the amor warped and crumpled in on itself. Tendrils of darkness seeped into the cogs, ripping apart the inner mechanism. The knight finally went limp. As soon as I released my hold on the creation, the metal clattered to the floor in a useless heap. No sooner than it did, a second set of whirling cogs thrummed to life. My head snapped up just in time to see another knight drop from the upper terrace. I wasn't quick enough to avoid the blow that sent me flying across the room. I slammed into one of the pillars. The sickening snap of bone filled my ears and pain shot up my arm.

This knight possessed no weapon, and it didn't move nearly as quickly as the previous one. It was easy to evade the next punch it threw in my direction. Its fist collided with the pillar instead, removing an entire chunk of granite in the process. I rushed back to the broken scrap of metal in the center of the room, rummaging through the mess until I located the key, and then I was racing for the closest door. I dared a glance over my shoulder only to find that the knight had launched itself off the ground, traversing the room in a single leap. My shadow curled around one of my discarded daggers and hurled it through the air. The blade lodged itself in the slit of the helmet. Had it been a person of flesh and bone wearing the armor, they would've been dead, or at the very least have lost an eye. The weapon didn't do nearly as much damage on one of Scias's creations. However, it did cause the knight to falter, which gave me the time I needed to reach my exit.

With my dominant arm rendered useless, my fingers struggled to get the key into the lock. When I finally managed to get it in, my relief was short-lived—the key only turned halfway before getting stuck. I had chosen the wrong door. I tried to yank it out again, but the key refused to budge. The whirring of cogs in my ear warned me of an oncoming assault. On instinct, I dived to the side. The knight missed its target and struck the door instead. The lock shattered and the door swung open on its hinges. Grinning, I quickly slipped under the knight's arm and into the next room. Its helmet twisted toward me as though in a glare, but it remained on the other side of the door, unable to cross the threshold. My shadow reached out to pluck the dagger from its eye socket, gliding it back into one of the many sheaths lining my body, before I turned to face my next challenge.

I had been in the House of Tribulations for well over an hour. There couldn't be many more rooms left for me to solve before the house decided to finally spit me back out.

This room resembled an underground tomb, the stone walls lined with flaming torches, illuminating the murky water that separated me from the next exit. Beneath the surface, reanimated corpses were chained to the bottom, their flesh bloated and their fingers grasping for their next meal. The message was quite clear: Don't fall into the water. I stifled a groan as I studied the variety of stones that would allow me to hop from this side to the next. Some of those stones would allow me safe passage over the water, while others would sink me to the bottom to join the undead horde. Scias did love her puzzles.

I peered about the room, searching for some sort of clue that would reveal which stones were safe to walk on, when a spider scuttled across the floor. I squished it beneath my boot. It was with great horror that I realized that there were dozens more scattered throughout the room, their grotesque bodies colored with a single crimson streak. The sight sent an ominous shiver down my spine. I debated turning back to fight the knight again. Perhaps I could trick it into kicking down one of the other doors. I glanced over my shoulder. The knight hadn't moved. Its hulking frame was still blocking the doorway, removing that option from the table.

I continued searching for some form of symbol or pattern that would hint at how to safely navigate the water. Yet the only thing I discovered were more spiders nestled within their webs. A nagging feeling tugged at the back of my mind as my eyes darted from the spiders to the flaming torches to the water. Understanding dawned on me. The spider was the sacred animal of Pasaphae, who was spurned by the god of fire when he chose to marry the goddess of the sea. Spiders. Fire. And water. Those were the clues. The love story of those three gods was riddled with tragedy and bitterness, but I doubted this had anything to do with the curse Pasaphae placed on the newlywed couple. No, this must be referencing one of the stories that came before, back when Lios would command the sun to set in the sky so he could sneak away to be with the one he truly loved. Under the cover of darkness, Tammearia would weave a bridge from moonlight, allowing the couple to cross the waves to an island hidden away from Pasaphae's wrathful gaze.

The answer quickly became obvious: The sun first had to set before the moon could guide the way. I commanded the shadows to snuff out the fire of the torches, plunging the room into darkness. A moment later, a faint glow of silver light streamed in through the cobwebs to illuminate a pathway of stones to the other side. I began hopping between them. I was halfway across the water when a tingling sensation crept from my shoulder toward the back of my neck. My blood turned to ice in my veins as I realized that one of the spiders had dropped down from the ceiling to land on me. Before I got the chance to swat it off, the creature slipped beneath the fabric of my tunic. I ripped off my combat uniform. Pain burst from my broken arm in protest against the movement, but I ignored it as I yanked my clothes over my head.

In my panic, my foot slipped off the edge of the stone and water rushed up to swallow me whole. I quickly tried to kick my way to the surface.

Unfortunately, it was too late. The corpses chained to the bottom of the pond already had me in their clutches. Fingernails dug into my skin as they pulled me down. Grabbing one of my daggers, I hacked at them blindly, their distorted faces barely visible through the murky water. My blade connected with flesh, but it did me little good. The dead did not feel pain. I needed to be more strategic with my attacks. I sliced my dagger through their fingers, releasing me from their hold only to have one get creative and sink its teeth into my calf. Bubbles of air rushed out my lungs in a scream. I jammed my dagger between its jaws, struggling to pry them back open, and eventually the pressure on my leg released. The water grew even darker with my blood as I finally broke to the surface. I clawed my way back onto the floating stone, my left arm straining to lift my entire body weight out of the water. I rolled onto my back, my chest heaving and my muscles aching.

Gods, I hoped there weren't any spiders in the trials.

I forced myself back onto my feet and continued to cross the moonlit stones until I reached the other side. Pushing the door open, I was greeted by soft green grass and an orange setting sun. It seemed that the House of Tribulations had decided that it was finished with me. Perhaps it thought my performance was satisfactory, or maybe it was just irritated that I broke one of its armored knights. Either way, I was grateful to be out of it.

No sooner had the door closed than it was flung open again. Akira strode out, her sleek black hair loose of its braid and her face smeared with soot as thick plumes of smoke wafted out from the room behind her. The quiver on her back was empty, the bow in her hand possessing a snapped string, and yet her expression retained an eerie sense of calm. "You should find a healer," she said, gesturing to the scratches on my chest. "Injuries from the dead are prone to infection."

"I need to go to the remedial house anyway. I'm fairly sure my arm is broken."

She scowled at me, which was the closest she came to showing affection. "You should be more careful, Koven. There may come a time when a healer won't be there to put you back together again." She began to walk down one of the many pathways that twisted through campus. This one led to the combat fields, where the remedial house was also conveniently located, the healers readily available to help stanch heavy bleeding and reattach severed limbs.

"Emrys told me that we're all on the same team for the trials," she said as I fell into step beside her. "We're going to have to be on our guard. Brazial enjoys twisting the exams into a battlefield. It's no secret that he rewards his vassals for prized kills. Faelan and I will undoubtedly have bounties on our head. Emrys might have one as well. The church claims that the two pantheons coming together for the exams is a symbol of unity and cooperation, but there is a reason the trials call forth the omens of war. The gods crave blood, and the trials are how they get it."

I didn't need the reminder. I was well aware of how dangerous the trials were, just as I was well aware that the Kaltan and Athearian gods enjoyed pitting their vassals against each other to see who would emerge the strongest. "If you're asking me whether I have qualms about spilling Kaltan blood, the answer is no," I told her. "If vassals of war come for us, I won't hesitate."

She gave me a long, appraising look before nodding. "Good, because they certainly won't hesitate, either, the bloodthirsty bastards."

The remedial house came into view as we crested a small hill, the building surrounded by a garden of medicinal herbs, the earthy scents of sage and thyme clinging to the wind. Akira veered toward the combat fields. Apparently, the House of Tribulations hadn't proved enough of a challenge for her.

As I walked into the remedial house, the water sluicing down my body left small puddles in my wake. Serenity was busy examining a patient. The injured boy was stretched out on one of the beds, cradling his arm in such a way that I suspected I wasn't the only one who had broken a bone that day. Upon my entrance, one of the other healers gave Serenity a nudge. She turned around to look at me, her gaze tracking everything from the water dripping off my hair to the claw marks that tore across my chest. She gave a disbelieving shake of her head, but I didn't miss the way her lips tugged into a slight smile.

I made a silent promise to myself that if I survived the trials, I would sweep her into my arms and finally learn what those lips tasted like. My shadow curled around my boots as though it rather liked that idea, and as darkness rose up to claim the sky outside, I was reminded that just as it was in the sun's nature to yield to the night at dusk, it was also in the night's nature to yield to the sun at dawn.

CHAPTER 10

The last week at the Cenobium was a tedious string of tests and assignments that covered everything from theology and economics through to war philosophy and diplomacy. Each of the different houses on campus also had specialist fields of study. Architecture and engineering were the domain of Scias. Astrology and divination were studied by those marked with the gift of foresight. Students from the House of Death undertook advanced military tactics and combat training. As a vassal of Celdric, espionage and subterfuge were my strengths. My final assignment from the spymaster was supposed to be the easiest one of the week, and yet I stood frozen like a statue, unable to speak. Master Moore stared back at me from behind his desk, his fingers drumming against the polished oak as he awaited my response. I needed to give one, but my throat had constricted and my tongue had turned heavy in my mouth. The spymaster exhaled a deep breath through his nose, a subtle yet alarming sign that he was beginning to lose his patience with me.

"The final assignment is not difficult," Master Moore said, his voice stretching out each word as though he thought me a simpleton. "You are close with the young lord of House Hardcastle. It's no secret that you desire to join his shadow court upon graduation. Emrys is an exceptionally talented vassal, but he has grown . . . reserved in recent years. He's not as vocal about his prophecies and visions as he was when he was a boy." The spymaster leaned forward in his seat, his bloodshot eyes glinting with intensity. "He's obviously fond of you. I'm sure he confides some of his secrets in you . . . you need only tell me them and then you're free to go."

Emrys's mind was a vault of secrets that not even my lockpicks could crack. What little information he did share with me was hardly anything that warranted repeating. Perhaps it was a deliberate choice on his behalf for this very reason—so that when this day came, when I was ordered to twist my loyalties, I would have very little to actually betray him with.

He thinks of his gift as a curse, the voice reminded me.

I *definitely* couldn't tell the spymaster about that. Such blasphemy could have Emrys kneeling in front of an inquisitor before the sun managed to set in the sky. I supposed I could divulge the fact that Emrys had foreseen the trials . . . but that could lead to a line of questioning that ultimately resulted in me breaking into the reverend's office to rearrange the groups. At best, that would earn me a trip to the penance room. At worst, Ashearan would absorb me into his undead horde for interfering with his exams—or, more accurately, for *getting caught* interfering with his exams. There were no good options, so I decided to take a page out of Faelan's book and try talking my way out of my current predicament.

"House Hardcastle has always been a devout follower of the one true faith. By serving them, I will in turn serve the church. After all, the gold of House Hardcastle has generously supported the church since the gods descended from the celestial realm to live among us. With my protection, the house will remain strong and thus be able to continue to support the church through the next generation. However, I cannot perform my duty if my liege lord suspects me of disloyalty. And as you have so astutely pointed out, Emrys is a gifted seer. It would not be wise for me to betray him."

Master Moore was quiet for a long stretch of time before responding. "That was eloquently said, Wickwire." That might've been the first compliment the spymaster had ever given me, but from the flicker of annoyance that crossed his expression, it was clear that he wouldn't let me slip away so easily. "It's true that by serving a faithful house, you are in turn serving the gods. However, appearances can be deceiving. Your first and foremost duty must be to the church. A position in a shadow court comes with many advantages, not because it gives you the opportunity to look outward, but because it gives you the opportunity to look inward. House Hardcastle is one of the wealthiest in Athearia. What if they are that way because they have been skimping on their tithes? Your duty would command you to report the disloyalty to a House of Inquiry."

Master Moore had once said that the art of conversation had the potential to be more deadly than any sword. This certainly felt like one of those times. "Are you suggesting that Essian would be blind to one of his own vassals stealing from him?" I countered.

"It's merely a hypothetical," Master Moore replied smoothly. "One that I expect you to answer."

Would I turn Emrys in if I knew that his family was deliberately whittling away at their annual donations to the church? Honestly, I would probably ask them to give me a cut. Master Moore, however, had the same ancillary ability that I did. He could detect a lie the moment it rolled off a person's tongue, which meant that I had to be very careful with my words. "I agree that in those circumstances my duty would require me to report such treachery to the House of Inquiry."

Master Moore proceeded to do something that made me extremely nervous. He opened his leatherbound book and scribbled down some notes. I forced my face to remain a mask of calm even as my heart began to pound in my ears. "I'm still waiting for you to tell me some of the young lord's secrets," the spymaster said, his gaze scrutinizing as he peered up from his pages. "That is my final assignment for you. Either you do it, or you will seek atonement for your failure with Reverend Richards."

I tried to search my memory for some innocuous pieces of information to placate him but quickly stopped when I came to the realization that this wasn't just about passing the assignment. He was asking me about Emrys specifically—the person I would watch over like a shadow for the rest of my life. If I gave away his secrets now, I would be expected to do so in the years to come. It wouldn't just be this one small betrayal; it would be hundreds over the course of a lifetime. I would have to hold my devotion to House Hardcastle in one hand all the while having a dagger hidden in the other.

I resisted the temptation to touch the retainer's relic that was tucked into the golden sash at my waist. Master Moore would notice such a movement and figure out just how anxious I really was. The thought of the penance room made everything inside me writhe like twisting snakes.

Then tell the spymaster what he wants to know, the voice reasoned.

Except then it might be Emrys in that penance room instead of me. And I wouldn't betray my best friend. Not now. Not ever. "Unfortunately, Emrys doesn't confide in me to the extent that you seem to believe he does. He mostly keeps his own counsel."

Master Moore gave me a skeptical look. "So, you have absolutely nothing to share? You haven't collected a single secret in all the years you have known him?"

It was all I could do not to grind my teeth in frustration. He wasn't making this easy for me. "As you have already noted, sir, Emrys is reserved. If there is perhaps someone else that you wanted me to glean information from, then I would be happy to—"

"No," Master Moore said curtly. "This is not a negotiation, Wickwire. This is an assignment, and it seems as though you have no intention of completing it. I would thank you not to waste any more of my time. I'll be sure to let Reverend Richards know that he can expect you in the penance room shortly. I would advise that you take the time to reflect on your failures and reconsider your priorities. Celdric lifted you up from the gutters. You were nothing until he shared his blood with you, and what the gods give, they can take away just as easily. You would do well to remember that."

The threat carried a foreboding undertone that made my mouth go as dry as desert sand. I gave the spymaster a firm nod to let him know that I was well aware of just how precarious my position was. The Cenobium reminded me of it at every opportunity. I was a vassal of the gods, blessed with power for however long they deemed me worthy of it, and if Celdric found me lacking, he could purge every last drop of blood from my veins. Even if I wasn't lacking, he could still choose to do it for no other reason than to satisfy his own amusement. That was what it meant to be a god among men.

Master Moore scribbled down another sentence in his leatherbound book, the scratch of the quill against the page sending an ominous shiver down my spine. "You may go," he said dismissively.

Whatever the spymaster was writing about me, I doubted it was good. In that moment, my instincts were urging me to spill every word that Emrys had ever said to me over the course of our friendship—to sacrifice him upon a pyre so that it would not be me who burned—because I was fairly certain that the penance room was not the only punishment Master Moore was recommending for me in that damned book of his.

This was why the Cenobium encouraged alliances over friendships. The latter were such pesky things. They came with annoying little inconveniences such as loyalty and scruples.

You're a fool.

Yes. Yes, I was.

With an inward sigh, I left Master Moore's office. Once I was out of his sight, I reached for the emerald ring around my neck, allowing the touch of it to soothe my fraying nerves. Master Moore was wrong. I didn't owe everything I had to Celdric. The god of thieves and shadows would've paid me no mind if it hadn't been for Emrys's scheme. I knew exactly where my priorities needed to be, and it would take a whole lot more than blood and pain for me to change them.

The penance room was located in the subterranean segment of the chapel. The church didn't like to use the term *dungeon*, but the windowless room certainly resembled one with its cold stone floors. A set of Rasalan shackles hung from one wall, and an assortment of whips dangled from a rack on the wall opposite it. The minutes stretched on to feel like hours as I stared at them with growing dread.

The door eventually creaked open and Reverend Richards stepped into the room wearing a mask of disappointment. "Master Moore tells me that you have faltered in your faith. That your loyalty to the gods has been called into question. That you need purification through pain in order to reflect on your failings."

A bead of sweat rolled down the back of my neck, but I refused to brush it away and give him the satisfaction of seeing my fear. I had survived the penance room before. I could do it one more time. In a few days, I would graduate and I would never need to come down here again.

Yes, you will, the voice argued. *How else will you chain the reverend with these very shackles? How else will you flay the skin from his back and have his blood coat these very stones beneath your feet?*

It was an idea that I had entertained at great length during the hours I'd spent rotting down here. And though anger helped keep me sane, that didn't mean it would help keep me alive. Killing a member of the church would either have me hauled off to Ismadore to be locked away for the rest of my days, or if the gods were feeling merciful, they would order me executed on the spot. I was smarter than that.

"You know the drill," the reverend said, gesturing toward the empty table. "Take off your clothes."

I placed my daggers in neat rows in the corner, adding my retainer's relic to the collection. I folded my gilded sash and positioned it next to the blades. I drew in a deep breath before pulling the cassock over my head. The reverend's stare raked over the various scars carved into my back.

Gouge his eyes out.

It was tempting. Gods, it was tempting. But what good would it do me to trade a brief moment of satisfaction for a very permanent coffin?

I moved to kneel in front of the shackles, my forehead pressing against the stone. The reverend locked the manacles onto my wrists, and I bit down on my bottom lip to keep from crying out as the metal burned into my skin, cutting me off from the divinity in my blood and making it impossible to escape. The reverend walked over to the rack to select his instrument of choice. He didn't move for a long time, and that silence was a form of torture in itself—waiting for the first crack of the whip. When it finally came, it ripped into my skin like a hot knife. I swallowed my scream and it came out as more of a groan. It seemed that the reverend had chosen a single-tailed whip, which meant fewer but deeper lashes than the ones with multiple appendages. He struck me again and again until I was no longer able to stifle the sound of my screams.

Peel the flesh from his bones, the voice hissed. *Carve out his still-beating heart and feed it to him. Make him choke on it.*

It was a glorious image, and I latched onto it like a sailor lost at sea might latch onto a piece of driftwood.

The reverend methodically cleaned the leather and returned the whip to the rack before approaching me again. I knew from experience that any movement would cause the manacles to shift farther up my arm, burning me all over again, so I forced myself to remain perfectly still, mentally bracing myself as the reverend threaded a thick needle. His breathing grew ragged as he started weaving the needle between the fresh gashes across my back, drawing the wound closed with a painful tug. Nausea swirled in my stomach, my vision blurring as the world tilted in and out of focus, but my mind clung onto consciousness, stubbornly refusing to give me the reprieve of oblivion.

"Why do you make me do this?" Reverend Richards said, his breath hot on my neck. "I don't enjoy hurting you."

A lie.

He plunged the needle back into my skin. My eyes started to burn, but I refused to cry. I couldn't deny him my blood, but at the very least I could deny him my tears.

"I just want you to be better."

A lie.

"Pain is the purest form of love."

A lie.

"This is for your own good."

He believed that one. He truly believed it with every fiber of his tarnished soul. Perhaps he needed to in order to justify all the lies that came before.

When he finally tied off the last stitch, every part of me was shaking. I flinched as he trailed his fingers down my back, collecting droplets of warm blood like a leech at a banquet table. "Do you seek forgiveness for your past transgressions, my child?"

The only thing I seek is your head on a spike.

I had once listened to that voice and told the reverend all the creative things he could go do with that clemency of his. I quickly discovered that my defiance was not worth his ire. "I seek forgiveness," I said, my voice hoarse and fractured from screaming.

"Then may this pain be your penance and cleanse your corrupted soul. I forgive you, my child, and I will pray for the gods to do the same."

Forgiveness would do my soul little good at this point. Paradise was no place for madmen. My soul was condemned from the moment the voice began whispering in my ear.

The reverend unlocked the manacles, allowing me to slump to the floor. I didn't want him to see the pain etched into my face, so I continued to stare at the wall, listening to the sound of his footsteps as he strode across the room. Except he didn't leave. He lingered. I didn't know what for until I heard the scrape of metal as a blade was withdrawn from its sheath. He was examining my retainer's relic.

"Ah, yes. Master Moore mentioned you had ambitions to join the shadow court of House Hardcastle. Unfortunately, he has made the determination that such a position would not be in the interest of the church. I will be writing to Lord Bastian to inform him of our decision. He's a pious man—truly devout to the one true faith and eternally grateful that Sheara blessed his barren wife with a son. I'm sure that he will take our recommendation into account." Reverend Richards slid the dagger back into its sheath. "You will no longer have need of this relic. I will see it safely returned to the lord of the house."

I didn't have the strength in me to turn around and watch as he stole my future from me. With my back shredded and my body in agony, I knew it wasn't just the retainer's relic that had been taken from me; it was also my chances of surviving the trials. No healer would touch me while fresh penance marks still stained my skin. The final exams were designed by the gods to weed out the weak, and I would be walking into them already broken and bleeding. I was as good as dead. It was only once the reverend left and the door clicked closed behind him that I finally allowed my tears to slip free. As my blood dripped onto the cold stone floors, I did something that I hadn't done in a very long time: I prayed, and I asked Celdric for something in return.

Celdric, I offer you my blood, blessed as it is with the power you gifted me. I ask for the reverend's blood in return, ripped from his veins with all the violence and the pain he relishes in.

The shadows in the room shifted around me, the darkness eating away at the bloodstains until there was nothing left. I didn't know if Celdric had heard all the other prayers that came before, but he most certainly heard that one.

CHAPTER 11

Every inch of my ruined flesh felt as though it was on fire. I had to wait for the sun to set in the sky before I managed to dredge up the strength needed to return to my room. Faelan's amber eyes widened at the sight of me. I dragged my feet toward the bed and collapsed face-first on top of the pillows. Reverend Richards had given me more lashes than usual, likely as a parting gift to remember him by once I graduated—though the prospects of me actually surviving the trials were looking rather dismal at this point. Faelan said nothing for a good long while, which was how I knew it was really bad. "What happened?" he asked finally, his voice uncharacteristically subdued.

"I don't want to talk about it," I replied, my voice so thick and rough that it sounded unrecognizable to my ears.

"Koven, we leave for Spire the day after tomorrow." I could hear the concern in his voice. He didn't need to remind me. I was well aware of just how fucked I was. Vassals of Sheara wouldn't touch me in this state. It was forbidden for them to aid sinners bearing marks of penance until the wounds had healed of their own accord. With the extent of my injuries, I wouldn't be able to fight. I wouldn't be able to do much of anything. I would be a liability to my team in the trials and probably get myself and everyone else killed as a result.

"You're not helping," I muttered, turning my bleary eyes on Faelan. His bronze skin glimmered in the lamplight like a polished shield beneath the sun. A set of old claw marks tore across the lean muscles of his chest, reminding me that he had once wrestled a wolf of war with his bare hands. If he could survive that, he should be able to make it through the trials just fine without me. Except he wouldn't leave me behind to die. He was far too noble for such a thing, which was a rare trait in the House of Shadows. He would probably fend off whatever horrors were lurking in the maze with a sword in one hand and me hauled over his shoulder with the other, valiant and heroic, true to his title as a prince of Athearia. Then he would have yet another insufferable story with which to enthrall the ladies of his cousin's court.

I think I would rather be fed to Ashearan's undead horde than be forced to endure such a fate.

Faelan moved in closer to examine my injuries. I must've slipped in and out of consciousness, because my eyelids fluttered closed, and when they opened again, the room was empty. Then I blinked and Emrys was peering back at me, his eyes more gray than blue, as though the sky had given way to storm clouds. He lifted a vial to my lips. The unmistakable scent of shaewood root wafted out from it as he poured the pungent liquid into my mouth. Some of it slipped down my chin to dampen the pillow, but I managed to swallow the rest. The effect was almost instantaneous; my pain started to dull along with the rest of my senses.

"I didn't tell him anything," I tried to say, but my tongue was like lead in my mouth, distorting my words. Emrys's face softened. His lips parted as though he wanted to tell me something, but then the world around me faded into oblivion.

When I next awoke, daylight filtered in through the window. Faelan was nowhere to be seen, but Emrys was sitting on the floor next to me, his head cradled in the crook of his arm as he slept against the edge of the bed. Dried blood coated his fingertips, and there was a pile of crimson-stained bandages on the floor next to him.

Without the night to help keep the pain at bay, it racked through my entire body. My attempt to get up from the bed lasted all of a split second before I sank back into the pillows with a grimace, the movement causing my skin to strain against the stitches. Emrys stirred from where he slept, lifting up his head in a daze as he peered at his surroundings. "You shouldn't move around too much," he advised.

"I'm completely fucked for the trials." My voice fractured as I spoke. I sounded weak and broken, which was exactly how I felt.

I hated it.

"Don't worry. It will be fine. I'm not going to let you die." He said it with such confidence that I could almost believe him . . . but it wouldn't be fine. How could it be when my body was in shreds and Reverend Richards had completely shattered my future as though it had been made of nothing more than glass?

"The relic—" I started to say, but I couldn't bring myself to finish the sentence. My retainer's relic was gone and my place in his shadow court had disappeared along with it. What was I supposed to do now? Without a commendation from the Cenobium, another noble house would be less inclined to allow me a position on their shadow court. My tutelage under Reverend Richards didn't make me eager to pledge myself to the service of the church, but maybe that was the only option I had left. "I can't join your shadow court," I informed Emrys, trying and failing to keep my voice even as I said it. "Reverend Richards has made it clear that the church won't allow it."

Dipping a rag into a bowl of water, he wiped away some of the sweat from my brow, the damp cloth cold and soothing against my burning skin. "Amari has already spun your fate, Koven, and she will not let it be easily changed." The notion wasn't nearly as comforting as he made it sound. A person's destiny was woven from threads, not carved from stone. Threads could be unraveled. Threads could be cut. Destiny was not definitive, and even if it were, fate could be just as cruel as the rest of the gods. Right now, it certainly felt that way.

"Your stitches are too tight," Emrys said as he produced another sleeping draught. "Now that there's enough light, I'll take them out for you. Get some rest, Koven, and let me worry about everything else."

He tipped the liquid into my mouth. The world once again faded into something dark and distant.

As the sun disappeared beneath the horizon, the shadows in the room slowly began to shift toward me as though taking on a life of their own. They coiled themselves around my legs and wove their way between my fingers. They caressed my flayed skin with a touch so soft and cold it made me shudder. I remained locked in sleep, unable to move or open my eyes, aware that I was trapped inside a nightmare that I was powerless to wake up from. Someone crouched down next to me, leaning in close enough that I could feel their breath against my ear.

"Such a vicious little prayer you offered me." Although I hadn't heard Celdric's voice in years, I recognized it instantly. The god of shadows was in my room, looming above me like a specter in the night. "I can grant it for you, but a death pact like that will cost more blood than this." At his command, the shadows spilled over to coat my bed like a blanket, lapping up the crimson stains on the sheets. "Fortunately for you, I'm a patient god. I can wait. I can collect your offerings drop by drop."

A hand reached out to stroke my hair.

"You should avoid disappointing me during your trials, or I might just be tempted to collect the payment in one go."

My eyes shot open, but the room was empty. It was just a dream, and with that realization, the thundering heart inside my chest settled back down to a steady rhythm. I struggled into a sitting position. Courtesy of the night lending me its strength, the pain was bearable. The windows had been thrown open, allowing a cool breeze to flow into the room. Someone had also left a plate of food for me on my bedside table, which contained an assortment of bread, cheeses, and grapes. My stomach twisted with hunger, reminding me that it had been more than a day since I last ate. However, my body in its weakened state refused to let me swallow more than a few mouthfuls.

The door creaked open, and Rita peeked her head in through the gap. "Ah, you're finally awake," she said, stepping into the room. Her blond hair was done up in a ponytail, showing off the variety of metal studs lining her ears. Instead of her academic robes, she was dressed in a loose linen shirt and a pair of breeches, her muddy boots coming up to her knees. Her gaze lingered on the shredded skin of my back before returning to my face. "Not a very clever move pissing off the faculty right before graduation, Koven."

"I'm aware," I replied flatly. She went to my cupboard to pull out a casual pair of trousers and matching dark shirt to go with it. She handed it over to me. I arched an eyebrow at her in question. "Are we going somewhere?"

"Yes, we're going to Ravenrook. Now, hurry up and get changed. We need to be back before morning."

Rita loved the seedy underbelly of her hometown and the chaos that engulfed the streets as soon as the sun set in the sky, and while I didn't share the same attachment to Ravenrook that Rita did, I usually didn't mind her requests for the occasional visit. However, I was not currently in the mood for a nostalgic trip down memory lane. "Rita—"

"It's not for me, it's for you," she said before I could voice my refusal. She paused a moment in thought. "Although we are going to be in the same group for the trials, so I guess it is for me as well. I don't really want to be stuck trying to drag your ass across the finish line because you're too injured to do it yourself. I know a healer who owes me a favor. She'll get rid of those lashings on your back. Let's just hope we can find her before dawn, because otherwise you'll be stuck like this for the exams."

She didn't need to tell me twice. I shrugged on the trousers. The shirt was a little more difficult to get on. She quickly grew impatient with my failed attempts at trying to pull it over my head and did it for me. "Gods, you really will be useless if we don't get you fixed up," she muttered under her breath. "Reverend Richards was a bit overzealous in doling out your punishment."

"It was a farewell gift," I said dryly, "because he's going to miss me so much."

Rita gave a humorless snort. No one in the House of Shadows liked to admit to needing help, so neither of us acknowledged it when she crouched down to lace up my boots for me. When she rose back to her feet again, she cast a curious glance at the rumpled mess that was my bed. "Did you change your sheets?" she asked. "When I came in to check on you earlier, this place looked like a war zone. There was blood everywhere."

I twisted around to find that the sheets were free of any crimson stains. The floors were also spotless, having been wiped clean of the trail of blood that I had left in my wake when I stumbled into the room last night. Faelan had never cleaned up a single thing in his life, so it couldn't have been him. It wasn't out of the realm of possibility that Emrys had taken the time to put everything in order . . . but then I spotted the pile of bandages that had been gathered into a wastebasket at the foot of my bed. They were as white as freshly fallen snow.

The hairs on the back of my neck bristled. It hadn't been a dream. Celdric had been in here, collecting my blood just like the shadows had done in the penance room. Prayers rarely got answered, and even when they did, the gods often took more than they gave. Deals with them were dangerous things. I hadn't thought it through when I reached out to Celdric in my anger and desperation, but it was too late to regret the decision now. The deal had been made, and more than a small part of me was pleased with the idea that Reverend Richards would be forced to face the wrath of one of the gods that he enjoyed evoking in his charade of forgiveness—but harming a member of the clergy was punishable by death, and while Celdric might be beyond the scope of divine laws, I most certainly wasn't.

"Emrys helped to tidy everything up," I lied.

"For a noble, I'll admit he isn't the worst." Coming from Rita, that was the highest form of praise. "He refused to leave your side today. You would think he was the one joining your shadow court, not the other way around." I fell quiet, all too aware of the absence of the retainer's relic upon my belt. Rita must've sensed the shift in my mood, because she quickly changed the topic. "Shall we get going?" she said.

I called upon the shadows and the darkness opened up at our feet, dragging the two of us down into the shadow domain.

The realm Celdric had created was devoid of all color, the world painted in various hues of gray and black. I emerged on the outskirts of a ruined city, the House of Shadows now little more than a pile of rubble behind me.

A thick mist clouded the air, the sky barren of both the sun and the stars. It was a desolate and lifeless place. The only movements were the wisps of shadow that flickered across the ground and climbed over the walls.

Some of the shadows circled my feet like winding snakes, but Celdric's blood in my veins kept them from trying to consume me. As a shapeshifter, Rita couldn't access the shadow domain like I could, but she could walk through it unharmed if a shadow-walker opened the gateway for her. While the realm was a useful way to travel, unfortunately, it had a vehement dislike for outsiders. I had once brought Emrys here, and without Celdric's marking to protect him, the shadows had viewed him as a trespasser and retaliated accordingly. The darkness here was a feral and violent thing. It went beyond my abilities to control. I'd barely managed to drag Emrys out of there alive, and it was not a mistake I planned on making again.

Rita and I began walking to the town square, the abandoned streets eerie and silent as silhouettes flitted in and out of view. Twisted roots of long-dead trees strangled the decaying buildings, the city half concealed beneath a heavy blanket of fog. The mist parted and congealed without any discernible pattern, occasionally revealing bones that littered the ground. Shadows roamed over them, searching for scraps of meat to strip away. When they discovered there was nothing left for them to devour, they slunk away again.

Although I had traveled through the shadow domain many times before, I'd never actually seen another shadow-walker inside it. I wasn't sure if that was due to the sheer size of this place, or because there were only a handful of us in existence. Either way, I liked that it didn't get many visitors, as though this world of swirling mist and slithering shadows was a treasure so rare that only a chosen few were allowed to enter it. The gateways were what made the shadow domain truly remarkable, a collection of hidden doors that connected this place to locations across the continent. Throughout my explorations, I'd managed to find a painting that transported me into the heart of the Marcaida Fortress and an archway that led out onto a balcony of the royal palace. I had located dozens of gateways scattered within the ruins of this realm, but I doubted that was all of them.

Rita and I entered the town square, which was almost an exact replica of Ravenrook's, down to the cracked cobblestone streets and the three-tiered fountain that stood in its center. This water, however, had grown stagnant with disuse. Rita stepped into it first, disappearing beneath the surface as though the water was a lot more than just a few inches deep. A distorted reflection of her peered back at me from the other side. The water rushed up to engulf me as I stepped in after her, and while it was cold to the touch, it didn't drench my clothes as I slipped through the gateway and back into the mortal realm. The unnerving silence of the shadow domain was replaced by the sound of the trickling fountain, the water now clear and free of algae. This water did try to seep into my clothes, but my boots managed to keep me dry as I waded to the edge and clambered out.

I followed Rita through the winding streets, which were sporadically lit by lanterns that dangled above tavern signs. It was already that time of the night when men and women were stumbling through the darkness and retching against the side of buildings. One particularly merry drunk was bellowing a folk song at the top of his lungs. Rita smiled as though she found it endearing.

The debauchery only intensified as we crossed over into the Dregs, which was the rougher part of town. It was also the district Rita had grown up in, earning her meals by picking the pockets of the people who had come in search of Ravenrook's infamous gambling dens and harlot houses. I was forced to step over a man who was dead in the gutters, likely the result of an unpaid debt or a robbery gone wrong. Children in rags eyed me from the opposite side of the street, obviously deliberating whether I would be an easy target, but then Rita scratched her neck with two fingers. It must've been a signal of some sort, because they proceeded to scatter in search of other prey.

"You miss it here," I noted.

She lifted a shoulder in a shrug. "It's home," she said simply.

The Dregs was a confusing maze of narrow streets. More than once I was forced to avoid the downpour of sewage that was tossed from the windows, the foul scent of it hanging heavy in the air. We had to stop at several drinking establishments before Rita managed to get reliable information about where the healer could be located. I expected that a vassal of Sheara who had somehow found herself in the Dregs would be tending to the poor souls dying of consumption in the streets, or perhaps cradling young children in one of the orphanages. Instead, we found ourselves on the top floor of a building that looked like it was one termite infestation away from collapsing in on itself.

Rita attempted to knock on the door, but as soon as her fist connected with the frame, it came off its hinges. She took that as an invitation to let herself in. A lone candle burned low in the center of the floor, illuminating the small room in a soft orange glow. The space was scarcely furnished, with little more than a moldy blanket rolled out in the corner and a selection of clothes hung on a washing line strung between two opposing walls.

The woman inside brandished a small knife in warning but lowered it when Rita stepped into the light. "Your door is broken," Rita informed her.

"I'm aware," the woman replied dryly. The wariness in her eyes returned when she noticed me standing by the entrance. "A friend of yours?" she asked Rita. She didn't wait for a response before she said, "Well, don't just hover there like a reaper waiting to collect my soul. Either come in or leave me in peace."

I stepped inside, wondering how a god-blessed healer had ended up in a place like this. She appeared to be nearing her fourth decade, but the silver streaks in her hair were too prominent to be just a mark of age. She had crossed the line before, dipping into her own life force to heal that which either shouldn't or couldn't be healed, and now the years she had traded away for more power were starting to catch up to her.

"Please, make yourself at home," she said, gesturing at the imaginary chairs she didn't own.

"I've come to collect on that favor you owe me," Rita said, leaning back against one of the walls with her arms folded across her chest. "We leave for the trials tomorrow, and my friend has penance marks he needs to be rid of."

"Penance marks?" the woman repeated, and then shook her head. "That's against the church's doctrine. It's dangerous work and students are reckless, easily found out. It could cost me my head. Find someone else."

Rita didn't move from her position. Instead, she propped up one knee, making herself more comfortable. "We made a deal. A favor for a favor . . . or perhaps you would like me to share your little secret with the high inquisitor."

The woman scoffed. "Oh please, you would hang for it, too."

"Only if they manage to catch me, and unlike you, I can change my face."

The woman held her gaze as though trying to assess whether the threat was real or merely bluster. When Rita didn't so much as blink, the healer sighed. "A favor for a favor," she agreed. She slipped her knife back into a holster around her ankle before approaching me. Taking hold of my hands, she studied the burn marks around my wrists.

"Your wrists will still be visible, so I won't touch them," she told me. "As for your back, you can hide that beneath your clothes. However, you will need to appear as though you are still in pain to avoid suspicion, so I'll heal most of the damage, but not all of it."

"That sounds sensible." No sooner were the words out of my mouth than her power poured into me, strong and demanding. My flesh stretched and rippled as it began to close. My knees buckled from the force of it. The agony was blinding—all-consuming—and it was all I could do not to scream. Then she let go of my hands and the agony faded down to a dull throb. Struggling back to my feet, I rolled my shoulders, and though my body was still tender, the pain wasn't nearly as debilitating as it was before.

"Thank you," I said.

"Good luck with the trials," the woman replied, though her voice was notably devoid of the compassion that her sisterhood was renowned for. "You're going to need it."

Rita pushed herself off the wall. "Pleasure doing business with you," she said before giving me a small nod.

I called upon the darkness, and it responded by swallowing us whole. We tumbled back into the ruined city of the shadow domain, the air swirling with mist and the silent silhouettes dancing across the abandoned buildings. The two of us began making our way back to the crumbling version of the House of Shadows.

"She was a bit jaded for a healer," I muttered.

"You would be too if you spent your life working in a house of inquiry," said Rita.

"Why would a healer join a house of inquiry?"

"To put the prisoners back together again so that the inquisitors can keep trying to pry the truth out of them."

"Well, yes, but what I meant was why would she *want* to join a house of inquiry."

Rita thought about it for a moment and then shrugged. "That's a question better asked of your seer. The money is good, but seeing how she lives, I doubt that was her reason."

"Is that why you want to join? For the money?"

Rita gave me a sideways glance. "I would be lying if I said it wasn't a factor, but there are other perks that come with the position. I don't hear of many inquisitors who are subjected to the art of their trade."

As we came to the end of the road, the mist thinned to reveal broken blocks of obsidian scattered across the ground. A snake-shaped pillar lay in pieces, its sockets devoid of the topaz stones that served as its eyes. Somewhere in these ruins, there was a tarnished mirror that connected to a shinier version of itself in the mortal realm. A touch was all that was needed to spit someone back out into the House of Shadows on the other side.

"I suppose I now owe you a favor for a favor," I said to Rita.

"How about drinks on you after we survive the trials?" she countered, and my lips curved into a teasing smile.

"Oh, I don't know about that. I have a feeling that you know how to run up an expensive tab."

"A *very* expensive tab," she assured me.

Considering that she had probably just saved my life, that was still a bargain. "Very well," I agreed. "Drinks on me after graduation."

CHAPTER 12

Students slowly filed onto the ship, the sigils of their patron gods stitched into the back of their combat uniforms, each one carrying a variety of weapons and shields in preparation for the trials. Reverend Richards was standing at the bottom of the gangway, holding a bejeweled bowl that contained a mixture of ashes and blood that he used to mark the foreheads of each student before they boarded the ship. When it was my turn to stand in front of him, it was a constant effort not to reach for one of my daggers to wipe that amiable smile off his face.

"Do you vow to faithfully serve the gods from this day until your last?" Reverend Richards said, and I forced myself to bow my head in a show of reverence.

"I do."

"Do you pledge your life in honor of your patron deity, Celdric, god of shadows and illusions, of mischief and deception, of travelers and thieves?"

"I do."

"Should your blood be spilled and your final breath drawn, do you offer yourself as a sacrifice upon the altar of your patron god?"

His words made me pause. If I died in these exams, it would constitute a sacrifice. And not just any sacrifice, a blood sacrifice—one of the most powerful forms of worship. For the first time, I wondered if maybe the trials were more than just about assessing who was worthy to bear the gift of the gods. The reverend's stare was a heavy thing as he awaited my response. The back of my neck began to prickle, sensing that something was amiss, but I didn't have any other choice than to complete the ritual.

"I do," I said. Reverend Richards dipped his fingers into the ornate bowl. He smeared the mixture of blood and ash across my forehead.

"May the gods deem you worthy, or may your soul find peace in paradise." He proceeded to place a hand on my shoulder as though in comfort. Then he squeezed it, putting pressure on one of the slashes left behind by his whip. While the wound was now shallow, the pain of it still caused me to grimace. The reverend's eyes glinted with a malicious sort of delight, yet his voice was kind as he said, "I hope you have heeded my lessons, Koven, and that you face your final trials freed of the burdens of your shortcomings."

I forced myself to replicate his smile. "Thank you, Reverend."

As I stepped onto the gangway and made my way onto the ship, I withdrew one of my daggers and sliced into my palm. I allowed my blood to trickle into my shadow, each drop disappearing into the darkness.

Once all the students were aboard, the massive set of sails unfurled and the ship lurched forward, gliding down the Rift that separated Athearia from Kalta. The stretch of water sliced the continent in two, the Athearian gods taking everything south of the border and the Kaltans taking everything north of it. The current wasn't too strong this far away from the sea, and it would've been possible for an ambitious swimmer to traverse the distance between the two countries, but hungry creatures were known to lurk in these waters. As I leaned over the edge of the railing, I noted several dark shadows prowling just beneath the surface.

Emrys came to stand next to me, a silver-wood staff in his hand. It had been a gift from the god of foresight for his tenth birthday, given to him along with a drop of Essian's blood. A large crystal ball was cradled at the top of it, the tips of the staff curling around it like a nest cradling an egg. The wind whipped at the loose fabric of his combat uniform, his frail limbs making it seem like he could be whisked away at any moment. The gods might have blessed him with a formidable power, but the body in which he housed it was delicate and fragile. I tried not to think about how easily those bones of his would break in the grip of a vassal of war, or how quickly that pale skin would blister under the onslaught of fire. Instead, I reminded myself that he had already seen the upcoming trials, which meant he knew the path he needed to take in order to make it through alive.

"Your injuries?" Emrys said. From the way he dropped his voice to a whisper, it was obvious he already knew about my illicit encounter with the healer in Ravenrook.

"Not bad enough to kill me anymore," I replied. His gaze dropped down to my bleeding hand, which was dripping over the railing into the water below. The scent of it must've excited one of the sea creatures, because a scaly tail briefly flicked out of the water and then disappeared back into the depths with a splash.

Emrys rummaged through the supply satchel that hung over his shoulder and pulled out a fresh bandage to bind the wound. "Did you offer up a prayer to Celdric this morning?" He didn't sound ecstatic about the idea.

"In a manner of speaking," I said. With the extent of his foresight, it sometimes felt impossible to keep a secret from him. He might very well already know what I'd prayed for, but if he did, neither of us dared to acknowledge it. Prayers were sacred pacts made between mortals and the divine. Most prayers were harmless, trivial things. A plea for good health, or a child, or forgiveness, or wealth. However, the more insidious deals were best not spoken aloud or you risked earning the wrath of the very god who held your prayer in their hands.

"Celdric is an unpredictable god, his shadows concealing him from even my sight," Emrys said as he tied off the bandage with a knot. "You should tread carefully with him."

I kept my gaze fixed on the horizon as the Rift grew wider until it eventually rolled out into the sea. The island of Spire appeared as a speck in the distance, the location of the final trials drawing ever closer. Without my place secured in Emrys's shadow court, I wasn't sure what fate had planned for me after graduation, but that was a problem for another day. First, I needed to survive through this one.

"Tell me, seer, is death what awaits me in my future?" My tone was teasing, so that Emrys would know the question was merely in jest, but from the morose way he leaned against his staff, his eyes turning as gray as storm clouds, he looked like he was taking it very seriously.

"We're all going to die at some point, Koven. That is what it means to be mortal."

It was high noon by the time we arrived at the docks of Spire. It was easy to see why the goddess of love had claimed this island for her own. The water was a stunning shade of crystal blue, the waves sparkling beneath the sun like a thousand tiny diamonds. Tall palm trees dotted the sandy beaches, the long fans of their leaves swaying gently in the breeze. It would've been perfect if not for the fact that the heat was so intense it felt like a physical weight on my shoulders.

The docks were bustling with activity as I stepped off the gangway, the scents of salt and fish hanging heavy in the air. The harbor opened up into a marketplace. Dozens of small stalls with thatched roofs were busy selling a range of goods, from colorful clothes and silver bangles to freshly baked breads and exotic fruits. At the sight of our black-and-gold combat uniforms, the residents whispered among one another with varying degrees of curiosity and awe. Just ahead of me, Faelan winked at a group of local girls. The heat seemingly had no impact on his mood. On the contrary, the bright sunlight brought out the bronze hue of his skin and made him appear as though he was glowing. The girls all giggled, a sound that grew even louder after he traded a few coins for some flowers to gift them with.

I came to an abrupt halt when I noticed the red-and-gold uniforms that marked someone as a student from Kaltan Academy. One particularly mean-looking boy with thick muscles and a scar that bisected his upper lip strode forward, the glint in his eyes making it clear that he was searching for trouble. I naturally broke away from the rest of the students to blend in with the busy marketplace. I wasn't the only one. Rita had already taken up a position atop one of the roofs, her body lowered in a crouch. It was forbidden for vassals to kill each other before the start of the trials, but one could never be too careful when it came to those marked by the god of war. They weren't exactly known for their self-restraint and sunny temperaments.

The boy came to a stop in front of Faelan, the back of his uniform bearing the snarling wolf of Brazial. Faelan proceeded to offer him a rose. "Would you like a flower, too?"

The curiosity of the crowd gave way to caution as people began to edge away. The boy slashed through the rose with his sword and then pressed the tip of it against Faelan's throat.

"I'm going to take that as a no," Faelan muttered.

"We were told that a prince of Athearia would be here," he said, his mouth slowly lifting into a malicious grin. "A vassal of Celdric, who is said to be as pretty as a vixen. I assume that's you."

"As pretty as a vixen," Faelan repeated, sounding delighted by the comparison. "Consider me flattered."

"Brazial has placed a premium price on your head." The vassal of war dug the point of his sword just deep enough to cause blood to trickle down Faelan's neck, but Faelan stood his ground, undaunted by the threat. I crept forward, my shadow slowly extending across the sand. "Apparently, the mad bitch Scias has chosen to be the next queen of Athearia is also undertaking the trials this year. Brazial has promised a mighty reward for her as well."

A crack appeared in Faelan's carefree facade, his eyes darkening with anger. Celdric's blood in my veins began to hum in anticipation of the chaos that was about to ensue. My shadow quietly enveloped the boy's legs. On the rooftop, Rita palmed a dagger. Faelan flexed his fingers, a sign that he was getting ready to fight. Then an arrow sliced through the air. It sailed past the vassal's head and embedded itself in a wooden support beam of a nearby stall. A warning shot.

Akira stepped forward, a hunting bow poised in her hand. The boy's upper lip curled into a snarl as he attempted to lurch forward, but my shadow already had ahold of him. The tendrils of darkness wrapped around his limbs like chains. He struggled against my restraints as he was forced down to his knees. I commanded the darkness to tighten its grip, but with the sun still visible in the sky, I wasn't at the peak of my strength. I wouldn't be able to keep him restrained for long.

"Who the fuck are you?" he demanded as Akira came to a stop in front of him.

"I'm that mad bitch Scias has chosen to be the next queen of Athearia," she replied evenly. He stared back at her with obvious skepticism. From the horrifying stories about her family, he probably expected her to be over six feet tall with wild, untamed hair and a cackle that could curdle blood. Instead, Akira was the very picture of calm, with silky black hair that was tied back in a neat braid and a round face that lent her a more youthful appearance.

When the boy's gaze narrowed on the jagged scar that tore across her throat, he must've realized that she was being serious, because he barked out a laugh. "You? You're a descendant of House Marcaida? The legend of your bloodline must be built on a mountain of lies, because I could crush you with my bare hands."

Once again, he fought against my restraints. The shadows slipped slightly, and his face flashed with triumph as he managed to stagger back to his feet. I moved closer to him, a bead of sweat trickling down my forehead as the shadows strengthened their hold, yanking him back down to the ground. He shot a glare in my direction, and I got the distinct feeling that Brazial didn't need to put a price on my head in order for me to make this boy's personal hit list.

"Then may fate see fit to have our paths cross during the trials so that we may determine who out of the two of us would emerge victorious," Akira said, seemingly unconcerned with the bounty Brazial had placed on her head.

The scene had started to attract the attention of other students, the air growing thick with tension as vassals from both Kalta and Athearia drew closer. Akira surveyed her surroundings and then signaled for me to release my hold on the boy. I hesitated for a moment, unsure of whether that was the best course of action, but I did as she instructed. Considering that he was a vassal of war, it was hardly surprising when the first thing he did was pick up his sword and rush forward, intent on separating Akira's head from her shoulders.

Faelan threw himself in front of her, reaching for his own sword as well. A wall of flames erupted in the space between them before a fight could materialize. The fire quickly died back down, though the scorching heat of it remained, rolling through the market like a shock wave. A young man stepped forward, his face marked by a smattering of freckles that danced across his nose and cheekbones. His hair was the fierce shade of red that was often favored by Lios, the god of fire. His piercing blue eyes, however, were as cold as ice as he regarded the vassal of war.

"You know the rules. No killing before the trials," he said, his voice carrying an undertone of warning. "Put your sword away before I make you."

The mean-looking boy fell into a sullen silence, his displeasure a palpable thing as he begrudgingly returned his blade to its sheath. "Fate be willing," he said to Akira. Then he glowered at me one last time before stalking away.

"Apologies for that," the redhead said diplomatically. "Vassals of Brazial are always eager to test their mettle. Please, take it as a compliment that he deemed you to be a worthy opponent."

"No apologies necessary," Akira replied. "Damien Knight, I presume?"

My interest piqued at the sound of his name. This wasn't just any vassal. This was the surrogate son of the god of fire and the goddess of the sea. Damien's lips lifted in the smallest hint of a smile. "It would seem that I'm preceded by my reputation."

Akira's gaze was scrutinizing as she considered him, but her face remained unreadable, giving no indication as to what she could be thinking. "I don't put much stock in someone's reputation. I prefer to make my own evaluation."

"Then you and I are alike in that regard. May the gods grant you their favor in the coming trials, my lady." He bowed his head to Akira. He repeated the gesture for Faelan as he said, "Your Highness."

He paused for a moment as he regarded me, seemingly contemplating whether I warranted some form of acknowledgment. Apparently, I did. "Shadow-walker," he said with a slight inclination of his head before turning around and taking his leave. The back of his combat uniform didn't just bear the dragon of Lios. It was also stitched with the horse of Tammearia, which meant that the stories about Damien Knight were true. He hadn't just been marked by one god. He was one of the very rare individuals who had managed to survive being marked by two.

Emrys stepped out from between two market stalls to intercept him, looking like a sage of old with his white hair and silver-wood staff. "Turn left at the crossing of the red lady and the crowned king," he advised with a disconcerting smile. Damien's brow furrowed at the strange words, but he continued walking. "Oh, and you should beware the wolf with no bark," Emrys called out, "for he gives no warning before he bites. You would do well not to turn your back on him."

Damien halted as though the warning meant something to him. He regarded Emrys with a mixture of curiosity and suspicion. "You're that seer with the barren parents," he noted.

"That's a rather blunt way of putting it. I do prefer to be called by my name, which is Emrys."

"Damien Knight," he replied by way of introduction.

"I know."

Damien shifted uncomfortably beneath Emrys's all-seeing gaze. Apparently, he decided that he didn't want to linger, because he left without saying another word. Seers did tend to have that effect on some people.

Faelan leaned down to pick up the severed rose from the ground. He brushed away the grains of sand clinging to its petals before holding it out. "Would any of you like the flower?" he asked.

CHAPTER 13

The deep bellow of horns echoed through the air like a war cry. I turned toward the sound, watching as enforcers in hooded white robes emerged from the brush to line either side of a pathway leading deeper into the island. They came to a stop, their faces all hidden beneath gilded masks devoid of emotion, and though they didn't speak a word, their message was clear. The vassals were being summoned. The trials were about to begin.

I followed the rest of the students as they converged on the trail. The tree canopies curved and bent to form a tunnel overhead, their branches weaving together like clasping hands. The enforcers stood as still as statues as they watched the vassals progressing deeper into the island, a set of shiny Rasalan whips curled at their sides, their presence serving as a silent warning for students not to venture off the designated route. The pathway eventually opened up into a clearing, where a grand feast had been prepared.

The long banquet tables were draped in expensive gold cloth, offering a lavish selection of food, from marinated fish and freshly picked fruits to pastries drizzled in honey and spit-roasted pigs, their mouths propped open with shiny red apples. A young woman in a flowing pink dress sauntered up to Faelan, her skin the deep shade of caramel that was dominant in the Spider Province of Kalta. She flashed a smile of pearly-white teeth, her eyes heavily lidded and her lips painted rouge. She was perhaps the most beautiful woman I had ever laid eyes upon.

"I didn't think the gods made men so pretty south of the Rift," she mused, her voice just as mesmerizing as she was. Faelan grinned as she ran a finger seductively along his jawline. Her gaze briefly flicked in my direction before she seemed to decide that I was beneath her interest.

An inexplicable wave of jealousy rose up within me.

"And I didn't think perfection could be achieved by a mortal, and yet here you stand before me," Faelan replied.

Her mouth curved into a suggestive smile. "I imagine that tongue of yours has more talents than just whispering sweet flatteries into a girl's ear." Her touch traveled down his neck and over his shoulder before traversing the length of his arm. Her fingers brushed over his family ring, which bore the crest of House Honora: a star framed by a set of antlers. "You wear such a lovely ring," she said, her voice practically a purr. "When I was a little girl, I would often dream of a prince giving me one just like this. How it saddened my heart when that dream never came true."

Faelan took off his family's ring as though it were nothing more than a trinket and slipped it onto her finger. The jealousy in me swelled as I was reminded that, with neither gold nor title to my name, I had nothing to offer her.

"Someone such as you should have everything your heart desires," Faelan said. Lifting her hand to his lips, he pressed a kiss to her knuckles. Her eyes glinted.

"I couldn't agree with you more, my prince." Linking an arm through his, she guided him to one of the banquet tables. "Come. Enjoy the feast that the gods have prepared in your honor."

I glanced around for Emrys and Akira, but they had disappeared among the mass of students. My feet moved of their own accord, following Faelan and the woman with him. The food decorating the table did smell good, intoxicatingly so, the air a delicious mixture of spices and braised meat. The heat of this island made me pick up a goblet of wine to quench my growing thirst. I raised it to my lips.

It's obviously been laced with poison, the voice whispered. *This is a trick, and not even a very clever one.*

I lowered the cup, my brow furrowing. My gaze scanned the banquet table, noticing for the first time that there was more than just one extraordinarily beautiful woman in attendance. There were dozens of them, adorned in flowing pink dresses, pouring wine into goblets and encouraging vassals to sample the various delicacies, and not all looked young enough to still be students.

Something was wrong.

The woman who was busy admiring the way Faelan's ring looked on her finger suddenly shifted her attention to me, her gaze narrowing on my yet untouched drink. As she drifted closer, her eyes locked on mine, and I couldn't bring myself to look away. I was a fly trapped in a spider's web. "You should drink," she said, her hand roaming across my shoulder blades. "Enjoy yourself."

She was right. I should enjoy myself. I began to slowly lift the goblet up again.

Slit her throat, the voice snapped. The command wasn't fueled by rage but rather panic. Something deep within me recognized that the woman who stood before me was a creature to be feared—that all the power and gold in the world would be reduced to naught but ash and dust at a mere whisper of her lips.

This woman was a vixen, a vassal of the goddess of love.

I dropped the goblet. It clattered to the table, the wine spilling out to drench the gold cloth. With a dagger in my hand, I whirled on the woman, who took a startled step back, her hypnotic eyes wide with shock. The core of her power resided in her voice, so I listened to my instincts and sliced at her neck. Faelan grabbed my wrist, preventing me from killing my target.

"What are you doing, Koven?" he demanded, anger plain on his face.

"She's a vixen," I hissed. "This is a trap."

The revelation did not have the desired effect on him. In fact, it had no effect on him whatsoever. "Don't be ridiculous, Koven. This isn't a trap. It's a feast. We're meant to be enjoying ourselves."

He was already under her spell. I glanced down at the banquet table again. The rest of the vassals were regarding the vixens with open adoration, happily accepting the food and drink that were being offered to them. They had all fallen prey to the charm-speakers. I needed to block my ears with wax before I was next. I dug into my pockets.

"Be still," the vixen ordered, her voice vibrating with power. The words wrapped around me like a chain, freezing me in place. Her surprise melted away into something that resembled mild curiosity. Tucking a finger beneath my chin, she lifted my head and forced me to get lost in her eyes.

Carve them out, the voice urged, but I couldn't. My body was no longer my own, and as I peered into the dark depths of her gaze, I thought that maybe my heart no longer belonged to me, either.

"Such a strong will," she said as she caressed my cheek, her hand warm and soft against my skin. "I admire that in a man. I didn't notice before, but you have such interesting eyes, green like polished jade and sunlit emeralds."

If it would please her, I would pluck them from my head and lay them at her feet like an offering to a goddess.

"And you carry so many daggers. You must be very dangerous."

She was right. I *was* very dangerous. She touched my hand, and my fingers unfurled of their own accord, allowing her to take the blade away from me.

"Would you protect me?" she asked, batting her eyelashes.

I would lay down my life for her.

"Yes," I said, unable to look away. "Unto death."

"Unto death," she repeated, sounding pleased with the declaration. "How loyal."

"I can be loyal, too," Faelan said, piercing me with an annoyed glare.

She tutted at him and gave a disappointed shake of her head. "Good boys don't speak to me unless spoken to. Be a good boy and sit back down. I'm sure you can find something to entertain yourself with." Her mouth curved into a wicked smile. "Admiring your own reflection, perhaps?"

Faelan sat back down as she commanded, dejected and forlorn, until he caught a glimpse of himself in a bronze tray. Tipping over the collection of petite raspberry tarts, he used the tray like a mirror. "Eyes like liquid honey. Skin like polished oak. Hair like spun copper." He twisted his head in all directions, studying every angle. "Gods, I really am gorgeous. I can't find a single flaw."

The vixen turned her attention back on me, gently pushing me down into my seat and offering me a fresh goblet of wine. She combed her fingers through my hair. "Drink," she ordered, and I took a sip. "It's delicious, is it not? So refreshing. You want to drink it all."

I frowned. The liquid was unpleasantly warm, having been left in the sun for too long. She leaned in closer. Her breath was hot on my ear as she whispered, "It would please me greatly if you drank it all. Don't you want to make me happy?"

There was nothing in this world I wanted more.

I drained the goblet and placed it back on the table. She swung herself onto my lap, her hands hooking around my neck. I twirled a piece of her brown hair around my finger. It reminded me of someone, but as soon as I tried to grasp at the memory, it slipped through my fingers like sand.

"Loyalty is a rare trait," she said, her voice tinged at the edges with what almost sounded like longing. I put my arms around her as she rested her head against my chest. "Loyalty, true loyalty, cannot be commanded. It must be freely given. Pasaphae thought she had that with Lios, the great god of the sun, lord of fire and dragons. Do you know the story?"

Everyone on the continent knew the story, but I had a feeling that she wanted to tell it, so I remained quiet.

"Fire is such a fickle element, capable of such great warmth and also such great destruction. Lios had pledged Pasaphae his heart, but his devotion was just as fickle as his fire. One night, he saw the goddess of the sea dancing beneath the moonlight and fell hopelessly, desperately in love with her. You see, love is also a fickle emotion if it doesn't have loyalty to anchor it.

"The betrayal was unforgivable, so on the eve of their wedding, when all the gods were to present their gifts to the newlywed couple, Pasaphae gifted Lios with both a blessing and a curse. She told him that his heart would never again be fickle. He would love his wife for all eternity, but when he next touched her, he would burn her until she dissolved to ash in his hands."

The vixen ran her hand down the length of my arm. "It's sad, is it not? To be destined to love someone but forever be torn apart. Sad but beautiful. I suppose that is why so many poets have tried to capture the story in their songs." She peered up at me with her lovely dark eyes. "Can I tell you a secret?"

"I love secrets," I said with a smile.

"People think that Pasaphae is the goddess of love, but I've always thought she was much more suited to being a goddess of vengeance. There is nothing quite so terrifying as a woman scorned. Don't you agree?"

"I've always found spiders to be a much more frightening prospect." I had never said it aloud before. At the Cenobium, fears were a weakness that could be twisted against me. But this woman had just shared one of her secrets with me, so it was only fair that I shared one of mine with her.

"You're scared of spiders?" She laughed, a sound so pure it could've washed the continent free of sin. "You do know that you have one sitting in your lap right this very second?"

I pressed my forehead against hers. "And I'm practically quaking in fear," I retorted, my voice teasing.

"You should fear me," she said, but the severity of her words was undercut by the endearing way she nudged her nose against mine. "My voice is far more deadly than any venom. I once asked a man to rip the heart from his chest just to see if he would."

"Did he?" I asked, curious.

"He died screaming with his hand still stuck in his rib cage. It was not nearly as romantic as I envisioned."

The shiny tray slipped out of Faelan's hands. He wobbled slightly before his eyelids drooped downward and his face slammed against the table with a painful thud.

I told you it was poisoned, you idiot, the voice chastised, but it was muted and distant, as though being shouted underwater. I was vaguely aware that I should be alarmed by the dozens of vassals that were all falling unconscious at the banquet table, but with the vixen in my arms, I couldn't bring myself to care about much else.

"And what would you ask of me?" I said, brushing a thumb over her knuckles.

She made a soft humming sound as she thought about it. "I think I would like to know your name."

It was such a simple request. Fulfilling it was hardly a true show of my devotion, but I did it anyway. "My name is Koven."

"Well, Koven, I have another secret for you." She held up a gold coin for me to admire. One side was carved with the spider of Pasaphae, the other was marked with the crow of Ashearan. "I like you, so I'm deciding to give you an advantage. You will need to survive the first trial on your merits, but this coin can buy you out of the second. The second trial is single combat to the death, so this advantage might just save your life. Make it through the maze and offer up this coin, and you'll be spared. But be warned, other vixens will have whispered about the existence of these coins into the ears of your competitors. They will be searching for them. You would do well to keep it hidden."

My mouth curved into a lethargic smile as she slid the coin into my pocket. "And what is the third trial?" I asked her.

"I think you should worry about surviving the first two trials, my darling, before you start worrying about the third." She pressed a kiss to my cheek. "May fate see fit to favor you," she whispered before my body grew heavy and everything went black.

CHAPTER 14

My eyes snapped open as I was jostled awake. It took a moment for my sight to adjust to the dimly lit tunnels. Emrys had said that we would be thrown into a maze, but he'd neglected to mention that the labyrinth in question was also a catacomb, the walls all coated with bones belonging to both humans and animals. A skeleton draped in tattered robes clasped a flaming torch in its hands. Another one flickered at the far end of the tunnel, providing a sporadic source of light that hindered me from seeing very far into the dark. It would've been convenient for me to snuff them out completely, plunging this place into utter darkness, but with Emrys looming above me, the crystal ball embedded in the top of his staff shining like a beacon of light, I was reminded that he couldn't navigate his way through this maze if he couldn't see where he was going.

He pointed to his ears, twisting his head to show me that he had already blocked them with wax. I rushed to do the same, remembering all too well how easy it had been to fall under a vixen's spell. My fingers clasped something small and cold in my pocket. The coin. The advantage that would spare me from having to compete in a fight to the death. My gaze spanned over the rest of the team. Did they know what awaited them after they managed to survive the maze? I should tell them. That way we could come up with a strategy to make sure we collected enough for everyone.

But what if you don't manage to get enough coins for everyone? the voice questioned. *Maybe they will turn on you. Maybe they will slit your throat in order to save themselves. Friendship is easily broken beneath the shadow of death.*

The thought caused trepidation to sink its claws into me. While I was loath to admit it, the voice had a point. This was the first part of the trials—the mind games—and if I made the wrong decision, it could fracture the team. It would be safer to collect them by myself and distribute them at the end. I left the coin safely tucked where it was and pulled out the ball of wax. As I sealed my ears, the world fell eerily silent.

Akira was busy counting the arrows in her quiver, making sure that none were missing. Faelan was rubbing the swollen lump on his forehead, his face no longer flawless as a bruise blossomed on the side of his temple. One person was notably absent from the group.

Where is Rita? I signed.

Scouting ahead, Emrys signed back. Offering me his hand, he pulled me to my feet. Shadows coiled impatiently around my boots, the power of their darkness seeping into my blood and warming my veins like finely aged liquor. Night had fallen. It seemed that the gold coin was not the only advantage that fate had seen fit to bestow upon me.

Emrys led the group down one of the tunnels, the utter quiet making this labyrinth seem like what it actually was: a mass graveyard. Emrys turned left at the first intersection. Two bodies lay dead on the floor, their black-and-gold uniforms marking them as vassals of Athearia. Their faces were unrecognizable, having been caved in by a bludgeoning weapon such as a mace or a war hammer, likely the work of a vassal of Brazial.

I was no stranger to death, but my stomach still churned at the sight of the bodies and what they represented. The gods had thrown us all into a maze together, and while I didn't doubt that there would be a variety of dangers lurking around every corner, perhaps the biggest danger was the one we all posed to each other. Beyond the bounties that Brazial had placed on vassals he deemed to be worthy kills, the addition of the coins had given students yet another reason to turn on each other. As though to prove my point, Rita was crouched next to the bodies, searching their clothes and rummaging through their supply satchels. With the wax in her ears, she hadn't heard us approach, but the white light on Emrys's staff eventually announced our presence. She abruptly stood back up.

A group of Kaltans went farther down this tunnel, Rita signed. *I recommend going in the opposite direction.*

Emrys glanced at the nearest skeleton that clasped a flaming torch in its hands. This one was different from the last, with a head of a deer and legs of a fawn. Perhaps they were location beacons of some kind, allowing students to map the winding passageways and alerting them to when they managed to travel in a circle.

Unfortunately, that's also the path we must follow, Emrys signed. *Our first objective is to get out of the maze. The longer we stay in here, the more dangerous this place will become, so it's in our best interest to move as quickly as possible. Once we get out of here, we can worry about the second trial. For now, we need to focus on staying alive. It seems like Akira and Faelan both have bounties on their heads, so be wary of any Kaltans we come across. Koven, I want you up front. Faelan, I want you to watch our backs and make sure nothing sneaks up behind us.*

I crept farther down the tunnel. The shadows on the wall crept alongside me like a dog at the heel of its master, awaiting the order to attack. Peeking my head around the corner, I caught a glimpse of movement as someone disappeared into another tunnel to the left. Emrys signaled for me to turn in the opposite direction. I did as he instructed. I came across the next skeleton, this one clad in tattered white robes instead of dark ones, red tears staining its cheekbones as though it was weeping.

There was no one down any of the passageways when I stepped into the next intersection, and yet the hairs along my arm all stood up, a sixth sense warning me that something wasn't quite right. With the labyrinth of bones rendered completely silent, the only thing I could hear was the pounding of my heart in my ears, a sound that quickly turned into the rapid beat of a war drum when the long, spindly legs of an arachnid prowled out one of the nearby shafts. I couldn't quite tell what manner of creature stood before me. She was neither completely human nor completely arachnid, but rather an unholy abomination that fell somewhere in between. A cluster of beady black eyes dotted her forehead, her hair as white as freshly spun silk and her naked torso blending into the bulging body of a spider. Her charcoal lips split into a disconcerting smile, revealing a set of pincers that curled on the inside of her mouth.

Fear washed through my body like a tidal wave. It froze me in place as the woman rushed forward, her legs scurrying with unnatural speed. An arrow sliced through the air, heading straight for the center of her chest, but she easily maneuvered around it by scuttling up the walls. She was nearly upon me when my survival instincts chased the ice-cold fear from my veins. My shadow lurched toward her. She darted to the side just as the darkness collided into the wall with enough force to shatter the skulls that were embedded in it. However, as the creature moved to avoid my attack, Akira fired another arrow, and this one found its mark. It pierced through the woman's sternum and she stumbled back, her mouth opening in a screech so loud that I could hear the muffled echo of it through the wax seals in my ears.

Although Akira's aim had been impeccable, the injury hadn't managed to kill the monster, only enrage her even further. As the woman yanked out the arrow, a sickly yellow ooze bubbled out of the wound. My shadow made another attempt to grab her, but those hideously long legs of hers managed to save her yet again. She leaped to the other side of the tunnel and then immediately bounded toward Akira, the pincers inside her mouth extending as though ready to devour her prey. Akira didn't try to run. Instead, she nocked another arrow with lethal efficiency at the same time that my shadow pivoted, and Rita threw a dagger, and Faelan hefted his sword. Akira released the bowstring and time seemed to slow down, a single second stretching to its absolute limit. Rita's dagger hit first, the blade burying itself between the woman's ribs. Faelan's blow came next as he hacked off three of her legs with a single swing of his sword. Then Akira's arrow speared through the woman's throat and, a heartbeat later, my shadow smashed into the monster so violently that she was splattered against the far wall.

A sticky yellow slime burst out from her carcass, and as her remains slid down to the floor, the crevices between the bones became clogged with clumps of matted hair and shredded pieces of meat. My mouth twisted with disgust. Spiders were the sacred animal of Pasaphae. Considering that she was involved in creating the exams this year, it wasn't surprising that she had found a way to incorporate them into the trials. But whatever that wretched creature was, it exceeded the confines of my imagination, and it made me worry about what other monstrosities were trapped inside this maze, vicious and eager for the taste of human flesh.

A group of vassals appeared at the end of the tunnel. The red fabric of their tunics immediately put me on edge, and my shadow swelled around me, a dark snake poised to strike at the first sign of trouble. A vixen stood at the front of their group, easily distinguished from the rest of the students due to the pink dress she wore, and unlike most of the vixens at the feast, this one was definitely young enough to be a student. Her face was a mask of fragility and innocence, even as her gaze clocked everything, including the dead monster that lay in a distorted heap on the ground. She raised her hands in a peaceful gesture. Her lips began to move, but when she realized that her words couldn't reach our ears, her expression became more cautious and she took a tentative step backward. She proceeded to say something to the rest of her team, and then all five of them retreated down a different passageway. I breathed out a sigh of relief and my shadow settled back down next to my feet.

Emrys placed a hand on my shoulder and then pointed in the direction we needed to go. I gave him a quick nod before taking up the lead again.

I eventually came across another dead body. The horse stitched into the back of his tunic marked him as a vassal of Tammearia. It looked as though something with very sharp teeth had taken bites out of him, leaving behind gaping wounds along his legs, throat, and torso. I suppressed a shudder as I stepped over the corpse.

I came to a sudden stop when a glowing light appeared in front of me. A girl cradled a flame in her hand, and though I didn't recognize her, I certainly recognized the mean-looking boy at her side. It was the vassal of war who had threatened Faelan and Akira in the marketplace, and from the menacing glint in his eyes, it was clear that he had every intention of collecting the bounty Brazial had placed on my teammates. He said something to the girl. I was fairly certain it was an order to burn me alive, because the vassal of Lios lifted her hands to do just that.

Scorching orange flames funneled down the passage. My darkness rushed forward to meet it, and the two elements clashed. For a moment, the wall of fire and shadow seemed locked in a stalemate, but a vassal of Lios was at their strongest in the day, and I was at my strongest during the night. The darkness quickly overwhelmed her, smothering her flames until they were nothing more than harmless puffs of smoke. While the shadows restrained her, the vassal of war dashed forward with his sword raised. A wave of darkness shoved him to the side, pinning him against the wall. Back at the Cenobium I had told Akira that I wouldn't hesitate to spill Kaltan blood if that was what it came to, and yet as his muscles strained against the darkness, his feet dangling helplessly in the air, that was exactly what ended up happening: I hesitated.

Do it, the voice urged from the back of mind.

The vassal bared his teeth in a snarl, making him look just like the wolf stitched into his uniform. I knew that if the positions were reversed, he would end my life without so much as a second thought. I reminded myself that he had threatened to kill Faelan. He had threatened to kill Akira. And if I let him go, he would probably add me to that list as well. I steeled my heart, my emotions going as numb and cold as ice, and then I tightened my hand into a fist. The darkness constricted around him with enough force to crush his ribs and rupture his lungs, and yet he remained perfectly intact.

An arrow flew toward him, only to bounce harmlessly off his head as though his skin were a shield. It was no wonder that he paraded himself with such arrogance. This vassal had inherited Brazial's gift for invulnerability, and the only thing known to cut through it was Rasalan steel, which only enforcers were allowed to carry. Killing him was going to be a tedious task. It would probably require wearing him down little by little until his power weakened, but that would take time and energy, neither of which were ideal for me to waste.

A feral grin spread across his face as Akira approached him. His lips moved, likely spewing a string of profanities and depraved insults directed at her family. She removed another arrow from her quiver and experimentally raked it down his face. The metal glinted off his skin as though being pressed against a grindstone. His grin grew wider. After a moment of consideration, Akira let the arrow hover above his eye. That triumphant smile of his vanished very quickly.

Wielding the arrow like a blade, she attempted to bury the metal tip in one of his eyes, but he quickly slammed them shut and the weapon simply ricocheted off his eyelid. Hooking her bow over her shoulder, she used her free hand to force his eye back open. With the other, she slowly drove the arrow through the opening. His mouth opened in a silent scream as the metal sank into the soft tissue. She continued to drive the arrow deeper until it pierced his brain. He stopped flailing. There was not one ounce of remorse on her face as she plucked the arrow back out and returned it to her quiver. That cold, calculating precision with which she killed her opponent was a terrifying reminder of what family she came from.

I was very glad that she classified me as a friend and not an enemy, and I almost pitied the poor souls that Brazial had sent to hunt her down.

My shadow lowered the body to the ground, and as that ruined eye of his stared back at me, I forced myself to stare back. There was a reason why the goddess of mercy didn't allow her vassals to participate in the trials. Mercy in a place like this was a death sentence.

My attention shifted to the girl who was still trapped within my cage of darkness. She was petrified, her eyes wide and her face streaked with tears. I highly doubted that she would try to come after us again. Yet the voice in the back of my head reminded me that she had tried to burn me to a crisp only moments ago, and its need for vengeance permeated through me, demanding retribution. She began to thrash against the dark chains that kept her bound, and when that didn't work, her lips started moving in a frantic plea that I couldn't hear. However, it wasn't her desperation that eventually had my shadows receding. It was the way she looked at me, as though I was her nightmare brought to life, the same way I had looked at that monster, and that fear cracked the layer of ice that had formed around my heart.

The darkness slunk away from her, returning to the night, and her expression shifted into one of cautious hope as she stood up on trembling legs. She slowly backed away down the tunnel. Her gaze kept darting to the dak patches of shadow on the floor like she was afraid this might be some cruel trick, and as soon as she had put enough distance between us, she turned around and ran as though her life depended on it. She disappeared around one of the corners, and the voice proceeded to let me know just how disappointed it was by wielding its dissatisfaction like a battering ram against the inside of my skull. The throbbing pulse threatened to give me a headache. I rubbed at my temples, but unfortunately, the action did little to soothe the sensation.

We should keep moving, Akira signed. She didn't wait for a response as she moved to check the next intersection for any signs of danger. Emrys was close behind her, using the light on his staff to inspect the nearest skeleton, likely trying to gain his bearings amid all the confusing twists and turns that made up the maze.

I'll take the rear, Rita offered, and Faelan gave her a grateful pat on the shoulder before quickly following them, his sword still clutched tightly in his hand. Rita didn't appear to be in any hurry to join them, and as I cast a speculative glance at the dead vassal of war, I wondered if she intended to rummage through his pockets just like she'd done with the two bodies she'd come across earlier in the tunnels. I must have lingered too long, because her gaze narrowed on me.

You know about the coins, she signed.

Not only did I know about them, I had one of my own. But it was probably for the best that I didn't tell Rita about that. She always put survival before sentimentality. If it came down to it, she would steal my advantage for herself, and I wouldn't even blame her for it. She had never pretended to be anything other than what she was. That was one of the reasons I liked her so much. *A vixen told me about them*, I signed. *Let's collect them together. Then we can divide them with the rest of the group if we have enough.*

She pursed her lips as she contemplated the offer. *Fine*, she signed. *I'll check this body. You check the vassal of Tammeria back there.*

I hurried toward the half-eaten vassal, trying not to think about what could have made those bite marks on him as I searched his body for a gold coin. I even went so far as to tip out his boots, but there was no advantage to be found.

Anything? Rita signed at me.

No, I signed in response. *What about you?*

Nothing.

Akira stood at the intersection, squinting in our direction, but she couldn't see us hidden in the dark. She looked like she was about to come searching for us when Rita and I finally stepped out of the shadows to join the rest of the group. Emrys took the lead as he strode deeper into the maze. I stayed close to his side, and as the minutes stretched on, the air began to grow stale with the unmistakable stench of death. It seemed like two groups had ended up in a skirmish, because the corridor was littered with bodies from both Kalta and Athearia. Emrys froze, his complexion growing paler than usual, and as he stared at the carnage, fear flickered like a burning flame inside his eyes. He had made a mistake. This was the wrong path, and judging by his expression, it was a very dangerous one.

His mouth moved to form one word over and over again. *Run. Run. Run.*

The bodies on the ground began to twitch, and all the hairs on the back of my neck rose in warning. There was a necromancer close by, and the dead were not opponents that I wished to face. There were only two ways to deal with them: burn them to ash, or break them to the point where they could no longer be wielded as a weapon. My shadows rushed forward to swallow the bodies. The darkness spat them back out again as little more than blood and gore.

However, when the necromancer appeared on the other side of the tunnel, he wasn't wearing the uniform that marked him as a student from the Cenobium. Though his face was concealed beneath the shadow of his hood, his identity was woven into wings that protruded from his back, the feathers sleek and dark like that of a crow.

This was the god of death himself.

Terror burned through my veins. Pure, unbridled terror. And yet, I couldn't bring myself to look away from him. Ashearan moved with a deadly sort of grace, as though his entire body was a weapon, one that he wielded with brutal efficiency. He extended his arm. The action was slow, unhurried, and I got the impression that it didn't matter how quickly or how far I managed to run, because death would catch me eventually. Whether that be today, tomorrow, or years from now, death came for us all in the end.

A hand gripped the fabric of my tunic, dragging me back, but it was too late. Ashearan snapped his fingers. A death curse burst out from him, the dark miasma rushing down the passageway like a flood. I commanded my shadows to rise up like a shield, reinforcing them with every ounce of power the night could lend me. As the death curse collided with the darkness, it created a shock wave so powerful that it threw me backward and caused bones to dislodge from the ceiling.

My head slammed painfully into the ground, my vision blurring as a thick cloud of dust obscured the air. The white light of Emrys's staff appeared through the haze. I clambered to my feet and stumbled after it, a high-pitched ringing in my ears. Then the light went out and I was left with nothing to guide me. My shadow dragged itself behind me, having exhausted itself fending off Ashearan's attack. I gripped one of my daggers, but it was highly doubtful the weapon would protect me from the wrath of a god.

Something grabbed ahold of me, yanking me through an archway of skulls and into a small room. I acted on instinct, striking with my blade. The person let go of me with a muttered curse. As my eyes adjusted to the dark, I found Faelan peering back at me. Behind him was a stone altar coated in dried candle wax, a ten-pointed star serving as the centerpiece. This appeared to be a prayer room. Faelan examined the bleeding wound on his arm and then scowled at me.

I barely managed to weave an apology on my fingers before slumping against the archway. The world was still spinning, the ground feeling as though it was shifting beneath my feet, and that horrible high-pitched screech hadn't faded, either. If anything, it was getting worse. I pressed a hand to my ears, only to discover that the wax seal in one of my ears was missing. Dread filled me as I came to realize that the shrill sound wasn't the result of an explosion. Someone was screaming.

Not just someone.

Rita.

I attempted to rush back out into the network of tunnels, but Faelan dragged me back inside the prayer room. He held one finger to his lips and then shaped his hand into three simple signs.

Death. Is. Coming.

With my heart pounding like a hammer against my rib cage, I forced myself to take in a steadying breath and focus on my hearing. My stomach twisted into sickening knots when Rita's sharp cry of pain was accompanied by the sound of ripping flesh. But there was another sound as well, one of boots crunching against the brittle bones that littered the floor outside. Ashearan was stalking the tunnel. My breath caught in my throat as his shadow darkened the archway. Faelan and I flattened ourselves against the wall, neither one of us daring to make a sound. The footsteps continued to echo through the catacomb and eventually faded into the distance.

This time when I darted for the archway, Faelan didn't try to stop me. I didn't make it more than a few steps before a reanimated corpse threw itself at me. The boy's complexion was an ashen gray and marked with a web of inky black veins. He bared his teeth in a feral snarl, but I didn't have time to get myself drawn into a prolonged fight. He swiped an arm at me, and I slid beneath it, quickly leaping back to my feet on the other side. A vicious growl reverberated behind me as Faelan leaped for the corpse, his body shifting to resemble a wolf as his jaws wrapped around the boy's throat.

Trusting that Faelan could handle himself, I sprinted toward Rita. She was still screaming. I tried to tell myself that was a good thing. Screaming meant that she was still alive. That notion died the moment she came into view: Three reanimated corpses were tearing into her even as she hacked at them with her dagger. But the dead didn't feel pain, and they couldn't die a second time. They didn't so much as flinch as the blade sank into their flesh. The shadows darkening the walls flared back to life, and the corpses screeched in anger as they were dragged away from their feast. My knees buckled as the darkness ground their bones to dust, and it was all I could do to crawl the remaining distance to Rita.

She clutched at her ruined abdomen, and for the first time in my life, when I looked into her azure eyes, I found fear reflected in their depths. "I don't want to die," she spluttered, each word punctuated by a desperate intake of breath.

Tears leaked out down her face as I pulled her against me. Cradling her head against my chest, I removed the wax seals from her ears. "It's okay," I murmured, running a soothing hand through her hair. "You're going to be okay."

"That's a pathetic lie," she rebuked.

"Very well . . . Do you think they have taverns in the afterlife?"

A weak laugh escaped her lips. "Fuck, I hope so. You still owe me a drink." She coughed and a trickle of blood leaked out of the side of her mouth. Her bottom lip started to tremble. She buried her face into the crook of my neck in an attempt to hide it. "Please, don't leave me. Don't leave me to die alone."

"I'm not going anywhere."

"I don't want"—she choked back a sob—"I don't want to become one of *them*."

She didn't want Ashearan to absorb her into his undead horde, twisting her into a mindless weapon that feasted on blood and flesh. The Kaltans had a custom of burning their dead to prevent vassals of Ashearan from having an army at their disposal in the event of another Holy War. For the same reason, Athearia embalmed their dead and kept them preserved in mausoleums. It was considered a great honor to sacrifice one's body for the strength of one's country, but having witnessed the savage nature of reanimated corpses and the equally savage nature with which they were destroyed, that particular honor seemed highly overrated in my opinion. Although Ashearan would consider it blasphemy, if I was given the choice, I would prefer the pyre to the crypt. I couldn't blame Rita for wanting the same.

"I won't leave you in here," I promised her.

"Will you take me home?" she asked, her voice barely more than a whisper.

"I'll take you home."

With a shaking hand, she reached into her pocket and produced a gold coin that was marked with the spider of Pasaphae on one side and the crow of Ashearan on the other. "You can't die just yet. If I meet you on the other side any time soon, I'm going to kick your ass."

The comment brought a smile to my lips. "I would expect nothing less."

I pressed a kiss to the top of her head as her breathing became ragged. Then her lungs stopped their relentless struggle and her body grew limp in my arms. She was gone.

CHAPTER 15

The shadows trembled and spluttered as they slowly encircled Rita's body. Her face was so serene in death's embrace, her skin smooth and her face wiped clean of any expression. It didn't suit her, not the untamed girl who was born and raised in the Dregs. Though my power had worn thin, with the last of my reserves I unlocked the darkness and Rita slipped from the mortal realm into the shadow domain, far away from this underground labyrinth and safely out of Ashearan's reach. I struggled back to my feet, trying not to think about how my combat uniform clung uncomfortably to my skin, the fabric warm and sticky with blood, but as the metallic scent of it filled my nose, nausea welled up within me. My stomach gave a painful twist, and a moment later, its contents burned up my throat to splatter against the ground.

Rita was dead. Her life had been cut short by the cruel talons of fate, and it was with no small amount of horror that I realized any one of us could be next. Monsters could be killed. The same held true regarding other vassals. The gods, however, were eternal. If they were inside the maze, if they were hunting us, then we needed to get out of this place as soon as possible.

A white light emerged farther down the tunnel and I breathed out a sigh of relief when Emrys and Akira came into view, both of whom looked like they'd managed to survive the ordeal with minimal injuries. Faelan made an appearance shortly after them. He attempted to wipe the blood from his mouth using the back of his hand, but that only caused it to smear more across his face.

Where is Rita? Akira signed.

I forced my numb fingers to slice across my throat, a sign that most people understood even if they didn't know Scias's hunting dialect. Faelan braced himself against the wall, his jaw flexing and his eyes darkening with grief. Rita had been his friend, too.

May her soul find peace in paradise, Akira signed.

While it was a nice sentiment, Rita would hate an eternity of peace. She would have a better time befriending the fiends that roamed the firepits of damnation than she would living forever in the harmony of paradise.

I turned to look at Emrys, who stared back at me with a mournful expression. I knew that he would find a way to blame himself for this. He would tell himself that this happened because he made a mistake, or because he didn't spend enough hours scouring the future, or because he missed some tiny yet crucial detail that could have warned him of what was to come. Emrys was a skilled seer, but he wasn't omnipotent. He was mortal just like the rest of us.

It's not your fault. Despite my shaking hands, I managed to weave the silent words on my fingers. The guilt that darkened his expression made it clear he disagreed with my assessment, but this was neither the place nor the time for him to lose himself to emotion. If we were to get through this maze alive, then Emrys needed to focus, and the rest of us needed to know what other dangers lay ahead, including which other gods could be waiting around the next corner to kill us. I tried to string the sentence together, but my fingers refused to obey me and the question came out a jumbled mess. Fortunately, Emrys seemed to understand what I was trying to ask him.

It's only Death, he signed in response. *He's the Athearian god who set the trials this year, and there's one particular vassal who has him in a foul mood.*

Before I had the chance to get more details, a horde of reanimated corpses stumbled into the passageway, their steps disjointed and their gazes listless. However, when they caught sight of me, drenched in blood like a well-marinated steak, their eyes grew wild with hunger, and I was reminded that unless I wanted to join Rita in the afterlife, I needed to push her from my mind and focus on my own survival.

Akira let loose a volley of arrows as the corpses sprinted forward. She aimed for their knees in an attempt to hinder their movements, but the attacks did little more than slow them down. My shadow shuddered slightly before sinking back to the ground. My power was spent. Several more corpses appeared on the opposite end of the tunnel, leaving only one route for escape: the same corridor where the god of death had first made his appearance. My boots crunched on the broken bone shards that were scattered across the floor like seashells on a beach, the tunnel visibly decaying where my darkness had collided with the death curse. Large cracks were carved along the walls and the ceiling as the curse seeped into its surroundings.

The undead merged into one ravenous, unrelenting mob as they raced after us. However, Emrys was not a gifted athlete. As a seer, he spent more time reading and meditating than he did running laps around the combat fields. He quickly started to lag behind the rest of the group, whereas the dead showed no sign of tiring. He wouldn't make it.

Let him serve as bait, the voice suggested. *While the dead are preoccupied with their meal, you will have time to escape.*

It was the logical thing to do and just the sort of tactic someone would expect from a vassal of Celdric. I could no longer serve in Emrys's shadow court, so there was little benefit in keeping him alive now . . . but he was more than just a convenience. He was my closest friend. This world was cold, and it was cruel, and it was brutal, and it wasn't worth suffering through it alone.

You're going to get yourself killed.

With a dagger in each hand, I skidded to a halt and faced down the snarling faces that were intent on ripping me apart. Emrys came to a stop beside me, his face red from exertion. His feet slid into a defensive stance as he twisted around and whacked the first corpse in the head with his staff. It fell to the ground and he proceeded to hit it again and again until its skull was caved in. I took the next one, my dagger severing its jaw so that it couldn't sink its teeth into me, but it continued to claw at me and my blades didn't have the heft needed to cut off its hands. The rest of the horde wasn't far behind, and they were closing the gap with alarming speed.

Akira slid in next to me, dropping down on one knee as she nocked an arrow and let it fly. It sailed upward, embedding itself in one of the cracks in the ceiling. The soil crumbled slightly from the impact, dust and debris falling down like rain. She let off several more shots in the same spot and the ceiling gave way, burying the undead horde beneath a landslide of dirt and bone. That left just the one that was busy digging its fingernails into the soft flesh of my neck until Faelan sliced off its head with his sword.

Staggering out of the collapsed tunnel, I waved a hand in front of my face in an effort to dispel some of the dust in the air. Emrys sagged against the wall, his chest heaving and his white hair now splattered with streaks of crimson. He eventually removed a waterskin from his satchel and took several long gulps before passing it around. Faelan rinsed his mouth and picked out a sliver of flesh that was stuck between his teeth before taking a sip of his own. I sank to the ground, grateful for the reprieve—however temporary it might be.

Emrys removed the wax seals from his ears. Akira surveyed the tunnels, ensuring they were empty, before doing the same. "I assume things did not go as planned," she said flatly, "or was meeting the god of death on your itinerary for tonight's events?"

Emrys leaned his head back against the wall, his eyes drifting closed for a moment. "This is the correct route. It's the shortest way through the maze from our starting point; we just passed through it at the wrong time. Time is a difficult thing to measure being underground with neither the sun nor moon to serve as a guide." His eyes drifted back open to look at me. "Thank you for not leaving me back there."

"I expect your weight in gold as payment," I retorted, and his lips twitched into some semblance of a smile. He dug a gold coin from his pocket and tossed it at me. My eyes widened at the sight of it.

"Consider it a down payment," he said.

"What's that?" Faelan asked, peering at it inquisitively.

"An advantage," Emrys explained. "That coin allows a student to buy their way out of the second trial."

Akira plucked it from my hand to examine it more closely. Then her gaze landed on Emrys. "What does the second trial consist of?"

"Single combat," he said.

"To the death," I added, causing her expression to darken. "At least, that's what the vixen told me."

"This is a division tactic." Akira shifted her attention back to the coin, her lips flattening into a tight line. "The gods want us to turn on each other. One advantage isn't going to help all four of us."

Emrys's gaze found mine again, and even without him saying anything, I knew that he knew. He waited, as though curious to see what I would do. After a moment of consideration, I reached into my pocket to extract the other two coins. The four of us all exchanged weighted glances, united in a common understanding: We only needed to find one more.

The tunnel came to what appeared to be a dead end. The path was blocked by a wall of stacked crypts that reached all the way up to the ceiling. The names carved into the stone were written in Old Athearian, an optional language class at the Cenobium that I had chosen not to attend. Akira, however, moved closer to brush her fingers over the ancient glyphs. "These aren't names," she said softly, sounding as though she was speaking more to herself than anyone else. "This is a riddle." She paused for a moment, taking a step back to read the entire wall, and her lips curved into a rare smile. "No, not a riddle. Instructions."

Using the metal ring handles, she scaled the crypts until she reached the top, where she tried to pry one open. The stone slab grated in protest as it slowly moved forward. She repositioned herself, pressing one boot against the wall in an effort to get more traction as she yanked on the handle again. The stone slab gave way with less resistance than she must've been expecting, because she fell backward along with it. Faelan rushed forward with his arms out to catch her. It wasn't his most graceful rescue, and the two of them ended up as a heap on the floor.

When I peered up at the tomb, I discovered that it wasn't a tomb at all. It was a secret passageway.

"That shaft will help us bypass most of the labyrinth and everything down here that wants to kill us," Emrys said as he shoved his staff through the opening. "If we can steal an advantage from another student, then none of us will need to compete in the second trial. However, other vassals will also be vying for an advantage, and some would prefer to have a battle in here rather than leaving their opponent up to chance in the next trial. If it becomes too dangerous to acquire the last coin, then we forget about it and run straight for the exit. Our first priority has to be getting out of this maze alive. Are we all in agreement?"

Everyone gave a nod of understanding.

"We should seal our ears," Emrys advised. "I don't know what will be waiting for us when we drop down on the other side."

I shoved the balls of wax back into my ears, hating how the world grew silent once more. Emrys climbed into the secret passageway, the corners of which were covered in old cobwebs, the husks of long-dead spiders hanging from the silk like executioners trapped in a noose of their own making. Fear prickled across my skin as I crawled in after him, hoping that there weren't any eight-legged creatures still skulking about inside.

The air was stale and musty, the tunnel uncomfortably narrow and pressing in on my shoulders, but at least nothing scuttled over my hands as I shimmied down the passage. The route had no deviations, just a straight line with a gradual incline that never seemed to end. Emrys finally paused ahead of me. I lifted my head and tried to peer past his shoulder to see what was happening. The passage was blocked by a slab of heavy stone that he was attempting to push open. He slammed his hands against it again and again, to no avail.

Something cold and scaly slithered next to me. I glanced down at Faelan, his forked tongue flicking in and out of his mouth as he glided past Emrys and slipped out through a crevice in the stone slab. A few moments later, the stone began to shift and then suddenly it was gone. Emrys shoved his staff out the exit before twisting onto his back. He partially shuffled out of the gap, grabbed ahold of something, and then clambered out. I crawled forward and stuck my head out. I was at the top of a very large mausoleum, which curved farther than the eye could see in either direction, as though this was just one of the outer rings of a tree trunk and venturing farther in would lead to its center.

Hundreds of crypts lined the walls, and we weren't the only vassals to have made it this far. Some were scaling down the high walls, having found secret passages of their own. Others were filtering in through entrances on the ground. Two skeletons flanked a massive archway on the inner wall, one wearing a pretty pink dress like that of a vixen and the other possessing a set of dark wings. The flaming torches in their hands were raised high in triumph, marking the end of the first trial. However, as I stared down at the distance that separated me from the exit, I realized that the world below was quickly morphing into a pit of chaos as some vassals rushed for the archway, while others began fighting each other in a desperate bid to find an advantage.

Grabbing the metal ring of the neighboring crypt, I hauled myself out and began my descent, climbing from crypt to crypt until the distance shortened enough for me to drop down the rest of the way. Landing in a crouch, I came face-to-face with a girl from the House of Sight. She was a mousy thing, short and quiet, with shaggy brown hair and large, fearful eyes. She didn't appear to be with the rest of her team, and from the blood that was sprayed across her face, I didn't want to know the details of what happened to them. She cast an apprehensive glance in the direction of the archway, but as the more ruthless students turned the mausoleum into a battleground, she didn't seem particularly eager to traverse the distance alone. I gestured for her to come with me, but then she looked over her shoulder at the tunnel behind her, as though afraid something or someone was chasing after her. She bolted for the exit.

The girl didn't make it very far before a javelin rammed into her chest. I stared at her fallen body, startled, as a vassal of war appeared by her side in a blur of motion. He began searching her body for a gold coin, his face splitting with a grin when he found one. Anger coiled deep within my gut. There was no need for him to have killed her. With how frightened she had been, she probably would have handed it right over if he had asked for it. He'd murdered her purely because he was a vassal of war and the trials gave him an excuse to revel in the violence that tainted his blood. I unsheathed one of my daggers, but a falcon swooped down from the sky before I had a chance to throw the blade, its talons aiming to snatch the golden coin out of the vassal's hand. Unfortunately, the vassal was quicker. He plucked the bird from the air, and with a vicious twist, he broke its wing.

My eyes widened as Faelan fell back to the ground in his human form, his face contorting with pain as he clutched his broken arm to his chest. The vassal of war wasn't content to stop there. He stomped on Faelan's leg, and though the world was silent to my ears, I could've sworn I heard the bone split with a resounding snap. I threw the dagger, cursing myself when my shaking fingers knocked it off course. Instead of the blade burying itself in the vassal's spine, it ended up embedded in his thigh. His leg buckled beneath the injury, but he still managed to twist toward me, his face red with outrage. He yanked the javelin out of the girl's body and sent the weapon flying through the air. I barely had time to roll out of the way as the tip of the javelin pierced into the dirt mere inches away from me.

At that point, Akira had finally managed to climb down from the secret passageway. When the vassal of war noticed the jagged scar that marked her throat like a necklace, recognition flared in his eyes. His patron god had a bounty on her head, and that scar made it very easy to identify her. With gritted teeth, he yanked the dagger out of his thigh. His arm whipped back as he prepared to throw it. I yelled out a warning to Akira, and frustration flooded into me when I realized that she couldn't hear me. I desperately reached for the darkness, but it remained unresponsive, and I could do nothing but watch as the dagger hurtled toward her.

An arrow collided with the blade midair, knocking the weapon to the side. I blinked in astonishment as Akira reached for the final arrow in her quiver. The vassal of war tried to avoid the impending attack, and with his gift of speed, he might have succeeded if not for his wounded leg, which caused him to lose his balance the moment he shifted his weight onto it. The arrow narrowly missed its mark, ending up in his shoulder instead of his heart. He rolled onto his back, writhing in pain. Akira stalked forward, wrenching the javelin from where it was embedded in the ground as she closed the distance between them. She was just about to finish the job when a blast of ice sent her stumbling back.

I rushed to her side, brandishing my dagger in warning as a pair of Kaltans moved to protect the wounded vassal. Dread filled me when a third one joined them and I realized that we were outnumbered as well as outmatched. If this descended into a battle, Akira and I probably wouldn't emerge alive. Yet the Kaltans were watching us with equal an amount of wariness, and after a long, tense moment, one of the girls slowly lowered her weapon and proceeded to drag the wounded vassal away, the other two flanking her as they retreated as well. It was a conscious effort not to sag in relief, but as more and more vassals were beginning to pour in, that sense of dread returned in full force.

The strength of our team had been thoroughly diminished. My shadow was still weak after the run-in with Ashearan, Akira was officially out of arrows, Faelan was severely wounded, and Emrys wasn't a strong combatant. The chances that another Kaltan would try to claim the bounties on Akira and Faelan were high, and considering the state we were in, one of us would likely end up dead if we lingered in the maze any longer. My gaze darted to the exit. Defeating one person in single combat would probably be easier than trying to get our hands on another advantage. Emrys must've come to the same conclusion, because he slung Faelan's arm over his shoulder and helped him limp across the distance on his shattered leg. Akira and I exchanged a look. Then we were racing for the exit as well.

A group of Kaltan students managed to reach the archway before we did. However, they didn't go through it. Instead, they formed a barricade, preventing anyone else from crossing over. I didn't know if it was because they wanted to collect the bounties, or if they wanted to force us to hand over any golden coins that we might have. Either way, I prepared my dagger in anticipation of a confrontation. I might not have liked my odds, but I would be damned if I didn't go down fighting. Akira, however, simply reached into her pocket and pulled out the advantage that had been given to her for safekeeping. She allowed them a chance to look at it before throwing it to the far side of the chamber. The group of Kaltans fractured as half of them dashed after the coin and the rest were left behind in disarray. Taking advantage of a gap in their line, the four of us stumbled through the archway.

Faelan collapsed on the other side, bringing Emrys down with him. As I peeled the wax seals from my ears, I was immediately overwhelmed by the shouting of the vassals who were still battling in the mausoleum behind me. A white-robed enforcer moved forward to greet us, her face hidden beneath a gilded mask and a wisp of long blond hair peeking out from beneath her hood.

"Congratulations. You have survived the first trial," the enforcer said. "If any of you have an advantage, now would be the time to play it. Those with an advantage will be spared from the second trial and will be allowed immediate access to a healer. You will also have a chance to rest before the third trial begins. If you do not have an advantage, then you will compete in the next trial, where you and another contestant will take part in a duel to the death."

I reached into my pocket to extract my advantage. Emrys unfurled his fingers, revealing the golden coin that was nestled in the palm of his hand. However, Akira no longer had hers and Faelan was in dire need of a healer, which meant that we had a very difficult decision to make.

CHAPTER 16

My gaze lingered on Faelan, his skin slick with sweat and his face etched with pain. With a broken arm and leg, he wouldn't survive the next trial. He needed to be taken to a healer, which meant that one coin had to be used on him, leaving one for the rest of us to decide what to do with. *Two of the coins were yours*, the voice whispered. *You should use one on yourself before the others try to steal it from you. Why should another reap the reward that you earned?*

"We need to be strategic about this," Akira said, her voice calm and reasonable despite the growing tension. "Faelan is too injured to continue, so he should get one of the coins. The next logical person who needs the advantage is Emrys. He's the weakest combatant, which means that he has the lowest chance of survival. Koven and I should continue on to the next trial."

My shadow curled around my feet in agitation. The night had started to bleed in to the early hours of the morning, and the power that the darkness lent me was fading along with it. As soon as dawn broke and the first rays of sunlight claimed the sky, exhaustion would seep into my bones and I wouldn't be much use in a combat scenario, either.

"You're out of arrows," Faelan pointed out.

"At least I have two working arms and legs, which is more than you have at this moment," she retorted. "And I do know how to use a sword. You'll just have to lend me yours."

"Akira, if you go out there, you'll die," Emrys warned. "I've seen it happen."

His somber words made everyone pause. She fell quiet for a moment, her arms crossing over her chest as she leaned against the wall in thought. "Well, then, who will survive the trials?" she asked him. When he didn't answer, she gave a slow nod of understanding. Not everyone was going to make it. "The future is not set in stone, but death comes for us all in the end. If that is to be my fate today, then I will not fear it."

All of a sudden the coin in my hand was starting to feel very heavy.

"Absolutely not," Faelan said, struggling to pull himself onto his feet. "You're not going."

"And who will go in my stead?" The question was clearly rhetorical, but Faelan reached out to gently cup her face, his eyes so full of devotion that she must've known what he felt for her, even if she was unable to acknowledge it.

"I'll go." The notion of his impending death must've made him brazen, because he dared to brush his thumb against her cheekbone, but that was a step too far. She pulled away from him.

"Don't be ridiculous, Faelan. You won't last a minute out there."

She was right. He could barely even stand. "Then I'll die gladly for my friend." His smile turned sad around the edges as he added, "And for my queen."

Emrys moved toward the enforcer, who held out her hand to accept his coin. "Are you playing this advantage for another, or are you playing it for yourself?" she asked.

His expression was apologetic as he looked at Akira. "I'm sorry, but you're too important to the stability of the country and its future to put at risk." He placed his gold coin into the enforcer's hand. "I'm playing this for Akira of House Marcaida."

A crack appeared in her composed demeanor. "What do you think you are doing?" she demanded, her anger leaking into her voice. "That choice should've been mine to make."

I stared at Emrys, wondering what was going on in that mind of his. My gaze dropped back down to the advantage that was still mine to play. If I didn't use this on Faelan, he would need nothing short of a miracle to survive. However, Emrys wasn't a strong combatant even on his best day; he possessed some defensive capabilities, but not enough to compete on equal footing with most other vassals. And if I didn't play it for myself, I would be gambling with my life . . . but I still had a little bit of time before dawn. Fate had seen fit to favor me so far. Maybe she would continue to do so.

I placed the gold coin into the enforcer's hand.

"Are you playing this advantage for another, or are you playing it for yourself?" she asked.

"For another." My gaze darted between Faelan and Emrys, but it wasn't much of a choice. While I was willing to gamble with my life, I wouldn't gamble with the life of my best friend. "I'm playing this for Emrys of House Hardcastle."

I stared out the metal grate that separated the small waiting room from the arena. The stadium located in the heart of the maze was large enough to house thousands of spectators, but the seats were mostly empty, consisting of only the students who had managed to buy their way out of the second trial with an advantage. The sky was finally visible, the darkness having already given way to a deep shade of blue that signaled the coming of dawn. The fighting pit was ringed by a wall of fire, casting an orange glow across the sand where two vassals battled each other, one wearing a tunic stitched with the horse of Tammearia and the other in a flowing pink dress that marked her as a vixen.

From my vantage point, I could only see the divine dais, which hosted the five Athearian gods. I recognized them from the paintings that were hung in the theology wing at the Cenobium. However, Scias and Essian were notably older than their official portraits, which depicted them in the peak of their youth, strong and powerful, their golden eyes a beacon of immortality. It was a stark contrast to see Scias with silver hair beneath her antlers, and though the age helped lend credibility to her title as the goddess of wisdom, it also made her look human, a comparison that I doubted any god would appreciate. Essian, who sat next to her, was even older than she was, his host having grown into a relic of a man with liver-spotted skin and a bushy white beard. Despite the battle taking place, he had managed to doze off, his head tucked against his chest.

The sight caused an uncomfortable feeling to stir in my chest. The gods were the most powerful beings in creation, and yet all that power was contained inside a fragile human shell. They could live in the mortal realm only because they had a host to anchor them, and when I imagined what it must have been like for those vassals to have their soul cleaved from their body so that their patron god could wear their skin, any awe I might've felt in their presence quickly gave way to a very real, very visceral fear. That fear had me averting my gaze, an instinctual part of me knowing that the gods were the apex predators in this world, and unless I wanted to end up as prey, I needed to find a way to impress them and prove that I deserved the divine blood in my veins.

The vassal of Tammearia sent volley after volley of arrows crafted from ice, and the vixen could do little else but hold up a shield to ward off the attack. I got the feeling that the two of them might have been friends. It would've been easy for the ice-wielder to end the fight, but instead she drew it out, and there was no look of enjoyment on her face as the vixen suffered beneath the assault, only one of dismay.

Ashearan must have finally grown bored of stalking the tunnels, because he strode onto the dais to join the rest of his brethren, his dark wings flanking him. He sat down next to his twin sister, who was draped in saffron robes similar to the ones worn by her healers, and watched the battle below reach its inevitable conclusion. Frost began to coat the vixen's shield, and it must've been too cold for her to hold on to, because she dropped it. With tears in her eyes, the vixen fell to her knees, and her opponent hesitated in delivering the killing blow.

"Please, I know you don't want to do this," the vixen pleaded, and the acoustics of the arena carried her voice to my ears. "You're as dear to me as a sister." The vassal of Tammearia must've taken precautions to seal her ears, because a spear of ice appeared in her hand. She looked up at something, probably her patron goddess. Whatever she saw caused her face to harden with resignation.

"Someone save me!" the vixen screamed, and my shadow lurched forward of its own accord, ready to do just that. But I wasn't the only one watching who was spurred to action by her plea. The vassal of Tammearia burst into bright-blue flames, her cries echoing through the stadium as her body was consumed in the fire. The vixen, however, didn't rise in triumph. She curled in on herself and wept. From the divine dais, Celdric laughed and held out his wine cup for an attendant to replenish. My knuckles grew white as I gripped the grate. How did this prove our worth as vassals? By showing them that we could be just as cruel as they were?

The only one who viewed the spectacle with distaste was Sheara, who leaned into her brother, burying her face into his shoulder as though she couldn't bear to watch anymore. He raised his pale hand to stroke her hair, and it struck me as strange that a creature so cold and callous could also be a source of comfort.

Enforcers strode in to remove the girl's remains, her body half crumbling into piles of ash as they lifted her onto a stretcher and carried her out of the arena. The penance marks on my back were beginning to ache again, and I eyed the sky nervously. Dawn was close. Dawn was very, very close. However, it seemed that fate was still being kind to me, because an announcer called out my name next and my grate began to rise. I had been given enough time to rest, and as I strode out onto the sand, my shadow lapped at my heels. I twisted around in a slow circle, taking in the entire stadium, from the spectators to the gods.

The patron deities of Kalta sat atop a dais on the opposite side of the arena. The goddess of fate was noticeably absent, but she was an enigmatic creature that rarely interacted with the rest of her kind. However, the other four gods were present. The woman wearing a dress of webbing was obviously the goddess of love, possessing a voluptuous figure and the sort of beauty that mothers often warned their sons about. The hulking man with a crooked nose that looked like it had been broken one too many times must've been Brazial, his skin covered in battle scars. The god of fire sat next to him with flaming red hair that came to his shoulders. His wife, Tammearia, wore a crown of coral and a shimmering blue gown, her face painted with scales and a pair of seashells dangling from her ears.

My eyes narrowed on the god of war, and anger burned through me at the wide grin that was spread across his face, as though he was enjoying every second of this. That was the god who'd fractured the pantheon in two and claimed Kalta for his own. The god who was so desperate for another Holy War he snuck across the border and marked Cahal with his blood, enraging Ashearan in the process. The god who had placed bounties on my friends, so that his vassals would hunt them down for sport. Brazial sat upon a seat covered in wolf pelts, drinking a large tankard of mead and looking like a mighty king atop his throne. I imagined what it would be like to put an end to his bloodlust by calling upon the night to crush him into dust. And yet, when his golden eyes fell upon me, I quickly found myself looking away. He was a god—a loathsome god, but a god nonetheless. Such thoughts would only lead me into an early grave, so I did myself a favor and banished them from my mind.

I finally came to a stop in the center of the fighting pit, and my blood began to thrum in my veins as I prepared myself for battle. However, my heart sank when my competitor's name was announced. A grate on the opposite side of the stadium drew open and Faelan limped out, leaning heavily on the silver-wood staff that Emrys had given to him.

I peered up at Celdric, who had moved to stand at the edge of the balcony, eager to witness how this battle between two of his vassals would unfold. The gods had made us work together to survive the first trial, and now they twisted us from allies to enemies. There could be no room for compassion. In this world, the strong survived and the weak fell.

Faelan's steps were staggered and slow, so I moved to meet him on his side of the arena. His grim expression matched my own as the two of us faced each other. Emrys must've known this was how things would end up, which was why he'd prevented Akira from participating. In his current state, Faelan would be an easy kill. My stomach churned. For the first time in my life, I thought I might just regret stealing that emerald ring after all.

No, you don't, the voice retorted.

A gong sounded, signaling the start of the fight, but neither one of us moved.

Faelan glanced up at the sky. When he realized that dawn had yet to break, he heaved a sigh. "Can I tell you a secret?" he said.

He's trying to delay you until the sun rises and robs you of your strength. Kill him now.

But I couldn't bring myself to make the first move.

"I think Akira marrying my cousin would've killed me anyway." Faelan scanned the arena as though trying to see her one last time. She was in the front row, her long black hair dancing in the wind like tendrils of midnight, and though her expression was as impassive as stone, her eyes glimmered with unshed tears. "I've loved her since we were children, but she was never destined to be mine. Fate can be cruel that way."

I slowly shifted into a fighting stance. "Fate can be cruel," I agreed.

The edges of Faelan's mouth curled into one of his classic smirks. "Best two out of three?" he said, then he was leaping forward, his body shifting to resemble a wolf of war. I rolled out of the way and he landed with a yelp as his broken paws buckled beneath his weight. My shadow darted forward, but the painful whine that tore from his throat made me falter at the last second. It gave him the opportunity to lash out at me, his claws raking painfully against my ribs. My blood leaked out onto the sand, only to be swallowed up by my shadow a moment later. From the dais, Celdric's grin widened.

This time when the darkness surged toward Faelan, I didn't hesitate to wrap my shadow around him. He slipped from its grasping fingers, slithering out as a snake, but he had used that trick on me before and this time I was ready. I steeled my heart. It was him, or it was me. I brought my boot down on him, and the sickening crunch of bones filled my ears. But my aim was too low, leaving him with enough room to whip his head around and sink his fangs into flesh just above my ankle. I stumbled back with a curse, the venom slowly burning up my leg.

Faelan returned to his human form, his body splayed across the sand and his teeth clenched in pain. However, he didn't let that stop him. With his one good arm, he flung daggers at me. My shadow swatted them away, but then my vision blurred and the world tilted on its side as the venom worked its way through my body. In my disorientation, a dagger pierced into my thigh, making my knee buckle. Anger flooded into me as I yanked it out and returned it to him. The blade sank into his shoulder and he rolled onto his back with a groan.

I didn't allow myself to hesitate this time. My darkness surrounded him like a cage and the fight in his eyes flickered out. He was trapped.

You love this, the voice snickered. *The power at your fingertips.*

I couldn't deny it, not to myself. I loved the way the darkness bowed to me and hailed me as its master. I especially relished it when the night filled my lungs like air and made me feel like the entire world could be mine if I so willed it. The power to wear my shadow like a cloak, as though I were a creature not of this world. The power to crush my enemies with a snap of my fingers. The power to slip through the darkness like a door, as though I held the keys to the entire continent.

I blinked at the thought, an idea taking route in my mind. My opponent wasn't Emrys, a seer marked by the god of foresight. Nor was it Akira, a vassal of Scias, marked by the goddess of wisdom. I was fighting Faelan, who also just so happened to have Celdric's blood pumping through his veins. There was one place he could go that the others couldn't. Celdric was the god of mischief and deception, so he might love a good trick, but there was no predicting how he would react. He had already warned me not to disappoint him in the trials or he might be tempted to collect the payment that had been promised in my prayer. Would he smite me for denying him the prince's life, or would he applaud my guile?

I shook the idea from my head. Killing Faelan would be safer. Doing anything else would be a risk. I tightened my fist and the darkness tightened with it. Then Faelan let out a sharp cry and my resolve shattered at the sound.

If I was going to pull this off, then it needed to look real. Limping forward, I dropped down on top of him and ripped the blade out of his shoulder. I sliced into him, nowhere vital but enough to make him bleed. I did it again and again, and between his agonized cries, Faelan peered back at me with such betrayal that I almost couldn't bring myself to go through with it. I knew what this must've looked like to all those who were watching. Malicious and brutal. The gods smiled down at the scene as though pleased with the performance.

But this was the only way we might both survive.

When the venom began to make my hands shake, I knew that I didn't have much time left. My shadow rose up to completely envelop him. Then

I unlocked the darkness. Faelan was sucked into the shadow domain and I compelled the darkness to spit out all the blood that had leaked from his wounds, making it appear as though he had been crushed into nothing.

I was victorious.

The spectators gasped and muttered at the shocking death of the prince, but I knew that Celdric would not be so easily fooled. Eventually, the world would also come to know the truth when Faelan made his miraculous reappearance. However, that would only serve as further proof of the cunning nature of Celdric's vassals. I dared to look up at my patron god, who regarded me with eyes of gleaming gold. His lips lifted into a crooked smile and he raised his wine cup in a salute.

Relief washed over me. I had survived the second trial, and as the first rays of sunlight brightened the horizon, it had come not a moment too soon.

CHAPTER 17

I had been hoping that I would see Serenity when I stumbled back through the gate, but it was another healer who attended to me. Apparently, Reverend Richards had kindly let them know about my penance marks, because she refused to heal my wounds. She did, however, clean and bind them with a bandage. She also gave me a concoction to combat the snake venom, which tasted so vile that I wasn't entirely convinced she hadn't tried to poison me for robbing the world of its beautiful, precious prince. The climb up the stairs to the spectator stands was a struggle, the strength of the night leaching away and leaving me exhausted in its wake. I used the silver-wood staff for support as I scaled the last few steps. The students from the Cenobium had claimed one half of the stadium, while those from the Kaltan Academy sat on the opposite side. There were fewer than half of us that had attended the banquet feast the previous day, and I tried not to let my mind drift toward Rita as I made my way to the front row.

"You could have told me the plan," I said to Emrys as I returned his staff.

"That's exactly what I said," Akira muttered under her breath, shooting him a sideways glare. It seemed Emrys had already informed her that Faelan was alive in the shadow domain. He would just need to crawl out of one of the gateways and find himself a healer. Nevertheless, she wasn't happy with him.

"Celdric is the god of deception," Emrys said by way of explanation. He rubbed the fatigue from his eyes, his white hair still streaked through with crimson, and I was reminded that I wasn't the only one who was exhausted. "He would've known if you and Faelan were merely acting, and it needed to be real. He wants to be entertained. Look at them. They all do."

He was right. Sheara was no longer on the dais, probably having reached her capacity for violence for the day, but the rest of the gods were watching the battles below as though it was a grand theater performance, enjoying food and wine, their mouths curving into vicious smiles as mortal blood seeped into the sand. This was entertainment for them. One of Brazial's vassals took down a boy marked by Lios, and true to his title as god of war, Brazial let out a roar of triumph. However, what was more disturbing was the reaction of the fire god. He didn't lament the loss of his slain vassal. Instead, his eyes fluttered closed and he shuddered as though in pleasure, relishing the blood sacrifice that was made in his name.

The bitter taste of ash filled my mouth. We were just pawns in a game to be used and discarded on a whim. These trials weren't about proving our worth as vassals. They were just an excuse for the gods to get drunk on power.

"It's a good thing for them to be entertained," Akira said, and I couldn't help but scowl at the comment. "The alternative is that they entertain themselves with another war, and a lot more people end up dead in that scenario."

It was such a clinical analysis of the trials that it took a moment for the significance of it to sink in. My attention shifted to the goddess of wisdom, noting how her gaze spanned from Celdric all the way across the arena to Brazial, her shoulders relaxing slightly as she observed how they were both watching the gruesome spectacle with obvious delight. Was this the secret to their three hundred years of peace? Sating their bloodlust and their boredom with the sacrifices of their vassals?

It's rather ingenious, the voice begrudgingly admitted.

However, the notion made me feel as though I were nothing more than livestock that had been raised for the slaughter. "This is wrong," I murmured.

"This isn't about right and wrong," Akira replied. "This is about the stability of the continent." Judging from the way the corners of her mouth turned downward as the enforcers carried a body out of the arena, she didn't find it any more tasteful than I did. "Only one more trial to go and we'll be finished. Don't let yourself lose sight of that goal."

Peering over my shoulder, I looked at the rest of the vassals who had managed to survive up until this point. The stadium was notably devoid of any students from the House of Death, which struck me as odd. The vassals of Ashearan were renowned warriors on par with those blessed by the god of war. They should've dominated the trials, and yet there was not a single one of them in sight.

"The next vassal that will be taking to the arena has made a special request," the announcer declared, and my brow furrowed. "He collected thirteen advantages, but instead of playing one for himself, he asked if he could trade them in exchange for choosing the opponent he would face in the arena. Pasaphae and Ashearan set these trials, and so it was left to their discretion whether or not to grant his request."

One of the metal grates opened, and Cahal Blackwood strode out with one sword in his hand and two spares strapped to his back.

"Impressed by his fortitude and strength, the gods decided to grant it," the announcer continued, and more grates began to slide open. My eyes widened as the entire cohort of students from the House of Death stepped into the arena.

"What the fuck does he think he's doing?" Akira muttered. Moving to grip the railing, she surveyed the scene with growing apprehension. I thought it was fairly obvious what he was doing. He was settling a grudge. The trials gave him free rein to destroy his competition, and by the laws of the gods, he was within his rights to kill every single one of them.

The god of war let out a cackle of pure delight as he moved to stand at the edge of the dais. He stared down at his illicit vassal—the one who should have belonged to Ashearan until he crossed the Rift seven years ago and claimed Cahal for himself. The god of death rose from his seat as well, and the air grew taut with tension as the two gods regarded each other. This wasn't just another battle. This was personal.

"Perhaps we should discuss this first," Scias said sharply, but gods were wily creatures beholden only to their true nature.

"The boy wants to test his mettle," Brazial shouted back, his voice booming through the arena like thunder. "I say we let him."

"I concur," Ashearan replied in a tone so cold it sent a chill down my spine. "Sound the gong."

"Wait—" Scias started to say, but it was too late.

The gong was struck and Cahal became a blur as he rushed for the closest set of vassals. They dropped dead before they even had time to rally a defense. Then the sand began to move and shift, making it difficult for him to keep his balance. There must have been a graveyard beneath the arena, because embalmed bodies began to crawl to the surface. He quickly decapitated the first wave of them and continued hacking away at his opponents until he was drenched in blood and his sword snapped in half. He reached for one of his spare weapons and resumed his onslaught. It was a bone-chilling display of violence, one that almost made it seem like his divine blood had been corrupted by madness, consuming him in the clutches of bloodlust. Yet there was no maniacal laughter that bubbled up from his chest as he ripped into his enemies, and each move he made had a calculated edge. This was his anger, raw and untouched by insanity, which was a terrifying thought in and of itself.

The speed that Cahal had inherited from Brazial made him a formidable opponent at the beginning of a battle, but he struggled to sustain it for any length of time. When he finally began to show signs of slowing, the vassals of death grew bold enough to attack. As they circled around him with slashing scythes, he unsheathed his final sword so that he could fight them with a weapon in each hand. With a snarl of fury on his face, he continued to cut them down one by one. In an act of either great cruelty or great desperation, one of the crows extended her arm. I sucked in a sharp breath as the girl snapped her fingers and a dark miasma burst out from her like a flood. It wasn't as potent or as powerful as that of her patron god, but it was deadly enough. The rest of her brethren dropped to the ground, the curse not discriminating when it came to those who were slaughtered in its wake. Their veins turned an inky shade of black as they clawed at their throats, their mouths gasping for air before growing still.

Cahal tried to flee out of the curse's reach. He almost made it, but the miasma must've brushed his fingers just before it dissipated, because his hand started to turn a dark shade of gray. He raised his sword and severed the infected limb before the curse had a chance to spread to the rest of his body. With a cry of pain, he fell to his knees, blood gushing from his open wrist. Only one vassal of Ashearan still remained standing, though she looked like her legs might also give out at any moment, the death curse having exhausted her. With gritted teeth, Cahal staggered back to his feet and stalked toward her. Glowering at him, she readied her scythe in preparation for his next attack.

He pushed forward with one last burst of speed, and with a mighty swing of his sword, he cleaved the girl in two. Dropping to the ground beside her, he stabbed his sword into the sand and rested his forehead against the pommel. He had emerged victorious, but he was gravely wounded. Serenity bolted out of one of the gateways, her orange robes flapping in the wind as she sprinted across the arena. For a heartbeat, the world fell silent, as though it was holding its breath. That hadn't just been a battle. It had been a crushing defeat aimed at humiliating the god of death in front of the rest of his brethren.

"We should go," Emrys said right before Ashearan raised his arms, his mouth twisting with a vicious sneer. The god of death was pissed. The entire stadium began to shake and the sound of cracking stone filled the air. I gripped the railing to keep myself from falling. Dozens upon dozens of feral snarls echoed from deeper within the labyrinth, and my blood grew frightfully cold as the memory of the mausoleum drifted to the forefront of my mind. There had been hundreds of crypts in there, and it sounded like Ashearan was determined to summon forth an army.

Spurred on by the challenge, Brazial grabbed one of his battle-axes. Then he sprinted forward and a large chunk of the balcony shattered beneath the power of his final step as he leaped from the platform, his shadow a speck on the sand as he sailed through the air. On the opposite dais, Scias's eyes widened in alarm, while Celdric's lips curved into a sly smile. He loved this. The chaos.

Horror flooded into me as the vassals of death littering the sand began to rise up again, their eyes glassy as they set their sights on Serenity. Cahal pushed her behind him, striking down all those who drew near, but he was exhausted and it was a struggle for him to repel multiple attacks with just one hand. My thoughts suddenly veered toward Rita. I imagined Serenity in that state, her body left in ruins after falling prey to the undead, those warm brown eyes closing forever.

"We need to get to the docks," Akira said, rushing to grab her bow.

Emrys, however, remained strangely calm as he said, "I know a way out of here."

"I'll meet you both there." I vaulted over the railing, tucking into a roll as I hit the sand. I gripped the wounds at my side as I picked up one of the discarded swords and raced forward. Above me, Brazial had reached the pinnacle of his jump and was coming back down straight toward the god of death. Celdric's smile grew even wider as Sheara made a reappearance, her golden eyes bright with panic. She rushed forward, positioning herself between her brother and Brazial with her hands raised as though trying to calm a pair of wild animals. Ashearan moved to shove her out of the way, but Brazial landed before he was able to, the battle-ax slashing into her.

Gods were eternal. They weren't supposed to die. I didn't know what I was expecting, but her end was a lot more graceful than those who had lost their lives upon the sand. Instead of blood and gore, she disintegrated into golden dust. The gravity of that moment slammed into me like a battering ram, robbing my lungs of air. The goddess of healing was dead. There would be no coming back from that, which could only mean one thing.

Athearia and Kalta were now at war.

Ashearan let out ferocious scream, and his undead horde all shrieked along with him, a chorus of grief and rage tearing through the arena. The world descended into anarchy as the remaining students tried to flee. It seemed they had come to the same realization that I had: The trials didn't matter anymore. If we didn't get off this island soon, we were all going to die.

I hacked into the corpses surrounding Cahal and Serenity. He didn't look ecstatic about the help, but he also didn't make any snide comments as the three of us raced for one of the open grates. Serenity led the way, the hem of her dress clutched in her hands to keep her from tripping, while Cahal and I fended off the torrent of corpses that were beginning to pour in from the gateways. There were too many of them, and it wouldn't just overwhelm us; it would overwhelm everyone in here. Lios unleashed his fire, which spread across the arena like a tidal wave, burning the dead with a stunning array of orange, blue, and purple flames. I might've gone so far as to call it a miracle, except he wasn't doing it to save us. He was doing it to save himself, and he paid us no heed as his fire engulfed the entire arena. Pain lanced up my arm as fire licked at my skin, causing it to blister and sizzle, but adrenaline and fear were a powerful combination. I didn't stop running until I was out of the arena.

Either Serenity didn't care about my penance marks, or she decided that this qualified as an extenuating circumstance, because she gripped my hand and stitched my wounds back together like a seamstress with a piece of torn cloth. It was a truly marvelous power, the gift of life and healing rather than death and destruction. It struck me that now that Sheara was gone, she wouldn't be able to create any more vassals, and Serenity would be a part of the last generation of divine-blessed healers. In less than a hundred years, there wouldn't be a single one of them left. It was a tragic thought, and from the tears brimming in Serenity's eyes, I wondered if she was thinking the same thing.

With a trembling hand, she led me back into the labyrinth. "The healers walked through a tunnel that connects this maze to the docks," she said, her chest heaving as she tried to catch her breath. She spun around at an intersection, looking a little lost and confused, her breath continuing to come in quick, shallow pants.

I squeezed her hand and her eyes found mine. "It's going to be okay," I told her. It was a lie, but sometimes lies were necessary. She squeezed my hand in return.

"It's this way, I think." She didn't sound so sure, but I gave her a nod of encouragement as she followed the path until we reached what looked to be a remedial room. She let out an audible sigh of relief at the sight of it. "Yes, this is it."

The room was in disarray, with bloodied blankets lying forgotten on the empty beds. My boots crunched against glass from broken vials. It seemed everyone had evacuated the room in a hurry. Serenity's face fell as she stared at the tunnel on the far side of the room, which had been sealed shut with a wall of ice, probably to stop any reanimated corpses from chasing after them. Cahal battered away at it with his sword, but his swings were uncoordinated and lacking his usual power. He barely made a dent before his weapon broke with a loud ping. He growled in frustration and kicked one of the apothecary tables, flipping it over in the process. Serenity's grip on my hand tightened.

"Why don't you cool down?" I told him.

He whirled on me. "Cool down?" he barked, and pointed at the tunnel. "There is a whole undead army out there that wants to kill us, and our escape route has been sealed off. Not to mention my muscles are starting to seize up from overuse and my hand is gone!"

All of which was nobody's fault but his own. He had wanted to take on a whole cohort of Ashearan's vassals and humiliate the god of death before an audience. These were the consequences, but it probably wouldn't help the situation to point that out.

Voices and footsteps echoed down the hallway outside. A moment later, Damien Knight appeared in the doorway, his hair windswept and his tunic covered in gore that reeked of death. My shadow spluttered uselessly at my feet, so I could do little else but hold up my sword in warning. "I'm not here to fight," he said quickly.

Cahal yanked the sword from my hands as he strode forward and leveled the weapon at Damien's throat. "Of course you're here to fight. We're at war now, which means that we're enemies."

"Are we enemies?" Damien questioned with a raised eyebrow. "You're a vassal of Brazial, and what you just did out there ensured that Ashearan wants you dead."

Cahal gave a derisive snort. "That's hardly anything new. He's wanted me dead since I was ten years old."

"So that's what this was all about? Settling a grudge?" Damein huffed out an annoyed breath. "Vassals of Brazial," he muttered with an incredulous shake of his head. "I don't have time for this." Raising his hand, he engulfed the sword with ice and hit Cahal with another blast that sent him staggering back into one of the abandoned beds. Damien discarded the sword. "War hasn't officially been declared yet and what is happening out there will kill us all if we don't get off this island. I already told you that I'm not here to fight, but it would not be wise to test my patience. I've had a really long night."

He strode into the room and a line of vassals followed him, consisting of a mixture of students from both Athearia and Kalta. Damien placed his palm against the wall of ice and conjured forth flames that melted through it within seconds. The students rushed forward, disappearing down the tunnel. Emrys skidded to a halt in the doorway, sweating and red in the face. He looked at me and huffed out a breath of relief. "Oh, good. You made it," he said, as though he hadn't been so sure that I would.

I was just about to ask where Akira was when I heard the twang of a hunting bow. "They're closing in fast," she announced as she burst into the room, slamming the door behind her. She hurried to push one of the tables against the entrance, the wood creaking beneath the pounding of hungry fists. Akira must've found an armory on the way here, because she now had a half-restocked quiver.

She scowled when her eyes landed on Cahal. "That was *not* a clever move," she said, leveling an angry finger in his direction.

"Maybe not," he conceded. "But it was a long time coming."

"There's no time to argue," Damien announced. "Everyone into the tunnel now!"

None of us needed to be told twice, not even Cahal. We ran for the escape route, and as the door gave way and the undead poured into the room, Damien lifted an arm and sealed it off with another thick wall of ice.

The walls of the tunnel eventually began to blend into a cave system, filling the air with the scents of salt and damp stone. The calming lull of the sea drew ever closer until we found ourselves standing in ankle-deep water, the sunlight filtering in through the exit ahead. It opened up onto a sandy beach that neighbored the docks. Sails dotted the horizon, a mass of ships having already fled the island. "I suppose this is where we part ways," Damien said, but Emrys grabbed his shoulder before he could leave.

"Now that war threatens to consume the continent once more, Amari is willing to answer your prayer," Emrys told him. "However, she needs something from you in return. Go now to her in the mountains and she will grant you what you seek."

"How could you know about . . ." Damien's voice petered off as a crinkle formed in his brow. "The vassal of war, the wolf with no bark, tried to kill me in the maze. You warned me it would happen. Why would you help me?"

Emrys gave him a small, secretive smile. "Because the goddess of fate needs you, and she's not just your salvation. She's the salvation to us all."

He left Damien confused and speechless in his wake as he made his way to the docks. The nearby marketplace was in a frenzy as people hurried to board the last few remaining ships with baskets containing what little belongings they could gather on short notice. We needed to make sure we boarded one of those ships as well.

Akira's expression hardened as her steps drew level with Emrys. "You knew this would happen," she said, the accusation clear in her tone. She pierced me with a glare as though I, too, had deliberately kept her in the dark. I held up my hands in a declaration of innocence, but I couldn't blame her for her anger. While Emrys was entitled to his secrets, this was an awfully big one to keep to himself.

"I knew it was a possibility," he confessed. "War was inevitable. It wasn't a matter of *if*; it was a matter of *when*. Now that it has come to pass, fate has given us an opportunity, and we must make haste if we are to seize it."

As I watched thick plumes of smoke unfurl in the distance, I couldn't understand why Emrys hadn't warned anyone that this was coming. At least that way the world could've been prepared for it, or maybe war could've been avoided altogether. Now, people were screaming as they fled their homes and massive flocks of birds took to the skies as their forests burned behind them. "Information is a powerful weapon," I said, "but it's not much use being kept in its sheath. If you had told us, then perhaps we could've found a way to prevent—"

"We couldn't stop it from happening," he replied, picking up his pace as he headed for the docks. "Another Holy War between the gods was always destined to break out, but at least in this the destruction is isolated to a single island and the casualties will be relatively low. The spark for this conflict was always going to be lit, but that doesn't mean it can't be extinguished if we act quickly. We have nearly all the pieces in place to bring this war to a quick and decisive end." His eyes scanned over us much like a strategist surveying a skirmish board. "We're just missing one."

"Who?" Akira asked.

Emrys held her gaze for a long moment. His voice turned somber as he said, "Your brother."

I sucked in a sharp breath, unease coiling deep within my gut. If Emrys wanted her brother, that could only mean one thing: His plan involved death.

CHAPTER 18

The Marcaida Fortress was located near the east coast of Athearia, which should've taken us the whole day to reach, but the winds were favorable and we reached the harbor earlier than expected. While I had slept through most of the voyage, completely exhausted after the grueling trials, I still woke up tired, every muscle in my body aching and in need of more rest. However, Emrys insisted we press on, and so we all endured several hours of hard riding before the stronghold finally came into view. Night had fallen by the time we passed beneath the thick metal grate that marked the entrance of the fortress, the sharp spikes lining the bottom of it making it appear more like a guillotine than a blockade. Torches flickered along the courtyard and banners of war were displayed along the bastions, which meant the news of what transpired on Spire had managed to arrive before we did.

In one of the tower windows, Akira's grandmother held a candle and stared out at the world with no particular attention, her cheeks sunken and her gray hair unkempt. She was a woman who had belonged more to the dead than the living ever since her son and daughter-in-law died. It had been three years since the incident, and rumor had it that she hadn't spoken a single word since. A gust of wind whistled past my ears, the sound eerily reminiscent of a scream, and I suppressed a shudder. Growing up in a place like this probably would drive me insane, too.

Faelan was the first to make an appearance as he rushed into the courtyard, and I couldn't help but wonder if the gateway to the Marcaida Fortress had just so happened to be his closest exit, or if he had crawled the additional distance because he knew that the first thing Akira would do after completing the trials was to return home. His broken limbs had been healed, most likely the work of Akira's sister. Though the woman was known to have more of a penchant for breaking bones than mending them.

He enveloped Akira in a hug, holding her close against his chest, his one hand stroking the back of her head. "The news of what happened on Spire reached us this afternoon. Falcons were flown out to all the noble houses, informing them of Sheara's murder and rallying our armies to war. We were told that the island was overrun. That so many lives were lost. I'm so glad that you're okay."

Akira froze for a moment as though unsure of how she should respond. Then her arms wrapped around him. "I'm also glad that you're okay. Your presence would've been missed."

Faelan's gaze met mine, and I shifted uncomfortably as my relief at seeing him alive battled with my guilt over what I'd had to do in order to make that happen. "I took no joy in what I did to you," I told him, hoping that he would understand. His throat bobbed as he swallowed.

"I understand why you did it." He tried for one of his good-humored smiles, but it didn't quite reach his eyes. "My miraculous resurrection will be sure to entertain all the ladies of the royal court, and at least you avoided disfiguring my face. Now *that* I wouldn't be able to forgive."

The head of House Marcaida stepped into the courtyard, the temperature of the air dropping upon his arrival and causing a cold shiver to run down my spine. His long, dark hair fell down his back, and one hand rested on the pommel of his sword as though he was always one heartbeat away from battle. He was dressed for war, his chest protected with armor and a black cape billowing from his shoulders. "I'm heartened to see you alive, little sister," he said, though his tone was as cold and impassive as stone. "The reports we received were most concerning."

Akira stood a little straighter in his presence. "I'm fine, but we have much to discuss." Her eyes flitted briefly to Emrys, who gave a slight bow of his head in greeting. Rin looked at him and then at Cahal, who was lingering in the back, his fingers constantly flexing and clenching as though he didn't like being without a weapon.

"There are so many lords in my home this is starting to feel like a party," he said.

"Or a war council," Emrys countered.

Rin's lips lifted into a disconcerting smile. "Like I said, a party. We were just in the middle of one. Feel free to join."

The interior of the fortress was decorated with art that was almost as morbid as the family's history, with a collection of antique weapons displayed on the walls and a bloodred carpet lining the floor. The god of death had favored the men in this bloodline for generations, which led to the creation of some of the most fearsome warriors in the country. I stopped before a woven tapestry depicting one of the most powerful necromancers in the Marcaida lineage. The Corpse King, Akira's great-grandfather, who wasn't actually a king despite the morbid title he had earned himself. In his waning years, the man had grown rather fond of feeding those that displeased him to the reanimated corpses of his ancestors—which was exactly what he was doing in the tapestry. He sat atop a throne of bones, his head thrown back in a maniacal laugh and a necklace of teeth draped across his chest. The tapestry faded into a mass of scarlet thread as his victims flailed and wept.

Rin flung open the doors to his war room. The large table in the center took up most of the space, the surface aglow with flaming candles that illuminated the Marcaida family crest painted in its center: a screaming skull impaled upon a sword. Half the seats at the table were already filled. In one of them sat Rin's twin sister, a woman I tended to avoid at most of the social gatherings that Emrys had dragged me to over the years. Mei Marcaida had a deceptively graceful face, possessing long fingers that would be the envy of any musician. She was busy stroking something in her lap, which I assumed to be a pet of some kind, until I caught sight of the dark feathers of a crow. The bird attempted to fly away, but Mei kept it firmly locked in her clutches.

Numerous advisers were crowded around the table, one of them wearing the deep-blue robes that marked him as a seer serving in a noble court. I expected the head of the table to be empty, the seat reserved for the lord of the fortress, but I quickly dropped down onto one knee at the sight of the king, a circlet adorning his brow. Zyair of House Honora had been in his final year when I joined the Cenobium. His features had matured since then, his hair now twisting down to his shoulders in dreads and a neatly trimmed beard shadowing his jaw.

Akira dipped into a curtsy, and behind her, Serenity attempted to copy it. The king stood up. "Please, let us forgo the formalities," he said. "We're all acquainted with each other and we have more pressing matters to attend to."

When I saw Emrys and Cahal rising back to their feet, I followed suit. The king moved around the table, his eyes deepening with emotion as he took Akira's hands in his.

"Zyair, I wasn't expecting you to be here," she said, startled.

"I wanted to surprise you. This was intended to be a celebration of you completing the trials, but I'm afraid that celebrations will have to wait."

She looked down at her tunic. She was covered in dried blood and sweat, her hair in disarray from the long ride to the fortress. "Forgive me, I'm not presentable."

"Nonsense," the king said, lifting her hands to his lips so he could lay a kiss atop her knuckles. A blush rushed up to color her cheeks. "Blood splatter is a very becoming look on you, my queen. You should endeavor to wear it more often."

The king then turned his attention to me. "I believe that I owe you my cousin's life, Koven. You have my eternal gratitude. It's a shame that Emrys has long since staked his claim on you, or else I would be tempted to offer you a position in my shadow court as a reward."

I dipped my head in a bow. "Thank you, Your Majesty."

"Unless the young lord would be willing to part with his retainer?" the king added.

It was a great opportunity. The prospect of holding a position in the royal court should've made me excited, yet my chest tightened at the question, making it difficult to breathe. I cast a sideways glance at Emrys. Was this what my future had in store for me with my retainer's relic gone?

"Maybe once my bones turn to dust and I'm scattered in the wind," he replied, and air rushed back into my lungs, filling me with relief.

With a chuckle, the king gestured toward the empty chairs at the table. "Come, let us continue with the discussions. Your counsel would be much appreciated."

As Akira and Cahal moved to claim seats, Serenity and I exchanged a look, unsure if the invitation also extended to the two of us. Emrys also hovered by the entrance. "Actually, Your Majesty, there is a sensitive matter that I wish to discuss with Lord Marcaida, which would be best done in private."

The king peered at Emrys curiously. "Does it pertain to the war?"

"It does."

"Then I wish to hear of it. This is my country, and I will not be left ignorant as to what my best general is scheming behind closed doors." He turned to face the table. "The rest of you are excused. We will pick this up tomorrow."

The advisers got up and shuffled out of the room. However, Cahal made no sign that he intended to get up from the table, nor did Akira. "Absolutely not," she said. "I'm the future queen of this country, which means that I have just as much right to hear whatever Emrys has to say."

The king offered her an affectionate smile as he returned to take his place at the head of the table. "I would not have it any other way, and I do believe that your place is farther up this table on my right-hand side."

It was a rare thing to see Akira smile, but a hint of one touched her lips as she moved closer to him. Faelan averted his gaze and turned to leave, but I placed a hand on his chest, stopping him. He stiffened at my touch. He was definitely still upset about the trials, even if he didn't want to admit it. But that particular discussion would have to wait. Right now Emrys didn't just owe an explanation to the king and his future queen. He owed one to all of us.

"No more secrets," I said pointedly to Emrys. "We all need to know what plan you have to stop this war."

He was quiet for a moment. Then he turned and closed the doors to the war room. "I was hoping to speak to Rin first, but the plan does involve all of you. Everyone, take a seat."

I gave Mei a wide birth as she cooed at the bird in her hands, choosing a seat on the far side of the table. Serenity peered around, looking a little lost in what she should do, until I pulled out a chair and gestured for her to take it.

"What is it that you wished to discuss with me?" Rin asked.

"A way to put an end to this war before the gods set the continent on fire and leave our country decimated in its wake," Emrys said, leaning his staff against the wall before joining the table. "The gods think that Sheara is dead, a casualty of Brazial's bloodlust, but that is a lie."

I stared at him, perplexed by his declaration. It was impossible, yet his voice rang with truth. "I witnessed Sheara die with my own eyes," I told him.

"Many of us did," Emrys said. "It was a trick. An illusion conjured up by the god of mischief. It must've been, because I have seen Sheara in my dreams, her wrists bound in chains. A prisoner trapped to Celdric's whim, but definitely alive." He paused for a moment, and he looked like he might start picking at his nails, but then he placed his hands in front of him, weaving his fingers together. "Few know this, but Ismadore wasn't just designed to imprison vassals. Hidden in the dungeons, there are cells designed to hold the gods themselves. It's a secret that has mostly been lost to time, but Celdric must know of them, because that is where Sheara resides, and will continue to reside unless we find a way to free her."

I recalled the sly smile on Celdric's face as Sheara rushed to place herself between her brother and Brazial. If Emrys was right, that might not have been Sheara at all. It was quite possible that she had been nothing more than an illusion, one designed to fan the flames of war and plunge the world into chaos. Celdric loved his tricks, and he had just pulled off the greatest trick of the century. Next to me, Serenity lifted a hand to her mouth to stifle a sob, tears of relief spilling from her eyes, reminding me that not all vassals feared their god. Some loved them.

"Then why haven't you informed the Sacred City of this?" the king asked. "Surely if you were to inform Ashearan that his sister still lives, his wrath could be tempered and the war avoided? Sheara has long been an advocate for peace between the two kingdoms. If she is alive, it changes everything."

War is the natural way of things, the voice whispered. *Maybe the best course of action is to let the world burn and rebuild it from the ashes.*

That was terrible advice. Contrary to what vassals of Brazial believed, war was not glorious. War meant famine, poverty, and death. The strength on both sides also ensured that no one would really emerge the victor. Witnessing the extent of the violence and destruction on Spire made it abundantly clear that war was not something to be desired. In a battle between gods, it was always the mortals who lost.

"Accusing Celdric without proof would be a very dangerous thing to do," I cautioned. "He can travel through the shadows, which means that he can move faster than the other gods. Celdric will have the cell emptied before anyone has the chance to investigate, and then he will make an example of us. No one can accuse a god of such treachery without proof, not even someone of royal blood. It would amount to blasphemy."

The bird trapped in Mei's hands let out a distressed squawk, interrupting the conversation. The king cast an uneasy glance in her direction but made no comment.

"Maybe you should let it go," Serenity suggested. Mei made no sign to indicate that she heard her.

Rin unfurled a map of the continent, placing a stone in each corner to weigh it down. The map displayed everything from Kalta in the north to Athearia in the south, and the dozens of tiny islands that dotted around it. Ismadore was a barren spit of land that bordered the Unchartered Waters, prone to heavy rain during the storm season and surrounded by pebbled beaches that were often littered with the washed-up carcasses of deep-sea creatures. It wasn't far away from Spire, so it was possible that Celdric could've taken her there without too much trouble. Rin tapped a finger over the island. "If what we require is proof, then we need to find a way to break Sheara out. From there, we can return her safely to her brother's side. Her compassion has always served as an anchor, weighing down his worst impulses, so perhaps that will be enough for him to agree to a ceasefire."

"It's impossible," Cahal said. "Ismadore is impenetrable. Believe me, I know."

The statement made the king frown. "Careful, Blackwood. While you have my deepest sympathies for what happened to your brother, that does not mean I'll abide treason."

"Rest assured, no treason was committed, Your Majesty. The gods granted me leave to visit my brother. I'm merely remarking upon what I saw. Ismadore is made of Rasalan steel, which means as soon as a vassal steps inside it, their power is rendered useless. The building itself is a fortress that puts this one to shame. The guards are also carefully selected, beholden only to the gods, and they take additional precautions when they aren't on shift, such as wearing Rasalan cuffs to prevent compulsion from vixens."

"That's a bit of a thorough analysis for just one visit," the king muttered. Cahal didn't respond.

"Breaking into the fortress would be a perilous task," Emrys agreed. "The architect was a gifted mind. The underground prison designed for the gods is even more difficult to reach. It's sealed with a blood lock and the cells require a separate key to get into, which I can only assume that Celdric has in his possession, and trying to steal the key from him would be nothing short of impossible. Regardless of how we look at it, our chances of success seem slim . . . but maybe that's because we are trying to tackle a divine problem with a mortal solution."

The crow in Mei's lap managed to free one of its wings. When she tried to tuck it back in, the bird opened its beak and bit her finger. Annoyance darkened her features as she wrung its neck and tossed it aside like a broken toy that no longer held her interest. And that was exactly the sort of behavior that had made Scias decide to consider alternative candidates for the next queen of Athearia. Serenity stared at the dead bird on the floor with a mixture of revulsion and horror until my darkness seeped over it and dragged it down into the shadow domain. Everyone fell into a grim silence. Akira touched the scar on her neck in a subconscious gesture, but she caught herself and quickly lowered her hand again.

"It's been a trying few days and we're all weary," Emrys said, breaking the silence as he rose from his seat. "We should get some sleep and reconvene in the morning. We will want to be well rested for what we'll be discussing."

He departed the war room, not bothering to collect his silver-wood staff or wait for an official dismissal from the king. I resisted the urge to follow him. He looked as though he needed a moment alone with his thoughts.

"Mei, we've talked about this," Rin said, his tone like that of a disappointed parent.

"It bit me," she retorted. "It needed to be taught a lesson."

I like her, the voice declared.

Of course it liked her. She was also borderline insane.

CHAPTER 19

I examined my back in the mirror that hung on the wall, a thin crack running along its surface. Reverend Richards had really given me a parting gift. Grabbing one of my daggers, I traced the scar along the palm of my hand and let the blood drip to the ground. The shadows, however, didn't rush forward to consume the offering. Perhaps the darkness wasn't hungry tonight, or maybe it was in the mood to savor its meal. Either way, I was too tired to find out. I crawled into bed, eager for the first decent night of sleep in a long time, but the fortress refused to let me rest. The old floors creaked and groaned, making me think that someone was stalking the hallway outside, but when I got out of bed to check, the corridor was deserted. Then the wind began to batter at the shutters with a loud howl, reminding me of all the stories that claimed this place was haunted by the restless ghosts of the mad Marcaida ancestors, who had become so entwined with death that reapers simply forgot to collect their mortal souls.

The door creaked open and I tightened my hand on my dagger as a glowing orange light filtered into the room. Emrys appeared in the entrance, his face shadowed and his body hidden beneath a full set of sleeping robes. With his white hair and deathly pale skin, I almost mistook him for one of the apparitions that were rumored to walk these halls. I lowered my weapon as he offered me a self-conscious smile. "I struggle to sleep in the best of times," he said, and then he glanced over his shoulder as though expecting to find something lingering behind him. "Do you mind if I stay here tonight?"

I was secretly grateful for it. This place would quickly drive me to paranoia if I was left with nothing but my own thoughts to keep me company. I moved over to make room for him as he placed the oil lamp on the bedside table. "Can I keep the light on?" he asked.

“You do realize the irony of being afraid of the dark while also being friends with me?” I said.

“Oh, there are certainly times when you terrify me, too,” he replied, and though his tone was teasing, he wasn’t lying. He crawled beneath the covers, weaving his fingers together as he stared up at the ceiling. “I don’t like being here. There’s something inherently wrong about this place. It’s as though the very foundation of this fortress was built upon bricks of grief and sorrow.”

That was a rather poetic way of saying it was downright creepy. A scratching sound echoed just behind the walls as though to prove my point. I tried to convince myself that it was just rats. “It’s easy to see how this place can drive its residents to madness,” I muttered before twisting over and attempting to close my eyes. Unfortunately, the small light given off by the oil lamp felt as though it was reflecting off the back of my eyelids, making sleep feel like an impossible feat. With a sigh, I rolled onto my back again. “Why doesn’t Essian know about this? He’s the god of foresight. Trying to fix this mess should be his job, not yours.”

Emrys continued to stare vacantly up at the ceiling. For a second, I thought he might not have heard me. Then he blinked and twisted onto his side to face me. “I can only imagine that he has grown weary in his old age. He has lived for more than a millennium, peering into the future and charting its course, being forced to bear the knowledge of all the consequences that result from every decision he makes. I think he can’t bring himself to look anymore, and I don’t blame him for it. I’ve only been doing it for a few years and it’s exhausting. I couldn’t imagine doing this for the rest of eternity.”

He sounded tired, so very tired. More so than someone his age should be. “You do know that you don’t have to bear the weight alone, don’t you? If the secrets you carry are too heavy, you can share them with me.”

The edges of his mouth lifted into a small smile. “Good night, Koven.”

He slowly drifted asleep, and after a while, sleep managed to claim me as well.

The screams woke me up. I lurched upright, my heart hammering in my chest, my shadow rising around me as though preparing for battle. Emry was thrashing violently in his sleep, the blankets twisting around his flailing limbs. I let out a deep breath as I realized that no one was dying; it was just one of his nightmares. Grabbing him by the shoulders, I shook him awake. He battered his hands against my chest as though trying to ward off an attacker, his cheeks wet with tears.

"It's just me, Rys," I assured him. "It's me. I'm here. You're safe. You're safe."

He peered around the room in confusion, his eyes wild with panic. Once he realized where he was, he broke down into thick, uncontrollable sobs. He sagged against me, burying his face in the crook of my elbow, his entire body shaking. "It's all right," I said softly, repeating those two words over and over again. I lay back down next to him and, gradually, his tears began to grow dry.

"Want to talk about what you saw?" I asked.

"I already told you. The foundation of this fortress was built upon grief and sorrow. It wants someone to remember its history. Pain doesn't like being forgotten."

That wasn't really an answer, but I decided it was best not to press him for the details as he swung his legs over the edge of the bed. He opened the window shutters and inhaled the crisp night air.

He peered back at me, his pale eyes made red from crying, and tried for a weak smile. "I don't think I'll be able to go back to sleep any time soon, but you should get some more rest."

"You probably need to rest more than I do. When was the last time you slept through the night?"

"As a vassal of shadow, I could ask you the same thing." It was an obvious deflection, but he didn't allow it to get drawn out into an argument as he picked up the glowing oil lamp from the bedside table. "Sorry for disturbing you. I should've known better. This place never fails to give me nightmares."

He left the room, closing the door behind him. The floorboards groaned beneath his footsteps as he walked down the hallway. The room fell into darkness as I sank back down into my pillows. I rubbed at my eyes, certain that I wouldn't be able to go back to sleep, either, but the last few days had left me thoroughly exhausted. However, this time when I slipped into unconsciousness, a nightmare of my own chased after me.

I found myself standing on the remnants of a battlefield with bodies heaped atop one another so high they seemed like hills rolling in the distance, their silhouettes dark against the bleeding sky. An eagle slowly circled the field as though inspecting the carnage. In front of me was a figure clad in blue robes, possessing white wisps of hair. A cat wove between his ankles, nudging its head against his boots. Then the fields began to burn, hot flames consuming everything in their path and clogging the sky with smoke. It was spreading fast. I tried to run toward him, but I was too late.

He was gone and the world around me dissolved into ash. A soft purr reverberated from the ground below. I glanced down to find that the cat was now winding its way between my ankles. It looked up at me with eyes like that of a mirror, and I stumbled away from it, terrified of the twisted reflection that peered back at me.

I was beginning to feel a little bit like Emrys when I jolted awake from the nightmare. Dawn hadn't yet broken, but I didn't bother trying to go back to sleep a second time. I frowned when I saw that my blood was still splattered on the floor, the shadows having ignored my offering. Unease snaked through me. Walking to the cupboard, I grabbed the clothes that had been provided for me, a dark ensemble with matching boots that was typically worn by members of a shadow court. I didn't even know if I was qualified to wear it, but I didn't have any other options to choose from. I slid my daggers into place and then left the room, roaming the halls with no particular destination in mind, making me feel like one of those restless spirits that were rumored to still dwell here.

I found myself wandering into a hall that must've served as the chapel to the fortress. It was lined with pews that led up to an altar with a figurine displaying a ten-pointed star. It wasn't like the chapel at the Cenobium, with its gloriously painted ceiling and beautiful stained glass windows. This space was cold, impersonal. I was about to turn around when all the hairs on my arm stood up. I was not alone in here. I tried to pinpoint what it was that had triggered the feeling, but there was no one to be seen and the place was quiet. I took slow steps down the center aisle, pausing when the stench of death tickled my nose.

I shrouded my steps with silence as I crept toward one of the archways that led into a personal prayer room. I couldn't see the man's face, just the back of his brown hair and his hands, which were coated in so much blood it looked like he was wearing crimson gloves. "You're going to have to do better than that if you want to sneak up on me." Celdric turned around to face me, amusement bright in his eyes. "I have a gift for you. Would you like to see it?"

He stepped to the side to reveal the small stone altar that was used to make offerings to the gods. I sucked in a sharp breath. Several jars of blood had been arranged in a circle and in the center was the severed head of Reverend Richards. This was my prayer brought to life.

I offer you my blood, blessed as it is with the power you gifted me. I ask for the reverend's blood in return, ripped from his veins with all the violence and the pain he relishes in.

"He died pleading for his life," Celdric said, a wicked smile curling at his lips as he raked his fingers through the reverend's hair. "I thought you might enjoy that little fact."

I did, actually. A lot.

However, my dark sense of satisfaction was short-lived as I wondered what Celdric was doing here, why he had chosen now of all times to answer my prayer. Did he already know that we planned to rescue Sheara and expose his scheme? Was this meant to serve as some kind of warning of what would happen to me and my friends if we dared to stand against him? The thought caused my stomach to churn, but I hid my fear behind a mask of cool indifference.

"You impressed me at the trials, Koven. You have a knack for scheming. I should hardly be surprised. I always did have high hopes for you." Celdric reached out to stroke my cheek, and I forced myself to remain still as he smeared wet blood over my face. "I think you're just the sort of person I need to solve a problem that I've been having. I assume that you've heard of the Corpse King? He is rather infamous around these parts."

When I realized that he wasn't here because of the war council meeting that took place last night, relief flooded into me. It was a conscious effort to keep the emotion from leaking into my expression, but I couldn't bring myself to relax just yet. The direction of this conversation was already sounding too dangerous for my liking.

"He was entombed with a couple of his trophies. Rings with family crests. Lockets with portraits inside. Eyeballs that he kept in jars. What I'm particularly interested in is the necklace of teeth that he made from his victims. I want you to get it for me."

"A necklace of teeth," I repeated. "Why would you want that?"

Celdric shrugged. "Let's call it morbid fascination."

It didn't make any sense, especially considering that the Marcaida family crypt was just outside in the courtyard. If Celdric wanted it, he could go and get it for himself quite easily, which meant there was a catch. "What sort of problems have you been having in trying to get it?" I asked.

He smiled as he leaned back against the stone altar. "I'm so glad you asked. You see, the crypt is sealed with one of those pesky little death curses. Anyone who tries to open it drops dead before they are able to. It's quite inconvenient."

Yes, I would say that would be quite inconvenient. However, gods weren't familiar with the word *no*, and considering the grisly display of blood and body parts behind him, I wasn't feeling particularly inclined to refuse his request outright. "If you haven't been able to steal it, what makes you think I can?"

"Oh, I'm sure you'll figure out something." He gave my cheek one final pat, his eyes flashing in warning. "If not . . . well, my time with the reverend was a lot of fun. I wouldn't mind a repeat performance."

He disappeared into the shadows, leaving his threat to linger in his place. I stared at the jars of blood and decided it was best to get rid of the exhibition before another stumbled across it and started asking questions that would be difficult to answer. As my shadows rose up to erase Celdric's handiwork, it wasn't pleasure, or relief, or vindication that filled me. It was dread. If Celdric had kidnapped Sheara, and I helped to expose him, my head could be the next one to end up displayed atop an altar. Gods were dangerous creatures, and I had a sinking suspicion that this was not going to end well for me.

CHAPTER 20

I was the last one to join the war room. Mei had another creature in her lap, but this time it was a reanimated cat with matted fur and half-rotten flesh. It hissed at me as I moved to take one of the empty seats, and Mei calmed it by feeding it a scrap of raw meat from the platter in front of her. At least she wouldn't be able to kill this one because it was already dead. The king was once again positioned at the head of the table, holding one of Akira's hands, his thumb brushing gently against the ridges of her knuckles. She had put effort into her appearance this morning, wearing a dress sculpted to look like armor with her hair braided around her head like a crown.

"Now that everyone is here, perhaps we can begin?" the king said, looking pointedly at Emrys. "I believe you were saying that we cannot tackle a divine problem with a mortal solution."

"Yes," Emrys replied, and then he sucked in a deep breath as though preparing himself for a difficult conversation. "There is something that we could use to break into Ismadore. Something that will help solve all our problems, even ones that are yet to come. What we need is something sharp enough to cut through anything. Something that will cut through solid Rasalan steel and break the chains that bind Sheara. There is a weapon that can do this. It's called Ashanti . . . and it's located in the Shadowlands."

If I didn't know better, I would think he was jesting, but his tone was deadly serious. This couldn't be a solution. The Shadowlands was a realm that fell deeper than even the shadow domain. It was the realm of dead souls—the proverbial afterlife—and that was something beyond my reach so long as my lungs still drew breath.

"The Shadowlands," Akira repeated incredulously. "And how exactly are we supposed to get this sword?"

"The Shadowlands is a place where only dead things can enter and living things can leave," he said, reciting the well-known phrase as though the answer was obvious. It was lost on me, but Akira's eyebrows rose.

"So, you want one of us to die? That is your great plan?" Her voice was scathing. "That isn't a plan, Rys. That is lunacy. Even if one of us died and somehow managed to procure this legendary weapon, how in the name of the gods is that person supposed to return from the land of the dead back to the land of the living?"

The reanimated cat hopped up onto the table, impatient and hungry as it began to devour the selection of meat on the platter. Mei ran her hand along the ridge of its back. "I thought you were supposed to be the clever one, little sister," she said, her tone taunting. "If it can cut through anything, does it not stand to reason that it might be sharp enough to cut through the fabric that separates the realms?"

That seemed to be a bit of a leap for me, but the look on Emrys's face indicated otherwise. Akira was right; this plan was utter lunacy. If we cut a gateway between the mortal realm and the realm of dead souls, that wouldn't just allow one of us to come back. Anything that lurked on the other side could pass over into this world, and the Shadowlands was home to creatures that were better left existing only in myth and legend.

"What's to stop the rest of the dead from seeping back out?" I asked. "And not just the dead but all the creatures of darkness that live there. Reapers. Furies. Soul eaters."

"It would be anarchy," the king agreed. "The destruction of our world would be far worse than anything this war could bring."

Emrys leaned forward in his seat, his eyes taking on a vibrant sheen, making them shimmer like pools of silver mercury. "Not if we closed the gateway soon after it was opened," he countered. "If a piece of fabric tears, then you just need to sew it back together again."

I was tempted to point out that the sage advice of seers wasn't all that helpful if no one could understand what they were even saying, but then Akira nodded like the plan was starting to make sense to her. "You wish to use the thread of fate to seal the gateway."

From the other side of the table, Serenity looked at me as though hoping I would be able to translate what was happening, but I just lifted one of my shoulders in a shrug. My lessons in the House of Shadows hadn't prepared me for discussions about legendary swords and the power of fate. This was the domain of seers and scholars.

"Here's my plan," Emrys said, turning first to Cahal. "Your family controls the territories along the Rift, which is likely to be the first place Brazial will land with his armies. You will need to prepare defenses and keep him occupied for as long as you can. We want to try keep this war from spreading to the rest of the country. You are a vassal of war yourself. You know how they think. Use that to your advantage. Don't expect much help from the gods. After the stunt you pulled, Ashearan wants your entire family dead, but if this all goes according to plan, then you will also be in a position to ask for his clemency."

Cahal's mouth twisted downward as though chewing on something sour. "His clemency? I was well within my rights to kill my opponents in the trials. He was the one who—"

"Oh for fuck's sake, Cahal," Akira snapped. "Don't be an idiot. You're a decent strategist when your mind isn't clouded by your anger. Pride is not something worth dying over."

The king watched the exchange curiously. "What happened at the trials?"

She heaved an exasperated sigh. "I'll tell you about it later."

The reanimated cat began to prowl along the table and Serenity shrank away as it hissed at her. Faelan, who was sitting next to her, hissed back at it with just as much vehemence. It flicked its tail at him in annoyance before continuing to stalk farther down the table. Then it collapsed, suddenly lifeless. Mei shot an accusatory glare in her brother's direction.

"It's being a distraction," Rin said evenly. "You can have it back when we're done."

She slumped back in her seat with a pout.

"We will need to procure the string of fate," Emrys continued. "Which means that Akira, Faelan, Koven, and I will head to the Irashkai mountains in search of Amari."

A strained silence settled over the room. The Irashkai mountains were crawling with monsters. Most people that ventured into them were never heard from again. That was the very reason Amari resided there, hidden behind creatures so terrifying that only the truly desperate would dare to seek her out. I stared at Emrys in disbelief, but he didn't so much as blink, apparently unperturbed by the impossible task that lay before him.

"I think this is where I need to stop you," the king said with a frown. "The Irashkai mountains are fraught with peril. While I appreciate your insight, Emrys, you simply aren't equipped to handle such a task, and I would not risk my queen on such a dangerous endeavor. If we need the string of fate, then I will send some of my retainers to acquire it, men and women who have trained for this sort of mission. You're still young. You don't have the experience necessary to undertake something of this magnitude."

I couldn't help but feel a tinge of relief at the king's declaration. I had just survived the horrors of Spire. The last thing I wanted to do was travel through monster-infested mountains.

"You were young when you ascended to the throne," Emrys retorted. "No one has ever accused you of lacking the necessary experience for the position."

Every muscle in my body went rigid as my relief gave way to shock. Although Emrys was descended from one of the great noble houses, this was the *king* he was talking to. Everyone at the table fell eerily quiet as the king's expression hardened, the tension palpable as he pinned Emrys beneath the weight of his stare. When he finally spoke, there was an edge of warning in his voice. "The crown has always valued the counsel of House Hardcastle, favored as you are by the god of foresight, but you would do well not to overstep the bounds of our friendship."

Emrys rubbed at his temples like he was trying to ward off an oncoming headache. He must not have gotten much sleep after his nightmare woke him up, because he looked absolutely exhausted. "Forgive me, Your Majesty. My phrasing was poor, but the point I was trying to make remains the same. Age is not always an accurate measurement of competence. There isn't another seer alive who can do what I do. I'm the only one who has the level of foresight needed to navigate through those mountains. It has to be me, just as it has to be Koven, and Akira, and Faelan. This plan cannot succeed otherwise. This is not a matter of politics, or strategy, or notions of self-grandeur. This is a matter of destiny. Fate has already chosen its champions for this war, and unfortunately, she's chosen us."

A smug grin spread across Faelan's face as he leaned back in his chair. "I rather like the sound of being the chosen one."

I rolled my eyes at him, but deep down something stirred within me, as though there was a part of me that rather liked the sound of it, too.

The king grew pensive while he considered Emrys's words. A declaration of destiny was not something to be trifled with. Despite residing in Kalta, Amari was considered to be a neutral deity, belonging to neither pantheon. She did not rule in palaces of ivory and gold like the rest of her brethren, yet there was no denying the influence she exerted over every living soul. I didn't know much about the power of fate, but I did know that it typically didn't end well for people who tried to play games with it. If this quest was one of destiny, then not even a king would be foolish enough to stop it.

Zyair shifted his attention to Akira, his voice softening as he said, "I don't like the idea of you venturing into Kalta in the midst of a war. I especially don't like the idea of you traveling through those mountains."

Akira looked every bit the warrior queen she was poised to become, wearing a metallic breastplate that flowed into rippling silver fabric, an iridescent cloak tumbling from the pauldrons that jutted out from her shoulders. Her face was the definition of regal calm, making it impossible to guess what she was thinking. "Destiny is woven from thread, not carved into stone," she said carefully. "I don't need to accept it. My kingdom is at war. My place is here."

"There are consequences that come with denying destiny," Emrys warned. "Yes, you can choose to stay, but if you do, Amari will reweave your fate so that instead of saving Athearia, you'll be forced to watch it burn."

Akira bristled. "Is that a threat?"

"No, that's a fact." His expression was haunted, his eyes darkening with so much grief, pain, and rage that Akira swallowed whatever retort she had been about to throw at him. She must have realized the same thing I had: Emrys had seen it. He had seen the fall of this kingdom. "Please, Akira, this is the only way."

She was quiet for a long moment before she said, "I will hear the rest of the plan, and then I'll make my decision."

Emrys hesitated, but then he nodded and turned to Serenity. "We're going to need a healer, but the Irashkai mountains will be dangerous, and so I'll leave it up to you as to whether or not you would like to come."

Serenity shifted uncomfortably in her seat as all the eyes in the room fell upon her, awaiting her response. The thought of her putting herself at risk made my stomach churn, but it was her patron goddess who was in need of rescuing, and I would not deny her this choice. Cahal, however, seemed to have no such qualms. "She's not going," he snarled.

"I don't believe that's your decision to make," I told him, which earned me a glower.

Serenity straightened her shoulders, her features hardening with resolve. "If my goddess is in need of my help, then I want to come with you. I'm also a retainer of House Hardcastle, and I would be remiss in my duty if I let you face such dangers without a healer by your side."

"You're not the only healer in the room," Mei muttered.

"Maybe not, but I am the only one that doesn't torture animals for my own amusement," Serenity fired back. Mei lurched up from her seat and Serenity did the exact same, the two girls glaring at each other from across the room.

Now this is entertainment, the voice said, sounding delighted. *Fifty gold pieces says that my girl beats your girl.*

You don't have any gold to bet with, I thought back. *You don't even exist.*

You're no fun, it muttered, but I could sense that it was pleased, and I silently berated myself for interacting with it. This was how people ended sliding down the path that led straight to a cold, desolate cell in Ismadore. And that was one fate I refused to embrace. Death would be a kinder alternative.

"You're a disgrace to the order," Serenity said, and Mei dived across the table with murder glinting in her eyes. I reached for a dagger, but Rin was faster, lifting his sister off the table and pushing her to the far side of the room.

"Calm down," he told her, but she just clawed at his arms. Grabbing her by the throat, he pinned her against the wall. "I said, *calm down*." That tone was as cold as ice, and it froze everyone in the room, Mei included. She stopped fighting and let her arms drop back to her sides, lowering her head until her hair fell over her face like curtains.

"Are you going to put me down like you did with Father?" She made it sound like a challenge, as though daring him to do it.

He removed his hand from her throat. "You're not nearly as dangerous as he was."

She flinched like he had just slapped her with an insult. He sighed, and a moment later, the cat leaped back to life on the table. It let out an angry mewl before jumping to the ground and crossing the room. Mei picked it up and cradled it to her chest as she threw open the door and stormed out.

"My apologies," Rin said, retaking his seat. "My sister can be a bit overzealous at times, but she's practically harmless. Let's continue. I believe that we were just about to get to the part where you try to convince me to kill myself."

I sank farther back in my seat, sensing another Marcaida family domestic about to break out as Akira's eyes widened. She whirled on Emrys. "No, absolutely not. My brother is the most powerful vassal of death that Athearia has seen in generations. We need him to reinforce our borders for the war."

"He is a formidable vassal," Emrys agreed, "but that is the very reason why it needs to be him. He's the only one who can succeed in getting the sword that we need."

Her chair scraped against the floor as she rose to her feet, both hands gripping the edge of the table as though she was trying to hang on to the last threads of her composure. "You're not sending my brother to his death. This plan of yours has so many variables. One thing goes wrong and everything else will unravel. He might not come back, and I don't have much family left. My parents are gone. My grandfather flung himself out the window. My grandmother is but a shell of who she once was. I won't put my brother at risk. I just won't."

If Akira's words moved Rin, he didn't show it. Instead, he regarded Emrys with a calculating gaze and drummed his fingers against the armrest of his chair. "Three years ago, the young lord of House Hardcastle advised me to have my father committed to Ismadore. I refused to listen to him, and because of that, he slaughtered my mother and nearly took my sister's life as well."

Akira's hand went to her throat, touching the jagged scar that her father had given her when he succumbed to the madness that plagued her family's bloodline.

"I won't make the same mistake again," Rin declared. "Emrys is a gifted seer. It was prophesized that he would be the greatest seer of his generation. If he says that this is the best way forward, then I will stand by his plan. Subject to my king's approval, of course."

Akira turned to face Zyair, clearly expecting the king to immediately disavow the plan, but his expression was thoughtful and he remained quiet, as though he was actually contemplating it. "Assuming that I agreed to this plan and it worked, it may quell the god of death, but what about Brazial?"

"If we succeed in this, Brazial will no longer be a problem, because with the power of Ashanti at our disposal, we *will* win this war," Emrys declared. "This is the best course of action we can take for the future of Athearia."

It was a bold claim, and the king didn't seem entirely convinced until I said, "He's telling the truth, Your Majesty."

A grim form of resignation settled over his features. He finally met Akira's gaze, and her shoulders sagged a little at the apology in his eyes. "I'm sorry, my love, but if this plan can win us the war, then the reward outweighs the risk. And if this is what has been preordained, then you know as well as I do that denying it would come with its own set of dangers." She opened her mouth to argue, but his tone was definitive as he said, "While I will always value your counsel, the final decision is *mine* to make."

Hurt and anger flashed across her features before she quickly concealed her emotions behind a cold veil of calm. "If this is to be your decision," she said in a voice as hard and unforgiving as steel, "then I will do my part. I will cross the border and convince Amari to give us the string of fate, and I will pray that House Marcaida doesn't fall into complete ruin under the leadership of my sister." The king reached out to place a comforting touch on her arm, but she quickly pulled away from him. "Please, excuse me. I need some air."

The king exhaled a long breath as she departed from the war room. Faelan quickly got up from his seat. "I'll go talk to her, Your Majesty," he said before chasing after her.

Once he was gone, Emrys turned to look at Rin. "I will need to tell you where to find the sword once you're in the Shadowlands, but you and I can have that conversation separately."

"Well," the king said slowly. "It seems that we have a plan."

Rin was going to die, steal a sword from the Shadowlands, and then cut through the fabric that separated the land of the living from the land of the dead so he could return from the other side. Meanwhile, I was going to venture into enemy territory to find the reclusive goddess and somehow convince her to give us the thread of fate, so that we could seal the gateway left in Rin's wake. The sword could then be used to free Sheara from Ismadore and hopefully bring an end to this war, saving countless lives in the process.

It sounded like a simple enough plan. What could possibly go wrong?

CHAPTER 21

The Marcaida family crypt was dark and cold, the air infused with the stale scents of dust and death. The stone walls were carved with weeping statues of women who held flaming torches in their hands, which reminded me a little too much of the skeletons that had lit the labyrinth during the trials. The funeral procession had already left for the reception that was being held in the grand hall, but I lingered behind, staring at the stone tomb that was laden with crow feathers. Rin was dead, which meant that the first phase of the plan had been put into action.

"How exactly did he go?" A man in a long dark coat moved to add a crow's feather to Rin's tomb. He had a handsome face and black hair that was cropped short. He wasn't someone I recognized. "I heard that he hung himself with a rope braided from his own hair. Though another story claimed he followed in his grandfather's footsteps and threw himself out the highest tower. Every tale that makes it to my ears seems more gruesome than the next, but one expects nothing less from a Marcaida. You know how the saying goes: All crows go crazy in the end."

I was beginning to wonder if maybe this man was one of them, from the way his lips curved into a disconcerting smile. "I believe that he fell upon his sword," I said, and the man heaved a sigh.

"How disappointing. The Marcaidas always have a flair for the dramatic when it comes to dying. I was hoping for something a little more . . . tantalizing." He canted his head to the side as though in thought. "Though, they do say that the next head of the house has been flirting with insanity since she was a little girl, so perhaps there is still hope."

I narrowed my eyes on him as the back of my neck began to prickle. "Celdric?" I said. It was just a suspicion, but the god was a shapeshifter. He could take on any form he pleased.

His eyes flashed gold for a split second. "Very astute, Koven," he said, and then began to wander deeper into the crypt. I got the impression that I didn't have much choice but to follow him. He came to a stop in front of a tomb, the name of Akira's great-grandfather etched into the stone. The old husks of insects littered the floor as though it was poisoned, and I decided to keep a healthy distance from it.

"Now *that* was a Marcaida who had a dramatic death," Celdric said with a nostalgic lilt to his voice. "In fact, he was rather dramatic in life as well. He would reanimate his hounds and have them hunt his victims through the forest up to the lake. Not many of them knew how to swim, but they still chose to drown rather than be ripped apart. Scias wasn't very fond of the twist he put on her sport. She wanted him sent to Ismadore, but the Marcaida line has produced some fearsome vassals. Even the god of death himself was hesitant to oppose him. When he crafted a crown of bones and declared himself king, I thought a civil war would break out, but then his children butchered him while he was bathing."

Celdric hovered a hand above the stone, looking like he might be tempted to touch it. "This death curse was placed upon the tomb by his eldest son. It should've weakened by now, but it still holds strong. It's quite an accomplishment for a spell woven by a mere mortal." When footsteps echoed down the crypt, drawing closer, he pulled his hand away. "Good luck in finding a way to break it," he said before walking away. When Emrys made an appearance, he gave a respectful dip of his head as he passed. Emrys returned the gesture, and he proceeded out into the courtyard.

Emrys was wearing mourner robes, but black wasn't his color. He always looked better in blue; it brought out the hue in his eyes. Black made him look even paler than he already was, as though he belonged more to the dead than the living. "Any particular reason as to why you're lurking back here?" he asked me.

I hesitated for a moment, unsure of whether or not to tell him, but his foresight gave him access to so many secrets. Maybe he knew of something that could circumvent the curse. "Celdric has ordered me to get him the necklace of teeth that is inside this crypt. That was who that man was, by the way." Emrys peered back as though to double-check, but the god was already gone. "Who knows why he even wants it, but he hasn't really given me a choice in the matter, and apparently it's sealed with some sort of death curse."

Emrys was quiet for a moment, concern flickering across his features as he examined the crypt. "The Marcaida bloodline has been favored by the god of death for centuries. It's not just a necklace of teeth, Koven. It's a talisman of protection, steeped in power derived over the course of generations. It effectively makes someone immune to Ashearan and his vassals. The undead will not touch them, nor would a death curse. If Celdric wants this, then he's planning on using it as a contingency. If news about what he did to Sheara gets out, he wants protection from Ashearan's wrath. It's vital that he doesn't get his hands on it."

I leaned back against the stone wall, crossing my arms over my chest as I contemplated my options, but I didn't have many. "Are we sure that we want to be doing this? The god of mischief is not exactly someone I want to piss off, which is exactly what will happen if we expose his scheme."

Emrys heaved a weary sigh and then leaned against the wall next to me, pressing his shoulder against mine. "It's not ideal," he admitted. "But I need you to trust me. If everything goes according to plan, then the gods won't be a threat anymore. We can do this—you and me working together. I've seen it."

I believed him, but the future was a fickle thing, and it didn't always go according to plan. I stared at the crypt. Perhaps the necklace could be more than just Celdric's contingency plan. If he really wanted it that badly, maybe it could be used as a bargaining tool. But first I would need to find a way to break the curse on the tomb. "How do I open it?" I asked Emrys.

He gave me a weighted look. "I'm not going to tell you, Koven."

His comment caused irritation to well up within me. My patience had reached its limit when it came to his secrets. He couldn't keep them all. Not when everyone's lives were hanging in the balance. Not when I had proved my loyalty over and over again and it still wasn't enough to earn his trust. If he wasn't going to tell me willingly, then I needed to force his hand.

I strode toward the crypt. Emrys rushed to yank me away from it, but his arms were as thin as reeds and I didn't so much as budge. "What are you doing?" he demanded, panic flooding his voice.

"I'm going to open it," I retorted.

He tried to block my path, extending his arms out to either side of him. My shadow simply wrapped around him and dragged him out of the way. "Please, Koven—"

"Tell me how to open it," I said. When his lips remained sealed in a stubborn line, I reached for the cursed stone.

"Sheara's blood!" he exclaimed, and I froze. "You need Sheara's blood. That is the only power that can counteract a death curse." He blinked the tears from his eyes as my shadow let him go. "What you just did was cruel, Koven."

Most people needed some cruelty in them if they were to survive in a world as brutal as this one. If he wanted an apology, he wasn't going to get it. I had bled for him in the penance room. I had risked my life for him more than once during the trials. The least he could do was help me open one little tomb.

Emrys fled the crypts, visibly upset, and a flicker of guilt rose up in me. However, instead of chasing after him, I regarded the tomb one more time. If Celdric had given me this task, that probably meant he didn't know the secret to circumventing the curse. It would seem that rescuing Sheara was the answer to more than one problem.

The courtyard was deserted when I exited the crypts. The day was overcast, the clouds blocking out the afternoon sun and turning the sky a dismal shade of gray. A lone tree stood in the center, the flowers on it just beginning to bloom, coating the branches with a smattering of pink petals. Faelan stepped out of the great hall, shutting the door behind him as though to stop the loud chatter inside from following him out. He began pacing the courtyard, his hands clenching and unclenching at his sides.

After what happened in the trials, I wasn't sure if he would want to see me, so I approached him slowly. He looked up at me, paused for a moment, and then continued pacing. "Something is wrong," I noted, and he huffed out a morose laugh.

"This whole situation is wrong," he muttered. He stopped and then shook his head. "I hope Emrys is right about this, because if Rin doesn't come back . . ." Faelan looked at me, apprehension reflected in his amber eyes. "Akira is distraught. She hasn't spoken a single word today, and she's refusing to eat. I don't know how to help her."

"Rin will come back," I placated. I reached out to place a comforting hand on his shoulder, but then thought better of it. "Even if he doesn't return, she'll be okay. Akira is a force of nature."

Faelan gave a slow nod, but he didn't seem quite convinced.

"Come on, let's go find her," I suggested, leading him back inside the fortress. The family banners hung from the walls in the great hall, bearing the symbol of the skull impaled upon a sword. The floral arrangements displayed along the tables were dead, their petals having long since dried up, as was customary for a funeral. The charade of mourners flitted about the room, whispering vicious rumors about the tragedy like vultures feasting upon a carcass. That was probably the reason why Akira was no longer in the room.

Faelan and I roamed through the rest of the fortress until the sound of sobbing drew us down a narrow corridor. The scene nearly cleaved my heart in two. For as long as I'd known her, Akira had been as sharp as a sword and as resilient as a shield. She gave off the illusion of being unbreakable.

Now, she was bent over as though in physical pain, one hand gripping the windowsill as she tried to keep herself upright. Her dark veil had been ripped from her face and cast upon the ground. The painted black tears were smearing down her face as real ones poured from her eyes like rain.

Faelan looked as though he wanted to run up and sweep her into his arms, but then the king appeared from the opposite corridor and placed a comforting hand on the small of her back. She collapsed into him, her fingers gripping the fabric of his tunic into tight knots. Her legs gave way beneath the weight of her grief and she fell to her knees. The king dropped to the ground with her. He pulled her into his arms and smoothed back her hair as she wept against his shoulder.

Faelan pivoted and rushed back down the hallway. I hurried after him, struggling to keep up with his pace. I was just about to ask him to slow down when he suddenly stopped and punched the wall. He did it again and again until the skin had been stripped from his knuckles and the walls were stained with wet streaks of blood. I watched in stunned silence as he slowly slid down to the ground.

"I . . . I just . . . It's just—" Faelan tried finding the words, but then his voice cracked. Life had given him wealth and beauty while at the same time making it so that he could have anything he wanted except the one thing he truly desired. Fate could be kind, but she could also be cruel.

I slid down next to him. "Give it time," I said. "It won't always feel this way."

Faelan stared down at his bleeding knuckles. "Gods, I certainly hope not." He leaned his head against the wall. "Maybe it would've been best if you had just killed me and put me out of my misery."

Maybe it would have, the voice agreed.

"Don't be so melodramatic," I said, suppressing the urge to roll my eyes at him. "You got your heart broken. You're not dying from some festering disease."

"A festering disease would be better," he muttered, and this time I did roll my eyes at him.

"Faelan, I'm sure you'll eventually find some other girl to love." I jostled my shoulder into his. My voice turned teasing as I said, "You certainly aren't lacking for choice with that hair like spun copper, and that skin like polished oak, and that *flawless* face."

"Oh, gods." He buried his face in his hands. "That was mortifying. I blame the vixen."

"The vixen only told you to admire your reflection. You came up with those adjectives all on your own."

His fingers slipped down his face to reveal his eyes, which sparkled with humor as he said, "I do have pretty great hair."

I reached out to tug on one of his curls and laughed when he swatted my hand away. He laughed with me, and a weight slowly eased from my chest. "About the trials—" I began, but he quickly held up a hand to stop me.

"I'm not mad that you gave the coin to Emrys. He isn't much of a combatant, and the two of you have been inseparable since the first day you arrived at the Cenobium. I wouldn't have expected you to use it on me, but the fight was . . . unpleasant. I don't think it was a very enjoyable experience for you, either. The important thing is that we're both still breathing. I think we should just leave it at that and move on." After a pause, he added, "Though, I keep waiting for Celdric to hunt me down for failing the second trial. I can barely sleep because of it, afraid that the moment I close my eyes, he'll slink in through the shadows and rip the blood from my veins."

The resignation in his voice sent a prickle of trepidation down my spine. I'd thought I was saving his life when I shoved him into the shadow domain. It was only now that I was beginning to realize maybe all I'd done was condemn him to a slower, more painful death than the one he would've received in the arena . . . but when Celdric had approached me in the crypts earlier that morning, he'd seemed too preoccupied with his own schemes to spare much thought for anything else. Perhaps he simply didn't care whether Faelan lived or died, or perhaps he was biding his time, allowing Faelan to stew in his fear before the consequences of his failure finally caught up to him.

"I think Celdric has bigger concerns at the moment," I said carefully. "Besides, no one managed to complete the trials. We all had to flee the island before the entire thing went up in flames."

I didn't know what that meant for me—for any of us. From the grim look Faelan gave me, it was clear he didn't know, either. "Do you think they'll make us go back once the war is over?" he asked.

"Gods, I certainly hope not."

It wasn't a thought I particularly wanted to dwell on. Faelan fell quiet as though he, too, preferred not to think about it. Standing back up, I offered him my hand. He took it and I hauled him to his feet. He peered over his shoulder at the bloodstains on the wall and raised his sleeve as though to wipe them off. Then he seemed to reconsider. He took a step back, admiring how they looked between the framed painting of a drowning woman and a set of mounted swords. "You know, I actually think it goes with the decor of the house."

CHAPTER 22

Emrys was standing at the end of a hallway, peering out one of the windows at the night sky, his expression pensive as he studied the constellations like he could find an answer to some great question hidden within them. I moved to join him by the window. The moon was a thin silver crescent in the distance, providing little light. That was good. It would make sneaking through enemy territory a little easier. The group would need as much cover as the darkness could give them, especially considering that I wouldn't be able to be with them for the first stretch of the journey.

Emrys turned away from the window and regarded the supply satchel that was slung over my shoulder, his eyes turning sad as he realized where I needed to go and what I needed to do. "I have a promise that I need to keep," I told him. "The shadow domain has a lot of gateways. Is there anywhere I can meet up with you after you've crossed over into Kalta?"

"Xyllon is relatively close to the border," he said. "We'll wait for you there."

I nodded. I started to walk away but then hesitated. "Will you be okay without me for a few days?" I wasn't technically his retainer; I didn't need to ask his permission, but I also couldn't bring myself to leave his side without knowing he would be all right. Athearia and Kalta were at war. If he was caught on the wrong side of the border, it would not end well for him.

"I'll still be alive, if that's what you're asking." He winced as he peeled off a sliver of skin from around one of his fingernails. When he moved to pick at another one of his fingers, I grabbed his hand.

"You need to stop doing that."

"I can't help it when I'm nervous." He averted his gaze and drew in a deep breath. "I have seen us succeed, but I have also seen us fail a dozen times over."

I resisted the urge to sigh at him. That would've been useful information to share at the war council, but it was too late to change our minds now.

"You no longer have the luxury of doubt. You have chosen the path. Now you must be the one to guide the rest of us down it."

Rather than taking my words as the encouragement they were intended to be, they caused him to deflate as though I had just added to the invisible weight upon his shoulders. "I'm so tired of walking through it alone."

I stepped forward, and clasping one hand behind his neck, I pressed my forehead to his. The gesture had many meanings depending on the context. A show of the bond shared between brothers. A show of the comradery shared between soldiers. A show of the affection shared between lovers. Regardless of the situation, it carried one common thread. It was a sign of loyalty, and Emrys relaxed beneath it. "Even if you end up straying down the wrong path, you won't be alone," I promised him. "I am your shadow, which means that I will always be by your side. I don't need a retainer's relic to know that much."

He blinked as I pulled away from him, a dazed look in his eyes, as though he had just woken up from a dream. "That wasn't an apology for the stunt you pulled in the crypts."

"And you're still not going to get one," I retorted.

A ghost of a smile found its way to his face. "I think I might like arguing with you."

The floorboards groaned, and I glanced over my shoulder to find Mei drifting down the hallway in a nightgown, her loose hair flowing all the way to her waist, her half-decomposed cat now limp and lifeless in her arms. She didn't bother greeting us as she turned up the flight of stairs that led to the sleeping quarters. "House Marcaida will really flourish under her reign," I muttered under my breath.

"Fate be willing, she won't stay the head of the house for long," Emrys said. "Though, she's not lacking in intelligence. She's just a bit . . . unstable."

That was certainly one word for it.

Perhaps she would like some company tonight? the voice suggested, which was the sort of advice that fell within the same category as letting the world burn and rebuilding it from its ashes.

I turned to leave, but then Emrys grabbed hold of my wrist. "I do trust you, Koven. I know you won't betray my confidence, but that's not my concern. I worry about the things you might be tempted to do if you knew the things that I knew." All his declaration did was make me even more curious to know just what sort of things he was so terrified that I might do. His grip on my wrist tightened. "But please also trust me when I say it's for the best that Celdric doesn't get his hands on that talisman."

The gravity in his voice made me pause. The last thing I wanted was to make Celdric even more dangerous than he already was. If I could find a way to stall him, I would. Only after I nodded did Emrys let me go. "I'll see you in Xyllon," I told him before turning up the stairs that led to the sleeping quarters.

Once I reached the top, I walked down the hall, wondering which room belonged to Serenity until I heard raised voices from behind one of the closed doors. She and Cahal were in the middle of an argument. I considered knocking, but then decided I didn't like the idea of her being alone in a room with a man that had a temper. I flung the door open and invited myself in. The room was lit with multiple oil lamps. A jar of incense burned in a dish on the bedside table, filling the air with the calming scents of lavender and cedarwood. Serenity had traded her saffron dress and sandals for a pair of trousers and sturdy walking boots. Her bed was covered with a selection of herbs and food provisions. She was packing the supplies into a travel pack, much to Cahal's displeasure.

"It's my decision," she snapped at him.

"Well, it's a stupid decision," he growled back.

"Am I interrupting?" I asked, knowing full well that I was. Cahal glowered in my direction. Then, in a blur of motion, he was standing right in front of me.

"I made a promise to my brother that I would keep her safe." He jammed an angry finger in my face, and I had to quell the shadow that rippled at my feet, itching to sever his remaining hand from his body and leave him devoid of fingers altogether. "If you turn me into a liar, you will meet the same fate that she does. Do you understand me?"

"I'll watch over her," I replied evenly, "but not because of any threat from you."

He strode past me, deliberately bumping his shoulder into mine as he left out the door. I swung it shut behind him.

"Sorry about that," she said, and I tutted.

"I thought we agreed that you wouldn't apologize for that asshole." My gaze scanned over her provisions. When I noticed a distinct lack of weaponry, I pulled out one of my daggers and offered it to her. She held up her hands, shying away from the blade.

"I'm a healer. I made an oath not to take a life."

"An oath doesn't double as armor, I'm afraid. But if it makes you feel more comfortable, I'm sure that, as a healer, you know all the nonlethal places where you can stab a person."

Her lips twitched into a smile. “I suppose that I do.”

I extended the weapon toward her, urging her to take it. “Hopefully you won’t need this, but I stand steadfast in the belief that every girl should have a hidden dagger on her person at all times.” She wavered for a moment before finally accepting it. “I’ll be gone for a few days, but I will meet up with the rest of the group once you have crossed over into Kalta. Fate be willing, there won’t be any trouble in my absence, but I made a promise to Rita that I need to keep.”

Her eyes deepened with understanding, and she reached out to squeeze my hand. “You don’t need to explain yourself. Go do what you must, and I will be here if you need me once you get back.”

My gaze dropped down to her mouth. It was a bad idea, especially right before we were about to leave on a journey where we would be forced to share each other’s company. The last thing I wanted to do was make her uncomfortable. My shadow, however, decided to go rogue as it coiled its way between our hands, and she stared at the wisps of darkness as though mesmerized.

Gods, she was beautiful.

Her gaze flicked up to meet mine, a bright blush coloring her cheeks, and I realized that I’d said my thought aloud. She stepped closer until her chest was pressed against my own, each breath like a caress against my skin. Heat seared through me where her body touched mine. Caution and reason faded to the recesses of my mind as I leaned down and brushed my lips against hers. It was a tentative kiss, gentle and sweet, just like her. She paused for a moment, her eyes wide as though that hadn’t been what she was expecting, and my heart sank at the realization that she didn’t want this. I was about to apologize for overstepping when her arms hooked around my neck and she dragged me back for more.

It took me by delightful surprise, the forcefulness with which her mouth collided with mine, as though she had been waiting for this moment for a very long time. I kissed her back with equal fervor, my fingers raking through her hair, leaving tendrils of shadow in their wake. She must have recently drunk a cup of jasmine tea, because traces of it still lingered on her lips, and I couldn’t help but smile at the taste of flowers that hummed on the tip of my tongue. When we finally broke apart, I was breathless, as though she had managed to steal the air from my lungs. Her eyes had grown so dark they almost appeared to be black, and yet there was a shine to them that wasn’t there before, making them look like glittering stars in the night sky.

I could get lost in eyes like those, spend hours and hours staring into them with no desire to find my way back out. Before I could give in to the urge to do just that, I pressed a kiss to her temple and took a step back.

"Be careful," I told her, and then I dissolved into the darkness.

I emerged within the ruined city of the shadow domain. There were no moon or stars in this sky, only an endless shade of gray. The Marcaida Fortress stood behind me. The metal grate blocking its entrance was rusted and the roof had caved in, the tangled roots of dry trees rising up the walls in an effort to sneak in. Shadows flitted near the bastions, giving off the impression that the building really was haunted. I stared out at the world that stretched out before me, the ground carpeted in thick swirls of mist, and I sighed. Trying to find Rita's body was going to be a challenge.

Time was a difficult thing to measure in a place without sunlight, but after hours of aimless searching, I eventually needed to dig some of the pieces of dried fruit from my satchel to stave off the hunger that was gnawing at my stomach. I continued my search, examining the bones littering the ground for any sign of whether they could belong to her. Eventually, I curled up inside one of the shells of a home and attempted to fall asleep while wild wisps of shadow roamed over me as though trying to figure out if this body on the ground was cold enough to eat. They eventually slunk away in disappointment.

I repeated the process again and again, roaming through the city as my shadow slithered ahead of me, dissipating the mist enough for me to see the ground. I was beginning to think that the search might be futile—that perhaps I should go on ahead to Xyllon and come back to continue this another time—but then the mist cleared to reveal the remains of someone wearing a black-and-gold tunic, the fabric shredded as though hands had torn it apart.

I crouched down next to the bones to examine them more closely. I pulled the chain from her neck and found a key threaded on it. This was definitely Rita. My chest began to ache with a painful combination of relief, regret, and sorrow. The memory of the night we broke into the reverend's office clawed its way back to the surface. I had told her to join my team. Perhaps if I hadn't, she might not have died, or perhaps she would've died in another way. There could be no knowing, and so I shoved the thought from my mind lest it drive me to insanity. But I couldn't shelve the thought of Celdric shuddering in pleasure as she was torn apart, her blood offered up to him in sacrifice. It made my entire body simmer with anger. While death would come for us all one day, she deserved better than to have met her end like a sheep upon an altar, dying for the amusement and bloodlust of the very god she had sworn to serve.

He deserved to have his scheme exposed and to earn the ire of Ashearan. He deserved to know the same fear that he instilled in his vassals. All the gods did. Sheara was probably the only one who deserved her title, and she was rotting away in an underground prison cell, betrayed by one of her own. I didn't have much faith in divine justice, but divine retribution was another matter altogether, and perhaps it was time that Celdric got a taste of what it was like to be on the receiving end.

The darkness that dwelled here had picked Rita's remains clean, its loyalty apparently only extending to Celdric's kin that still drew breath. My shadow reached out to envelop her. The sound of shattering bone reverberated through the abandoned city as I pulled out a cloth from my supply satchel. After my shadow deposited the bone dust on top of it, I folded it carefully and made my way to the three-tiered fountain in the city center. It must've still been daylight in the mortal realm, because the water inside was missing, which meant that the gateway was locked. I made myself comfortable as I waited for the sun to slip beneath the horizon and the stagnant water to reappear inside the fountain. As I stepped into it, the world flipped over. The sound of trickling water filled my ears as I climbed out the gateway.

Weaving my way through the streets of Ravenrook, I headed toward the bad part of town. When the street kids eyed me from across the road, I scratched two fingers down my neck, remembering that was the sign Rita had used the last time we were here. They slunk back into the alley. I wandered through the streets, looking for a good place to scatter her ashes, but between the rats and the sewage rolling through the gutters, nowhere seemed ideal.

"You look a little lost, luv," said a woman who was leaning out the window of a harlot house. A smoking pipe was balanced delicately in her hand, and a half-finished bottle of wine rested on the ledge. The sleeve of her dress slipped down her shoulder as she leaned down, her red-painted lips curving into a seductive smile. "Maybe I can help?"

Living in this part of town, perhaps she could. Though it likely wouldn't be the sort of help she was referring to. "I'm looking for a place for my friend," I said, unfurling the cloth to reveal the bone dust inside. "She was from here."

The harlot lifted up one sculpted eyebrow and then took a long drag of her pipe. "Died in a fire, did she? How tragic." Her tone was playful, as though she knew that wasn't what happened. Cremation was illegal on this side of the Rift, but that didn't mean it never happened. She gave a wave of her pipe, gesturing across the entirety of the street, from the men converging on the gambling dens all the way down to the old woman who was hunched over on the street corner with a threadbare shawl wrapped around her shoulders and ragged cough that threatened to be the end of her if she didn't see a healer. "Scatter her anywhere you please. If she wanted to come back to this shithole, then I don't think she's the sort of girl who would mind."

I thought about it for a moment before deciding she probably had a point. I gave the cloth a flap and the white dust took flight on the wind. I wasn't certain about what to do next, but the gravity of the moment compelled me to give a final farewell, so I said, "May you wreak havoc in the firepits of eternal damnation."

The harlot gave a snort of laughter. "I'll drink to that," she declared before raising the wine to her lips. When she proceeded to offer it to me, I took a generous sip as well. A little farther down the road, a man shouted from outside one of the gambling dens. A girl with strawberry blond hair raced past me, a coin pouch in her hand and a triumphant grin on her face. I couldn't help but smile at the scene.

"Welcome home, Rita," I said, and then I tipped over the wine bottle, pouring its contents out onto the street.

CHAPTER 23

I walked through the remnants of Xyllon, which was considered one of the greatest cities on the continent before it was destroyed during the last Holy War. The air here was cold, unnaturally so, and my breath turned to mist in front of my face. Once populated by tens of thousands of people, it had been a multicultural city that had thrived from trade. It proceeded to grow into the capital of knowledge and higher thinking. Scholars and philosophers from all over the continent had flocked to it and the grand libraries it housed. All of it was reduced to ash when the city fell to Lios. The evidence of that great tragedy was still visible. The fire had burned so hot it even managed to warp stone, leaving behind shapeless distortions of what used to be grand halls and theaters.

Xyllon used to house a fifty-foot-tall statue of Scias holding a stack of scrolls in her hands. There was almost nothing left of it now, only the creases of the dress that covered the bottom half of her legs and a foot that was missing three of its toes. Deep slashes cut across what remained of the statue like claw marks. There was only one creature that could've cut into marble like that—Vicarius, the dragon that the god of fire rode into war. I traced my fingers over the grooves with a mixture of fear and awe. The dragon was the last of its kind, having grown reclusive in its old age, but there was an era when it had set the entire continent ablaze, and I didn't doubt it would do so again once Lios summoned it to battle.

I began searching for any signs that indicated Emrys and the others had passed through here. The ground cracked beneath my boots like fractured glass, still fragile from the death curse Ashearan had placed upon the land after it had fallen into the hands of the enemy, rotting away what little remained of the city. The stories claimed that nothing would ever grow here again, but after hundreds of years, small weeds were beginning to break through the hostile environment, a splash of green bursting through the cracks in the stone. It seemed that the city was slowly beginning to recover, but the world continued to believe it was both cursed and haunted. Most travelers avoided it, which made it a perfect location for people to hide when sneaking into Kalta.

I crouched down, placing a hand against the fractured ground, but I couldn't see any immediate signs that a group of people had passed through here recently. Perhaps everyone else got waylaid and I had arrived first. I began looking for a building that would serve as adequate protection against the cold for the night when the soft crackle of burning wood pulled me deeper into the city. The windows were missing their shutters, but blankets had been hung in the gaps, dimming the light of the hearth within, but not concealing it completely. Someone was here.

Erring on the side of caution, I commanded my shadow to move ahead of me, pushing open the decaying door. An arrow flew straight at me. When my darkness snatched it from the air, Akira lowered the second shot she was about to send in my direction. I stepped into the house, which was small but warm due to the fire, a rabbit slowly cooking on a spit above it. Slivers of moonlight filtered in through holes in the roof to illuminate the thick layer of dust that coated the floor, but it provided a decent enough shelter against the elements.

Akira placed her hunting bow back down. Crow feathers were woven into her hair—a sign that she was still grieving the loss of her brother. Emrys was leaning against the far wall, wearing a plain brown traveling cloak with a hood that he could easily be pulled up to hide the distinctive color of his hair. Serenity was curled up on her side, asleep, the purple flowers she wore having withered after days of travel.

"You're late," Akira scolded. "This is our second night here."

"I came as soon as I could," I replied. She made a noncommittal grunt as she settled down next to the hearth and turned the rabbit over. Sensing that she was not in the mood for conversation, I set my supply bag down next to Emrys's silver-wood staff before joining him on the floor. My shadow slowly slithered across the room to return the arrow to Akira's quiver. There wouldn't be any armories to restock her supply where we were going.

"Did you manage to find her?" Emrys asked.

"I did," I said. "Any trouble on the way over?"

"Nothing that Faelan couldn't sweet-talk his way out of," he replied, and as I looked around the room again, I noticed that he was missing. As though summoned by the sound of his name, a bird's wings flapped overhead before it glided in through one of the holes in the roof. Faelan shifted back into his original form as he landed on the floor. He shook out his arms as though they were aching from overuse and then offered me a smile.

"Glad you could make it, Koven. I don't know if I could spend another night here. This place gives me the absolute creeps." His gaze briefly flicked to Emrys, who had probably screamed his lungs off from the nightmares this forsaken city had given him. "Anyway," he continued, shifting his attention onto Akira. "There's a patrol a few miles to the south, but I've scouted the path that leads to the mountains and we shouldn't run into any problems."

"That's good," she said with a nod. "We'll eat first and then we'll leave. Traveling at night is still the best way to get to the mountains unseen. It shouldn't take us more than two weeks to reach the tunnels that were marked on the map."

"We could get there quicker if we also traveled during the day," Emrys suggested.

"It's too risky," Akira replied coldly. I looked between her and Emrys as the air grew taut. She didn't like his plan, but with the king's approval and her brother now dead, she didn't have much of a choice but to see it through.

Akira's tone hadn't suggested that the matter was up for debate, but Emrys decided to argue with her anyway. "We don't have time to waste. The quicker we can—"

"Don't talk to me about wasting time when we have been stuck here waiting for your retainer," she said, cutting him off. "And if you had warned us that all this would come to pass earlier, then we could've avoided—"

"There was no avoiding war," Emrys snapped. "It could've been delayed, but then a worse fate would have befallen the continent. At least this way we have a chance to stop the destruction once and for all. I couldn't tell you what was coming. Any of you. It risked changing the future altogether, and this was the best path forward."

"I find that difficult to believe."

The rabbit, having been neglected above the fire, was beginning to char. "The two of you need to stop with this argument," Faelan said, rushing over to save the meat before it could burn. "It's happened. It's done. Quarreling about it won't change the past."

The raised voices caused Serenity to stir from where she slept. She rubbed her eyes and then blinked when she saw me. One of the wilting aster flowers dropped to the ground, and my shadow plucked it up from the ground to place it back in her braid. "Koven," she said, and then she gave me a smile that made me think that perhaps dawn was breaking on the horizon. "Welcome back."

Your taste in women bores me, the voice muttered.

If the voice at the back of my mind didn't like her, I took that to be an excellent sign.

"Evening, sunshine," I said with a smile, and a rosy hue traveled up her neck to tint her cheeks. She brushed her fingers over her bottom lip as though remembering the kiss we had shared. I held her gaze, a silent promise simmering in my eyes, and I could've sworn something like excitement flashed across her face, but she turned away and began rolling up her blanket before I could be sure.

Faelan grinned as he squatted down next to me. "I'm here if you ever need tips," he whispered as he handed me a portion of the meat. "Or if you ever need me to fracture a bone or two," he added with a wink. "Healers can't resist a broken boy in need of mending."

"I'm going to chart the stars for omens," Emrys announced, rising to his feet and fetching his silver-wood staff. "I'll be outside when everyone is ready to go."

"You should eat something," Faelan called after him.

"Not hungry."

As Emrys disappeared out the door, Akira began pulling the blankets down from the windows and packing away the supplies. "Eat quickly," she instructed. "I don't want to linger here any longer than we already have." She paused for a moment to look out at the ghost town, utterly destroyed in the violence of war. Her breath turned to mist as the chill of the night crept in. She shivered, though I doubted that had anything to do with the temperature. "Gods, I hope this doesn't happen again," she muttered to herself.

Suddenly, I wasn't feeling all that hungry, either.

Faelan scouted from the air above as the rest of us traveled below, using the trees and the cover of darkness to avoid detection. Occasionally, Faelan would swoop down to let us know of any nearby encampments or patrols, and we would take a detour in order to avoid them. At daybreak, Akira found a hollow beneath a bank of trees for us to take refuge in, offering to take first watch as everyone else got some sleep. She kept her bow in her lap, her eyes vigilant as she scanned the horizon.

I tried to close my eyes, but the sunlight felt like a direct assault even with my eyelids closed, and the day was too warm for me to hide my face beneath the blanket. I eventually gave up and went to sit next to Akira. Pulling out the whetstone from my supply satchel, I began to sharpen my daggers.

"So, what's the plan?" I asked her, lowering my voice to a whisper. "We sneak into Amari's sanctuary, steal the string of fate, and then sneak back out?" Akira gave a small snort. It was a derisive sound, but circumstances being what they were, I decided to let it slide. "I'm going to assume that means we're *not* going to steal it."

"The string of fate cannot be taken, only gifted. It's Amari's power imbued within it that gives it the power to change fate. Without her touch, it will be nothing more than a useless ball of twine. I thought every child hears the stories about them growing up. My mother used to sing me a lullaby about it."

I tested the edge of my blade. When I still found it lacking, I returned to dragging it against the stone. "Well, I didn't exactly have parents to sing me lullabies before I went to sleep."

She gave me a sideways look. "Are you really going to try playing the orphan card with *me*? My father murdered my mother in front of my eyes and tried to kill me as well."

She had a valid point. There weren't many people who could win against her in a game of tragedies. "I wasn't playing the orphan card," I corrected, switching my daggers over to sharpen the next one. "My mother is dead, but who knows whether my sorry excuse for a father has joined her in the afterlife?"

"Ah, so the dead mother and the deadbeat father card."

I flashed her a grin. "Exactly."

The corners of her mouth curved upward ever so slightly. "I understand why Emrys likes having you around so much. Not at first. At first I was rather annoyed with this disheveled boy who followed him around like a shadow at school and then later to all the social gatherings he was required to attend. I thought for certain you were a snake trying to slither your way into his coffers, but that was my own prejudice fueling my suspicions. I think sometimes vassals of Celdric all get painted with the same brush, which isn't always fair. After all, Faelan didn't change much after he was marked."

She peered over at him. Having exhausted himself flying through most of the night, he'd had no difficulty falling asleep. His mouth was hanging open and a loud snore reverberated from the back of his throat. I expected her to wake him up and tell him to turn onto his side, but she left him undisturbed. "He does go through women like a gambler goes through coins," she muttered, "but I don't think that particular vice can be blamed on Celdric's blood in his veins. He means well, though, and he's always been a good friend. That part of him has remained the same."

Her eyes shifted to me, and I tried not to squirm as her gaze dissected me with a look sharper than any sword. "And you, Koven, have a quality that the entire fortune of House Hardcastle cannot buy. Emrys knows it, which is why he keeps you close." That sounded like a compliment, but coming from Akira Marcaida, I almost didn't believe it. "If you ever decide that you want to serve in my shadow court, I would accept you."

My dagger froze halfway down the whetstone. I wasn't sure if the offer was because she thought I deserved it, or because she was mad at Emrys and wanted a way to lash out at him. Either way, it certainly wasn't an opportunity to be sneered at. But loyalty was not a set of clothes that could be tried on and changed at a whim. It was either something someone had, or they didn't. And I already knew where mine belonged. "I will take your offer under advisement," I told her, which was the diplomatic way of refusing her request.

She didn't say anything in response, only returned her attention to the horizon, her gaze searching for any signs of movement between the trees. She picked up her bow as something shuffled in the underbrush, but she relaxed again when it turned out to just be a squirrel with round cheeks and a bushy tail.

"How does the lullaby go?" I asked.

"It tells of how the string of fate can come in different colors. Each one has a power associated with it. What we need is a golden string, which fixes something that is broken."

"Like a tear in the fabric between realms?" I said, and she nodded. "Will you sing it for me?"

"Absolutely not."

"Come on, please?"

"No."

"Not even if I played the dead mother and deadbeat father card?"

Her eyes narrowed on me as though annoyed, but I could tell that she was fighting the urge to smile. "If I do, will you leave me in peace?" she asked.

I placed a hand over my heart. "Akira of House Marcaida, if you sing me a lullaby, I vow to leave you in peace."

She checked to make sure that everyone was still sleeping. Then she closed her eyes and drew in a deep breath. When she started to sing, it took me completely by surprise. Unlike the rest of her, which was sharp and rigid, her voice was soft and harmonious, making her sound like someone else altogether.

From fate I need some thread
For my wife I need it red
So that when she goes I will not cry
For I'll find her again when I die

When something is broken and needs repair
It's gold stitching that will help me there
When my house has fallen or my friend has strayed
This is the thread I need to braid

If I wish to start life anew
I need the thread to be blue
I do not like the fate I've known
So with this gift a new one is sewn

If the string is black, I'll make a noose
With blood I'll knot it so it won't come loose
Then in the fire it will go
And with it burns my hated foe

Her eyes flicked back open to catch me staring. The tune had been so slow and haunting that the final note still lingered in the air, the ghost of the chorus like a caress against my cheek. I never knew she could sing, especially not like that. When it became clear that I wouldn't be going to sleep anytime soon, she surveyed her surroundings one last time before leaning back and kicking her boots up on a tree root. "Well, if you're not going to get some rest, then I will," she declared, making herself comfortable. "Wake me up if you hear a patrol close by."

I turned my attention back to sharpening my daggers. I had almost finished going through all of them when a snake slithered out from beneath a pile of leaves, its scales black and gleaming beneath the sun. I was content to just let it be, but then the voice in my head whispered, *What if it's a vassal of Celdric that has come to spy on you?*

I froze, my hand tightening around my dagger.

I tried not to listen to it, tried to tell myself that Celdric didn't know we were here, that there was no cause for me to worry . . . and yet the longer

I stared into the snake's beady eyes, the more unsettled I became. While Celdric did not possess Essian's gift of foresight, he was a collector of secrets with a whole host of spies at his disposal. He would have vassals lurking in every corner of the continent. All it would take was one whisper of our treachery to reach his ears and we would be exposed. One whisper and our lives would be forfeit.

What if it slithers back to its god and warns him that you have crossed the border to conspire with the goddess of fate?

I threw my dagger. The snake flailed and writhed on the ground as the tip of the blade pierced into it. Then it went still. Nothing happened. It was just a snake.

I think you might be going paranoid, the voice taunted.

I ignored it, even as the thought filled me with a very real fear.

CHAPTER 24

Serenity crouched next to a stream as she refilled her waterskin, blissfully unaware of me standing a few feet away, leaning against one of the trees with my arms folded across my chest. The Irashkai mountains were only a few more days away, yet dark clouds loomed in the sky, as though warning us to turn back while we still had a chance. The storm had been chasing us since the crack of dawn, and now that it had finally caught up, I couldn't help but feel it was an ill omen. I instinctively scanned my surroundings for any sign of enemies lurking nearby, and though nothing moved beyond the rustle of leaves in the wind, I still found myself searching the shadows as though expecting to find a pair of golden eyes staring back at me. I shook my head, silently berating myself. I refused to allow the voice in my head to drive me to paranoia.

My gaze settled back on Serenity. The aster flowers she usually wore had long since fallen free of her braid. She looked oddly vulnerable without them, like a knight who had been stripped of her armor. The only weapon she carried was the dagger at her hip, but I had yet to see her actually unsheathe it. The dagger was not intended to be a decoration, and before we entered the mountains, I needed to make sure she understood that.

"You're lucky I'm not an enemy." She shot to her feet at the sound of my voice, but the startled expression on her face quickly melted away once she turned around to look at me. The trek through Kalta had left my hair permanently tousled and stained my clothes with a healthy layer of dirt. From the way her gaze roamed over my body, lingering and wistful, I wondered if perhaps she preferred this slightly wilder version of me. My blood heated beneath the intensity of her stare, but I didn't allow myself to get distracted by it.

"Take out your blade," I ordered.

She frowned at the request. "Why?"

"Monsters of old still dwell in the mountains. It wouldn't hurt to learn a few defensive maneuvers before you walk into them."

"I highly doubt a dagger would do me any good against such creatures. I was just planning on staying very close to you." Her voice was nothing but sincere, as though she didn't understand the significance of what she'd just said, but I heard the words that remained unspoken. She trusted me to protect her, trusted me with her *life*, and that trust was not something I planned on breaking. Hopefully, it would never get to the point where she needed to wield a weapon, but I would rather she learn how to use it just in case.

"I like your strategy, sunshine." My voice was smooth as I stepped away from the tree and moved to stand in front of her. "But I still want you to take out your blade."

She held my gaze for several long seconds before discarding the waterskin on the ground and drawing her dagger. I proceeded to adjust her grip on the handle. Once I was satisfied that she was holding the weapon correctly, I demonstrated a few easy moves for her to replicate. There wasn't enough time to teach her much beyond simple slashes and thrusts, but it wasn't her technique that I was worried about. She would never be a blade master, especially not in the span of a few short hours. What I was more concerned about was her motivation to actually use the weapon if the situation demanded it.

After she practiced the movements enough times, I gave a small nod of approval and then said, "Good. Now, I want you to attack me."

Her brows knitted together in confusion as though she hadn't heard me correctly.

"Attack me," I repeated, my voice deadly serious. "Come at me with everything you got."

She glanced nervously between the blade and me. "But I could hurt you."

My lips curled into an amused smile at the comment. "Well, I guess it's a good thing you're a healer, so you can put me back together again."

For a moment, I thought she would refuse, but then she took a deep breath and slashed at me. The movement was slow, reluctant—exactly what I wanted to make sure *didn't* happen if she ever needed to defend herself. I easily caught her wrist before she was able to make contact.

"You're too slow," I chastised, "and you need more power behind the strike."

"But I don't want to hurt you."

"You won't."

"That's an arrogant assumption."

"Then prove me wrong."

Her lips flattened into a thin line at the challenge. Then she came at me again, with more force this time, but it still wasn't nearly enough. I wanted her to be able to bury that blade down to the hilt if necessary. I caught ahold of her wrist again, and this time when I let her go, I gave her a little push. She only stumbled back a few steps, but it had the desired effect. Annoyance flickered across her features.

"Again," I said, and this time when she charged forward, I met her dagger with one of my own. Our weapons locked, and a different kind of intensity burned in her eyes.

"Again."

She aimed her next thrust at my abdomen.

I deflected it.

"Again."

She tried to drag the blade across my thigh.

I sidestepped the attack.

"Again."

Her strikes were stronger each time she came at me, and once she realized this training wouldn't leave me wounded and bleeding in her wake, the last of her hesitation vanished. Satisfaction swelled within me at the determination etched into her face. She took a swipe at my ribs. This time, when I blocked her attack, she didn't retreat. Instead, she leaned into it, throwing her body weight behind her blade. She strained against me, her chest heaving and her hair damp with sweat. All I needed to do was take a step back and she would lose her balance, but I met her resolve with some of my own, pushing against her until her arms were shaking from exertion.

I flashed her a taunting grin. "Is that the best you can do, sunshine?"

I was hoping the comment would rile her up even more, but then her gaze dropped to my mouth and something shifted in her expression. A heartbeat later, she arched onto her toes and kissed me. That smug grin was wiped clean off my face at the first brush of her lips. She lowered her dagger, and my own weapon became a forgotten thing as my free hand snaked around her waist. She deepened the kiss, her tongue slipping into my mouth, hungry and searching. I responded in kind. She was still kissing me when the tip of her dagger stung my throat, drawing forth a tiny trickle of blood that rolled down the side of my neck. I huffed out a laugh as a triumphant smile spread across her face.

"I don't think that trick will work on the monsters," I said.

She lifted her shoulders in a shrug. "Maybe not, but it does feel pretty good to best a shadow-walker." She returned her weapon to its sheath, and with a caress of her fingers, she erased the small incision she'd made on my neck. "I still don't think a dagger will do me any good once we're in the mountains."

"It could buy you a few seconds. Sometimes that's all you need. If something comes at you, don't hesitate. You drive that dagger into the bastard with as much force as you can muster." She didn't say anything in response, only averted her eyes. It was the first indication she'd given that she was actually afraid of what was to come. I tucked a finger beneath her chin and gently guided her gaze back to mine. "I won't let anything happen to you."

Her expression softened, and gods help whatever monsters were lurking in those mountains, because I would grind their bones to dust if they tried to touch her. My hand moved to cradle her face, and as I stared into those beautiful, dark eyes, I started to wonder what other delightful expressions she was capable of making. I had to bite down on the growl that wanted to tear free from my throat. It was much too soon for me to be having such indecent thoughts about her . . . and yet I couldn't bring myself to stop thinking them.

I was only half-aware of my actions when I picked up Serenity. An intoxicating blend of surprise and anticipation flickered across her face as I pressed her against one of the trees. She arched her neck, and I obeyed the silent request, leaving a trail of kisses down her throat. Tendrils of shadow traveled up her legs, her arms, her torso, the darkness deliberate in its desire to claim her. Her fingers threaded through my hair, a low moan of pleasure rolling off her tongue. Emboldened by the response, I grazed my teeth against her skin. My mouth curved into a slow smile when she shivered against me.

I could've spent countless hours coaxing forth more lovely reactions from her body, but unfortunately, the sound of crunching leaves and snapping twigs alerted me to someone approaching. Her eyes widened as she heard it, too. With a bitter tang of disappointment, I quietly lowered her to the ground and held one finger to my lips. She gave a nod of understanding, and it was with no small amount of pride that I noticed her hand went to rest on the hilt of her dagger. I stalked deeper into the woods, readying my weapons in case it was a Kaltan soldier. However, it was only Faelan, who appeared to be going out of his way to stomp on every piece of debris on the forest floor, as though he suspected what we might be doing and wanted to give us enough warning to stop doing it. I expected him to make some witty remark upon his arrival, but his face was tight, completely devoid of humor, and that immediately set me on edge.

"I just returned from scouting ahead," he said, his voice grave. "There's a Kaltan regiment based a little farther up north. I decided to drop down and have a listen to what's been happening while we've been away."

"From your expression, I'm assuming it's not good," I said.

"No, it's not good."

No one spoke after Faelan recounted the gossip he'd overheard from the Kaltan war camp. Brazial had already launched his first attack on Athearia, claiming one of the main strongholds along the northern border. He had led the attack himself, and while the Athearian forces were formidable, the might of men could not withstand the power of a god. Ashearan was the only one powerful enough to take on Brazial in a direct fight, but apparently he was so grief-stricken over the loss of his sister he had yet to make an appearance on the battlefield. If the rumors were to be believed, he was hauled up in the Marcaida Fortress, content to let Athearia bleed while he hid himself away behind stone walls. From the comments the Kaltan soldiers were making, it sounded like that first battle had been an absolute massacre.

Emrys sat perched atop one of the logs that littered the ground, age having turned the wood to a dull shade of gray. He hadn't looked up once the entire time Faelan was talking. The shadows beneath his eyes seemed more pronounced than usual, his face gaunt and his expression somber. His continued silence eventually earned him a withering glare from Akira.

"I'm sure Scias will come up with some brilliant plan to stop Brazial," I said in an attempt to alleviate some of the tension between the two of them.

"Maybe," Akira said, though she didn't sound convinced. "Scias couldn't find a way to defeat him last time. In case you've forgotten, the last war ended in a bitter stalemate that split the continent in two and wiped entire cities off the map. With Sheara imprisoned and her brother refusing to fight, we're already down two gods. Three if we count Essian, whose host is too goddamn old to be of much use. The moment Tammearia readies her fleet and Lios summons his dragon, we are fucked."

She was right, and no one tried to argue otherwise. The war had only just started, and yet the odds were already stacked heavily against us. I raked my fingers through my hair, bewildered with how I had ended up getting saddled with the responsibility of saving Athearia from being decimated in another Holy War. I was supposed to be celebrating my graduation right now, enjoying festive tavern music and laughing with my friends. I pictured Akira with a rare smile, begrudgingly accepting a mug of ale from Faelan on account that this was a "special occasion." Faelan, of course, had managed to pay for the drinks with little more than a few charming words and a well-placed wink at the barmaid. Emrys would be watching the scene with quiet amusement, the liquor forcing a bit of color into his pale face. I imagined Serenity there with me, mirth sparkling in her eyes as I twirled her to the rhythm of the music.

A loud cheer drew my attention to the far side of the tavern where a pair of women were arm wrestling. The victor stood up, thrusting a fist into the air in a display of triumph, and something in my chest collapsed at the familiar sight of those blond curls. Rita shook her empty mug at me before adding it to the absurdly large stack that was forming on her table. Then, with a mischievous grin, she ordered another round and blew a mocking kiss in my direction, adding the drink to the ever-growing tab under my name. This was what I had promised her after we survived the trials. Nausea burned at my throat as the daydream collided with the memory of her dying in my arms, her body torn to shreds by the claws of hungry corpses. I blinked the image away until I was standing in the forest once more, the music and the laughter fading away until only a tense silence remained.

I surveyed the grim faces of everyone around me. Once we entered the mountains, we would be putting our lives at the mercy of fate. I had already lost Rita. I couldn't bear the thought of losing one of them as well. "What are we even doing?" I muttered under my breath. "The king was right. We're in over our heads. We've only just graduated. The fate of Athearia should not be resting in our hands."

"Technically speaking, because the trials were interrupted, none of us have officially graduated," Akira replied dryly.

"Considering the circumstances, I'm sure the church will make an exception this year," Serenity said in a voice so gentle and reassuring that I could almost bring myself to believe her. "The gods can't just fail an entire cohort of students, especially considering that what happened on Spire wasn't our fault."

"I think the gods can do whatever they want," Faelan retorted. He was flicking a dagger between his fingers. The blade slipped in and out of view with a practiced ease, giving him the illusion of being relaxed, but he wasn't fooling me. I had been friends with him long enough to know that was one of his nervous habits, in the same way that Emrys resorted to picking the skin around his nails and Akira resorted to making snappy comments. With a flick of his wrist, the dagger went flying through the air and embedded itself in a tree several feet away. "They could wipe us all out and no one would be able to do a damn thing about it."

The bitter truth of his words struck a chord deep within me, making me feel completely and utterly powerless, as though I was back in the penance room with Rasalan shackles clamped down on my wrists. The gods were the ultimate authority throughout the land. Even the king only ruled at their discretion. There was absolutely nothing stopping them from eliminating an entire cohort of students if that was what they decided to do.

"They're not going to kill us," Akira said firmly. "Noble families accept deaths during the trials because the gods claim that it separates the weak from the strong. If they started slaughtering us indiscriminately, it would cause too much discontent among the populace. Undertaking another set of trials is also unlikely. Even if we managed to put a stop to this war, the gods will be too preoccupied dealing with the fallout to prepare another round of exams. Serenity is right. The church will probably decide to make an exception this year."

Emrys finally lifted his head up from where he sat perched on the log. His eyes were the same shade as the clouds that darkened the sky, and just like the storm, he seemed on the verge of breaking. Between the limited rations and the long, strenuous hikes, his already thin body was beginning to whittle away into little more than a husk. It worried me, seeing him like this, worried me more than I cared to admit. "I hardly think graduation is our main priority right now," Emrys said quietly. "Fate does not choose her champions lightly. This is exactly where we need to be. So long as we follow the path of destiny, Sheara will be freed, the war will come to an end, and Athearia will emerge even stronger than before."

He didn't sound nearly as convincing as he had back in the war council meeting, and from the wary look Akira gave him, I wasn't the only one thinking it. A prickle of unease formed at the base of my neck as I recalled what Emrys had confided in me back at the Marcaida Fortress. He had seen this quest fail time and time again. The others deserved to know the full extent of the risks they were about to take . . . and yet giving them that information might fracture the group, and perhaps that was one of the dozens of reasons why Emrys had seen this quest fall apart. Doubt would be a dangerous travel companion to invite on this journey. Perhaps Emrys was right not to tell the others about it. He was the seer, after all. The boy born of a miracle and destined for greatness. I was just an orphan who happened to steal a ring. He was far better suited to make this decision than I was.

"Do you ever think that maybe destiny was wrong to choose us?" I threw the question out there as though it was merely a curiosity, but from the glint in his eyes, it was clear he knew exactly what I was doing. I was giving him a chance to voice any reservations he had before we entered the mountains and no longer had the option of turning back. As the first drops of rain began to filter in through the trees, he tilted his head back and let the water splatter against his skin, like it had the power to wash away all his regrets and uncertainties. When he looked at me again, he managed to lift his lips into some semblance of a smile.

"You're more than welcome to have that argument with Amari once we reach her. Personally, I'm not in the habit of arguing with a goddess, but you've never been lacking in courage, Koven."

While the thought was certainly amusing, not even I would dare to pick a fight with the goddess of fate. I was already playing a dangerous game with Celdric. The last thing I needed was to make an enemy of yet another deity.

Emrys stood up and retrieved his staff. "Let's keep moving. Even destiny has her limits when it comes to patience." His declaration was punctuated by a rumble of thunder, and once more, I wondered if maybe some higher power was warning us to leave this place. But I'd made a promise back at the Marcaida Fortress, and that promise had me quickly falling into step behind him. Even if he ended up straying down the wrong path, he wouldn't be alone. I would be by his side. Always.

CHAPTER 25

The storm had subsided, leaving the fresh scents of rain and damp soil in its place. Unfortunately, neither my boots nor my socks had managed to dry yet, which would likely leave my feet covered in blisters, but no one else was complaining about it, and I refused to be the first. I shifted my focus to the mountains in front of me, which possessed peaks so high the tips were lost to the clouds. Amari's sanctuary was located at the very summit. The problem was that there weren't many ways to get to the top. The rock face was notoriously unreliable, prone to giving out and crumbling away as soon as you managed to get a foothold. It was believed that the goddess and her maidens of providence used a series of ancient tunnels inside the mountain to reach the sanctuary, but how they managed to avoid getting eaten by the monsters was another mystery altogether.

Emrys, however, was under the impression that he could guide us through it like he had in the labyrinth during the trials. I resisted the urge to point out that not everyone in our team had managed to make it out alive the last time. It wouldn't help the group morale, which was running low after long nights and little sleep, our stomachs gnawing with hunger as our rations began to dwindle. Yet Akira decided to bring up the topic anyway. "The last time you served as our guide, we didn't all make it across the finish line," she said, her words causing him to stiffen.

"That's not fair," I told her, defensive on his behalf. "He said he could guide us through it, and he did. That maze was teeming with dangers in every direction. There was no way we could avoid them all."

She turned toward me, and the crow feather woven into her hair fluttered at the movement, reminding me that she had more to lose than anyone else if Emrys's plan ended in failure. "You treat him like he's infallible, but he's not. Blind faith is a good way to get us all killed."

"So is doubt," I countered, "especially when the only way to get through this alive is for us to work together. We don't have any other choice but to trust in his plan . . . unless you happen to know a different way to get to Amari's sanctuary at the top of the mountain?"

Her eyes darkened with irritation, but she remained quiet. This was the only option we had, and she couldn't argue otherwise. Either we managed to make it to the sanctuary and succeed in obtaining the thread of fate, or we failed and the war would wreak havoc across the continent. As Emrys peered up at the mountains with his silver-wood staff in his hand, the clouds parted in the sky and a stream of sunlight filtered through to illuminate him where he stood, making him appear like one of the mystical sages from the tales of old.

"This will not be any different to the trials," he warned. "I know the way through, but creatures of death and darkness dwell within these tunnels. It will be dangerous, so we'll wait until nightfall before entering the mountain. It will be to our advantage to have Koven at the peak of his strength."

Faelan swooped down from the sky, landing in a crouch as his wings extended into arms and his feathers smoothed over into dark battle leathers. Rising to his feet, he stretched out his limbs, his face worn down by fatigue. "No patrols in the near vicinity," he reported.

With the path ahead clear, Emrys stepped out of the protection of the tree line to cross the terrain that separated the forest from the mountain. Without the cloak of darkness to shroud me, I felt uncomfortably exposed as I followed him, but eventually the rocky terrain and abundance of caves quelled any concerns I had about lacking cover in case of an emergency. The Irashkai mountains possessed hundreds of tunnels to choose from, but Emrys kept traveling farther down the mountain path. Scorpions and centipedes scuttled across the dirt, their brown complexion allowing them to blend in seamlessly into their environment.

When I noticed Serenity lingering farther and farther behind the group, I slowed my pace until I fell into step beside her. I was about to ask if she needed a break when she came to a sudden stop and tugged on the sleeve of my shirt, pointing at something. I almost didn't see what had caught her attention, but then a large scorpion crept out from between two rocks. When my shadow rose up to crush it, her eyes widened with alarm.

"No, don't kill it!" she exclaimed. She quickly dug through her travel pack and removed a jar. "That's a desert-tail deathstalker. The venom serves as a fast-acting paralytic. I want you to catch it for me."

My lips lifted into an amused smile. My shadow slunk forward, the scorpion completely oblivious to the darkness even as it wrapped around the creature to form a cage. Serenity held out the jar, and the darkness lowered the critter into the glass. She screwed on the lid, beaming as she held it up for closer inspection.

"I do recall you mentioning that you were a poison expert," I mused.

"I need to be in order to know how to cure them. I can mend torn skin and fix broken bones, but poisons require a herbal remedy. I need to be able to recognize their symptoms so I can treat the patient. Some herbs also have both medicinal and lethal properties. Shaewood root, for example, is a very effective ingredient for sleeping draughts, but take too much and the patient will never wake up. It's important for a healer to know how much of something is needed to make a lethal dose."

"How fortunate for the world that your oath forbids you from murdering anyone."

The edges of her eyes crinkled as she smiled. "I suppose that it is."

Farther ahead, Emrys started to climb up a set of boulders, a task that required both of his hands, so Faelan grabbed the silver-wood staff with his talons and soared up to the top. Akira hooked her hunting bow over her back and began scaling the rocks with the sort of ease that came with years of practice. Serenity, however, grew a little pale as she stared up at the wall of rocks.

"I'm not the best climber," she admitted.

I placed a hand on her lower back, urging her forward. "I'll be right next to you. My shadow will catch you if you fall."

She hesitated for a moment. Then she drew in a deep breath and began the climb. I waited for her to gain some distance before following her. When her foothold slipped, my shadow darted up to stabilize her, but the incident must've shaken her confidence, because she ended up clinging to the spot, frozen in place.

"Keep going," I told her. "You're not going to fall. I won't let you." When she still didn't move, I climbed up beside her, noticing how her body trembled and her fingers turned white as she gripped the stone. Her eyes found mine, and a realization dawned on me. She was terrified of heights.

"I think I need to go down." Her voice was shaking almost as much as she was, but the path to Amari was up ahead, which meant that she needed to keep going.

"A wise person once said that there is no shame in having fear, only in the failure to overcome it." Some people made the mistake of thinking that a healer's kindness made them weak, but I thought it was the opposite. In a world filled with so much violence, it took a special kind of strength to choose compassion over cruelty. "You're not lacking in courage, sunshine. You can get to the top. I know you can."

The wind rippled through the brown curls of her hair as she rested her forehead against the stone. "My father had a bit of a temper," she said, and I had a feeling that the tremble in her voice was more than just about heights. "There was a tree just outside my bedroom window that I would use to escape when he was in one of his moods, but one time I wasn't quick enough. He tried to drag me back inside. I fell and shattered my hip on the way down. I was still a child at the time—before Sheara had given me her blessing—and I can still remember the weeks of pain that followed. I've never climbed out a window since."

It was fortunate the man was already dead, because otherwise I might've been tempted to kill him myself. The official story was that the man had drunk himself into the grave. The unofficial story was that House Blackwood had helped him along. From the sound of it, he had gotten what he deserved. But, in the end, death had claimed more than just Serenity's father. It had claimed her sister as well.

"I'm not going to let you fall," I repeated as tendrils of darkness gently curled around her wrists. She stared at them for a long moment before allowing the shadows to guide her hand to the next crevice she could use as a handhold. I lagged just behind her, ready to catch her should she slip again, but she didn't. Faelan helped pull her over the edge once she made it to the top. As I followed her, I discovered that there was another pathway carved along the side of the mountain.

Serenity staggered away from the edge before sliding to the ground. Closing her eyes, she tilted back her head and drew in an unsteady breath. When she opened them again, her gaze found mine and she mouthed, *Thank you.*

I gave her a nod before turning my attention to the large cavern located at the end of the path. The darkness swallowed up everything inside it, giving it the impression of an open maw ready to consume its victims. Something screeched from inside its depths—a horrible, guttural, inhumane sound unlike anything I had ever heard before. If Amari had picked this location because she wanted to be left alone, she'd done an excellent job. The only people who would dare to enter these tunnels would be the truly desperate, or the truly insane.

"Are you sure this is the right entrance?" I asked Emrys, who regarded me with a grim expression.

"It's the right one," he confirmed. There was another screech followed by the sound of nails scuttling across the stone floor. Even Akira's calm demeanor cracked as she unslung her quiver and began nervously counting her arrows.

Serenity took out a small chunk of shaewood root from her satchel, which she crushed using the flat side of the dagger. A pungent smell wafted out from it. She unscrewed the lid of the jar that contained the scorpion and then threw the root inside. She waited for its tail to droop and its legs to grow limp before tipping over the jar. I watched with growing fascination as she carefully extracted the venom from the scorpion's tail and applied it to the edge of the dagger. It was a clever strategy, especially considering her skill with a blade was limited. After the task was completed, she returned the scorpion to the jar and screwed the lid back on.

When the sun finally slipped beneath the horizon, its fading light casting an orange-red glow against the rocks, Emrys stepped up to the entrance of the cavern and tapped his staff twice against the ground. The crystal flickered to life. "Everybody stay close," he instructed before walking in. My eyes strained against the combination of light and dark, which prevented me from seeing much farther than anyone else. As we traveled deeper into the underbelly of the mountain, the less it seemed like a labyrinth and the more it seemed like an insect mound with interconnected tunnels shooting off in every direction. At one point, I had to stretch my shadow across the floor like a bridge to prevent everyone from falling into the deep holes that burrowed into the ground. I kept my shadow at my heels, ready to attack at a moment's notice, but as time stretched on and nothing ominous or deadly made an appearance, I began to relax.

That was my mistake.

A split second of inattention was all it took. The creature was so quiet that I didn't hear so much as a whispered exhale from its lips, but I did hear Serenity scream as she was dragged through one of the tunnels in the ceiling. That scream promised to haunt me in my nightmares. I leaped after her without even thinking, moving on instinct as I scrambled up the shaft after her. My vision blurred for a few seconds as the light was left behind me. Then my eyes snapped back into focus and I caught a flash of Serenity's boots as she was pulled into a horizontal tunnel located farther up the shaft. I began climbing even faster, hauling myself into the same tunnel that she had disappeared into.

My shadow rushed forward like a flood, a wave of darkness ready to drown my enemies in its wake, but it came to a sudden halt when I saw

Serenity crawling toward me, her hands blindly searching for the way out. When I grabbed her, she let out another ear-piercing scream. "It's me," I told her, cupping her face in my hands and wiping away the tears that were spilling from her eyes. "It's me."

She collapsed into me, her hands tightening to fists as she gripped the fabric of my shirt. "Koven, thank the gods!" she exclaimed. "Something grabbed me. I don't know what it was. I don't know if it's still here."

I wrapped an arm around her as I peered down the tunnel. I suppressed the shiver that wanted to run down my spine at the sight of the monster that lay twitching on the ground, her dagger embedded in its side. The creature had no eyes, just smooth skin and a mouth that was so large it appeared to split its face in two. An obscenely long tongue was curled on the ground next to it, which must've been how it snatched Serenity from where it was hidden in the ceiling. My shadow reached out to grab the dagger and return it to the sheath at Serenity's hip. The scorpion's venom had done its work, but she had said that it was more of a paralytic than a poison. Eventually, it would wear off and I didn't want this monster to come after her a second time. The darkness converged on it, and the sound of crunching bones echoed down the chasm.

I ran a hand through Serenity's hair as she buried her face against my chest. "It's gone," I assured her. "It won't be able to hurt you anymore."

She let out a shuddering breath and nodded.

"We need to start climbing down," I said, but she began to panic as soon as I pulled away from her, her grip on my shirt tightening.

"It's completely dark, Koven. I can't climb down. I can't see anything."

I gently took hold of her hands, wisps of shadow curling around her wrists. "It's okay, we can go slowly. I'll guide you. I promise, I won't let you fall."

I swung back over into the vertical shaft and helped her do the same. She clung to the edge, biting down on her bottom lip to keep it from quivering. I started descending slowly, but then a commotion broke out below. I heard the distinctive twang of Akira's bow, quickly followed by a wolfish growl that must've been Faelan. Then Emrys shouted and the light emanating from his staff winked out.

I let go and dropped the rest of the distance. The darkness reached out to catch me, softening the impact as I landed in a crouch. I looked around, but the tunnel was empty.

"Rys!" I yelled, and the name was repeated back to me as it bounced off the stone walls. "Akira!"

There was no response.

My stomach twisted into sickening knots. I had left them alone. I tried to tell myself that I'd had no choice, but that would be of little comfort if I stumbled across their corpses. I spun around in a circle, trying to ascertain which direction they had gone, painfully aware that each second that passed meant that they were more and more likely to be dead. I pictured Emrys splayed in the dark, his pale skin painted scarlet, his eyes hollow as he stared up at nothing. I was supposed to keep him safe. Without him, there was no path. Without him, the continent would wither and burn beneath the onslaught of another Holy War. As a deep sense of failure threatened to consume me, my fingers closed around the emerald ring that was threaded on my necklace. Without Emrys, my life ceased to have a purpose.

"Koven?" Serenity called out, sounding scared and confused. "What's happening?"

I quickly pushed the morbid thought from my mind, afraid that if I lingered on it too long then I would completely unravel. "The others are gone," I replied, and despite the torrent of emotions that threatened to rip me apart on the inside, I managed to smooth my voice into something calm. "We need to hurry. Let go. I'll catch you."

"Let go?" she repeated, and I could already tell from the fear in her voice that she wouldn't be able to do it, so I did it for her. The shadows that were curled around her wrists slithered up to pry her fingers from the stone. She yelped as she dropped. The darkness rose up to catch her and lowered her safely to her feet.

Grabbing ahold of her hand, I searched the area until I found something that made my chest tighten, the sensation squeezing all the air from my lungs. A blood trail led down one of the passageways. Arrows were scattered across the floor as though Akira had been knocked over and dragged away, causing them to fall out of her quiver.

Steeling my nerves, I followed the scarlet path deeper into the abyss, my shadow collecting the discarded arrows as I went. Fate be willing, Akira was still alive, and she would be needing them.

CHAPTER 26

Sweat beaded down the back of my neck as the sides of the tunnel slowly became coated in a thick layer of webbing. My shadow flickered uneasily with every step. I listened for any sign that my friends could be alive, but the path ahead was eerily silent. I tightened my grip on Serenity as the passage opened up into a large chamber. My gaze followed the blood trail until it came to an end in front of a giant spider that was almost as big as a merchant's wagon. It lay motionless on the ground, its hairy legs curled up to its abdomen, its beady eyes dull and lifeless. With my heart thundering in my chest, I peeled my eyes away from the spider and glanced up toward the ceiling. White cocoons were suspended in the air, each one big enough to fit a human body. Dread pooled in the pit of my stomach. The only way to be certain that none of the others had been captured was to open them up one by one.

"I need to go check on something," I said to Serenity. My voice was lowered to a whisper, but the vastness of the cavern latched on to the slightest of sounds, causing me to wince as my words echoed back to me. When nothing scuttled out from one of the tunnels, I let my shoulders relax. "You'll be safe here. I won't be far."

Serenity nodded. Letting go of her hand, I withdrew one of my daggers and commanded my shadow to leap up and twist around a cocoon, pulling it to the ground with a sharp tug. Crouching down next to it, I made an incision in the webbing and grimaced as the smell of rotting meat wafted out into the air. Whoever was inside had already been reduced to a juicy mess, which meant that the person had been dead too long for it to be one of my friends. My shadow pulled down the next cocoon and I opened it up with a similar result.

Third time's the charm, I thought as I sliced into the next one. I became hopeful when I wasn't immediately attacked by the stench of decomposing flesh. I quickly peeled back the webbing, hating how the silk clung stubbornly to my fingers. I couldn't have been more surprised to find who was inside. Damien Knight peered back at me, his blue eyes open but unseeing. I pressed my fingers to his neck. Although his skin was pale and cold to the touch, I managed to detect a weak pulse. Whatever he wanted from Amari must've been important, because he had risked his life traveling through these mountains in search of her.

I turned toward Serenity, who was holding her dagger out in front of her, ready to slash at anyone and anything that drew close. When I warned her that I was approaching, she slowly lowered the weapon and allowed me to guide her across the chamber. "It's Damien," I explained as she knelt next to him. "The Kaltan who we escaped Spire with. I think he's been bitten by a spider."

If she was surprised, she didn't show it. Instead, her features morphed into a look of concentration as her hands blindly searched his body until she found the smooth skin of his face. "His heart rate is slow. If it's because of spider venom like you claim, then I'm going to need a herbal remedy to counteract its effects. What sort of spider bit him? Did you see it?"

I cast an apprehensive glance at the monstrosity on the other side of the chamber. "It's hairy with fangs." Not wanting to cause her unnecessary alarm, I added, "It's a bit bigger than your usual spider."

She made a pensive sound from the back of her throat as she mulled over the information. "Let's try newalla root," she decided, removing her supply satchel and holding it out for me to take. "The skin of the herb has a red hue to it and a texture marked by small ridges. The properties are quite diverse, one of which is neutralizing a range of paralytic agents. We'll start with that and go from there."

I began riffling through the satchel, but there was too much inside it. I quickly grew impatient with it and tipped out the contents onto the floor. I examined several different ingredients before finding the one that resembled her description. I pressed it into her hand. Her fingers searched the curvatures of Damien's face before prying open his mouth. As she chewed on the root and then slipped it beneath his tongue, a high-pitched keening sound emanated from the other side of the cavern, which made all the hairs at the back of my neck bristle. I twisted around and watched in horror as a spider the size of a human head crawled out of an egg sac . . . followed by another and then another until there were dozens of them scampering straight for me.

My darkness swept through the cavern, flattening them against the ground with a disgusting squelch. However, more started to hatch, and soon they were rushing toward me in every direction. My shadow battered them away, but they were relentless. One jumped forward and landed on my arm. I sank a dagger into it, nausea rising in my throat as its legs convulsed against me. It screeched as it died, and the sound seemed to incite its siblings, because they became more vicious in their assault, an endless horde of nightmares determined to make me into their first meal.

My shadow grew wild and panicked, lashing out in every direction. Serenity let out an agonized cry. She clutched at her arm, blood seeping through her fingers. I froze, horrified that I had hurt her, and the spiders leaped at the opportunity that it afforded them. They crawled all over me. My shadow rose up to crush them, but it was too late. Their fangs ripped through my clothes to sink into my flesh. A burning pain laced through my body, making my limbs grow heavy. My shadow spluttered as it tore one of the spiders off my leg, squeezing it until it burst. Then everything turned cold and the darkness slipped through my fingers, leaving me defenseless.

I collapsed.

The spiders converged on me, working together to roll me over as they covered my body with webs. I tried to reach for my shadow, but everything inside me was numb. Having removed me as a threat, a handful of the spiders turned their interest to finding their next victim. Serenity was frantically tapping Damien's cheek, trying to rouse him, but he remained motionless. In the end, I couldn't protect her. I couldn't protect anyone. My eyes fluttered, threatening to close forever.

You are the commander of the night, the voice yelled, the sound dragging me back from the brink of unconsciousness. *The wielder of shadow. The harbinger of eternal darkness. This is not how you meet your end. I will not allow it.*

My shadow staggered forward and swallowed the cluster of spiders that were skulking toward Serenity.

You're supposed to be saving yourself, you idiot, the voice chastised right before a spider scurried over my face and sticky threads of silk taped my eyes closed. I tried once more to call upon the darkness, but it grew as still and silent as an untouched grave.

A sudden warmth filled the cavern, helping chase away the chill that had crept into my bones. When a spider attempted to crawl into my mouth, I tried to spit it out, but then a hand clamped down over my lips. It took me a moment to realize that it wasn't actually a spider that was making my tongue tingle. It was a bitter herb of some kind. The sensation traveled down my arms to make my fingers twitch. A hand tapped my cheek and my eyes flicked back open to find Serenity crouching above me, her face lined with concern. I twisted my head only to discover that most of the hatchlings had disintegrated into a pile of ash. Several of them were still on fire, shrieking as they fled like glowing lanterns in the night before finally succumbing to their gruesome fate. Damien was on his feet, cobwebs hanging from his battle armor. He held an orange flame in one hand, while gripping his knee with the other as though he was struggling to stay upright.

"Just a bit bigger than a normal spider," Serenity muttered under her breath, shooting me an unamused look from the corner of her eye as she hurried to peel the webs from my torso.

"I didn't mean to hurt you." The words that rolled off my lips were thick and clumsy, my tongue feeling like lead in my mouth, but they needed to be said. Some gods were loved, and some gods were feared; vassals were much the same. I didn't care much about how the rest of the world viewed me. On the contrary, there were advantages that came with being able to conjure terror in the heart of another, but I think something inside me would break if she started to look at me as though I were one of the monsters lurking in the mountain.

"It was barely more than a scratch," she said dismissively. It was a lie and not even a convincing one. Yet there was no trace of anger or fear in her voice, which was a relief.

"Water?" Damien croaked, his voice harsh and cracked like dry wood that had just been fed into a hearth. He didn't wait for a response before helping himself to the waterskin that lay among the other provisions scattered across the floor. He took a sip, looking as though even that small movement caused him a great deal of pain. The bitter root that Serenity had shoved beneath my tongue left an unpleasant tang in my mouth, making me yearn for a sip from the waterskin as well, but then Damien tilted his head back and drained every last drop of it.

"I know you," Damien said, his voice still hoarse. "You're the shadowwalker . . . from the marketplace." He looked around the chamber as though expecting to find more people. He frowned when he discovered that we were alone. "Where's the seer?"

The question was a stark reminder that I didn't have time to loiter. My friends were still missing. My muscles ached as I attempted to lift my arm. I managed to get it halfway up before it fell back down again. "We were looking for him." Gritting my teeth together, I tried to lift my arm again but to little success. "I need to keep going."

"You need to rest," Serenity cautioned, but I couldn't just do nothing while precious time continued to slip away from me.

The sound of shifting pebbles echoed from deeper within the cavern, and my heart rate began to gain traction. My shadow shuddered back to life for a brief moment before dropping back down again. "Fuck," I muttered just as another giant arachnid burst into the chamber. A shriek of utter fury threatened to rupture my ears when it discovered all its young had been burned to a crisp.

The spider's beady eyes turned on the three of us. It rushed forward. I tried to move, but my body spasmed as the paralytic venom clung to my muscles. Serenity attempted to drag me away, but she only had two legs and that revolting mishap of a creation had eight. Damien unleashed a pillar of fire, but it was quick to dart to the side, running up the cavern walls as the flames followed it, setting the silk aglow and causing heat to seep into the stone. Then Damien's fire shrank back down, his chest heaving with exertion and his skin slick with sweat.

The spider attacked. Flames sparked at the tips of Damien's fingers before sputtering out again. The monster suddenly tilted to the side and cried out in pain. Between the veil of darkness and Damien's fire, it was difficult for me to see the half-shadowed figure above the spider, but the sound of beating wings made me believe that it was Faelan, his talons gouging out the creature's eyes. Akira emerged from a nearby tunnel with a glowing silver-wood staff in her hand and a limp Emrys sagging against her. She lowered him to the ground before drawing one of the few arrows she still had left. She aimed a shot at the spider. The creature hissed and launched itself in her direction, but then Faelan dropped to the ground, and with a fierce growl, his jaws locked onto one of the spider's back legs and ripped it clean off.

With fire no longer responding to his summons, Damien drew out a spear of ice, and as the spider charged forward once more, he impaled it. Thick sludge poured out from the wound in its abdomen and the beast gave one last shriek before collapsing, its seven remaining legs shuddering as it died. Serenity lowered me to the ground next to Emrys, who looked to be asleep, his chest rising and falling with shallow breaths.

With the spider now dead, Akira leaned back against the cavern wall, stifling a groan as she pressed a hand to her rib cage. Her leather breastplate had been shredded down the side and blood leaked out of the gashes to drip to the floor. Serenity inserted a piece of newalla root into Emrys's mouth before quickly moving on to Akira. The pain on her face intensified when the wound began to knit itself back together. I struggled into a sitting position as the tingling sensation traveled down my legs to warm my toes. Emrys stirred next to me, and I brushed the white sweep of hair away from his eyes. He looked so fragile, susceptible to breaking at the slightest touch, and guilt moved in to fill the hollow left behind by my fear. He was alive, but that didn't erase the fact that I had failed to protect him in the first place.

His eyelashes fluttered open and he blinked in confusion. "I'm sorry that I wasn't there," I said, and taking ahold of his hand, I pressed it to my forehead in a plea of forgiveness. His skin was frightfully cold against my own, his lips having taken on a blue tinge, but he managed a weak smile.

"It's not your fault, Koven," he replied softly. He twisted his neck to look at Serenity. She had just finished healing Akira's wounds and was in the process of wiping her hands clean using the hem of her tunic, her fingers leaving bloody smears behind on the fabric. "I'm glad that she was returned to you unharmed." He slowly pushed himself upright as Damien limped toward him, one foot dragging awkwardly behind him as though he was still regaining control over the muscles in his leg.

"I know what I'm doing here," he said, his ice-blue eyes swirling with suspicion as he regarded the seer, "but what are you doing here?"

"We're seeking the same thing you are," Emrys replied, his tone oddly composed considering the circumstances. "You would like to be gifted with the thread of fate, and we just so happen to be in the market for the same ourselves. We can help each other."

My brow furrowed as I wondered how someone like him was supposed to fit into all this. War had been declared between our two kingdoms, which meant that Damien was an enemy. And he wasn't just any enemy; he was the surrogate child of Lios and Tammearia, the god of fire and the goddess of the sea. I didn't like the idea of relying on a Kaltan for this mission, and from the way flames sparked between Damien's fingers, he didn't like it much, either. Sensing a potential threat, I quickly brandished one of my daggers. "You're outnumbered," I warned him. "Don't even think about it."

"I almost *died*," he growled in response. "I never should have listened to you back on Spire. I don't know what I was thinking."

Walking over from the other side of the cavern, Faelan slapped Damien on the shoulder as though the two of them were friends, having bonded in their joint effort to take down one of the terrifying beasts that dwelled within the mountain. "Well, you're still breathing, so it all worked out in the end," Faelan said.

"You're the shapeshifting prince," Damien muttered, his brow furrowing with recognition. "Aren't you supposed to be dead?" The Kaltan cast me a sideways glance, no doubt recalling how I had supposedly killed the prince during the second trial.

"Apparently, destiny had other plans for me." Faelan flashed him one of his easygoing smiles, but the effect was somewhat dampened by the rivulets of dark blood that stained his teeth. "Welcome to the team, Damien."

Akira, who had been in the process of removing her shredded leather armor, stopped what she was doing to scowl at the implication that a Kaltan would be joining us on our quest. "Why do you need the thread of fate?" Akira questioned, her gaze narrowing on Damien with obvious mistrust.

Damien looked like he deliberating whether or not to answer her, but he must've realized that it would be pointless trying to keep it a secret. The only reason he was here was because Emrys already knew what it was. "Pasaphae cursed my parents to remain separated. I've seen how much they love each other and how much pain it causes them to spend an eternity apart. The thread of fate can rewrite their destiny. It can erase Pasaphae's curse. My parents would never allow me to come into these mountains, but after what happened on Spire, I knew they would be distracted enough for me to slip away. This is probably the only opportunity I will get to seek out Amari. I owe my parents everything. I just wanted to give them something in return." He paused for a moment as he considered Akira with an equal amount of wariness. "And why do you need the thread of fate?"

I glanced nervously at Emrys, uncertain of how much of the plan would be safe to tell him. He was a Kaltan, which meant that his loyalties wouldn't align with our own. The last thing we needed was the secret about Sheara to get out and tip Celdric off that someone might try to rescue her. Nor would it be wise to let the other side know that we were hoping to procure a weapon capable of breaking into the infamous prison that held some of the most dangerous vassals on the continent.

"We're hoping that the goddess of fate will be able to help end this war before it's had a chance to really begin," Akira replied, shooting a look of warning in Emrys's direction that told him that was the extent of the information she would allow to be shared on the topic. "I have no interest in allowing my country to suffer under the constant onslaught of fire and death for the next decade. If Amari's thread can reshape destiny, then perhaps she can make sure history does not end up repeating itself."

Damien fell quiet for a moment. Then he slowly lowered himself to the ground, wincing as he stretched out one of his legs. "Brazial has been yearning for another war since the last one ended, and his vassals crave conflict. They want this war to happen. They can't help themselves; it's in their blood. I don't know if fate has the power to rewrite all that."

Emrys let out a harsh laugh, a sound so strange coming from his lips that I thought he must've hit his head at some point during the commotion. "Do not underestimate the power of a fate-weaver, Damien Knight. What are the chances that in this endless network of tunnels, we would happen to come across you just when you were in need of our help? This was Amari's handiwork, weaving together a grand tapestry that goes all the way back to when you were but one of a hundred children to undertake being marked by two gods, emerging as the sole survivor. Fate has a plan for you, and it has led you to this very moment."

Damien stared at him as though he wasn't sure whether to be awed by his words or concerned for his sanity. "Amari didn't lead me here," he said skeptically. "You did."

My hand went automatically to the emerald ring that hung on my necklace. This wouldn't be the first time Emrys had used his gift of foresight to play games with destiny, and I had a sinking suspicion that this wouldn't be the last, either.

CHAPTER 27

The rest of the night thankfully passed with little excitement as Emrys led the way through the mountain, occasionally requiring us to crawl on our hands and knees through a shaft and into an adjoining passageway. When the only water we could find was a pond coated with a thick layer of algae, Damien conjured up some ice to melt, which we used to refill our waterskins instead. Although the cavern remained shrouded in darkness, I could feel that daylight had started to brighten the sky outside as my body grew weak with exhaustion. Eventually, we all agreed to stop to get some sleep. No one wanted to linger in this place one second longer than we needed to, so we only rested for a few hours before we set off again.

As the afternoon dragged on, the unsettling quiet of the mountain started to give off the impression that it would be just as uneventful as the morning, but I refused to be lulled into a false sense of security. Not after what happened last time. With Emrys and Serenity just ahead of me, I kept a careful watch on the numerous holes and crevasses that dotted the tunnels in every direction. I was right not to let my guard down. A childlike giggle reverberated through one of the passageways, the sound bouncing off the walls and making it impossible to determine where it had originated from. At first it was only one, but then more joined in until there was a whole chorus of them.

"That didn't sound good," I muttered.

"It's not," Emrys replied. He spun around in a slow circle like he was trying to figure out where the monsters would start crawling out from. A scratching sound like fingernails grating against stone emanated down a passage to the left. Then down a passage to the right. I glanced upward as a giggle traveled through a gap in the ceiling.

We were surrounded.

"Run!" Emrys shouted, already sprinting down the tunnel.

I bolted after him, keeping one hand on Serenity's back, urging her to run faster. The chorus of giggles grew louder and louder. I didn't dare slow my pace even when my legs began to burn and my lungs begged for reprieve. Sneaking a quick glance over my shoulder, I caught a glimpse of the creatures that were pursuing us. They were grotesquely human-looking, moving on all fours with matted hair and wild eyes. Damien unleashed a wall of ice, blocking the tunnel and allowing us a chance to catch our breath.

"What are those things?" Akira asked, but Emrys didn't have the chance to answer before the rough sound of scratching drew her attention back to the blockade. Whatever those creatures were, they were tunneling through the ice, clawing at it without any regard for the injuries it caused them.

"Keep moving!" I shouted, and then we were racing off once more. The shattering of the icy barricade vibrated down the cavern. Damien summoned his fire, blasting it down the tunnel, but no matter how many he burned, more of them appeared. I skidded to a halt as the creatures dropped down in front of me, their limbs twisting at unnatural angles as they scurried closer, their eyes a milky shade of white and their feral grins displaying an assortment of yellowed teeth.

Shoving Emrys and Serenity behind me, I threw a dagger at the closest one. The blade sank into the creature's forehead. As it dropped to the ground, the rest of the horde continued to snicker. A pair of them scampered up the wall to hang upside down on the ceiling, their tangled locks of hair dangling in the air. I hurtled daggers at both of them, each one hitting its mark, but more rushed forward. My shadow rose up like a shield, pushing the monsters away, but it was still daylight and I was quickly running out of weapons. Akira came to stand next to me, firing off arrow after arrow. While the two of us defended the front, Damien defended the back, but he was panting and drenched in sweat. I doubted he could go for much longer, and as soon as one of these fiends died, another was quick to take its place.

Damien sealed the tunnel with another wall of ice, his hands shaking with effort as he made it thicker than before. Then he staggered to the front and repeated the process until we were surrounded on all sides by a cage of ice. The creatures weren't deterred. They began digging at it, their excited chittering slightly muffled behind the barriers.

"We're trapped," Akira declared with a grim expression.

"It would appear so," I muttered.

I would like to take this moment to point out that if you didn't insist on this ridiculous notion of friendship, you wouldn't be in this predicament, the voice said.

You're not helping, I thought back.

Nor are you, it retorted.

"What do we do?" Damien asked, his gaze piercing into Emrys. "Come on, you're the seer. You were the one who said fate has a grand plan. If that's true, then this can't be where we die."

The ice fractured and a hand clawed through the gap, its fingernails cracked and coated in frost. With a swing of his sword, Faelan severed its arm. Damien quickly glazed over the hole, but more fissures were quickly appearing. "That's an excellent point, Damien," Emrys replied just as another creature managed to claw its way through. He whacked it back with his staff. "Have some faith. This is not where we meet our end."

One of the creatures managed to get its entire torso through a gap. I snapped its neck with a flick of my shadow. It hung there for a moment before one of its brethren dragged it out and proceeded to try crawling through the breach itself. An arrow buried itself in its eye and then it, too, went limp. "I'm running a little low on faith at the moment," Akira said as she withdrew another arrow.

A spindly body crawled through one of the holes and landed on the ground in a distorted tangle of limbs. Faelan hacked into its skull with his sword, a streak of scarlet splattering across his face in the process. I got the next one that slunk in through the opening. I sliced my dagger across its throat, its skin as soft and delicate as warm butter. While they were easy to kill, their threat was in their numbers, which still didn't appear to be dwindling. The cage of ice was quickly growing claustrophobic as the bodies piled up. I knew the situation was really starting to grow dire when Serenity withdrew her dagger to slash at the hands of those that were scraping their way inside.

The barricade in front me finally gave way, the sheet of ice collapsing like an avalanche on the floor. My shadow rose up to crush the first creature that leaped toward me. My dagger sank into the chest of another. The horde went unnervingly still, their twisted grins vanishing in an instant. Then, as though they were one entity, they all turned and fled into the network of tunnels. They disappeared in a matter of seconds. After witnessing so many of their brethren fall, I thought maybe they had fled in fear until I noticed an orange glow emitting from deeper within the tunnel. I lifted my blade in preparation for another fight but slowly lowered it again when I saw that it wasn't some fearsome monster intent on finding its next meal. It was a girl, one who couldn't have been more than thirteen years of age.

She was barefoot, with long, dark hair that flowed to her knees. She wore a simple white dress that was cinched at the waist with a belt woven from twine, and while I had never met a maiden of providence before, I'd heard the stories of what they looked like. This girl was one of the followers of Amari. In one hand she held a flaming torch, and in the other she clutched a branch of vibrant orange leaves that gave off an excessively sweet scent, like that of toffee and honeysuckle. As she came to a stop in front of me, her gaze briefly flicked toward one of the shafts that the horde had used to make their escape, but if walking among monsters gave her cause for concern, she didn't show it.

"My mother is expecting you," she said. "Come with me; I'll take you to her." She walked away without another word.

Emrys wiped the sweat from his brow with the back of his hand, the damp strands of hair clinging to the sides of his face. He smiled as though he had never been worried in the first place. "See?" he said, casting a pointed glance in Akira's direction. "Sometimes you just need a little faith."

She yanked an arrow out of the monster that lay dead at her feet and wiped the blood off on her trousers before returning it to her quiver. "I'll be sure to engrave that on your tombstone when you die," she retorted.

Serenity carefully picked her way over the carcasses on the floor as she followed the maiden of providence, but her foot still snagged on one of the severed limbs. I caught her before she could fall. She peered up at me, her lips lifting into a sheepish smile, but for once my gaze wasn't drawn to the warmth of her eyes. Instead, I found myself staring at the fresh scar that tore down the length of her arm. The gash was thick enough that it must have cut her all the way down to the bone.

What else did you expect? the voice whispered from the back of my mind. *Flowers wither and die when shrouded in darkness.*

She quickly tried to conceal the injury with her hand, but it was impossible. The scar was much too long. I had done that to her. When the arachnids were starting to overwhelm me, I lost control and one of my shadows lashed out at her. My stomach gave an unpleasant twist at the memory. I took a step to the side and gestured for her to go ahead of me. She opened her mouth to speak. When she couldn't decide on what exactly she wanted to say, it snapped shut again and she trailed after the others.

The tunnel that the maiden led us through became so narrow that we were forced to walk in single file. At the end of the passage was a flight of crudely cut stairs that had been chiseled out of the rock. My legs were shaking with fatigue by the time I made it to the top, but the light filtering in from above promised an escape from the horrors of the mountain below. I'd never thought I would be so happy to see the sun. As soon as I stepped out of the cavern, it was easy to understand why this place was called a sanctuary. The grass was thick and green and spotted with a variety of wildflowers. The sky was colored with striking shades of pink and purple, making the landscape look like something out of a painting.

The maiden placed the flaming torch in a holder by the entrance of the tunnel and then positioned the tree branch on the floor across the staircase.

"No gate?" I asked skeptically.

"The dwellers in the mountain do not come out in the sunlight, and at night the verrena leaves keep them away," she explained, pointing to a cluster of orange trees nearby. "They can't stand the smell."

Serenity stopped for a moment to admire the flowers, her fingers lightly brushing against the petals. I told myself not to linger, but before I could heed my own advice, she said, "Do you know what kind of flower this is?"

I paused to consider it and then shook my head. It was pretty, with curling white petals that faded into a crimson center, but botany was an area of study that fell solely within the domain of healers. Serenity leaned forward to inhale its fragrance. "It's a *corpos lillus*. Otherwise known as *the kiss of death*. The petals can be brewed into a tea that eases the pain of childbirth, but the milk harvested from the seeds is lethal enough to stop a man's heart with a single drop."

I studied the flower with renewed interest, marveling at how beauty and danger so often seemed to come hand in hand. "So, what I'm hearing is that I should never make you angry," I said, my tone deadly serious, and she laughed. It was a sound that I could get drunk on if I listened to it too much, but the scar on her arm had a deeply sobering effect. The wound stood out against her skin like a slash across an otherwise perfect canvas.

I wasn't sure what expression I was wearing, but it caused her own to grow somber. She traced over the line that started at her shoulder and ended past her elbow. "It doesn't bother me, if that's what you're worried about," she said. But how could it not when I was the one who had inflicted it upon her after promising to keep her safe? Yet there was no deception in her voice, and when her gaze met mine, there was something inherently sad in her eyes. "I have so many scars on the inside that it feels only right to have one on the outside as well."

She searched my face as though she was hoping to find a common understanding reflected back at her. While she hid a lot of her pain behind her smile, she still wove her grief into her hair every morning—she just chose to wear flowers instead of crow feathers. After the long journey through Kalta, her hair was matted with clumps of dirt and crumpled pieces of leaves, devoid of the color that usually brightened her dark curls. My shadow reached out to pluck the deadly flower from the ground and tuck it behind her ear.

"It suits you," I told her.

"You seem to be under the impression that I'm a lot more dangerous than I actually am." She slowly drifted closer to me, and between her blood-stained tunic and the dagger at her hip, she looked more lethal than a vixen. A better man would try to keep his distance from her, but I was a vassal of Celdric, and there was something about her that coaxed the greediest parts of me to the surface.

I reached out to brush a stray lock of hair from her shoulder, using it as an excuse to graze my fingers softly against her neck. "Oh, I beg to differ, scorpion tamer."

"I do rather like the sound of that title," she said, staring up at me with expectant eyes. I leaned in until our lips were so close that her breath mingled with mine, and gods was it tempting to close that last sliver of distance that still separated the two of us, but the better part of my judgment managed to hold me back.

"I hurt you, Serenity. We can't just ignore that."

"It was an accident," she replied gently. "I forgive you."

Those three words came effortlessly to her, as though she had said them many times before. I didn't want to be one of the people in her life that she had to make excuses for. "You forgive too easily," I told her.

Tilting her head back, she cradled my face in her hands, and looking directly into my eyes, she said, "It is *my* forgiveness, Koven. I can wield it however I please. If you wish to wallow in guilt, then that will be at your behest, not mine." Her thumb brushed against the line of my cheekbone. "I will not turn this into a fight. Once you have learned to forgive yourself, we can finish this conversation."

She pulled away from me to follow the others. I was just about to do the same when a soft purr reverberated from the ground. I glanced down to find a gray tabby cat winding its way between my boots, the action reminding me all too much of the nightmare that had visited me back at the Marcaida Fortress. However, this cat didn't have eyes like a mirror, but orbs that glowed a bright shade of yellow. Crouching down, I ran my hand over its back before it sauntered away and stretched itself out in a patch of fading sunlight. As I traveled deeper into the sanctuary, I spotted dozens of other cats lounging in the low branches of the trees or sprawled out on the grass, their tails flicking with disinterest.

The maiden of providence guided our group through a nearby apple grove, where a handful of women were harvesting the fruit. They all wore the same white dresses with belts of twine, their long hair covering their backs like a shawl. They cast curious glances in our direction, exchanging heated whispers with each other as we passed them. Considering the trip to get here, I suspected that they didn't get many visitors.

The grove opened up to reveal a clearing where a picnic blanket had been laid out. Fresh fruit was piled high in wicker baskets and a selection of pastries was displayed on rustic wooden platters. A child sat in the corner of the blanket with a panther curled next to her, its head resting in her lap as she scratched it between the ears. Her wavy hair rippled around her like a waterfall of liquid gold, and though she appeared to be barely more than ten years old, there was something unnaturally ancient about her eyes, as though she had seen much over the course of her life.

"I have brought them as you requested, Mother," the maiden of providence announced, and my eyebrows shot up in surprise. This wasn't a little girl that sat before me. It was Amari, the goddess of fate. However, unlike the rest of the gods, who were marked with eyes of gold, hers were the deep blue of the sea.

"Thank you, daughter," said Amari, and the maiden dipped into a curtsy before leaving. She turned her gaze on Emrys, and the two of them regarded each other like a pair of old friends. "I have been patiently awaiting your arrival, Emrys of House Hardcastle."

He gave a respectful bow of his head. "It's an honor to be in your presence, fate-weaver."

"You have had a long journey to get here. Come, let us eat." She waved her hand over the feast, and my stomach let out an audible growl. The panther lifted its head and yawned, showing off a sharp set of incisors. The goddess took the opportunity to tickle the beast beneath the chin. "This is Simara. Do not fret. She won't harm you while you're under the protection of my hospitality."

Kneeling down on the blanket, I cautiously cut myself a slice of the apple pie. The beast didn't show me any particular interest as she settled back down into Amari's lap. I took a bite of the crumble, welcoming the sweet taste of it after days spent nibbling on travel rations. The goddess stared at me with a curious look on her face, her head slightly tilted to the side, like she was studying something that she found incredibly interesting. I tried to ignore it at first, but when she didn't look away, I said, "Is something wrong, Your Divinity?"

"You're the spitting image of your father," she mused.

The comment took me completely by surprise—and not just me. Everyone was now staring at me. "You know my father?"

"I know of every mortal in this realm."

"He's alive?"

"Yes, but not for much longer. I'm sorry if that comes as a disappointment to you."

I hope his death is slow and painful, the voice snarled. The darkest part of my heart would rejoice in such a thing. The man had abandoned my mother like a candle in the wind, gone at the first sign of a squall. He deserved nothing less than to meet a bitter end worthy of the life he lived.

I lifted my shoulders in a shrug as though apathetic to the information. "I never knew him."

"Consider it a kindness. He's not a very pleasant man. His life will amount to nothing. However, each of his children will go on to achieve great things."

I blinked as the implication of what she just said sank in. My gaze slowly panned over to Emrys, who was suddenly taking an avid interest in the selection of sundried tomatoes. He *knew* that I had siblings on my father's side and he'd neglected to share that piece of information with me. A part of me wanted to be angry at him for it, but I couldn't blame him for keeping this particular secret. He had offered to tell me about my family's history, and I was the one who had decided that I didn't care enough to know about it.

Akira set her plate aside. She looked exhausted, her skin unusually pale and her tunic having been reduced to tatters. "Sorry to interrupt," she said, though she didn't sound apologetic in the slightest. "But we should discuss the reason why we came here. Considering that a war now looms over the continent, time is not a luxury that we can afford to waste."

"Mortals are always in such a hurry," the goddess said, running a hand along the ridge of her panther's back. "Perhaps it's because your lives are so fleeting, gone in the blink of an eye, but those of us who are as old as the stars know that time is not something that can be wasted, because time is infinite."

Akira's mouth opened as though she was tempted to argue, but Amari was not one of her fellow scholars who enjoyed a lively debate. She was a goddess. Akira hesitated for a moment and then lowered her head in deference. "Wise words, Your Divinity."

Amari's eyes sparkled like she knew that was not what Akira had actually wanted to say. "I know why you have come. Each of you needs a thread of fate. However, such a gift does not come freely. I would like something in return. You see, I am bound by certain rules. I cannot use my abilities on beings that are not of this realm."

Damien's face fell at the revelation, because if that was true, then this had been a wasted journey for him. "That means that the threads of fate won't work on the gods."

"I'm forbidden from doing so, but you are mortal, Damien Knight. You have no such restrictions. I cannot alter the fate of Lios and Tammearia, but should you use the thread, then it can be done. However, as I said, there is a price for it."

His expression hardened with resolve. "You need only name it."

"People often say that until the day comes for their debts to be collected."

Simara shifted and then stretched out her limbs before sauntering over to Emrys. My shadow flickered in agitation, but Emrys only smiled as he raised a hand to stroke her. I watched, bewildered, as the panther nudged into him, rubbing her head against his chest. Then she collapsed on top of him, her hulking form pinning him in place. He didn't seem to mind as he scratched at the fur around her neck. Yet, when Faelan drew closer in an attempt to pet her, the beast let out a low growl of warning. He quickly retreated to his corner of the blanket, and the goddess watched the scene with amusement before she continued speaking.

"When Lios came to this realm, he came on the back of his dragons, one of which is still alive. Vicarius has feasted on the flesh of my children and darkened my skies with his shadow for far too long. He has burned entire cities to the ground and will burn down more if given the chance. He's a creature of destruction that does not belong here. I will give you the thread of fate, but in exchange, I want you to slay Vicarius before he is called to war once more."

An image of Xyllon resurfaced in my mind, a city of ruins that had been consumed by death and dragon fire. Vicarius would have talons sharp enough to shatter marble statues and scales thicker than any shield. "You want us to kill a dragon?" I repeated incredulously.

It sounds like fun, the voice said.

No, it didn't. It sounded like a suicide. All I did was steal *one* ring, *one* time, and yet that brash, impulsive decision had somehow led to me getting stuck fighting a fucking dragon and trying to stop a war from ravaging the continent. Fate might look like a small, innocent child, but that clearly didn't stop her from having a twisted sense of humor.

"It will be a challenge," Akira agreed. "But Vicarius is a threat that has hung over Athearia for centuries. He will be older now, and slower. While daunting, taking down a dragon isn't impossible. They have been slain before."

That seemed like a bit of an overstatement in my opinion. A grand total of *one* dragon had been slain during the last Holy War, a feat that had required a battalion of men armed with a massive crossbolt that Scias herself had designed.

"And if we are unable to stop the war," Akira continued to say, "it will be a relief to know that the dragon won't set my entire kingdom on fire."

Damien's initial confidence waned into hesitancy. "My father is very fond of Vicarius."

"Then you have a choice to make," the goddess said. "If you choose to leave, I will have one of my maidens escort you safely out of the mountains, but if you go now, then you will be going without the power you desire. You have to decide what you're willing to sacrifice in order to get what you want. Power always comes at a price; not everyone is willing to pay it."

As Amari stood up, her golden hair swept against the ground. "You all have a decision to make, but for now, eat your fill and get some rest. My daughters will see that you are attended to." Her attention shifted to Faelan, and she gave him a weighted look as she added, "I have endeavored to protect my girls from the dangers of men. Some have been here all their life. They are naive and curious, easily lured in with the promise of a pretty smile."

As though proving her point, a group of maidens had gathered on the outskirts of the apple grove to get a closer look at the disheveled visitors. Faelan glanced in their direction, and even with his face marred by blood splatter and his curls having deflated from neglect, they let out a distinctive giggle—a sound that would now forever be entwined in my memory with the twisted creatures that resided in the dark tunnels of the mountains.

"Do not abuse my hospitality," Amari cautioned him, "or I might be tempted to revoke the favor I have shown you thus far." The edge in her tone was a harsh reminder that fate could be just as cruel as she could be kind. Faelan had the good sense to avert his gaze and look thoroughly chastised. The goddess walked away, her hair trailing behind her like a veil, and the panther eventually extracted herself from Emrys's lap to follow her.

"What was that about?" Akira asked him.

"What?" he said innocently.

"The two of you gave me the impression that you already knew each other."

"She's the goddess of fate," he said simply. "She knows all the mortals in this realm."

Akira was quiet for a long moment, but she must've decided that she was content with his explanation, because she picked up her plate and resumed eating. I, however, recognized the answer for what it was: a deflection. Emrys did know the goddess of fate. The only question that remained was just how well the two of them were acquainted.

CHAPTER 28

Steam rolled across the hot springs like a fine mist. The main pool was encircled by a ring of large, flat stones. Warm water seeped over the edge and trickled into ponds farther down, forming a cluster of small waterfalls. Candles had been placed around the perimeter to serve as a source of light, but it was hardly needed when the stars looked close enough for me to reach out and snatch them from their perch in the sky. I lowered myself into the water, enjoying the way my body relaxed as the heat of the spring worked its way into my stiff muscles. Sinking beneath the surface, I scrubbed my face clean of the dirt and gore that I had accumulated throughout the journey. When I emerged again, Emrys was busy climbing into the spring, his skin clinging tightly to his rib cage. The trek across Kalta had clearly taken its toll on him. My body was sturdy enough to withstand a certain level of hardship, but the gods had built Emrys as though he were a reed that grew along a riverbank—tall, thin, and easily broken.

His expression was serene as he stared up at the sky, and for once, he didn't look as though he was about to collapse beneath the weight of his exhaustion. He seemed oddly content considering the daunting task that still lay ahead of us. "I like it here," he declared. "It's peaceful. I think I might actually be able to get a decent night's sleep for once." He reached for the salt scrubs, and a playful smile tugged at his lips as he sniffed the contents. "Lilac and bergamot with a hint of rosemary. I'm sure the dragon will tremble in fear when he smells us coming."

When I didn't laugh, he sighed and returned the salt scrubs to the stone shelf. "Okay, out with it, Koven. What do you want to say?" I had so many questions I wanted to ask him, but what good would it do me to ask them if he only replied with vagaries and deflections? It was unfair that he seemed to know all my secrets—sometimes before I even knew them myself—and yet he shared so little in return. As though he could hear my thoughts, he said, "I can't answer all your questions, but I can give you the answers to some of them. We'll start with the first one. You want to know whether Amari and I have met before, don't you?"

"It's a very disconcerting thing being friends with a seer," I muttered under my breath.

"She sometimes visits me in my dreams," he told me. "The future is a difficult thing to navigate. If I drift too far, the current will sweep me away and dash my mind against the rocks, my sense of reality shattering along with it. It's the fate that befalls most seers who attempt to glimpse Amari's tapestry, but she has made an exception for me. She doesn't allow me to get lost. When I've strayed too far, she appears as a blue-eyed cat and guides me back to myself."

Something moved in the cherry blossom tree above me, causing the branch to shake and pink petals to flutter down and scatter across the pond. The water rippled as my shadow shifted beneath it, but then a cat with orange fur leaped out and landed gracefully on the ground. It stretched itself across one of the warm stones encircling the hot spring and proceeded to lick its paw. My shadow settled back down again as I reminded myself that this was Amari's sanctuary. While I was here, I was safe.

Are you? the voice questioned. *Celdric is the master of shadow and secrets. Do you think he wouldn't have eyes everywhere? Maybe this is one of his vassals, a shapeshifter hidden in plain sight.*

The comment planted a seed of paranoia in the back of my mind, and the darkness slowly began to creep toward the cat, but I quickly crushed the thought before it could grow roots. *I'm not playing this game with you again*, I thought back bitterly, and the voice laughed.

Emrys shifted closer to the cat, and it let out a soft purr as he scratched it between the ears. "Why does Amari help you?" I asked him. It struck me as suspicious. The gods never gave out favors without demanding something in return. If Amari was helping him cultivate his power instead of letting him slide into insanity, then she would expect to be paid for her efforts.

"Because the destiny she has woven for me would unravel the moment my mind fractured and I became consumed with madness . . . Though there are certainly times when I think that would be the kinder fate." His gaze met mine and he smiled, but it didn't quite reach his eyes. "I found you in a dream, you know. I followed Amari right to you and she showed me how to entwine my destiny with yours. I was a child at the time. I didn't fully understand what I was doing, but Amari knew that a light shines most brightly in the presence of the dark. We are two sides to the same coin. I cannot fulfill my destiny without you, nor can you fulfill yours without me. Each of us is one half of a greater whole."

He said it like it was meant to be some grand revelation, but as my fingers enclosed around the emerald ring on my necklace, he had just put into words something that I'd always known deep down. I had a connection to him that I couldn't quite explain. It went deeper than friendship and perhaps it even went deeper than love. Just as it was in the nature of a shadow to follow the light, my place in this world was at his side. "And what is this great destiny that we are supposed to fulfill?" I asked, but when his expression turned apologetic, I already knew that this was one of the questions he wouldn't be able to answer.

"Knowledge shapes our actions and actions define our future." Emrys eyed one of the pink petals floating on the surface, the current gently pulling it toward the edge of the pool that spilled over into the spring below. "Take this petal, for instance. I know it's about to fall because I can see where the current is directing it. With that knowledge, I can choose to let it continue undisturbed, or"—he snatched the petal just as it was about to be swept away—"I can choose to save it, altering its path and changing its destiny. If most people knew that they were about to fall, they would make different choices in order to prevent it from happening. Sometimes it works, but sometimes, no matter what they do, fate manages to drag them over the edge anyway."

I arched an eyebrow at him. "Is this your way of saying that I'm going to fall over the edge?"

He let go of the petal, and this time when the current took it, he only watched as it disappeared over the side. "It was merely a metaphor. Good or bad, it's for the best that you don't know what fate has planned for you."

I picked up a petal of my own to examine but quickly came to the conclusion that I wasn't much of a philosopher. With a sweep of my arm, a wave traveled across the hot spring and washed all the petals away. "You would make for a terrifying seer," Emrys remarked. His tone was teasing, but he was probably right. Information was a weapon, and unlike him, I would have no interest in keeping it sheathed.

"What about my family?" I asked, and the humor vanished from his expression.

He fell quiet for a moment. I thought that maybe this was another question that he couldn't answer until he said, "You already know that your father had a reputation with the harlot houses. It can't be that much of a surprise to know he sired other children."

It wasn't anything I had given much thought to before, but now that I knew they existed, I couldn't help but feel a mild sense of curiosity about them. "Will I ever meet them?"

"Do you want to?" he asked in response. I wasn't sure how to reply to that question, so I remained quiet. Emrys climbed out the hot spring and grabbed one of the linen towels hanging from a nearby tree branch to wrap around his waist. He slicked back his hair with his fingers as he glanced back at me. "It takes more than blood to make a family, Koven. I hope you know that."

Picking up one of the candles, he disappeared down the path leading to the villas. With a flick of my wrist, my shadow spilled out of the hot spring to snuff out the rest of the flames. The world plunged into darkness, and as I lay back to watch the stars glowing like diamonds in the night sky, I couldn't help but think that Emrys was right. The light did shine so much brighter when it was in the presence of the dark.

CHAPTER 29

I awoke to find two large blue eyes peering down at me. A cat was perched on my chest, regarding me with interest, but as soon as I raised a hand to stroke it, it leaped onto the sill of the open window and disappeared out into the garden. It was already bright outside, which meant that I had been allowed to sleep in for a few hours. I glanced over to the empty bed on the opposite side of the room only to find that it was empty. Either I had been truly exhausted, or Emrys had been as quiet as a dormouse when he left this morning, because I hadn't heard him go. Rubbing the sleep from my eyes, I climbed out of bed. A bowl of water rested on the table by the door, which I used to splash my face before drying it off with a small towel. My clothes lay in a neatly folded pile next to it, having been washed clean of bloodstains and dirt. I got changed and then slid my daggers into place before leaving the villa.

My steps slowed when I caught sight of a patch of purple aster flowers. Crouching down, I began to snap the stems and form a bouquet. I was almost finished when the sound of approaching footsteps caused me to look up. Serenity was draped in one of the plain white dresses typically worn by girls that lived here, a belt of twine cinching her waist. A slow smile spread across her face as she studied the flowers in my hand. "Are those for me?" she asked.

Standing back up, I scoffed at her audacity. "How presumptuous. Maybe I picked these for myself. I, too, deserve a little appreciation every now and again."

She laughed, and my shadow swayed at the sound as though dancing to its melody. I circled around her and started to pin the flowers into her braid, a smattering of purple petals against her dark curls. When she cast a glance over her shoulder at me, her smile was gone. "You look worried, sunshine," I said as I tucked the last flower into the end of her braid.

"That's because I am," she said before reaching into her supply satchel and pulling out a medicinal vial. Taking a hold of my hand, she pressed it into my palm and enclosed my fingers around it. "This is milk harvested from the kiss of death. I soaked the seeds in warm water overnight and blended them into a liquid this morning. A single drop of this is enough to kill a man, so handle it with care. I still don't know whether it was the right thing to make this, but what I do know is that we need the string of fate, and you're going to need every advantage that you can get if you're going to come back from this alive. I'm not sure how much use it will be against a dragon, or if you'll even get the opportunity to use it, but I would rather you have it just in case."

I stared down at the vial and then back at her. "You say that as though you aren't coming."

"That's because I won't be. I've already had this conversation with the others, but I will be no use in a fight against a dragon, and while I understand that the creature's death is necessary for the safety of the continent, that does not mean that I care to witness its demise."

She had a fair point. There wasn't much a healer could do if someone was consumed by dragon fire. Death would be instantaneous, and if that was to be my end, I was a little relieved that she wouldn't be there to see it. I also wouldn't have to worry about her being put in harm's way like she had been when we were traveling through the tunnels beneath the mountain.

"I hope you can forgive me for choosing to stay," she said, averting her gaze to the ground.

Tucking a finger under her chin, I lifted her gaze back to meet mine. "Never apologize for having a kind heart. Such a thing is far rarer than diamonds and more precious than gold."

A deep blush rose up her neck to color her cheeks. "You have been spending way too much time with Prince Faelan for such pretty words to roll off your tongue. You should be careful, or I might start to think you mean them in earnest."

My gaze dropped down to the scar that tore down the length of her arm, and though guilt dug its cold talons into me, I was all too aware of the fact that once I left this sanctuary, I might never return. I couldn't bring myself to leave her with any doubts about the extent of my affections. Cradling her face in my hands, I pressed a tender kiss to her forehead. "I've never once said something to you that I didn't mean in earnest," I told her. "And I think you're nothing short of astounding."

Her eyes shimmered at the confession. She opened her mouth to speak, but before she could, the sound of excited voices drew her attention to the trees. Faelan was weaving his way through the apple grove, his presence having captured the notice of the maidens picking fruit from the branches. He raised a hand to shield his eyes from the sun as he approached. It quickly became obvious that he was looking for me when he stopped at the edge of the tree line and gestured for me to wrap up my conversation.

"I must go," I said, but Serenity caught ahold of my hand as I tried to move past her.

"You better come back," she said sternly. "I don't have room in my heart for another gravestone. That is the sort of scar I won't be able to forgive you for." Her grip on my hand tightened as though she was scared that I would vanish the moment she let go. The warmth of her touch seeped into me, beckoning me to bring her knuckles to my lips, and wisps of shadow danced across her fingers as I dusted them with a kiss.

"Then I shall fight even death himself to get back to you," I promised.

"You really have been spending too much time with Faelan," she said, slipping her hand out of mine. "I will hold you to that promise, and perhaps after facing down a dragon, you will finally have the courage to do more than just kiss me."

Despite having a vial of poison and more than a dozen daggers on me, the comment left me feeling completely and utterly disarmed. She was careful to keep a tight hold on any words that could be construed as a final bid farewell as she walked away. My gaze continued to follow her, and if there hadn't been prying eyes nearby, I might have given in to the temptation to sweep her into my arms and carry her into one of the villas. Before my imagination had the chance to run wild with that particular thought, I peeled my gaze away from her and strode toward Faelan, who greeted me with a grin.

"We didn't even have to resort to breaking your bones," he said, sounding impressed as he hooked an arm around my shoulders. "If we return from this mad venture alive, I'll share with you my secrets, the ones that have girls lining the passageway outside my door. We have the blood of gods pumping through our veins, Koven, and that can be proved in the bedroom as well as the battlefield." The group of maidens had nearly doubled in size by the time he made his return trip through the trees. Their baskets lay forgotten on the ground as they whispered to each other. He flashed them a roguish smile and wiggled his fingers in a suggestive wave.

"Amari warned you to keep your hands to yourself," I reminded him.

"My hands are to myself," he retorted. "It's not my fault they're staring. If fate didn't want them looking at me, she shouldn't have blessed me with a face designed for marble." It was a dangerous thing to joke about. Amari could easily reweave his fate, making it so that he was struck down with an illness that left the smooth contours of his face riddled with pock marks or have his skin destroyed completely by the hot claws of fire. The wrath of a god was not something to be sneered at, and while Amari might've had the appearance of a child, that didn't stop her from being as ancient and powerful as the sun and the stars.

A white pavilion came into view as we exited the cluster of trees, the structure possessing a roof that was shaded beneath purple stalks of wisteria. Everyone else had already assembled. Emrys was crouched down next to Simara. The panther's eyes were closed, her head tilted back as he scratched her beneath the chin. Akira was watching the scene with an unreadable expression, a half-stocked quiver of arrows peeking out over her shoulder. The maidens hadn't managed to get all the bloodstains out of her tunic, but they had stitched together the torn fabric at her side. Even Damien was present, dressed in his full set of battle armor, his expression grim but determined.

The goddess was seated on one of the benches with her bare feet dangling just above the ground. "What a mess," she muttered to herself as she tried to untangle the ball of yarn in her lap. She heaved an exasperated sigh when the fidgeting only caused the knots to tighten. Reaching for a knife, she cut through the mess of strings. They glimmered before evaporating into the air. The sight of it sent an ominous shiver down my spine.

"There's been another battle," Akira said, her eyes still lingering on the empty space where the tangled heap of yarn had been a moment before.

"Brazial has claimed another stronghold along the northern border of Athearia," Amari confirmed. "Much blood has been spilled, but it is nothing to the destruction that will befall your kingdom if Vicarius takes to the sky. The god of fire is traveling to Lithios to awaken the dragon from its slumber. If he reaches the island before you do, then Athearia will be set ablaze once more."

Lithios was a remote island all the way on the other side of the continent. Home to a mountain that was once known to spew fire, the site was considered to be sacred to the god Lios. It would not be an easy location to get to. I cast a nervous glance at Emrys, but he was as calm as the sea on a windless day. His eyes looked more blue than gray today, his skin bright and free of the dark crescents that usually shadowed his face. I decided that if he wasn't concerned, then I shouldn't be, either. His foresight had managed to get us this far, and knowing that the goddess of fate herself helped steer him through the future, I reasoned that she would guide him down a path that would lead us to victory.

Victory doesn't come without sacrifice, said the voice in the back of my head. I tried to ignore it, but the thought still served to make me uneasy. Mortal lives were fleeting things in the eyes of the gods. If the final trials had taught me anything, it was that we were seen as little more than pawns to be used and discarded at their pleasure. Even if Amari had a vested interest in our success, that didn't mean she wouldn't be willing to sacrifice each and every one of us in order to get what she wanted.

"Lithios." Akira repeated the word slowly, sounding like she was struggling to keep a hold on her composure. "Forgive me if I'm speaking out of turn, Your Divinity, but it would take weeks to get there, and that's assuming we don't get caught by the patrols, which will grow even tighter the longer the war goes on. Whether we travel by horseback or sea, I doubt we could reach there before Lios does, and I don't wish to be gone from my kingdom for that length of time, especially considering that Brazial is spilling Athearian blood as we speak."

"You're forgetting that you are in the presence of a fate-weaver." The goddess severed a piece of string before moving toward a heavy stone pillar in the middle of the pavilion. It cradled a shallow basin of water, the bottom of which was engraved with a set of strange runes that I didn't recognize. "A drop of your blood is all I need and I can weave my thread to place you anywhere on the continent. I need only to unravel it and you'll be returned to your original location."

Amari held out a small knife. I stared at the blade with skepticism as Emrys stepped forward to accept it. He sliced open his hand and the water took on a slightly pink hue as he allowed his blood to drip into it. He offered me the blade next. I didn't trust Amari—gods were capricious creatures, loyal only to themselves. I did, however, trust Emrys. Taking hold of the knife, I ran the tip over the prayer scar that was carved into my palm and allowed my blood to mingle with his in the basin. The knife was passed down the line until only Damien remained.

He hesitated.

You can't trust him, the voice warned. *Having a dragon under their command is a massive strategic advantage for Kalta. Killing it would be tantamount to treason. He must be planning to betray you.*

From the way Akira's gaze narrowed on him, she didn't seem to trust him much, either. The thread of fate was a rare gift—the only thing with the power to break the curse that had been inflicted upon his parents—but was he actually willing to pay the price in order to get it?

Maybe he is, the voice said, *and maybe he will try to rid himself of all the witnesses to his crime after the fact.*

Suspicion settled like a stone in my chest as Damien finally grabbed the knife and sliced open his palm. His blood dripped into the stone basin. The goddess tied the ends of the string together before steeping it in the water, turning the thread from white to a deep shade of pink. "Long have I waited for this moment," she said, her voice both soft and distant as she wove an intricate pattern on her fingers. "When fate meets fire and ash falls from the sky like rain. When light binds itself to the dark and the queen of sorrow weeps tears of gold. When the prophecy of old comes to pass and the fallen stars all burn to dust. Only then can the sun rise on the dawn of a new age."

Despite her gentle tone, her words carried an undeniable heaviness with them. Her gaze locked with mine, and a ghost of a smile tugged at the edges of her lips, as though she knew something I didn't. Then her hands snapped apart and the strings grew taut.

I blinked and, suddenly, I was no longer in Amari's sanctuary. The wind ripped at my hair and clothes as I stared up at the mountain of fire. It was still and quiet, having fallen into a deep slumber like that of the dragon that dwelled within. It had been many generations since the mountain last erupted and vegetation had started to reclaim the land; a smattering of short shrubs and weeds at the base looked to be slowly climbing their way to the top. Faelan spun around, his eyes wide, as though he couldn't quite believe that he had traversed the continent in the time it took for his heart to jump from one beat to the next. Even a shadow-walker like me had to admit that it was quite a remarkable feat.

A giant archway was carved into the base of the mountain. Trenches filled with oil ran on either side of the passage. With a snap of Damien's fingers, the oil caught alight and burned a bright shade of gold, lighting the path forward. The others moved forward to enter the base of the mountain, but I lingered behind, glancing up at the sky. "Maybe we should wait until nightfall," I suggested.

"I'm at my strongest during the day," Damien countered. "And those of us who aren't marked by Celdric can't see in the dark. We should go now."

"He's right," Emrys said. "It's best if we go now."

My shadow flickered with displeasure as I stepped beneath the archway. The temperature of the passageway increased the deeper I traveled into the mountain until sweat caused my clothes to cling to my body. My lungs began to struggle for air, and the water from the flagon offered little reprieve as the heat seeped into it, making it unpleasantly warm as it slid down my throat. Emrys came to a grinding halt, hunching over as he rested his hands on his knees. I poured some of the water over his head, but as he shook out the droplets from his hair, his face remained a startling shade of red.

"You okay?" I asked him, and he exhaled a long breath.

"It's not much farther," he said, which wasn't an answer to my question.

Akira blazed ahead even as moisture beaded her skin like drops of rain. Her long black hair was tied back and the crow feathers woven into it stuck out awkwardly from behind one ear, reminding me that this would all amount to nothing if her brother didn't manage to return from the realm of the dead. Even if we defeated the dragon and procured the thread of fate, it would do us little good if we didn't have the sword needed to break into Ismadore. However, with her lips set into a determined line and her eyes hardened with resolve, Akira looked like a force to be reckoned with, and I didn't doubt that Rin Marcaida was wreaking all kinds of havoc on the other side as he tried to fulfill his part in the plan.

Eventually, we were all forced to stop when a large set of stone doors blocked the path, the surface of which was etched with a series of deep patterns and swirls. Faelan pushed against the barricade, his muscles straining with effort, but it refused to budge.

"These doors can only be opened by a vassal of Lios," Emrys said, casting a pointed look at Damien. Despite wearing steel-plated armor, he didn't appear to be suffering much from the heat, a trait I envied as my lungs burned and my legs threatened to buckle. The Kaltan stepped forward, and when he placed his hands in the center of the door, orange flames burst out from his palms and slowly spread through the pattern engraved in the stone. The lines began to glow like magma flowing through cracked rock. There was a whirring sound as Damien stepped back and the doors slid apart.

As I entered the chamber, a gust of air washed over me, cooling my burning skin. A stretch of blue sky was visible high above me. My eyes took a moment to adjust to the sunlight that filtered in through the gap, illuminating the treasure that stretched out before me, which glittered and gleamed like a river of gold. A mass of coins and jewelry were piled up into mounds in a collection that put the House of Shadows to shame. My fingers itched to stuff some of it into my pockets until I caught sight of all the bones scattered among the treasure. Most of the remains appeared to be from typical farm animals such as cows, goats, and sheep, but there were some distinctly human bones scattered among them as well.

Akira put a finger to her lips. Then she lowered into a crouch and crept forward. Quiet as a shadow, I snuck my way over to her and peeked around one of the mounds of gold, another gust of wind rippling through my hair as I did so. My blood turned cold as I realized it wasn't a draught blowing through the cavern. It was the exhalations of the massive beast that slumbered within the mountain. He lay atop his bed of sparkling gems and gilded chalices with scales the color of midnight and sharp spikes that ran along the ridge of his back. As I stared at Vicarius, the last of his kind, I couldn't help but think that maybe fate considered her thread too precious a gift to give away, because we hadn't even begun to battle the dragon yet and it was already starting to seem like an impossible task.

CHAPTER 30

The dragon's body rose and fell with each breath. He shifted one of his legs, the movement causing the jewels beneath him to come loose and jingle to the floor. I winced, thinking that the sound might stir the beast from his slumber, but he remained blissfully asleep. That was good. That meant that we had time to strategize. I began creeping back toward the entrance when a loud clang reverberated through the chamber. My head snapped in Damien's direction—his foot had struck a bronze vase. He offered me a sheepish look.

He did it on purpose, the voice hissed.

I wasn't so sure that he had, because his alarm looked quite real when the dragon's eyes snapped open. Vicarius shook his head as he awoke. Old scales peeled off him to fall to the ground like black flakes of snow as he clambered to his feet, the movement slow and languid. A low growl emanated from his throat as he sauntered forward, hunting for those who had dared to intrude upon his lair. Shrouding my steps in silence, I slipped behind a marble statue that was half-buried in a mound of gold. The others disappeared into hiding places of their own with Emrys moving to crouch beneath a piece of rock that jutted out the ground like a spear.

My heart thundered in my ears when the dragon meandered closer in his direction. Emrys peered at me from across the cavern, his eyes wide as the dragon's movements caused a wave of coins to spill across the floor, immersing him up to his knees.

You're fine, I signed with my hands. *It's just looking. It doesn't know you're there. Stay still.*

The dragon whipped his head around the rock, peering out at his sea of treasure, which was as still and quiet as a windless day. A thick rivulet of drool dripped from his jaws to splatter on Emrys below. His lips twisted into a grimace, but he didn't dare move while the shadow of the beast still darkened the ground around him. Then Vicarius slunk away and I sucked in a ragged breath of relief.

A squawk drew the dragon's gaze skyward, to the birds that were nested in the crevices higher up in the cavern. He let out a huff of annoyance before opening his mouth wide. A pillar of fire erupted into the air. The birds all took flight with startled cries, their feathers catching alight as they fell to the ground like stars falling from their mantle in the night. Satisfied that the culprits who had roused him from his sleep had been appropriately punished, Vicarius settled back down. I was beginning to think that maybe Amari was truly on our side after all until the dragon stretched out his wings as he made himself comfortable. Thick plumes of dust rolled off them to taint the air. Every muscle in my body stiffened while I waited. A few seconds passed in merciful silence. My shoulders relaxed as I told myself that everything would be fine.

Then Emrys sneezed.

The dragon's head snapped back up and he let out a roar so loud that it felt as though it was piercing into my skull. Vicarius rushed forward with a predatory glint in his eyes. Emrys frantically searched for another place to hide, but there was nowhere for him to go. He was trapped.

That friend of yours will be the death of you one day, the voice muttered.

I just hoped that day was not today.

I darted out from behind the statue, waving my arms in a desperate attempt to capture the dragon's attention. "Over here!" I yelled and was filled with instant regret as Vicarius turned toward me. He opened his maw, his dozens of sharp teeth on full display, and a heartbeat later, the back of his throat started to glow a brilliant shade of yellow that reminded me of the afternoon sun. It would've been beautiful if it weren't so damn terrifying.

Clearly, you didn't think this through.

No, I did not.

I slid down the mound of treasure just as a stream of dragon fire turned everything behind me into a river of gold and silver. As I sprinted for the nearest outcrop of rocks, I was grateful that the cracks in the floor siphoned away some the molten metal, slowing its progress and making it appear as though the cavern was growing veins of golden ichor. I finally reached the closest rock and managed to haul myself off the ground just as the glistening liquid collected in a puddle below me. I didn't even have time to be relieved as sweat turned my hands slick, making it difficult to grip the stone. My shadow quickly surged forward, helping me cling to the handholds as I crawled into a hiding place that would shield me from the dragon's sight.

Fortunately, Vicarius hadn't managed to relocate me yet. He strolled through the golden lake, his paws splashing through the bubbling liquid as though it were nothing more than a pleasantly warm bath. He was surveying the cavern, trying to find my seared remains among the carnage, when a high-pitched whistle echoed from the other side of the chamber. Even without looking, I knew that it was Akira. Vicarius stalked toward the sound, his mouth curling into a fierce snarl. Focused as he was on the ground, he didn't notice the falcon soaring overhead. Faelan landed on top of the dragon, and morphing into his original form, he attempted to pierce his sword into the curve of the beast's neck. The weapon shattered against the hard scales upon impact.

Faelan muttered out a curse as Vicarius swayed violently from side to side, like he was attempting to shake a flea from his back. Faelan grew wings once more, soaring into the air at the same time that an arrow embedded itself in one of the dragon's eyes. Vicarius let out a shriek so loud that it had me sticking my fingers in my ears to keep them from bursting. A gale ripped through the chamber as the dragon unfurled his enormous wings.

"Don't let him take flight!" Emrys shouted, which struck me as a rather unreasonable request considering the circumstances. I studied the golden lake simmering beneath me, my gaze narrowing on a dry segment of floor just a few meters away. Sending a silent prayer to Amari for luck, I vaulted myself off the rock. My landing was not graceful and my fingers grappled for a handhold as I rolled, coming to a stop just before I tumbled into one of the molten veins that ran across the bottom of the cavern. When I attempted to stand up, I was nearly thrown clean off my feet by the gust of wind that was created as Vicarius gave another flap of his wings. The appendages, however, were old and riddled with holes, and he struggled to gather the necessary momentum needed to launch himself into the air.

With the sun still beaming down from the sky above, there wasn't much I could do, but I reached out for the dragon's shadow anyway, commanding the darkness to rise up and wrap around the creature like chains. It was hardly a surprise when the dragon was able to tear through the restraints as though they were made of paper, but it did serve as a good enough distraction for Vicarius to retract his wings and swipe his tail at me. My shadow rose up to defend me. Unfortunately, it wasn't strong enough to repel the attack. I was sent flying into a pile of chalices and trinkets, which dug painfully into my back upon landing.

Akira surfed down a mountain of gold on the back of a shield, sending a volley of arrows at the beast. Vicarius breathed fire in her direction, but then Damien appeared between the two of them, and raising his hands, he diverted the flames to either side of him. Faelan decided to take advantage of the commotion to dive back down and attempt to gouge out the dragon's last remaining eye with his talons, but Vicarius noticed his approach. Faelan was forced to swerve out of the way when the dragon released another wave of fire into the sky. He picked up speed as he tried to get ahead of the flames, but he wasn't fast enough. A sharp cry of pain resonated through the chamber as his tail feathers began to burn. He plummeted to the ground and disappeared into one of the golden peaks on the far side of the chamber.

Another arrow flew through the air before burying itself in the dragon's second eye. Vicarius let out a bellow of absolute fury. Damien wrenched a halberd from one of the skeletons, its bones scattered among the rest of the dragon's hoard like long-forgotten trophies. He charged at the beast, his arm whipping back as he prepared to hurl the weapon down the beast's throat, but then his resolve fractured and he ended up freezing directly in front of Vicarius. The beast's throat began to glow and my shadow raced forward to yank him out of the way just as the flames burst forth to consume everything in its path. Damien fell flat on his back, his arms flailing as my shadow continued to drag him across the cavern by his feet.

Claiming the halberd for myself, I removed the vial of poison from my pocket. If one drop was enough to stop a man's heart, how much of it would be needed to fell a dragon? I decided it was best not to be conservative with the dosage. I poured the entire bottle over the edges of the weapon before turning to face Vicarius. The dragon drew in a deep breath, preparing to unleash another wave of destruction, when I yelled out. His head swung toward me, his nostrils flaring while blood seeped out from his ruined eyes. The stench of death and decay clung to his breath as he unhinged his jaw.

If I failed here and now, there would be no escape. Only death. My mind conjured an image of Serenity, her kind eyes wet with tears as she wept over my empty grave. That would not be her future, nor mine. I had made a promise to return to her, and I intended to keep it. Steeling my nerves, I tightened my grip on the halberd. I would only have one chance to get this right. I ran forward, closing the distance, and then launched the halberd. The weapon sailed into the dragon's mouth and impaled the back of his throat. He let out a sound that was halfway between a growl and a splutter. Angry red froth spilled out from his bottom jaw as fire and blood mixed together inside him. He staggered away from me, his body tilting dangerously to the side.

Your strategizing could use some work, the voice said right before the dragon collapsed with such force that the ground trembled beneath my feet. I watched with growing horror as the impact caused a spray of liquid metal to shoot high into the air.

"Koven!" Emrys called out. I turned just in time to catch the ornate shield that was thrown at me. I was skeptical as to how useful it would be. With the dragon etched into its center and a variety of precious stones encircling the rim, it looked to be more decorative than practical, but it was all I had. Dropping to a crouch, I raised it above my head as droplets of gold pelted down from above, splattering against the shield like rain. I shut my eyes, waiting for the gold to seep through like acid and burn my skin all the way down to my bones. When no searing pain tore through my body, I cracked my eyes back open. Gold was no longer falling from the sky, and the great and mighty Vicarius lay motionless on the ground.

The dragon was dead, and I was the one who slew it.

A dark thrill of pleasure rolled through me at the realization.

See? the voice crooned. *Didn't I tell you it would be fun?*

"Koven, are you all right?" Emrys asked. He was carefully traversing the cracks and puddles on the ground as he made his way over to me.

"I'm fine," I said, which was a lie. I was better than fine. Every nerve inside my body was humming. I had never felt so alive.

"I do believe that I owe you my weight in gold." A small smile curved at his lips as Emrys swept his arms over the dragon's hoard. "Hopefully this clears my debt with you."

I stared out at the sea of glittering treasure, all of which was now mine for the taking. There were enough riches to buy me a title if I so wished. I had never allowed myself to consider the possibility before. Such a thing had always been outside my reach, but now that the thought had entered my head, there could be no denying that I wanted it. I wanted it in the same way I had wanted the power Celdric offered to me as a child. A laugh threatened to erupt from my throat as I caressed the coins on the floor.

All the world could be yours.

"All the world" was a bit of a stretch, but I would no longer be the boy who had so little that he was forced to steal even his own name. I could buy myself any life that I desired. With this amount of gold, I wouldn't need to join a shadow court; I could stand by Emrys's side as an equal, a lord in my own right.

I was in the process of stuffing my pockets full of jewelry when Faelan limped forward, his leg an oozing mess of charred skin and his face battered and bruised from the fall. He examined the dragon's body with a morbid sort of curiosity, and then, with gritted teeth, he extended his arms and transformed back into a falcon. I momentarily paused my plundering to watch as he flew across the golden lake, diving and swooping through the air as he struggled to maintain a steady course until he eventually dropped down on the creature's head. Morphing back into his original form, he dipped his fingers into one of the streams of blood dribbling out of the dragon's mouth. My brow creased as I wondered what he could possibly be doing. Then a hand clamped down on my shoulder and I peered back to find Damien hovering behind me.

"You saved my life," he said, his voice somber. "I thought it only right to thank you." He cast an apprehensive glance at the dragon's body, but he was quick to avert his gaze, unable to bring himself to look at the last of his father's sacred animal, which he had helped to kill.

Before I had the chance to reply, the mountain let out a low rumble, causing the mounds of coins to vibrate and filling the cavern with the sound of clinking metal. Dread pooled in the pit of my stomach. "We need to leave," Akira stated, already making her way to the exit. Her expression was cautious as she surveyed her surroundings, and though my instincts told me she was right to flee, my boots remained firmly rooted in place as I regarded the hoard of treasure. I didn't know when I would next be able to return, and I couldn't trust that thieves wouldn't find this place in the interim.

Another rumble tore through the mountain, this one much more violent than before. Large chunks of rocks fell down from above, shattering on the ground below. It would seem this was one of the futures that Amari had not seen fit to forewarn Emrys about, because his panic was a palpable thing as he shoved me toward the stone doors. A crack split the air like thunder, and when I dared to look over my shoulder, I discovered that the floor was breaking apart to reveal glowing magma. Vicarius slipped into the bubbling inferno below and my heart sank in my chest as his vast collection of coins joined him, the possibility of buying myself a title disappearing along with it.

Such a waste, the voice lamented, but wealth would do me little good if I was dead.

I raced for the exit. The oil trenches were still burning, their flames lighting the passage ahead. I was so close. Then everything went black with ash. The air singed my lungs, clogging them like smoke, and suddenly I couldn't breathe. My knees buckled as the mountain trembled with all the wrath of a vengeful god. Maybe Lios had felt the moment his precious pet was stolen from him. Maybe this was the physical manifestation of all his grief and fury. I tried to inhale, but it was like swallowing needles, the sensation leaving my throat raw and my body writhing in agony. As heat scorched my skin, I was fairly certain that this was no longer the mortal realm. This was the infernal firepits of damnation, where I would burn again and again for daring to defy Celdric.

Someone latched onto me, weighing me down like an anchor in a storm. I didn't need to see in order to know it was Emrys. When the burning sensation faded slightly, I realized that he was attempting to shield my body from the elements. I should be the one protecting him, not the other way around, but what did it matter now? Neither of us would be able to escape this place alive. Yet I couldn't find it in myself to feel fear. My destiny was bound to his, which meant that even if death was to be my fate, I wouldn't have to face it alone.

I blinked as the darkness shifted to a bleary haze of sunlight. The colors around me all blended together like paints that had bled into each other on a canvas. My chest expanded and contracted as my body battled for each breath, my wheeze a pitiful thing even to my own ears. Emrys's face drifted in and out of focus. He was in my arms, unconscious, his skin blistered and his hair stained black with soot. My head rolled back to find a pair of deep-blue eyes staring down at me—eyes as old and as ancient as the stars. Then everything went silent and the world faded into oblivion.

CHAPTER 31

Emrys screamed. I staggered through the dark, desperate to find him as ash rained down from above. I yelled out his name, but his cries of anguish just echoed off the walls, assaulting me from every direction and making it impossible to pinpoint his location. Smoke clouded the air, choking my lungs and stinging my eyes, and someone laughed from beyond the abyss. Celdric pressed his lips to my ear as he whispered, "Neither victory nor defeat comes without a price, Koven." I spun around, but he had already dissolved into shadow. "If you want to play games with gods, then you must be prepared to lose everything."

My heart pounded against my rib cage as a hand reached out to caress my hair. I sliced out with my dagger and my eyes widened with horror as the blade opened Serenity's throat. She collapsed, her hands clutching at the wound as blood seeped out between her fingers. I gathered her in my arms, apologizing a dozen times over as my tears left tracks in the ash coating my face. "I thought you would never hurt me again," she spluttered, her voice full of betrayal. Then she slipped through my fingers to sink into the ground and flowers sprouted from her grave, only to wither at my touch.

Serenity's hands burst out of the soil a moment later, her skin a rotten shade of gray as it peeled away from her bones. She grabbed ahold of my legs and my shadow refused to save me as she dragged me down into the grave with her. I grappled for a handhold, my fingernails cracking and bleeding as I clawed at the dirt, but I could do nothing as I disappeared beneath the surface. My feet hit the floor and my eyes took a few seconds to adjust to the dim lighting. Celdric stood with his back to me, his hands coated with so much blood that it looked as though he was wearing crimson gloves.

"You're going to have to do better than that if you want to sneak up on me." The god of mischief turned around to face me, amusement bright in his golden eyes. "I have a gift for you. Would you like to see it?"

He stepped to the side to reveal the small stone altar that was used to make offerings to the gods. I sucked in a sharp breath. Several jars of blood had been arranged in a circle, and resting in the center was the severed head of Emrys. He peered back at me, his eyes colorless and unseeing, and everything inside me withered like one of those flowers on Serenity's grave.

"He died pleading for his life," Celdric said with a wicked smile as he raked his fingers through Emrys's white hair. "How did you think this was going to turn out for you and your friends, Koven? Did you really think you could best me? I am the god of deception, and you're nothing more than a mortal, living a life of such little significance that no one will spare you a second thought after you die."

As Celdric took a step toward me, I took a step back. "I will take all those you hold dear and deliver them to you one piece at a time." The god's shadow took on the form of a snake as it wrapped around me, locking me in place. "You would like that, wouldn't you? After all, you're just as twisted as I am. Worse, even. At least I don't pretend to be something I'm not. There's a monster lurking inside you, Koven, and one of these days you're going to let it out of its cage. I saw the glint in your eyes when you sliced Faelan apart in that arena. You enjoyed his pain, didn't you? You enjoyed the sound of his screams."

The floor beneath me dissolved into sand, forcing me back into the trials, and I was helpless to do anything but stab into Faelan again and again. He flailed beneath me, his body broken and bleeding, yet I didn't stop. He screamed, and he screamed, and he screamed. A laugh rippled through the arena, but it didn't sound like Celdric. It sounded like me.

I bolted upright in the bed, but the screams had managed to follow me into the waking world. My gaze landed on Emrys, who was thrashing in the bed on the other side of the room, crying out as he battled a nightmare of his own. I stumbled across the room to shake him by the shoulders. His eyes snapped open with a gasp, looking disorientated and confused as he peered around the villa with its white chalk walls and thatched roof.

"It was just a nightmare," I told him. "You're fine." And he was. Although soot still clung to his hair, the blisters and burns that previously marred his skin had since been healed. He reached for the jug of water on the bedside table, but his hand was shaking too badly for him to take hold of it. I poured him a glass and held it to his lips as he gulped it down.

"It wasn't a nightmare." His voice was thick and charred as though he had breathed in too much smoke. It took me a moment to realize what he meant. If it wasn't a nightmare, then it had to be a vision, a glimpse into the future of what was still to come. After fleeing the hordes of the undead on Spire and battling a dragon inside a mountain of fire, I didn't want to know what else Amari could possibly have planned for the two of us, but it wasn't fair for him to carry the weight of that knowledge alone.

"What did you see?" I asked.

He hesitated as though he might actually tell me. Then a shutter fell down over his expression. "We should get going," he said, shoving the blankets aside. "We fulfilled our side of the bargain. It's time for Amari to fulfill hers."

I could think of a long list of things I wanted to do before seeking an audience with the goddess of fate. Hunger gnawed at my stomach, and from the sweat and ash that coated me like a second skin, I was clearly in desperate need of a bath. However, Emrys didn't give me time to attend to either of those needs as he headed for the door and stepped out into the garden. I lifted a hand to shield my eyes from the morning sun, squinting at the figure in the distance. Akira was traveling back from the direction of the hot springs. She had borrowed a white dress from one of the maidens, which was a little too long for her, and so she walked with the hem bunched up in her hands to prevent herself from tripping over it. With her long hair hanging loose down her back, she could almost blend in with the rest of the girls in the sanctuary. Her scars, however, stood out like thorns on a rose stem, and she carried herself like a warrior with her head held high and an expression cold enough to freeze over the sandy dunes of the Matarran Desert.

Her lips pursed with displeasure when she came to a stop in front of Emrys. "I was hoping to have a chance to speak with you," she said in a tone that made it hard not to shrivel in her presence. "How fortuitous that fate has seen fit to grant me an audience with you so early in the day."

Emrys rubbed at the side of his temple as though trying to ward off an oncoming headache. "Akira—" he began to say, but she cut him off.

"You failed to warn me of the ash and fire that would rain down on the world after the dragon was slain. With all the secrets you refuse to share, I'm tempted to reconsider the alliance between our two noble houses. You better hope that my brother returns, because you will not find me to be in a forgiving mood until he does."

Emrys couldn't have warned anyone of the impending eruption because he hadn't known it would happen. I'd seen the truth of it in his eyes when the mountain began to tremble. I saw his fear, and his surprise, and his panic. If Amari was helping guide him through the future, then she had chosen to keep that incident hidden from his gaze, but Akira was the sort of person who considered ignorance to be a far worse offense than deceit.

This whole plan hinged on his gift as a seer. Any credibility Emrys still held with her would be lost the moment he admitted his fallibility. He must've known it, too, because all he said was "We successfully completed the task that was asked of us and we returned alive. That is all that matters."

She stepped closer to him, and though he towered over her in height, it was no competition as to which of the two cut the more daunting figure. "The future is not written in stone, which means there was a possibility that I and everyone else in your company could've died yesterday. I am no coward, Emrys. I'm willing to take the risks needed in order to ensure the success of this mission, but I should know what dangers lie ahead of me. You have no right to play so recklessly with my life."

She turned her attention to me when she said, "Did you ever think that maybe he knew Rita wouldn't make it out of the trials alive and he chose to remain silent so as not to change her fate?" Her words caused my shadow to shift uneasily at my feet. "Did you ever think that maybe he looked at all the futures that were laid out before him and deemed her sacrifice necessary to his own survival? And if he did that to her, what's to stop him from doing it to the rest of us?"

The question settled like a stone in the pit of my stomach. I looked at Emrys, who refused to look at me in return, and I decided that I didn't want to know the answer.

"You're not a god, Emrys," she said, her tone seething. "You would do well to remember that."

Akira continued down the garden path, leaving him to contemplate her words as she headed for the orchard. In the distance, I spotted Faelan leaning against one of the tree trunks, shamelessly tempting his fate as he accepted an apple offered to him by one of the maidens that formed part of his new entourage. He didn't appear to be limping, which meant that Serenity must have tended to him at some point over the course of the night. She must have attended to all of us. Worry flickered through me at the thought. The source of a healer's power came from within. There was only so much they could do before they were required to dip into their own life force, and she was the sort of person who would do it, too, sacrificing a part of herself in order to save another.

"I need to check on Serenity," I said stiffly. Emrys caught ahold of my wrist as I moved in the direction of her villa. I stared at him, waiting for him to address Akira's accusation.

"Come to the pavilion when you're done" was all he said before letting me go. He didn't give me an answer about Rita, and I couldn't bring myself to demand one. Perhaps a part of me feared the truth might fracture the faith that I had in him, but the bigger part was all too aware of just how easy it would be to forgive him for any sin that he laid at my feet, just as I knew that he would be able to forgive all of mine.

Shielded as the sanctuary was from the violence of the outside world, the doors had no need for locks. The entrance to Serenity's lodgings simply swung open as soon as I pushed it. Thin slivers of light snuck in through the shutters to decorate the floor with golden stripes. Not wanting to disturb her rest, I shrouded my steps in silence when I stepped inside, but the cat napping at the foot of her bed sensed an intruder and poked its head up to glower at me. Serenity's eyes were closed, her expression peaceful as though her sleep was deep and dreamless, but as I drew closer, I noticed that her lips were a frightening shade of blue. My gaze settled on the silver streak that stood out against her otherwise dark hair, and an invisible hand slithered through my rib cage to clench around my heart.

She had exchanged years of her life to make sure the rest of us survived. She had probably made the trade without so much as a second thought. I reached out to touch the silver streak that now stained her hair, and she stirred in her sleep before going still once more. She was too good for me, but my heart was greedy and selfish enough to want her anyway. I was tempted to take a seat on the edge of her bed and hold her hand until she woke up, but I couldn't stay, so I picked some flowers from the garden instead and left them on her bedside table before closing the door quietly behind me on my way out.

The sanctuary was a lot bigger than I remembered, and after coming out on the wrong side of the apple grove, I ended up finding Amari rather than the pavilion. She was pruning one of the rosebushes with a small pair of garden shears, the hem of her dress stained with dirt and grass. I was once again struck by her youth. It made me wonder whether she had been cruel enough to sacrifice a child to host her divine spirit, or whether her power over fate made it so that she had no need for a mortal host at all. She was different to the rest of her kind, with eyes of sea and sky rather than gleaming gold. She also didn't seem to enjoy the company of the other gods much, choosing instead to seclude herself in the mountains, content to live a simple life away from all the violence that her brethren reveled in.

"Koven," she said with a sweet smile. "My apologies for letting the nightmare through, but I was beginning to think that you might sleep the day away, and we have business that we must attend to."

My brow furrowed at the confession. "You sent a nightmare to wake me up?"

"I'm a fate-weaver, not a monster-wrangler. I cannot command a nightmare to do anything, but they feast on fear and pain and guilt. I suspected that you would make quite the meal for them." She sheared off another flower head before standing back to admire her work. Her lips twitched into a displeased frown and she moved in closer to snip at an untidy outcropping of leaves. "Contrary to popular belief, nightmares are not ill omens. They cannot reveal terrible things yet to come. They can only reveal what already exists inside you. They are a mirror of sorts, one that shows a distorted reflection but a reflection nonetheless."

Amari examined the roses once more, and this time, she hummed with satisfaction. She shifted her attention to me, and her strange blue eyes seemed to pierce into the very depths of my soul. "The greatest thing you fear is yourself. You fear the darkness that taints your blood, and you're right to fear it, Koven. You have no idea what you're capable of, but I do."

The goddess reached up and touched my cheek. The gesture was eerily reminiscent of my mother, so much so that it dredged up an old memory from the recesses of my mind. She was sitting on a moth-eaten rug that lay in front of the fire. Her hands were worn to the bone, her skin waxen and her face whittled away by exhaustion, but I hadn't noticed those details when I was a young boy perched in her lap. I gazed up at her, completely enamored, as she spun wild stories of how my father hailed from a noble line of ancient kings. One day he would return from his quest to reclaim his crown, and on that day, we would walk through grand halls and wear the finest clothes, and we would never go hungry again. That was before my mother got sick and her body was dragged away to the plague pyres. Before I was left alone with nothing but lies to keep me warm at night until the truth about my father finally reached my ears. He was a swindler who had abandoned my mother with a pile of debt that would take a lifetime to pay off, and he had no intention of ever coming back. Not for my mother, and certainly not for me.

I blinked as the memory faded and the world around me came back into focus. I must have gotten lost in my thoughts, because I didn't remember walking to the pavilion. Yet I was standing inside it, shaded beneath the purple wisps of wisteria. Everyone else was already in attendance, including Simara, who occupied herself by rolling a ball of yarn on the floor. She ended up getting both of her paws tangled in the thread. Amari regarded the scene with an endearing smile. Then she crouched down to help her pet escape the mess she had made.

"Vicarius is no more," the goddess declared as she collected the ball of yarn from the floor. "His shadow will no longer darken my skies, nor will his fire burn my children to ash. You have held up your side of the bargain, and now I will hold up mine."

She blew on the ball of yarn, and the thread began to shimmer like stardust. She first offered it to Damien, who stared at it with red-rimmed eyes. He had paid a heavy price for the power to rewrite the fate of his parents, but he wiped the last trace of remorse from his expression as he drew out a length of the string. It was one thing to have heard the stories of the string of fate; it was another thing altogether to watch the story come to life before my very eyes. I watched in astonishment as he severed the thread and it changed from a shimmering white to a deep shade of blue.

"Damien, son of fire and son of ice, you have been gifted the power to change one's fate," Amari said.

Damien stepped back with his head bowed in deference, and Emrys moved forward to take his place. He had no blade of his own to use, so I offered him one of my daggers. His gaze was heavy on mine as he accepted it, weighed down with words yet unsaid, but his eyes held a silent promise that he would share them with me. I nodded, letting him know that I understood. He shifted his focus back to the thread. He cut off a piece of it, and I frowned as it turned a brilliant shade of scarlet.

"Emrys of House Hardcastle, you have been gifted the power to bind two souls together," said Amari, and I tried not to panic at the declaration. That was *not* the power we needed. That was not the reason we had traveled all this way and battled a creature born of fire.

"We need it to be gold," Akira interjected.

"No, *you* need it to be gold," the goddess said, holding out the ball of yarn for her to take. "You all took part in the task; you will all reap the reward."

With her hunting knife, Akira cut the string and heaved a sigh of relief when it turned gold in her hands. "Akira of House Marcaida, you have been gifted the power to fix that which has been broken."

Amari proceeded to offer the ball of yarn to Faelan. Simara let out a low growl when he touched it. "Hush now," the goddess scolded, and the panther's upper lip dropped back down to conceal her canines. He flashed the creature a cautious look as he reached out for the string once more, but this time she only flicked her tail in annoyance. He cut off a piece of thread, and it turned blue in his hands. He had been gifted with the power to change fate, just like Damien. He stared at it with an arched eyebrow as though unsure of what exactly he was supposed to do with it.

Then it was my turn. Though the voice at the back of my mind didn't speak, its anticipation spread through me. As soon as I touched the string, the power imbued within it pulsated at my fingertips and I had to suppress the shiver of pleasure that threatened to travel down my spine. I sliced into it. When the thread turned as dark as my shadow, the anticipation gave way to a bitter disappointment. Amari smiled as though she had been expecting this—as though she had been looking forward to this very moment. "Koven, descendant of a bloodline long since forgotten, you have been gifted the power to end life."

Not wanting to offend the goddess, I was careful to keep my true thoughts from tainting my expression. Red. Gold. Blue. Those threads were capable of amazing feats. They could break curses, bind souls, repair ripped seams between this world and the next. All the black string of fate could do was give me the power to end another's life, a task I could easily accomplish with a flick of my dagger, yet Amari was staring at me like I was cradling the sun itself in the palm of my hand.

"You have all been given a great power," the goddess said, her voice grave. "You can only use it once; I recommend you use it wisely. It was a long journey to get here. You need not suffer the same fate upon your return. Take the day to rest and gather your strength. Tomorrow, with a drop of your blood, I will send you back home."

A starling swooped down from the sky to perch on the edge of the stone basin, using the water to preen its speckled feathers. The rest of the birds trilled from the treetops, a joyous tune that was in harmony with the singing maidens of providence. The sanctuary truly was a beautiful place, forcing all its residents to bask in the glow of its peace and tranquility. There would be none of that in the world below. War was spreading through the continent, and it would continue to do so until Rin managed to crawl his way back from the land of the dead. The last Holy War had lasted over a decade, each day filled with a torrent of blood, death, and despair. If Rin remained trapped on the other side, that would be the fate that awaited us all—but for some inexplicable reason, I found myself impatient to return home anyway.

Let's hope he fails in his endeavor, the voice whispered. *It would be a pity if this war was cut short before you had the opportunity to wet your blade.*

It was all I could do not to sigh as the reason for my impatience suddenly became clear.

CHAPTER 32

Steam rose up from the hot springs, warm and inviting. I quickly peeled off my soot-stained clothes, eager to step into the heated waters, yet I stood hesitant at the edge of the pool, unsure of what to do with the black string of fate in my hand. It seemed like a bad idea to leave it somewhere out of my reach. After a moment of consideration, I threaded the string around the emerald ring that hung around my neck. After securing it in place, I finally allowed myself to enter the spring. The water around me turned gray with ash as I slathered my body with salt scrubs. When my hair spilled forward to cover my eyes, I tugged pensively at its length. Having been neglected over the last few weeks, it was in desperate need of a cut. My shadow slunk across the ground to collect one of my daggers, and once it deposited the blade in my hand, I began hacking blindly at my locks. The end result was unlikely to be pretty, but fortunately, I didn't care for my appearance in the same way Faelan did.

"Would you like some help with that?" With a shy smile, Serenity stepped out from behind one of the cherry blossom trees. She looked as though she had only just woken up, her dress still creased and her hair bedraggled. "I wasn't trying to spy on you, I promise. I was hoping to use the hot springs myself."

My mind came to a stuttering halt in her presence, my body laid bare beneath her gaze. Only a murky veil of water kept me from being completely revealed. Yet her eyes didn't wander past the penance scars that were etched into my back. There was no pity in her expression, only tenderness and understanding, and that made me feel more exposed than any absence of clothing.

As she moved toward me, it was impossible not to stare at the silver that now streaked through her dark curls. She touched it in a self-conscious gesture. "It doesn't look too bad, I hope." How it looked wasn't the problem; it was what it represented. I opened my mouth to speak, but she beat me to it. "Please, don't lecture me. The choice was mine and I made it willingly. I don't regret it. A few years was a small price to pay, and if you think about it, lives are cut short all the time. I might die tomorrow, or next week, or next month, and the years that I gave away would amount to nothing."

I could understand the logic, but that didn't make what she did any less dangerous. If she truly believed the sacrifice was worth it, then she would do it again, trading away pieces of herself until she was nothing more than a withered husk. "Tell me that it scared you," I said, because at least then she might think twice before trying to replicate the feat.

She didn't heed my request. Instead, she hiked up the hem of her dress and sat on the edge of the spring, lowering her legs into the water and extracting the dagger from my hand. I was acutely aware of where the bare skin of her calves brushed against my sides while she evened out the rough edges of my hair. When she was finally finished, she placed the blade on the stone shelf and combed her fingers through my shortened locks. After a moment of consideration, her fingers slowly slid down to trace the scars along my back. The gentleness in her touch made me shiver. Then she leaned down to place a kiss on my shoulder, as though trying to erase the sting of the reverend's whip with her lips. "It terrified me," she said, her voice wistful, "but probably not in the way you're hoping it did."

I twisted around to face her. It was a mistake. Her proximity caused my eyes to darken, and the situation wasn't helped when her gaze roamed over the beads of water that rolled down my chest. "That level of power," she said, her voice barely more than a whisper, "it was intoxicating. The price didn't scare me nearly as much as the rush I got once I paid it."

I took her face in my hands. "Promise me you won't do it again."

"I can't promise that." She leaned forward to rest her forehead against mine. "If you were dying, I would pay that price a hundred times over to breathe life back into you."

Gods, I wished she hadn't said that. It fractured my self-restraint like it was made of nothing more than glass. My lips came crashing down onto hers. She wound her legs around my torso as I lifted her up and dragged her into the water with me. When my shadow glided up her thighs, she broke away with a gasp. I took the opportunity to mark her jawline with my mouth before swiftly moving down to claim her neck. She tilted back her head to give me better access to her throat, and the desire burning through my veins turned into something dark and consuming.

"Careful, sunshine." I slid my hand up her spine and knotted my fingers in her hair. "I'm not nearly as nice as you think I am. If I told you about some of the twisted thoughts in my head, you would run screaming."

It was supposed to be a warning, but she only pressed herself closer to me. "You don't frighten me, Koven. On the contrary, you make me brave, and perhaps a little bit reckless, but I like the way I feel when I'm with you. As though I could jump off a cliff without fear of falling because I know that you would be there to catch me."

The water had turned her dress semitranslucent, and her curves taunted me from beneath the thin slip of fabric. She shivered as wisps of shadow brushed against the scar that lined her arm. An image of her dying flashed to the forefront of my mind, her eyes full of betrayal as she sank into her grave, but I reminded myself that it was only a nightmare. That was my own fear reflected back at me, not a prophetic vision of what was to come. I would never hurt her again. I would sooner carve the heart from my chest.

Her fingernails dug into my shoulders as I pinned her against the wall of the hot spring. I traced my thumb over her bottom lip, the movement slow and deliberate as though I could memorize its curve with my touch. I didn't know how I could have ever thought there was innocence in those eyes of hers. She looked just as hungry as I did. "We should slow down," I said, hoping that she would have the strength to put a stop to this before we went too far, because Essian knows that I certainly didn't.

"I think I have waited for you long enough." She pulled me into another kiss and let out a low moan when my tongue brushed against her own. Her fingers slid down my chest. They inched lower, and lower, and—

When are you going to tell her that there are three of us in this relationship?

If the voice at the back of my head had a physical form, I would've commanded my shadow to shatter it into pieces for that interruption. Though I wanted nothing more than to ignore the comment, it needled its way into my conscience, making it impossible to do so. Snatching ahold of Serenity's wrist, I broke away from the kiss.

She was breathing heavily, her chest rising and falling in sync with my own. She stared at me with startled eyes like she thought she might have done something wrong. I needed to tell her about the voice, but the words got stuck in my throat, promising to choke me before they ever made it past my lips. "This is neither the time nor the place," I told her, my voice so thick and rough I almost didn't recognize it. "And before you make this decision, I want you to know who I am, even the parts of me you might not like."

Her expression softened. She lifted a hand to caress my cheek, and the edges of her mouth twitched upward at the prickle of my stubble. "You won't scare me away, Koven." She sounded so certain of that fact. It was as though she knew it in the same way she knew the sun would rise at dawn and disappear beneath the horizon at dusk. I didn't share in that certainty, but it was nice to allow myself to imagine, if only for a moment, what it would be like if she was right.

CHAPTER 33

Although I looked for Emrys the rest of the afternoon, he didn't make an appearance. He was even absent from the farewell feast the maidens of providence had prepared in our honor. I returned to the villa late in the evening, admiring the aster flower pinched between two of my fingers. It had fallen from Serenity's hair, and my thieving shadow had claimed it for me. I tucked the flower into my pocket and then opened the door. Emrys was hidden inside, sitting on the windowsill with his long legs pulled up to his chest. The moonlight filtered in through the open window to illuminate him, the silver tones reflecting off his pale skin and hair, making him look like a spirit that had been whispered back to life. He stared up at the stars with a forlorn expression, as though he fancied himself to be one of them, one that had fallen from grace and was forced to live in the mortal realm below.

"Sometimes, I have to do things I don't like for the greater good," he said, his gaze still transfixed on the stars. "But what happened to Rita was not by my design. She was always destined to die in the trials. The thread of her fate was weak and frayed; it could not be rewoven. It was going to be cut whether the blade that severed it was fire, or steel, or the hunger of death. Although I could not prevent her fate, I knew that you would put her in our team, and I chose to allow you to do that. At least that way she didn't have to die alone, her body forgotten and left to decay. I could ensure she would have that kindness if nothing else." He turned to face me, his eyes as gray and desolate as a sunless sky. "I can take Akira's ire for all the secrets that I keep, but I cannot take yours."

I moved closer to the window, leaning against the wall with one shoulder as I peered up at the sky. With its bright-red glow, the Eye of Maylore had always been the easiest constellation for me to pick out. Typically it was just a speck of red in the dark, but tonight, the crimson star seemed closer than usual, and it glared down at me with a stare that was both ominous and angry. It was as though it wanted me to be enraged. Yet all I could think was how Emrys had once told me that his foresight was more of a curse rather than a blessing, and how difficult it must be for him to bear the weight of that burden alone. He hadn't sacrificed Rita for his own gain; he had been forced to live with the knowledge that she was destined to die, knowing there was nothing he could do to stop it. "You did your best under the circumstances," I told him.

He gave a humorless snort and a bitterness crept in to taint his expression. "My best isn't good enough. I can't save everyone, Koven, no matter how hard I try. This world is so broken. It's no wonder Essian can't bring himself to look at it anymore. He helped ruin it, and now when the people need his guidance the most, he willfully turns a blind eye while Athearia's strongholds fall one by one. He makes me ashamed to carry his blood in my veins."

The world didn't need Essian to be its champion, because this land did not belong to the gods. They were merely guests in it, borrowing the bodies of mortal vessels so that they could reside in this realm alongside men. If gods were the ones that ruined our home, then they couldn't be relied upon to fix it. What the world needed was a mortal seer to serve as its guide, born of blood and bone instead of gold and stardust. Though a title of my own would be nice, it was probably better for my sanity that I didn't have one. There was humility in service, which was something the voice in the back of my mind had none of. If it was my fate to serve another, Emrys was more than worthy of my devotion. "Then tell me what we must do to save our kingdom," I said. "Lead and I will follow."

He swung his legs off the window, rising to his full height as he said, "I need access to the shadow domain."

I arched an eyebrow at the declaration. He had visited the shadow domain once before, insisting that he could walk its ruined roads as though he were a vassal of Celdric, and I had been too young and enamored by his attention to argue otherwise. The darkness had tried to consume him the moment he arrived. He'd barely managed to escape with his life. "The shadow domain will kill you," I reminded him.

"Not if it thinks we're the same person." He unfurled his hand to reveal the red string of fate. "If I bind my soul to yours, the darkness won't know the difference. I will be able to walk through the shadow domain just as you do."

I stared at the thread of fate for a long time. The binding of two souls was not something that could be undone, nor was it something that people did merely for power. My gaze lifted back up to meet his. "Is that the only reason you wish to bind yourself to me?"

He fell quiet for a moment, like he was deliberating whether or not to give me an answer, but this was not a question that I would allow him to circumvent. When he finally spoke, he did so slowly, as though selecting his words carefully. "You're half my soul, Koven. We are each one side of the same coin, woven to share the same destiny, but fate and power are not my only reasons for wanting to do this. Life in the mortal realm is short, so much shorter than the one after death. I would like to be able to find you again on the other side. This thread will allow me to do that."

He was fearful of life after death, which was a reality that all mortals had to face eventually, and he was scared of having to go through that journey alone. But he didn't need to. He was the light and I was the shadow; you couldn't have one without the other, and that held true both in this life and the next. I offered him my wrist, and he wound the crimson string around it. My skin began to prickle and burn as he tied off the thread with a knot. Between one blink and the next, the red string of fate disappeared and an invisible link was forged in its place.

"We leave tonight," Emrys said, moving to collect the silver-wood staff that rested in the corner of the room. "The Kaltan forces have advanced quicker than expected. The city of Arlow is under attack as we speak. Brazial's army will breach the gates if you don't stop them."

With his staff in hand, he returned to my side, staring at me expectantly. He hadn't wanted the power to walk through the shadows for some future expedition. He wanted me to open a gateway into the shadow domain *now*. Arlow was a fortified city in the northern territory of Athearia, but it wasn't the first stronghold, or even the second, or the third. It should have alarmed me how quickly the Kaltan troops were advancing. Yet my blood began to quicken in my veins at the challenge, the darkness of the night yearning to be unleashed like a tidal wave upon my enemies.

What are you waiting for? the voice demanded, impatient and eager for the taste of battle.

I studied my wrist, wondering if the thread of fate was enough to protect Emrys from the feral shadows once I opened the gateway, or if I would be sending him straight to his death. Even if he did manage to survive the shadow domain, if his plan was to exit into the middle of a battlefield, that would also come with its own set of risks. "We already accomplished what we came here to do," I said. "We got the golden string of fate. Surely we have done our part in this war."

"There are many things we still have left to do. Destiny has not given me an easy path, but that is why she also gave me you, so that I need not walk it alone. You are the sword needed to protect this realm, and I am the sight needed to direct your blade." Emrys reached out to clasp my shoulder. "You said that if I lead, you will follow. Open the gateway, Koven."

I had never been able to refuse him. A part of me wanted to lay the blame for that at destiny's feet, but I had a feeling that particular weakness was no one's fault but my own.

At my command, the darkness congealed into a puddle on the floor, dragging Emrys and me into the domain below. The world flipped over into one of gray skies and thick mist. I found myself in a section that I hadn't been to before, staring at a rotting pavilion, the wood cracking and the roof entangled with shriveled vines. The structure was hidden inside a grove of dead trees. I knew from experience that I couldn't shield him from the flesh-eaters of this place, but I still moved to stand protectively in front of Emrys as a shadow slithered down from one of the barren branches. The shadow prowled closer, and I fought the urge to reach for one of my daggers. At best, the steel would do absolutely nothing. At worst, it would encourage the shadow to rethink its long-standing tradition of not feasting upon any of Celdric's kin.

The darkness circled my ankles before moving to inspect Emrys. It paused as though unsure of what to make of him. I held my breath as the shadow inched closer, slinking over his boots until the leather was the color of ink. Then it slunk away again, retreating back to the trees. The breath that I was holding hissed out between my teeth. "It looks like you were right," I muttered.

"Well, I'm not often wrong."

I leveled a skeptical look in his direction. "The last time you convinced me to bring you here, you nearly died."

"I said that I could walk through the shadow domain just like any other vassal of Celdric, and I can, my prediction was just a tad bit early."

Early by several years.

Emrys strode forward, navigating his way through the decaying grove as though he had already walked this path before. A heavy fog rolled in to conceal the trees as soon as we made it out on the other side, the sanctuary disappearing behind a wall of mist in a matter of seconds. A barren wasteland stretched out before me with a city of ruins just visible on the horizon, but distance was often distorted in the shadow domain. Something could be a lot farther or a lot closer than it originally appeared. Fortunately, in this case, it was the latter. It didn't take very long to reach the crumbling buildings that were scattered along the city's outskirts like broken seashells littering the shore.

The tip of a turret jutted out from the ground, a flag hanging lifelessly from its point. I could already ascertain from the colors that one side bore the crest of the Athearian royal family in the form of a star framed by a set of antlers. An upside-down tree would be imprinted on the other side, its roots reaching for the sky while its branches twisted toward the ground—the symbol of House Blackwood. "Prepare yourself," Emrys said, and then grabbed the flagpole. He vanished from sight before I could inform him that his advice was too vague to be of any use. With a sigh, I grabbed the flagpole as well.

The silence of the shadow domain was replaced by a chorus of battle cries. I stood on the very peak of a battlement tower, the flag above me flapping furiously in the wind. The sky was painted black, the moon hidden behind sightless clouds, and the hamlets dotting the hillsides all burned like bonfires in the distance. Though the walls to the city were high, the Kaltans attempted to scale it with siege towers. Necromancers sent waves of corpses to fend off the invaders. Some of the Kaltans were slain beneath the claws and teeth of the undead horde, their screams drowned out by their gurgles as the corpses ripped open their throats. However, there were vassals of Lios hidden in the crowd, and the dead quickly turned to pillars of ash with a snap of their fingers.

It was complete anarchy. I didn't understand how Emrys expected me to be able to put a stop to this. The thought must have been written on my face, because he put a reassuring hand on my shoulder. "Don't worry about the frontal assault." His voice was raised to a shout in order to be heard above the noise. "It's just a distraction. They are using the cover of darkness to launch a sneak attack through the east gate. That is where you need to go. I'll warn the commander of the stronghold. You just make sure the gate holds until reinforcements come."

I gave him a nod to let him know that I understood, but when I turned my attention back to the battle, I struggled to find a viable route to the eastern side of the fortress. The wall walk was thick with bodies, the two kingdoms clashing in a disorienting haze of corpses, and steel, and smoke. It would be difficult to traverse all that chaos. My eyes narrowed on the ridges that ran along the interior wall, which I could use to get across, but it was an awfully long drop to the hard stone floors of the courtyard below. Even with my shadow to soften the blow, a fall like that might kill me.

Then don't fall, the voice reasoned.

My training in the House of Shadows had prepared me for sneaking in through windows and leaping between rooftops, but this was something else altogether. One wrong move and I would very likely plummet to my death. I cast a nervous glance at Emrys, but he didn't seem to share my apprehension. His eyes were steady as he stared back at me, his trust in me firm and unwavering. I sucked in a deep breath and slid down the tiles of the turret before my reservations could get the better of me. I didn't allow myself to linger once I dropped down onto one of the ridges below. I sprinted from one ridge to the next. When I made it halfway across without incident, I started to think that it was a masterful plan. Then a pair of grappling warriors knocked into me. I slipped off the wall. My arms rushed up to grab the stone, but my fingers only clawed at air. My stomach performed a somersault as I began to fall. I came to a painful and sudden stop as my shadow latched onto my wrists. It yanked me back up onto the wall, and I huffed out a breath of relief as I found my balance again.

I proceeded forward with more caution, the darkness shoving away anyone that drew too close. Once I reached the eastern side of the fortress, I jumped down onto the walkway, eyeing one of the dead soldiers lying on the ground. The stronghold was in the midst of a battle, so bodies alone weren't enough to cause suspicion, but the fact that the vast majority of them appeared to be wearing Athearian uniforms didn't escape my notice. I traveled farther down the wall walk. This section of the stronghold was quiet, which was to be expected when forces had been redeployed to fortify the main gate, but it was a little *too* quiet. My shadow stalked the battlement alongside me, ready to attack as soon as I gave the command.

Ahead of me, a pair of soldiers were conversing in hushed tones, but they fell quiet upon my approach. When the soldiers stood to attention, my suspicion swelled. I wasn't their commanding officer, nor was I dressed in the uniform of a fellow warrior. They should be demanding to know who I was and what I was doing here. My steps slowed as I studied their blood-splattered armor, which was too large on the one and too tight on the other. These were disguises, likely stolen off a soldier's corpse in haste. The men weren't Athearian soldiers; they were Kaltans. The pair exchanged a look. They must have realized that their disguises hadn't managed to hold up to scrutiny, because both of them moved to unsheathe their weapons. My shadow was quicker. I didn't hesitate, not when it was my life or theirs. The darkness came down on them like a hammer, crushing their metal breastplates until their ribs cracked and blood seeped out from their mouths. I didn't allow myself to think about just how easy it was to kill them, or how the darkness discarded them off the battlement afterward as though they were nothing more than broken toys.

I forced myself to stay focused on my objective, but as I raced toward the gatehouse, the rattle of chains reached my ears and I realized that I might already be too late. Someone was lifting up the gate. I forced my legs to pump even harder. My gaze narrowed on one of the windows, and I leaped through the air. I just managed to latch onto the ledge. With gritted teeth, I pulled myself up. The guards inside had all been slaughtered, their bodies torn to pieces. One man was cranking the wheel that controlled the gate, an impressive feat of strength that clearly marked him as a vassal of Brazial. Half a dozen others had managed to infiltrate the stronghold with him, their swords still wet with blood from their recent kills and their faces plastered with smiles as though the war was already won. When I dropped into the room, their smiles only grew wider. They didn't think I was a threat. Not when I was so outnumbered.

That will be their mistake, the voice growled. Its bloodlust leaked into me, spurring me to violence. *You don't even know the depths of your own power. How could you? You resist it at every opportunity, but I could show you what you're capable of; you just need to let me in.*

I couldn't fight a battle on two fronts, so I chose the one that mattered. I didn't try to suppress the violence. Instead, I breathed it in, allowing it to fill my lungs. From there, it spread through my body like a wildfire. The power that surged through me was a flood in comparison to the shallow well I typically drew from. I didn't even need to reach for the darkness; this time the darkness reached for me. The entire room went black. The shadows consumed everything, even the sound of splintering wood and snapping bone, leaving nothing but silence in its wake. The darkness dispersed as quickly as it had come, leaving behind cracked stone walls that were dripping with a fresh coat of red paint. The crank for the gate had been reduced to rubble. The Kaltans had disappeared. I didn't know where to until I noticed the entrails that dangled from the ceiling.

The sight filled me with a twisted sense of satisfaction.

I took a leisurely stroll across to the peephole that overlooked the gate, enjoying the way the crimson puddles on the floor rippled around me with each step. A smirk manifested on my lips as I peered outside. The portcullis had dropped back down like an anchor cut free of its ship. The invading force was stranded outside, their ranks falling into confusion and disarray.

A gust of wind blew into the room as someone rushed through the broken doorway. Cahal skidded to a halt, nearly losing his balance on the blood-slicked floor. He raised his sword, ready to jump into battle, but all the firelight in the room had been extinguished, leaving him blind to the enemies he had stormed in here to slay. His presence summoned forth something very cold and cruel within me. I thought hatred would be like fire that burned too hot to control, but for me it was as sharp and unforgiving as a blade of ice. Grabbing a piece of flint from the supply shelf, I struck sparks with my dagger, and one of the torches flickered to life once more. Cahal spun in the direction of the flames, preparing to strike with his blade. He paused when he discovered that the only person in the room was me. Lowering his weapon, he sagged back against the wall, his breathing heavy and his hair damp with sweat.

Now is the time to kill him. Look at him. He's exhausted. Weak. No one is here to witness it. No one will ever know.

The thought was appealing. My head canted to the side as I considered all the ways the darkness could rip him apart. He didn't deserve a quick death. It should be slow, so that he could feel every agonizing second of it, the pain drawn out just long enough for his arrogance to be supplanted by fear. That should be the last emotion he feels before my darnkess strips the flesh from his bones.

Cahal surveyed the scarlet-painted walls before his gaze darted up to the newly decorated ceiling. "What the fuck happened in here?" he asked. I decided to remain quiet, allowing his imagination to conjure up an image of what had transpired. All the blood must have painted quite a terrifying picture, because he tightened his grip on his weapon. "You got a look in your eye that I don't like, Wickwire."

I took a step toward him.

He took a step back, his sword raised in warning. "Come any closer and I'll—"

"You'll what?" I challenged. The night swayed in my presence, so eager to serve me as its lord and master. As the shadows in the room swelled, the torch weakened and the flame threatened to wink out of existence. I was forced to rein in my power. I wanted Cahal to be able to see what was coming for him. "You should be on your knees right now thanking me. I just saved this stronghold, something that you seem to be incapable of doing yourself. I'm surprised you haven't flung open the main gates yet and invited the Kaltans in for a celebratory feast. That must be what you've been doing these past weeks. I don't see how else the enemy could have advanced this far so quickly."

He bristled at the insult, his mouth twisting into a snarl. "You have no idea how difficult it is to defend a stronghold from the literal *god of war* without a god of our own to fight him. Ashearan, feckless coward that he is, seems content to sequester himself in the Marcaida Fortress until Brazial has decimated my family's territories and there is nothing left of my bloodline but bones and ash. This kingdom bleeds not because of me, but because Ashearan is a petty, self-serving cunt that would sooner watch his people burn than swallow his own pride."

"A petty, self-serving cunt that would sooner watch his people burn than swallow his own pride," I repeated thoughtfully. "Remind me, are you describing Ashearan or yourself?"

His nostrils flared, but he didn't rise to the bait. Instead, he cast a glance over his shoulder for the door. The darkness surged forward to block off his escape route, but he managed to slip out the exit in a blur of motion. Annoyance flickered through me, but I doubted he would make it very far in his condition. When I exited the gatehouse, I found him hunched over at the bottom of the staircase, his sword hanging low in his hand like it was struggle for him to keep holding on to it. I stalked down the stairs, slowly trailing after him.

"Go on," he spat. "Try and kill me, you mad bastard. I've survived far worse than you."

"Oh, I highly doubt that," I said as the darkness solidified into chains, binding his arms and feet, pulling him down to the ground. He fought the restraints, but he might as well have been chained with Rasalan steel for all the good it did him. I came to a stop on the final stair, enjoying the way he looked on his knees before me. I brandished a dagger. Perhaps I would start by cutting out that insolent tongue of his and making him watch as I fed the sliver of meat to my shadow.

An arrow zipped toward me. My darkness swatted it away like a fly. I looked up to discover that the scene had started to attract a small crowd of soldiers. This had been Cahal's plan, not to escape but to draw witnesses. I was left with only two options. I could release him, insisting it was nothing more than a mild disagreement . . . or I could get rid of the spectators. There weren't many of them. It would be easy enough. The darkness began to gather like a storm above the soldiers, its shadow invisible against the night sky. It poised itself like a snake about to strike, but then a rumble of boots made me reconsider my decision. An entire battalion had arrived to reinforce the eastern gate.

Begrudgingly, I allowed the chains binding Cahal to dissipate like smoke in the wind. He rose in triumph, his smug expression so infuriating that

I was almost tempted to murder him anyway, consequences be damned. However, a thunderous crack drew my attention to the gate. Golden eyes glowed like two beacons in the dark as Brazial rammed into the barricade again. My eyes widened as the metal bars warped beneath the attack, leaving me in awe of the sheer strength he possessed. It should've terrified me that such a being was trying to get inside the fortress. With that sort of power, he could probably rip the limbs clean off my body. But I had been chosen by destiny. If anyone could defeat a god, it was me.

"Must I do everything myself," Brazial growled as he gripped the portcullis and attempted to pry the lattice apart with his bare hands. It groaned as a piece of the metal snapped off, leaving behind a small hole. If he replicated the feat enough times, he would eventually be able to create a gap wide enough for him to crawl through, but clearly he didn't have the patience for that method, because he squatted down and began to heave the portcullis up. The reinforcements attempted to stop him with arrows and spears, but the mortal weapons all bounced harmlessly off his skin. With a fierce cry, the god hefted the gate high above his head, and the Kaltan forces started to pour into the fortress.

CHAPTER 34

Shouts filled the quad as the Kaltans stormed the stronghold. The Athearian forces rushed forward to meet them in a furious clash of shields and steel. My shadow flickered with impatience, wanting to join in on the fun, but my gaze settled on the true prize of the battle. Brazial's muscles bulged beneath the weight of the portcullis, but from the savage grin that spread across his face, he had no intention of letting that gate drop until his entire army had passed beneath it. It would be quite an achievement to kill the golden wolf; a feat like that would spawn many ballads and legends, a victory worthy of the analogues of history.

Koven, killer of dragons and slayer of gods, the voice mused. *I like the sound of that.*

So did I.

I charged into battle with daggers in both hands, slashing and stabbing at any Kaltan that managed to evade my shadow, carving myself a path toward the gate. Shards of ice rained down like spears from above. My darkness rose up to form a shield above me as the cries of the dying filled the night. I continued to press forward, the darkness feasting upon my enemies with a hunger that could never be sated. With burning lungs and bloodied blades, I came face-to-face with the god of war. Although Brazial had just witnessed me kill more than a dozen of his warriors in order to reach him, he made no move to drop the gate.

"You think you can take me on, mortal?" He laughed, a bellow so deep and resounding it sounded as though it belonged to a chasm. "I am a god! My skin is harder than steel and my fists can shatter rock. You cannot kill me, but give me your best shot, and I will give you a glorious death in return. It will be my gift to you for your courage."

No mortal weapon could pierce his skin, but even a mountain would eventually whittle away if the wind chipped at it for long enough, and I had all the power of the night to draw from. The darkness burst out from me with a vengeance, shredding the portcullis into pieces of shrapnel and sending the god of war flying backward. With the gate now lying in ruins, I walked out of the stronghold, not bothering to look at the bodies that were bent into distorted shapes on the ground. The Kaltan forces had halted in their tracks, hesitant to attack as their god picked himself up off the ground with a startled expression. Brazial stared at me as though appraising me anew. Then he smiled in approval. "Give me your name, mortal, and I will make a toast in your honor at my victory feast."

"You may call me god-slayer." I flashed him a vicious smile of my own. "After tonight, that is what the world will know me as. I might as well start getting used to it."

Brazial wrenched a battle-ax from one of his men. He proceeded to test the sharpness of the edge by lopping off the soldier's head. With the weapon proven to be lethal, his eyes gleamed with anticipation as he turned to face me. "I thank you for the laughter that will fill my halls when I announce your name while drinking mead out of your skull."

He raced forward with frightening speed, but I felt no fear as the darkness converged on him, slamming him into the dirt with enough force that a crater formed in the ground. Brazial managed to rise back to his feet even as the darkness continued to press down on him. He took one slow step forward, and then another, and another. The standstill of the two armies fractured when the Athearians took advantage of the god's distraction by rushing out the shattered gateway to attack the invaders.

My confidence tipped over into frustration as Brazial managed to close the distance. He aimed his axe for my neck, and though my shadow managed to block the swing, it didn't block the fist that slipped beneath the darkness to connect with my gut. I landed on my back several paces away, gasping for air that refused to enter my lungs. "Come on, god-slayer," Brazial taunted, lifting his axe to rest against his shoulder. "At least give the minstrels a bit more material to work with before you meet your end. This will barely fill a single stanza."

With my teeth bared in a grimace, I forced the darkness to wrap around him, twisting around him like a snake, squeezing him with enough strength to liquefy a full-grown man. But he was not a man. He was a god, one built with sturdier bones than a fortress. He wrangled the wisps of shadow until he was free of their grasp. Fatigue was starting to creep into my muscles, sweat running in rivulets down my skin, and yet Brazial showed little sign of tiring himself. I lost sight of him between one blink and the next. Then he was suddenly lifting me up by the throat and slamming me down into the ground. Pain radiated across my scapula as the bone fractured. I slashed out with my dagger, intent on burying it inside his eye, but he merely twisted his head and the blade skittered harmlessly across his cheek instead. "Vassals of Celdric are such pesky creatures," he said, his hand tightening around my throat, robbing me of air. "Much like fleas, so small and yet so bothersome."

Blackness was beginning to creep into the edges of my vision, my body threatening to slip into unconsciousness. Then a silver snake wrapped around Brazial's neck. He released me and began clawing at his throat. I spluttered and gasped, my chest heaving. However, my relief gave way to irritation when I discovered that my savior was none other than Cahal Blackwood, wielding a Rasalan whip that he must have taken from an enforcer. The metal sizzled against Brazial's skin, weakening him and making him vulnerable to attack. It was a good idea, one that I was a little bitter not to have thought of myself. "Now, Wickwire!" Cahal shouted. "We only have one chance."

I plunged my dagger into the god's chest, aiming directly for his heart. The blade shattered upon impact, and any hope I had of defeating the god of war shattered along with it. Brazial proceeded to wrap his hand around the tail of the whip and wrench the weapon out of Cahal's grip. The sacred steel had left a mark on the god, but it was negligible, only a thin red line that looked more like a rash than a burn.

"You think a bit of hallowed steel can defeat me?" he shouted, and as he snatched ahold of my wrist, my bones crunched like walnut shells inside his grip. "I am a *god*, not a watered-down imitation so weak it can only handle a few drops of my divinity." He tossed me aside and then turned to regard Cahal with a menacing glare. "You are *my* vassal. After your display during the trials, I thought you understood that. I will give you one last chance to bend your knee to me. Join my side and you will know the sweet taste of victory. Refuse and you will die on your knees anyway."

Cahal unsheathed his sword and then spat upon the ground. "I'm a lord of Athearia, descendant of one of the great warrior houses, bound to the same oaths as my ancestors before me. I will die before I bow to the likes of you." The god of war collided with his vassal in a confusing haze of motion that only lasted a few seconds before Brazial buried his axe in Cahal's side, denting his armor so badly that it split open. His legs buckled as the jagged edges of the metal curled inward to gouge into his torso.

"And now you will die on your knees like a faithless dog brought to heel," Brazial declared, wrenching out the axe.

"Fuck you," Cahal snarled, even as he clutched at the gaping wound at his side. Brazial lifted his weapon for a killing blow, laughter rumbling out of him like thunder, and when I looked at that open mouth of his, I saw an opportunity. Maybe he was built more like a dragon than a wolf, hard on the outside but just as weak and vulnerable on the inside. My shadows rushed forward, determined to funnel down his gullet and rip his organs to shreds. However, Brazial noticed the attack coming. He swiped Cahal's sword from the ground and launched it through the air like a javelin. The blade buried itself so deep in my thigh that the tip emerged out the other side. The shadows under my control were banished beneath the fire of agony.

I screamed as blood blossomed around the blade like a flower, and while I blinked away the tears that blurred my vision, I became acutely aware of the battle that was raging outside the stronghold. Men and women climbed over the bodies of their fallen comrades with snarls of fury on their faces, their boots splashing in pools of blood as they fought one another, and somewhere at the very top of the Irashkai mountains, Amari severed a tangled ball of thread and the soldiers continued to die in droves. This was anarchy manifested in physical form. It was violence and disorder, and it was—

Glorious, the voice said, but its bloodlust was fighting a losing battle against my pain, and with its grip on me loosened, all I could think was that I really had gone insane. What other explanation was there for me challenging the *literal god of war* to a duel to the death? I gave in to its dark desires so easily, my head filled with notions of grandeur and my heart yearning for violence in the same way my lungs yearned for air. I couldn't stay here. The city would soon fall, and if I lingered too long, I would fall with it. I needed to find Emrys; we needed to flee this place while we still could.

A reanimated corpse diverted away from the battlefield to leap onto Brazial. The god threw the creature off and stomped on its head until its skull caved in. While he was occupied, I attempted to crawl toward the gateway, which was a difficult task between my shattered wrist and my punctured leg. I didn't manage to make it very far before Brazial's form loomed above me, a fearsome figure built of scars and thick cords of muscle. "Where are you going, god-slayer?" he said, wrenching the sword out of my thigh. "I need a song to fill my mess halls, and this ballad of ours is yet unfinished."

My mind scrambled for a way to get out of this alive, but Brazial was too fast, too strong, too powerful. He was war incarnate, and death was the only thing capable of defeating him. Unfortunately, Ashearan was hundreds of miles away, content to abandon his people to Brazial's wrath. The god might have been hateful and cruel, but there was no denying that Athearia was in desperate need of his power. It almost made me wonder if maybe it wasn't grief over the loss of his sister, or petty vengeance against Cahal Blackwood, that kept him from fighting. Maybe he wanted to remind this kingdom just how quickly it would crumble without him there to protect it.

You don't need him, the voice practically purred into my ear. *The power of death is already here. You wear it around your neck.*

I grasped the emerald ring, and my heart leaped as my fingers brushed against the black string of fate that was wrapped around it. Amari had gifted me with the power to vanquish my enemies, but when I remembered the song that Akira had sung to me, my heart sank back down like a stone inside my chest. I needed to knot the string with blood and throw it into a fire, yet Brazial stood above me practically unharmed, as though I hadn't blasted him across the battlefield and broken my blade against his skin. There wasn't a single drop of golden ichor in sight, and if I hadn't managed to get him to bleed after all that, I wasn't going to be able to do so now. Escape was my only option.

I tried to call upon the darkness to swallow me whole and drag me into the shadow domain, but then Brazial pressed his boot to the wound on my leg. I cried out as white-hot pain seared through me, and my shadow shuddered before going still. In the distance, a crow gave a sharp cry. An omen of death. I was certain it was coming to claim me. However, Brazial froze as though he thought the omen was intended for him. Another caw sounded, and then another, and another until their cries drowned out everything else. A flock of crows flew over the battlefield, dozens of them, hundreds of them, enough to blot out the stars of the night sky. All the dead soldiers turned an ashen shade of gray, their limbs twitching as life was breathed back into their bodies. This level of power could only mean one thing. Ashearan, the god of death, was riding into battle.

Brazial's eyes darkened to a molten shade of gold and a feral grin spread across his face. He stepped away from me, an axe in one hand and a sword in the other, eager to fight an opponent worthy of his sweat. A strange stallion cantered toward the stronghold. Its coat was stained with algae and its mane was dripping wet, its hair matted with seaweed as though it had just emerged from the depths of a lake. A cloaked figure sat atop the steed, his face concealed beneath his hood, the pommel of a large sword peeking out from behind one shoulder.

Brazial dropped to his knees and severed the horse's front legs. However, instead of tumbling to the ground, the creature merely dissolved into a puddle of water. Before it disappeared completely, Ashearan leaped off its back and landed in a crouch. He reached for the weapon strapped to his back, and as the god of war pivoted and prepared to launch another attack, Ashearan gave a mighty thrust of his sword. The blade pierced Brazial's abdomen. The god peered down at it in shock as golden ichor leaked out of him. Ashearan yanked the blade back out, and with a decisive swing, he separated Brazial's head from the rest of his body.

The great golden wolf of Kalta disintegrated into a pillar of shimmering dust.

No mortal weapon could pierce through Brazial's skin, which meant that sword was no mortal weapon. The warrior threw back his hood, revealing that it wasn't the god of death who had ridden onto the battlefield like a vengeful spirit. Rin Marcaida stared back at me, having returned from the land of the dead, and it seemed like the sword was not the only prize that he'd brought back with him. His steed re-formed from the puddle of water on the ground, giving itself a firm shake that sent droplets splattering in every direction. "I assume that if you're here then your liege lord is here as well," Rin said, his tone eerily calm, like killing a god was a common occurrence, hardly worthy of his acknowledgment. "Inform him of my arrival. Tell him that I have what he asked for."

"Where are you going?" I said as he remounted his stallion.

"A nearby farmer told me that the Kaltans have grown bold in the face of their recent victories. It's time to remind them why widows weep and the voices of men tremble when they dare to utter my family's name." The horse reared up onto its hind legs, letting out a fearsome screech that did not belong to a creature of this world. Then Rin galloped into battle, bringing a battalion of undead soldiers with him, and in the wake of Brazial's death, he turned the tides of this war.

CHAPTER 35

The remedial tent was already overcrowded by the time I was carried in on a stretcher. The ground was stacked with so many injured and dying soldiers that the bone-menders barely had enough space to walk between them. Only a handful of god-marked healers were present, their expressions weighed down with exhaustion. I watched as one healer walked past the groaning man next to me, who had been burned beyond recognition, his skin charred to the point where I was surprised he was still breathing. The healer spared him only a cursory glance before abandoning him to his fate, the cost of saving him too great when there were dozens of others in need of help. If she were truly merciful, she would have plunged a knife into the man's throat and put him out of his misery. I didn't even warrant a cursory glance until I caught ahold of her hand. "Please—" I began to say, but then her eyes darted to the bandaged wound on my thigh and her gaze hardened.

"You will not die any time soon," she said abruptly, cutting me off. "A bone-mender will see to you shortly and stitch your wounds."

She wrenched her hand from my grip before I could ask her to send word to the young lord of House Hardcastle that I urgently needed to speak with him. I lowered myself back down to the floor with a grimace, clasping my shattered wrist to my chest. I would have to wait for one of the bone-menders to pass on my request, but as I glanced around the crowded tent, I wasn't hopeful that I would be attended to any time soon. The man next to me let out another pained groan. His body was the color of embers found at the bottom of a dying hearth. A bone-mender wouldn't be able to save him. They would just let him suffer until death came to claim him. I listened to his tortured cries for over an hour before I did the decent thing and jammed my dagger into the side of his neck. He exhaled one last strangled breath before finally falling silent.

"I was wondering whether or not you would do it." My head snapped up to find Cahal looming above me. I didn't know how long he had been watching, but he did so with the eyes of a hawk. Apparently, he was important enough to warrant a healer's touch, because he stood before me unharmed, his ruined armor having been traded in for a clean tunic. It was dyed an expensive shade of purple, the color of his house. "I was just speaking with Emrys. He sent me to come get you."

Cahal fell quiet for a moment, as though hoping the silence would unnerve me.

It did.

"I told him that you were slipping into madness," he said, and suddenly it felt like I was falling off the battlement wall again, except this time there was no shadow to catch me. If wielded correctly, a secret could be far more dangerous than a blade, and mine was out. "He claimed not to believe me, but considering the extent of his foresight, I think he's full of shit. I think he knows exactly what you are. He's just choosing to ignore it."

Although the statement made me uneasy, I was careful not to show it. "You say that as though you haven't threatened my life more than a dozen times. It's hardly a sign of madness for me to do it to you just once . . . If I woke up one morning and suddenly found your company agreeable, now *that* would be insane."

He gave a humorless snort, unconvinced by the lie. "Violence in and of itself is not madness. It's an inability to control the violence. You forget, Wickwire, that I've been to Ismadore. I have walked its forsaken halls, and I recognized the look in your eyes tonight. It might be gone now, but it will come back. It always does. If Emrys wants to wait for you to turn on him, so be it, but I won't have Serenity suffer the same fate. You will stay away from her, or I'll make you wish you had."

You should have ripped out his tongue when you had the chance, the voice muttered.

I ignored it. In fact, I was quite determined to ignore it for the rest of my life.

Cahal didn't turn to leave. Instead, he grabbed hold of the nearest healer. She just so happened to be the same one who'd ignored me when I first entered the remedial tent. My eyebrows shot up in disbelief when Cahal commanded her to heal me. Although I remembered her, there was no recognition in her eyes when she appraised my wounds again. Apparently, the lovely happenstance of our first meeting had not made an impression on her. "His wounds are not critical, my lord, and my power is nearly depleted," she protested. "A bone-mender will attend to him."

"Heal him," Cahal ordered, his tone indicating that this wasn't a matter up for debate. "I will not ask a third time."

Her expression hardened beneath the threat. "I'm not a mule to be whipped into submission, nor am I a soldier to be commanded. I am a vassal of Sheara, and her doctrines regarding the treatment of the wounded during wartime are quite clear. It is better to save ten men than expend all my energy saving only one. This man does not need a healer's touch in order to survive. A bone-mender will see to him."

She attempted to walk away, but Cahal didn't loosen his grip on her. "I'm going to be honest with you, I don't like this man very much. Quite frankly, if it was up to me, I would do the world a favor and snap his neck." She blinked, startled by the confession. While his words didn't surprise me, I did think it was a strange thing to say when he was trying to convince her to help me. "I'm not asking you to heal him out of a personal favor. It is better to save ten men than expend all your energy saving only one, yet it is also better to expend all your energy saving one commander than it is to divide it among ten men. Your doctrine allows for you to make an exception."

She stared down at me with a healthy dose of skepticism. "He doesn't look like a commander."

"No," Cahal agreed. "But, unfortunately, he is vital to the war effort. I need him healed, and I need him healed now."

She huffed out a breath of annoyance but did as he asked. She crouched down beside me and I gritted my teeth, stifling my moan as her power flowed into me, snapping my wrist back together and closing the gaping wound on my thigh. When she peeled her hands away from me, her complexion was pale and her lips were starting to take on a blue tinge. Her eyelids dropped down in a heavy blink like she was fighting the urge to fall asleep. Then she slipped into unconsciousness. I caught her as she fell forward and carefully lowered her head to the floor. Fortunately, there was no silver streak in her hair or new wrinkles at the corners of her eyes. She was just exhausted.

"Come with me," Cahal said, leading the way out the remedial tent. The night was beginning to fade into the early hours of the morning, and with the battle over, the stronghold had mostly fallen quiet. Cahal veered toward one of the turrets. The guards stood to attention upon his arrival. He threw open the door and I followed him into one of the rooms on the ground floor.

Banners bearing the Blackwood crest decorated the walls, along with several paintings depicting historic battles where cities burned like pyres and blood flooded fields like rain during storm season. A table was positioned in the center of the room with a large map of the continent rolled across its surface. Wooden pieces were placed on top of it, tracking troop movements. Emrys was standing next to the hearth. When the door opened, he turned to greet me with a weary smile. He held his silver-wood staff in one hand, and a large sword was strapped to his back, which was the same sword that Rin had wielded when he slew the god of war. That was the weapon he had stolen from the Shadowlands. Ashanti. The sword that was sharp enough to cut through anything, even the fabric that separated this realm and the next.

Think of its power, the voice whispered. *The power to fell even the mightiest of gods. The power to cheat death itself. It could be yours to wield. You need only take it.*

My fingers itched with the desire to touch it, so I shoved my hands into my pockets as though that could somehow cure me of the sensation.

It did not.

"I still think you should leave him in Ismadore," Cahal muttered before slamming the door shut, leaving the two of us alone. The comment hung like a noose in the air, tightening around my throat and making me wonder whether it would be easier to breathe if I allowed excuses and denials to roll off my tongue in order to save myself.

"We should go," Emrys said, handing me a pair of black leather gloves. He was already wearing a pair of his own. "Dawn will soon be upon us, and I would like to free Sheara from her prison before news of Rin's return reaches Celdric's ears."

My hands slunk out of their hiding place from inside my pockets to slip into the gloves. I flexed my fingers, hating the constraints of the fabric, but Ismadore was crafted almost entirely from Rasalan steel, so it was a necessary precaution. Emrys also handed me a supply satchel, which was mostly empty barring a water flagon and some food rations. He didn't address Cahal's comment, and I didn't know whether or not to feel relieved as I commanded the shadows to open up like a door.

We emerged on the outskirts of the ruined city once more, the world fading to a dull shade of gray. I stared at the horizon, knowing that across the barren wasteland was a lake, and inside that lake was the gateway that connected to Ismadore. Perhaps we could make it there before dawn, but we were going to have to hurry. Emrys must have been of the same mind, because he set off at a fast pace.

Typically, silence didn't bother me, but the endless dunes started to make me feel just as desolate as they were when Emrys didn't speak to me the entire time. Perhaps he was angry at me for keeping the secret to myself, or maybe he feared that I would fly into a fit of homicidal rage the moment he brought up the subject. I hoped it was anger rather than fear, but the only way to know for sure was to ask him. I mulled over the best way to start the conversation, but I wasn't a politician or a poet, gifted in the art of spinning words. I grazed my fingers over my wrist, the one that had been touched by the red string of fate, and it gave me the courage to finally force the confession out my mouth.

"I hear voices," I said, the admission earning me a sideways glance from Emrys. "Well, one voice, actually. It's violent, and cruel, and power hungry. I try not to listen to it, but it's a bit difficult to ignore when it's inside my head." When he didn't seem surprised, I heaved a heavy sigh. "But, of course, you already knew about that."

"We have had this conversation before," he admitted, "in my dreams. A dozen different times, a dozen different ways. Yes, I know about your voice."

"You could have said something," I grumbled.

"You could have as well," he countered. As we crested the dune, the lake finally became visible, appearing before my eyes like an oasis. A fine mist rolled over the colorless stretch of water, while dark shadows prowled just beneath the surface. "I'm not going to let Ismadore be your fate, Koven. We all have dark impulses—yours are just a little darker than most. You have a harder battle, but you're a stronger fighter than you give yourself credit for."

A comforting warmth encircled my wrist. He had known about the voice all this time and yet he still chose to bind his soul with mine, accepting everything that was good about me, and everything that was bad. Emrys started the trek down the sand dune toward the lake. I quickly followed him. "What dark impulses do you have?" I asked, my tone only half teasing. I doubted he had a voice in his head that urged him to gouge out eyes and paint the walls red with blood, but his comment had piqued my curiosity.

"I have the ability to shape my own future." He hesitated as though he had already shared more than he ought to. After a moment, he added, "I could damn this world in exchange for everything I have ever wanted, but then I would only be using my foresight to serve myself. I refuse to walk down that road, but sometimes I let myself dream of what would happen if I did."

His answer caused my curiosity to grow. Emrys was the heir to one of the richest families on the continent. If there was something he wanted that badly, surely he would be able to buy it? His expression became tinted with what looked like shame, and before I had the opportunity to ask him about it, he said, "I know that I shouldn't do it. Even if I convince myself that it's only a dream, the temptation remains even after I wake. That's the problem with power, and desire, and greed. It corrupts so easily. You would do well to remember that lesson."

His words sounded like any other warning a seer might issue, a piece of wisdom delivered in the form of a story, but the timing of it struck me as a little too convenient. My clothes were still stained with the blood of that lesson, my body still throbbing from freshly healed wounds, and then the realization hit me. He was the one who sent me to the gatehouse. He'd orchestrated the whole thing by forcing me into a situation where I would give in to the madness that tainted my blood.

"That was a lesson?" I said, my anger leaking into my voice. "I somehow convinced myself that I could fight a *god.* I broke several bones and almost got myself killed!"

Emrys winced as I listed my injuries, but he didn't look nearly as remorseful about it as he should have. "If it was a pleasant experience, it wouldn't make for a very good lesson. You needed to know that the darkness inside you cannot be controlled. It's an infection and pain is only a temporary treatment; it's not a cure. If you give in to it enough times, then eventually there will be no snapping back out of it. You will end up on a path that can only end in carnage and ruin."

The lesson was a simple one. The darkness was terrifying. *I* was terrifying. That was an easy enough thing to understand; it did not merit such extreme teaching methods. "What would you have done if I actually died?" I demanded.

He rolled his eyes like I was merely being dramatic. "That wasn't going to happen, Koven."

"But what if it did?"

He tilted back his head as though trying to seek refuge among the stars, but there were no stars here. He heaved a sigh. "I suppose I would've felt bad about it."

"You would've felt bad about it?" I repeated incredulously.

"Fine, I would've felt very bad about it. Happy?"

"No, Rys. I'm not happy. My best friend manipulated me, and apparently, he would only feel *very bad* if he got me killed in the process."

He stopped in his tracks, whirling on me with an annoyed expression. "Do you honestly think it wouldn't devastate me if you died?" he snapped, the vehemence in his tone taking me by surprise. "You know what else would devastate me? Sitting back and doing nothing while I watched you twist into a person I no longer recognized." Tugging on the chain around my neck, he pulled the emerald ring out from beneath the collar of my tunic. "And don't forget that the whole reason we're friends in the first place is because I manipulated you into stealing this. That is what seers do; they manipulate. They look at omens, and signs, and futures, and they use that information to steer others toward a certain course of action. But what I did tonight was not for me; it was for you. You needed to see what you would become if you allowed the darkness inside your head to infect all that is good inside your heart."

He prodded a finger against my chest, his stormy gray eyes freezing me in place. "Succumb to madness—let the violence twist you into a monster and have the world spit upon your name—or don't trade your principles for power and instead spend your every waking breath fighting the temptation. The choice is yours. I'm tied to you either way."

He continued down the dune, the sand shifting and molding beneath his feet, while I remained rooted in place, staring after him. He shot an impatient look over his shoulder once he reached the bottom, and as the moon of the outside world waned and exhaustion threatened to turn my feet to stone, I knew that we didn't have time to waste. I hurried down and waded out into the lake. Although the water didn't seep into my trousers to wet my skin, it still managed to drag against my legs, making slogging through it a challenge. Fortunately, the lake was shallow and its depths never made it past my knees.

"Fighting it with my every waking breath sounds like a lot of effort." I intended it to be a joke to lighten the mood, but Emrys didn't laugh.

His tone was morose as he said, "I know what it's like. I fight my own battle, a different one, but a battle nonetheless." The mist thinned to reveal a swirl of darkness skulking over some of the bones that littered the bottom of the lake, its dark tendrils spilling into the eye socket of a skull only to slither out its mouth a moment later. Then the mist solidified again, concealing the boneyard beneath its haze. "I wish I could say that it gets easier, but that hasn't been my experience." His expression softened when he looked at me. "But there are people in this life who make the fight bearable."

The comment was almost enough to banish the last of my anger. I didn't want to have this darkness that festered inside me to twist me into its puppet, but I also didn't want Emrys to do the same. "My life is my own, Rys. While I can understand why you did what you did, it can't become a habit. You cannot use your foresight to manipulate me every time something happens in the future that isn't to your liking."

"I always respect your choices, Koven, and I don't like a lot of them, but I let you make them. You can choose to let the darkness consume you; all I did was show you what that choice would actually cost you. Your life is your own and you can live it as you please. I might prefer the person you are now, but I've already decided there is no version of you that I can't accept."

The mist parted once more to reveal the lighthouse that marked Ismadore's shoreline. This one had toppled over, its lantern room partially submerged in the water and its stone walls dark with moss. Emrys disappeared from sight as he touched one of the columns that held up the storm roof. I didn't know whether he'd meant his words to comfort me or unnerve me, because they'd somehow managed to do both. I peered down at my reflection in the water, allowing my mind to warp the image into something darker, something unrestrained, and ruthless, and cruel. I didn't understand how such a twisted reflection didn't horrify Emrys, because it certainly horrified me.

CHAPTER 36

The first light of dawn spilled over the sea, its glow softening the fierce waves and frothing foam. As I admired the view from the top of the lighthouse, I wondered if this was how the god of the sun showed the world all the devotion he had for his wife. I eventually peeled my gaze from the sea to scan the shoreline. There weren't many patrols this far outside civilization. The fortress itself was considered impenetrable, and the journey to reach the remote island was fraught with peril. My eyes settled on a sea serpent that had washed up upon the rocks, its body long enough to wrap around a ship several times over. Yet, despite its impressive size, something else had managed to bite off chunks from its midsection, leaving behind gaping holes that showed off the creature's rib cage. The decay of its flesh tainted the air, attracting crabs and gulls to feast upon its remains.

I started down the spiral staircase that led to the pebbled beach. The prison loomed in the distance, built upon hard rock and constructed from cold gray steel. An ominous shiver traveled down my spine at the sight of it. If the church ever deemed me insane, this was where they would drag me off to, left to rot in a cell like one of the carcasses that had been spat out by the sea. With the wind whistling in my ears, I trekked toward the prison. Once I was closer to the outer walls, I crouched down behind a cluster of rocks to scout the way ahead, searching for prying eyes from atop the watchtowers, but it was a struggle just to keep my eyes open.

"Perhaps we should wait until nightfall?" I suggested.

Emerging from the protection of the rocks, Emrys threw caution to the howling wind as he headed for the prison. I balked at his recklessness. "What are you doing?" I hissed, keeping my voice low so as not to attract any unwanted attention in our direction.

"Fate is on our side, Koven. We will cross this land unseen. Amari will make it so." He didn't bother to look back as he said it. He expected me to follow him. I was almost tempted to stay behind if for no other reason than to prove him wrong, but my feet moved of their own accord, jogging to catch up with him.

"It's sunrise. I'll be next to useless in a fight," I warned him.

"Then we should avoid getting into a fight," he retorted.

I peered apprehensively at the watchtowers. No alarms had been sounded, but that didn't mean we couldn't be spotted at any moment. "This is unwise. We should find somewhere to camp for a few hours and get some rest. You've been awake all night. You're just as exhausted as I am. Don't pretend otherwise."

"Exhaustion is a close companion of mine," he said dismissively. He handed me his staff to hold and then he reached over his shoulder. He pulled the sword from its sheath, revealing the strange runes carved along its fuller. It didn't appear to be any sharper than another sword, yet I stared at its edge, mesmerized. It was a large weapon, one that required two hands to wield, and Emrys seemed to struggle with the weight of it. I tightened my grip on the silver-wood staff, yearning instead for the distinctive heft of steel. "If it's too heavy for you, I can take it," I offered, my tone nonchalant, as though it didn't matter to me either way.

He pinned me with a weighted look. "I might trust you with my life, Koven, but I don't trust you with this. I won't give it to you, but you are stronger than me. There wouldn't be much I could do if you decided to take it."

Do it, the voice demanded. *That is a sword fit for a god. Claim it for yourself. Make its power your own.*

I averted my gaze, ignoring the way my palms turned slick with sweat inside my gloves.

Emrys walked the perimeter of the wall until he finally came to a stop. He must have found the section that he was looking for, because he hefted up the sword and hacked into it. I expected to hear the clang of clashing metal, but the sword passed through it as though it were made of water. I watched in astonishment as Emrys carved out a small hole. However, with how thick the wall was, the block was difficult to move. My muscles strained with effort as the block slowly inched inward. It eventually crashed to the floor on the other side, a sound that made me grimace. I cast another nervous glance at the closest watchtower. When no guards came storming down to check on the commotion, I sent a silent prayer of gratitude to Amari.

With his narrow shoulders and wiry frame, Emrys managed to crawl through the gap with ease. It was a little more challenging for me, and in a moment of inattention, the side of my forearm grazed the metal of the wall, which seared into my skin like a hot poker. I muttered a slew of curses under my breath when I emerged out the other side. Everything inside the prison had a metallic sheen. The walls. The ceiling. The corridors. I became all too aware of my vulnerability as my shadow grew lifeless upon the ground.

Emrys led the way down a set of stairs, heading for the dungeons, where the most dangerous prisoners were located. My mouth turned dry as I recalled the horror stories of the deranged souls that dwelled where not even the sunlight dared to touch. Without Celdric's blood to aid me, I saw nothing but darkness as I peered down into its depths. Tapping the silver-wood staff twice on the ground, the crystal nestled at the top of it flickered to life, emitting a white glow. Most of the prisoners were asleep in their cells, curled up on musty blankets on the floor. The few that were already awake shied away from the light as though it hurt their eyes, twisting in on themselves like an injured animal that had come to associate light with danger and pain. My feet came to a grinding halt when I recognized one of the faces trapped behind the bars.

Grayson Blackwood, Cahal's older brother, squinted at me from the shadows of his cell, his cheeks sunken and his eyes encircled by dark rings. The last time that I saw him, he had been adorned in fine clothes, standing tall with all the self-assurance that came with being the eldest son of a great noble house. Dressed in the gray garments of an outcast, he barely resembled the proud man he once was. One of his ankles was chained to the wall, the Rasalan shackles causing blisters to appear atop scabs that had yet to heal. I had not been on the guest list for his wedding, but the tragic story of what transpired had reached my ears not soon after it happened. Ashearan's blood in his veins had caused him to go on a murderous rampage, killing his bride and several others in attendance. Yet, as I looked at him now, I couldn't see the insanity that was supposedly rooted within him. His eyes were that of a broken man, not a madman.

"I never thought the two of you would seek out a visitation with me," he said, his voice dry. "House Blackwood and House Hardcastle have never been the closest of friends, but no one ever comes to see me except my brother, so it's not like I'm in any position to be picky. Let me formally welcome you to my humble abode. I would offer you some refreshments, but"—he jingled the chain around his ankle—"I'm a little tied up at the moment."

"I'm sorry about what happened," Emrys said, and Grayson responded with a derisive snort.

"The gods giveth and the gods taketh away," he said, giving a one-shouldered shrug. "You know, being locked up in here gives a man a lot of time to think. I don't even know how long I've been here."

"Almost a year," Emrys informed him.

Grayson made a pensive sound from the back of his throat. "It feels like a lot longer than that . . . does Reverend Richards still preach at the Cenobium?"

My mind conjured up an image of the reverend's head atop a stone altar. "He was still preaching when we were there," I said, which was true enough.

"There's a sermon of his that keeps replaying in my mind. The one of how man first came to be tainted and our souls damned to eternal torment. Maylore, father of the faithless, looked upon the world with jealousy, for the gods created man, and man in turn worshipped the gods as their creators. He sought to claim the souls of these creations for himself, and so one night he snuck out of the Shadowlands and filled a mortal woman with his seed. The conjugation spawned a baby boy who was said to be so beautiful the sun itself dimmed in his presence. Maylore was clever, for he knew that gifting his son with such beauty would hide the darkness that festered within. The gods instructed the mortal mother to cast the babe into a fire, warning her that he would be the ruin of humankind, but as she gazed into the child's innocent eyes, she could not bring herself to see the corruption that tainted his heart.

"The boy grew into a man, and the man had children of his own, and those children had children, until all of humankind had been infected by Maylore's seed. We were children of the gods, but now we were children of the corrupter as well. However, Reverend Richards didn't blame the babe for the downfall of man. He blamed the mother, for she knew the divine light and wisdom of the gods, and yet she willfully turned her back on them. She was the first follower of Maylore, and her one act of defiance damned us all. Now, he has a claim on each and every one of our souls, able to twist us into kindling to be used in his firepits. A lack of faith is what led to man's corruption, and therefore, it is only with faith that we can be cured of it. That is why the only unforgivable sin is that of disobedience."

Grayson paused for a moment, as though he were lost in the memory. Then his lips curved into a disturbing smile and I caught a glimpse of the madness lurking within. "But how can the gods be our salvation if they themselves are the disease? When their blood touches our lips, it doesn't cure us. It only makes us sicker. They like to blame that part on Maylore, too, claiming that insanity is what happens when his corruption taints the divine blood in our veins, but I see through their lies. They suckle at the bosom of violence and bloodlust, unrestrained in their vices, and yet they punish their vassals for the same sins that they themselves commit. The gods are here walking among us, and yet Maylore hides himself in myth and legend. He isn't the corruption; they are. The gods cannot be our salvation if they are also our downfall."

"We should go," Emrys whispered to me, but it felt wrong to leave Grayson like that, chained like an animal with not even the sky to keep him company. I reached for the aster flower that was tucked inside my pocket, the one that had fallen from Serenity's hair back in the sanctuary, knowing that it would mean more to him than it ever could to me. I could still picture what Aster looked like, because she and Serenity were nearly spitting images of each other, both sharing the same dark hair and kind eyes. She must have made a beautiful bride.

I stuck my arm through the bars, unfurling my fingers to reveal the aster flower within. His face dropped at the sight of it. The shackle around his ankle kept him restrained when he attempted to lurch forward. He struggled against the chain, desperately grasping at the flower, but it was still out of his reach. I pressed myself up against the bars, and a hiss of pain escaped from behind my clenched teeth as the Rasalan steel burned into my cheek. As soon as Grayson managed to grab the flower, I jerked away from the prison bars and the searing pain faded to a dull throb. Although the petals were crushed and wilted, he cradled it as though it were the only thing he had left in the world. Dropping to his knees, he broke down into thick, heavy sobs. As I followed Emrys deeper into the dungeon, the echoes of his grief followed me, and I couldn't help but think how sad it was that not even love was a strong enough shield to withstand the might of madness.

The last cell was unoccupied. The gate creaked when it was swung open, as though it had long since fallen into disuse. Emrys knelt upon the ground, his gloved fingers gliding over the surface until he found a nick in the floor. It looked to be just a small blemish, one that was almost imperceptible to the eye. "This is a blood lock, one that only a specific bloodline can open," Emrys said. His expression was shadowed beneath the glowing light as he looked up at me. "Your bloodline is the key, Koven."

I crouched down next to him, examining the tiny hole in the floor with curiosity. "Why my bloodline?" I asked, confused.

"Beneath this cell, there is a hidden prison designed to contain the gods. The weapons given to enforcers are made of a weakened compound, containing only small shards of Rasalan steel, enough to cripple a vassal but not enough to harm the gods. The shackles in the cells down below are made of pure Rasalan steel, capable of restraining even the strength of Brazial. Your ancestors have warred with gods before. The architect of this place decided that your family could be trusted with the secret of this prison, but time erodes everything, even blood and memory."

Considering the fact that my mother was a pauper and my father was a crook, while the gods lived in cities of marble and walked streets paved with gold, things probably had not worked out well for my ancestors. Yet here I was about to make an enemy of the god of mischief, following dutifully in the footsteps of my forebearers. With a sigh, I unsheathed a dagger and made a small incision on my forearm. I let my blood drip into the nick on the floor. A mechanical sound grated against my ears, and the ground began to shift beneath me. A segment of the floor lowered to reveal a set of stairs that led into a deeper chamber beneath the dungeons.

I descended the stairs into the cramped space below. The air was stale and warm, like it had been breathed too many times without the possibility of escape. The prison cells took up most of the space, and from behind one set of bars, golden eyes glowed like two candles in the night.

I moved closer, and the light from the staff spilled into the cell to illuminate Sheara's face. Although I knew that her host was in her third decade, the goddess looked much younger than that, possessing a soft face and delicate features, her flaxen hair disheveled but bright. She was still in the same orange dress that she wore during the trials, though the fabric was torn in places and flecked with golden ichor. Shackles bound both her hands and feet, the touch of the metal causing her skin to bubble and blister. Judging from the fading bruises and scabbed-over cuts that littered her body, the restraints had managed to render her powerless, making her unable to heal herself.

Sheara stared at me with a startled expression, the despair in her eyes quickly replaced by a wild and frantic sense of hope. "Please," she pleaded, her voice cracking. "Please, free me from this place." When Emrys stepped into view, tears of relief began to slip down her cheeks, because whereas I was a stranger to her, she knew him. After all, she had helped to create him. She had laid her hands upon his mother's belly and nine months later he was born.

Emrys lifted up the sword and slashed at the prison bars, one strike aimed high and another aimed low. The bars clattered to the floor. He stepped inside, and using the sword, he cut Sheara free from her manacles.

"That sword," she said, staring at the weapon in awe. "I've never seen anything like it before. Where did you get it?"

"A relic of time long past," he said cryptically, an answer that revealed absolutely nothing and yet would be expected coming from a seer. As he guided Sheara out of the cell, ushering her up the stairs, my eyes lingered on the shackles, which lay in broken pieces upon the ground. They were made with pure Rasalan steel, potent enough to rob even a god of their divinity—a useful thing to have on hand once Celdric went looking for vengeance after his scheme was exposed. I shoved the chains into my satchel. I was just about to leave when a piece of ginger-colored silk caught my attention. It had been bundled up and discarded in the corner, lying forgotten between stale loaves of bread and bags of dried figs. Sheara must have used the fabric to attend to her wounds, because it gleamed with golden ichor. I shoved it into my satchel as well before following the goddess.

After I climbed up the stairs, the hidden door automatically closed behind me, and I couldn't help but wonder what sort of man had been able to create such a contraption. As Emrys led the way back through the dungeons, I realized that this was almost over. Sheara would be free, and with the god of war now dead and Kalta deprived of its last dragon, perhaps the northern kingdom would reconsider its position in this conflict. Besides, once Damien broke the curse on Lios and Tammearia, the two of them would likely have other things on their mind than war. An armistice could be brokered and peace would settle over the continent once more. It had all gone exactly as Emrys had planned.

However, when we passed Grayson Blackwood's cell on the way back, everything began to unravel. Something inside him became unhinged as he noticed the golden gleam of Sheara's eyes. The chain around his ankle grew taut as he threw himself at her, his lips twisting into a savage snarl. "You're poison!" he screamed. "You and the rest of your kind. I hope crows feast on your flesh and pick your eyeballs from your skull. I pray for the day that you all drown in a river of your own blood."

While his insults couldn't do any harm on their own, the commotion served to rouse the other prisoners. They, too, began to scream and rattle their chains. It seemed that any luck Amari had sent to aid us on this quest had finally run out. The sound of boots began to pound against the floor above as guards rushed to check on the prisoners. Although exhaustion had set in to my limbs, I forced my legs to move. I sprinted for the exit, bursting out the dungeon and nearly crashing straight into a pair of guards in the process. I acted on instinct, smashing the staff into the face of the closest one. She reeled back, blood pouring from her nose. The second guard reached for his weapon, but before he could put it to use, I rammed the staff between his legs. His eyes bulged as he doubled over, clutching at his valuables with a grunt of pain. I whacked him on the back of his head, knocking him out cold. Wielding the staff like a bat, I cracked it against the first guard, the wood snapping upon impact. She dropped to the floor along with the top half of the staff.

Emrys joined me in the corridor. Annoyance sparked in his eyes as he stared at the fractured pieces of his prized staff. He should be panicking right now. We had been discovered. We needed to leave, and yet he was just standing there as though we weren't about to be overwhelmed in a matter of moments. I didn't even know what the plan was for getting off the island. It probably involved commandeering a ship from the docks, a feat that would be near impossible now that they knew we were here. Discarding the other half of the broken staff, I armed myself with a pair of daggers. "I'll hold them off as long as I can," I told him.

Emrys, however, didn't seem to share my sense of urgency, even as more shouts echoed from deeper within the prison. A dozen uniformed men and women came careening down the far end of the hallway. My daggers wouldn't be enough. I needed something more. My gaze settled on the sword strapped to Emrys's back. With a weapon like that, I could fell several guards in a single swoop, splitting them open with the force of lightning splintering the sky.

"Give me the sword," I demanded, and he arched an eyebrow as though asking if I really wanted to have this conversation with him. "Give. It. To. Me."

He folded his arms across his chest. "No."

He did say that if I wanted it, I need only take it from him. He would be angry with me, but he would be alive, and I didn't see any other option for getting out of this situation without it. This wasn't for power; it was for survival. He had to know that, and yet his expression hardened when I reached for it. "Don't touch it," he said, his tone making it clear that it wasn't a request. It was an order, reminding me that he was more than just my friend, he was a lord, one that I had sworn to serve. I might not have said a formal oath bound in blood, but I held it in my heart all the same.

I froze, my gaze heavy on his, my hand hovering inches away from the leather-wrapped handle. "You're condemning us to death."

"Do not touch it," he repeated, and though it went against every instinct I had, I slowly lowered my hand. The guards were nearly upon us. I shifted to stand in front of Emrys as they raised their weapons. However, they all came skidding to an abrupt halt, their mouths falling open in shock as Sheara stepped forward to greet them. The guards swiftly dropped to their knees beneath her golden gaze, bowing their heads in reverence.

"Holy One, we had received news of your death," one of the guards said, her voice filled with awe. "Yet, here you stand before us. I know your face. I bore witness to your ascension over ten years ago."

"It seems that the continent has fallen prey to one of Celdric's schemes," Sheara said, and despite her unkempt appearance, she attempted to retain some her divine dignity as she held her head high. "I am very much alive, as you can see."

"Blessed be Sheara!" the guard proclaimed, reveling in the miracle of her return. The other guards were quick to repeat the chant.

"The goddess requires a ship and a crew to ferry her back to the mainland along with her two faithful servants," Emrys declared. "The continent weeps beneath the blood of an unjust war, and her presence will be a much-needed light in this time of great darkness." He shot me a sideways look, lowering his voice to a whisper as he muttered, "That speech would have sounded better with a staff in my hand."

"Forgive me for trying to save your life," I said dryly.

"You're forgiven," he replied just as dryly.

"I retract my apology."

"It has already been given and accepted. You can't retract it."

I glared at him, annoyed, and the edges of his lips curved in the faintest hint of amusement.

"If you're starting to have regrets, I could sever it, you know. The sword would be able to cut through the red string that binds us."

If not for the teasing lilt to his voice, I would have taken that as a threat. "It's too late. You're stuck with me."

"Always?" he asked.

"Unfortunately."

He laughed. The mirth of it crinkled the corners of his eyes and polished his gaze until it gleamed like twin stars in the night. He gathered up the broken pieces of his staff, and when he turned back toward me, his face was bright with a smile. "It's finally time for us to return home."

CHAPTER 37

The ship was sinking. We had almost made it to the mainland when fate saw fit to forsake us, for she was cruel just as she was kind, and though she had gifted us a boat, she had cursed it with a weak hull so that the waves could claim it and drag the wreckage to the bottom of the sea. Emrys was drowning, and I drowned along with him. I kicked my way toward the light streaming in through the surface. I managed to break through the water just long enough for a single gasp of air before I was sucked under once more. I fought the tides that sought to take me. I fought, and I clawed, and I kicked. But it refused to let me go. I was dragged deeper and deeper until the light above me winked out of existence and I was left stranded in a place of utter darkness. I was alone and had exhausted myself swimming against the current. I clutched at my chest, my fingers gripping desperately at the fabric of my shirt, confused as to how my heart still had the strength to keep beating when it was so very heavy. It would be so much easier to just let go. I stopped kicking and the last bubbles of air escaped from my lips.

My eyes started to droop down, threatening to close, but then a crimson light appeared, glowing like a candle in the night. A red thread was tied to my wrist, connecting me to Emrys. He floated in front of me, his body still and unmoving, his white hair swaying above him. I reached for him, and as my fingers brushed his skin, understanding filtered into me. I wasn't lost to the bottom of the ocean; I was lost inside his mind. It was no wonder he was afraid of the dark. This place was the pit of despair. So long as I was trapped in it, I would be forced to drown in the salty tears of sorrow and battle the currents of melancholy. I shook Emrys by the shoulders, trying to wake him up from this emotion, but his eyes remained closed.

My lungs burned for air, but this place, so dark and desolate, did not require breath. Although my chest tightened with discomfort, I dared not inhale and invite sorrow into my body. I glanced upward. I was so far down that there was no longer a light to guide me back out, but I was still determined to try. Gripping Emrys with one hand, I started to swim toward the surface, but his body refused to budge. His legs were tied down with a thick chain, anchored to something that was too far away for me to see. When I attempted to unhook the chains from his ankles, his emotions flooded into me, raw and all-consuming. Self-preservation demanded I let go, but I forced myself to latch on tighter, and it nearly ripped my heart to shreds to feel even a fraction of his pain.

He had mourned people who died centuries ago and those who had yet to be born. He had seen civilizations rise and fall and known enough tragedies to last a thousand lifetimes. He had watched everyone he loved die a dozen different ways. He was terrified of making a mistake and being forced to live with the blood of his friends staining his hands. The fate of the world rested upon his shoulders, and the weight of it was crushing him. He would live a thankless existence, and the only reward for his troubles would come in the form of loneliness and sorrow.

I was dying.

No, I wished I was dying.

Death would be better.

Death would be a mercy.

I wrenched my hand away from the chain, my heart racing even as the emotions ebbed away, and tears leaked from my eyes to feed the unrelenting tides of this chasm. His skin was frightfully cold when I took his face in my hands. "You're not alone," I said, but my voice was muted beneath the waves, and no matter how loudly I shouted, he would not be able to hear me.

If I couldn't free him from his chains, then I was just going to have to destroy the anchor. I swam down, following the chain deeper into the darkness. The red string that linked me to Emrys stretched as it followed me. Eventually, I found myself caught inside a riptide, and I no longer needed to kick because the water simply swept me toward the bottom. The first thing I saw were the teeth. Thousands of them, all jagged and decayed, and I realized too late that there was no bottom that could be reached. It was just an open maw, waiting patiently for its meal to drift into its mouth. I began struggling against the current, hoping to make an escape before it swallowed me whole.

Don't be a coward, the voice hissed. *Despair is not the only monster lurking within these depths. We can take him.*

I shouldn't listen to it. The more I allowed it in, the more I would descend into madness. Yet I wasn't the only one fighting an internal battle. My thoughts turned to Emrys, who floated helplessly somewhere above me, chained to the beast down below. I stopped fighting and allowed the current to drag me down into the creature's belly. This was a place of endless darkness, and when I called, the darkness answered. Despair groaned as it was forced to know the anguish it inflicted upon others, and as the shadows ripped it apart from the inside, its body rumbled with the force of fire-spewing mountains and fleet-sinking storms. Then the thread around my wrist snapped taut, yanking me out of the beast's maw and onto dry land.

I coughed and spluttered, relishing in the air that filled my lungs. Emrys leaned over me, his head blotting out the sun as droplets of water dripped from his hair to splatter against my face. He stared at me with an astounded expression, like he couldn't quite believe that I was here with him. After he helped me to my feet, I peered around at my new surroundings. I was standing in the middle of a forest, the scents of damp moss and fresh pine filling my nose, a welcome change from the dark depths that I had found myself trapped in only moments ago.

Clasping a hand around the back of Emrys's neck, I pressed his forehead to mine. "You're not alone," I said again, punctuating each word, making sure that this time he heard me.

He clasped a hand around the back of my neck in return. "Darkness and despair. We make quite the team." His voice shook when he spoke, caught somewhere between a laugh and a sob, and as tears slipped down his cheeks, I couldn't discern whether they sprang from joy or sorrow. He stepped back and wiped them away, his eyes turning a startling shade of blue in the wake of his tears, and the muscles along his jawline flexed as though he was working up the courage to say something. "Koven, I think I should tell you that—"

The rest of his words were cut off when a scream pierced the air. The sound rattled me down to my bones. Akira was here, and she was in trouble. I raced in the direction of the sound, weaving through the tall trees and leaping over fallen logs until she came into view. She was pinned to the ground by a monstrous hound, its eyes red and its thick body covered with matted fur. Froth bubbled along the edges of its mouth as it snapped its jaws. Akira managed to jam her bow between its teeth and the hound proceeded to shred the piece of wood into splinters.

"Akira!" I yelled, running toward her, but she didn't look my way. Grabbing a dagger, I rammed it into the beast. However, my blade didn't dig into its flesh as intended. My momentum carried me forward and my body passed through the hound as though I was nothing more than a ghost. Casting the dagger aside, I attempted to shove the monster off her with my bare hands, only for the same thing to happen all over again. It was as though I had become a shade cursed to roam the land of the living, forced into the role of a bystander while the world continued to spin around me.

My wrist began to burn as Emrys stepped through the brush, moving at a frustratingly slow pace. "How do we help her?" I asked him, and his expression turned somber.

"We can't," he replied.

"What do you mean, we can't?" I shouted back, refusing to accept that there was nothing I could do but stand there and watch.

"You have found your way into one of my dreams." He frowned and lifted up his wrist for closer inspection. A red ring encircled it like an angry rash. "It must be a side effect from the thread of fate. This is . . . unexpected."

I could do nothing but watch as drool dribbled down from the hound's jaws to drench Akira's leather armor. A wild screech echoed from within the forest, and the thunder of hooves grew louder as her brother burst forth from between the trees. He rode atop a monster of his own, a stallion that possessed a mane of tangled seaweed and a dripping wet coat, which was the same color as a murky river. Rin's long black hair billowed behind him, his expression murderous as he hefted the spear in his hand and rammed its tip into the hound. The beast gave a yelp of pain, but it did not die until the horse unhinged its jaw and took a bite out of the creature's throat.

Akira wiggled free from beneath its carcass, her features twisting with disgust as she wiped the slobber from her breastplate. Her brother's dangerous expression melted away, and he looked like he was almost tempted to laugh. "I thought the goddess of hunting favored you for her sport, little sister, and yet this kill tilts the tally in my favor."

Akira scowled at him. "Your stallion felled this beast; you did not. I believe that means we're currently tied."

He unslung a spare hunting bow from his back and tossed it to her. "I will not have you spin tales about how you would have emerged the victor if only your bow hadn't been broken."

She hefted the new bow, testing the weight of it in her hands, and then pulled back the string to assess its flexibility. Satisfied with its performance, she lowered it again. "I'll make you regret arming me, brother."

The challenge brought a smile to his lips. He offered her his arm. She gripped it and swung up onto the back of the horse with him. The stallion galloped forward and disappeared into a thicket of trees. As I followed them, a chorus of hisses began to whisper through the forest, making it seem like spirits were flitting about the trees. Monsters of old still dwelled in the ocean and lurked deep within the mountains, but the ones of the forest had been hunted to extinction centuries ago, cleared out to make way for man. It took me a moment to realize why they had made a sudden reappearance: Rin had cut a gateway between the realm of the dead and the realm of the living. These were the creatures of death and decay that had crawled out through that opening.

I entered a small clearing where four men lay dead, riddled with arrows and battle wounds, their eyes completely white and their naked bodies obscured with strange markings. On the edge of the clearing, the ground had been split open with a black seam, dark smoke churning in the space that separated this world and the next. Two skeletal hands reached out, gripping the edges and widening the gap as it tried to haul itself out. Akira crunched the fingers beneath her boot, sending the creature back to whatever dark rock it had crawled out from under. Then she pulled out something from her pocket. The sunlight caught the golden thread, the rays making it shimmer and gleam in the palm of her hand. She whispered something to it, something that I was too far away to hear, and then there was a blinding flash of light. I shielded my eyes, and when I looked again, the doorway to the Shadowlands was no longer there. Akira had managed to close it.

She grinned in triumph, completely unaware of the monster that was skulking in the brush, but I could see it clearly from where I was standing. The creature moved on all fours, its skin festering with sickly boils and sores, and ooze dripped from its body to shrivel the patches of grass below. It slowly crept toward her, its movements silent like a predator stalking its prey. I shouted out a warning, but I wasn't really here, so she didn't hear me. I could do nothing but watch as the monster prowled closer. Then a spear sailed through the air and impaled it. The creature twitched and spasmed before going still.

Rin trotted over to retrieve his weapon. "I do believe that the tally is back in my favor," he said, and Akira's smile slipped away into an aggrieved groan. A roar bellowed in the distance. The sound was loud enough to scare the birds from the treetops, and they took to the skies with startled squawks. Akira and Rin exchanged a look. Then they both raced toward the beast.

Emrys walked into the clearing to join me, not bothering to glance at the strange creatures that lay dead on the ground, or rejoice in the fact that

Akira had managed to repair the ripped seam. He had seen this all before. "So, this is the future?" I asked him, but he shook his head.

"This used to be the future," he corrected. "It has now become the past. This happened days ago." He peered after Akira and Rin, who had already vanished from sight, and somewhere within the forest, the beast from the Shadowlands let out another bloodcurdling bellow. "They have done their part. Now, it's time for us to do ours."

Emrys shoved me, and I fell backward. My eyes snapped open the moment I hit the ground. As the churning waves rocked the ship, my hammock swung from side to side, following the rhythm of the sea. A prickling sensation ran up the length of my arm, and when I glanced down at my wrist, I discovered that the skin was inflamed, a red streak encircling it like a crimson bracelet. It hadn't just been a fever dream. With a groan, I forced myself to crawl out of the cradled netting. The wood creaked beneath my feet as I moved to look out the porthole. Athearia's coastline came into view behind its water-splattered glass. The gateway to the Shadowlands had been closed and the goddess sprung free of her prison. The only thing left to do was return her to the god of death.

Emrys emerged from his hammock to come and stand next to me. When his gaze met mine, there was a vulnerability there that hadn't existed before. He knew my secret, and now I knew his. "No matter how difficult it is, you have to keep kicking against the current," I told him.

A sad smile tugged at his lips. "The sorrow has already made a home for itself inside my lungs. Sometimes, it feels as though each breath is a battle." He paused for a moment to stare out the porthole. "But I'm not in the habit of losing wars."

I rested a hand on his shoulder. "It's not a war you need to fight alone."

He brushed his fingers over the matching crimson streak that encircled his wrist, and some of the sadness that tainted his smile leached away. "Madness and melancholy," he mused. "Our enemies will tremble in fear at the mere mention of our names." He said it as though in jest, but I didn't laugh. It sounded like a formidable force to me, and I pitied any of the poor souls who would stand against us.

CHAPTER 38

The Marcaida Fortress seemed even colder than usual as I walked its empty halls. The hour was late and many of the servants had already retired for the evening. Yet the floors still groaned and creaked beneath the weight of invisible footsteps. A shiver traveled down my spine as the wind blew in through an open window to tickle the nape of my neck. I moved to close the shutters, but the wind was determined to get in, and it battered against the wood, causing the shutters to rattle against the metal latch. The ghosts of the fortress were restless tonight. I climbed the stairs leading to the sleeping quarters. From the rumors circling the harbor, it seemed that the god of death was still residing in the fortress. However, after confusing reports came in claiming that Brazial had fallen in battle, the troops under the command of House Marcaida had started preparing for an imminent departure up north, so they could ascertain the truth of the matter for themselves. Fortunately, they had not left the confines of their barracks just yet.

I came to a stop in front of the room typically reserved for the lord of the house, and as such, it would be the room with the most comforts and refinery. If there was a god living within these walls, I assumed this was the room they would claim for themselves. I raised my knuckles to knock on the door, but hesitated when my mind turned toward Rita. After everything that happened, the trials seemed like a distant memory, but time had not dulled the feeling of her body growing still in my arms, her skin turning cold as the warmth of her blood leached out to stain my clothes. All of the gods carried some culpability for what had happened to her, their lust for violence and blood sacrifices being the sole reason she was there in the first place, but it was Death who had stalked those tunnels like a reaper in search for souls, and it was his undead horde that had torn her apart in the end.

Then claim your vengeance, the voice urged. *The golden wolf of Kalta is dead, slain at the hands of a mortal. It can be done.*

Except battling a god had not gone well for me last time, and I used that memory like a shield to block the voice out. I would not allow myself to forget what happened to Rita, but I also wouldn't have her ghost drive me into an early grave. I needed to be strategic in the battles that I fought, and this was not one I could win. Not right now, anyway. I took my anger and shelved it before knocking on the door. My brow furrowed when the sound that followed was not the heavy thud of boots but rather the soft pitter of featherlight footsteps. The door cracked partially open and Mei peered out from behind the gap, her hair bedraggled and a thin sheet wrapped around her body. I blinked in surprise and then remembered that this was the room intended for the head of the household, which was the mantle she had taken up upon Rin's death. Ashearan must be in another room.

"Forgive me, my lady," I said, giving a polite bow of my head. "I didn't mean to disturb you. I must have knocked upon the wrong door."

No, this is definitely the right door, the voice said with a level of enthusiasm that made me eager to leave before it could fill my head with baser thoughts.

She was quiet for a moment as she regarded me. "I assume that if you're here then the seer's plan has either come to fruition or gone horribly wrong. Which of the two is it?"

"The goddess waits downstairs as we speak," I answered, but instead of relief, it was annoyance that sparked to life behind her eyes. "I must speak with Ashearan. I believe he has taken up residency here. Could you tell me which room he's staying in?"

Her expression twisted with displeasure. She looked like she was tempted to slam the door in my face, but then she disappeared back inside the room, leaving the door ajar for me to follow her. After a moment of hesitation, I pushed it open and stepped inside. One of the walls served as a bookshelf, housing a collection of thick, heavy tomes that would be the pride of any scholar, while the opposing wall hosted a collection of swords that spoke to the heritage of a warrior. Her dead cat was curled atop the sheepskin rug near the hearth, its ear partially rotted off and a white sliver of its femur visible along its front leg. The flames had faded down to glowing embers, but the remaining firelight still managed to catch the sheen of the pair of dark wings that lay discarded on the settee.

Maybe it was not his grief that kept Ashearan chained to this place after all, because he shifted from the bed, standing naked as he moved to wrap an arm around Mei's waist. Pulling her closer, he brushed his lips against the bare skin of her shoulders. I shuddered at what it must be like to be touched by Death himself, but her eyes darkened as though the only thing to be found in it was a deranged sort of pleasure. With neither his wings nor his foreboding dark hood to conceal his face, Ashearan could almost be mistaken for a man if not for his godly eyes. He had a square face, his jawline shaded beneath stubble, and though I always expected his hair to be as black as his wings, his locks shared the same golden hue as those of his sister. His gaze caught mine from across the room, and he smiled.

"You didn't tell me that we would be expecting company tonight," he said. "Is he here for your pleasure, or mine?"

"Neither," she replied. "He is a serpent of a shadow court, come in the night to deliver a message to you."

The god of death paused to consider me again, and a hint of disappointment fell across his features. "A pity. He has pretty eyes."

"Prettier than mine?" she challenged.

"It's not your eyes that keep me chained to your bed day and night," he said before biting on the bottom of her ear, the action a little too forceful to be considered playful. His arms slipped from her waist and he strode forward. My shadow flickered with agitation as he drew closer, knowing that gods did not ask for permission when it came to taking what they wanted, but he merely grabbed a dark robe from the back of the settee, which he tied together with a sash. "So, what news do you bring that is so important you would disturb me at this late hour?"

It would be far easier to just take him to his sister than to try and explain everything. "I think it's better if I show you, Your Divinity."

He did not look pleased with that suggestion, and he made no move to indicate he had any intention of leaving this room until dawn brightened the sky outside. Mei trailed her fingers down his arm as she came up behind him. "I'm not going anywhere," she told him. "I will still be here should you wish to return. Though you might find your shackles broken once you leave."

He brushed the hair away from her face, and though his expression was one of obvious lust, her own had shifted into something unreadable. "The appetite of a god is voracious thing." He made it sound like a warning as he leaned toward her. "You have not sated it yet, little mortal. If Brazial has truly been slain, then I will have my vengeance by feasting upon the wolves he sired. When I ride for battle, I will take you with me, and I will know what you taste like as I lay you down on a bed made of blood and bones."

He wrapped a hand around her throat and kissed her, letting out a low growl when she slipped her tongue into his mouth.

I was all too aware of my desire for violence. It bubbled up from the abyss as my yearning for vengeance coupled with a jealousy that did not belong to me. The night swayed outside, ready to bend itself to serve me, and I averted my gaze before I gave in to the temptation to call upon it. My eyes landed instead on the mirror in the corner of the room, its borders carved to resemble the distorted faces of tormented souls. I caught sight of my reflection in the silvered glass, but my features seemed darker than they ought to, my hair tousled and my cheekbones shadowed. The eyes that peered back at me were not my own. They were pools of greed, and wrath, and ruin. My lips lifted into a menacing smile. Then I blinked and the image was gone. The only thing reflected back at me was my own disconcertment.

Ashearan begrudgingly pulled himself away from Mei, his golden eyes simmering, and he gave me a threatening look that promised retribution if I proved to be nothing more than a waste of his time. I led him out into the passageway and down the stairs. The shutters were open again upon my return, the wind blowing in to haunt the halls, making the hair along my arms prickle. It made me uneasy as I traveled past the morbid tapestry that depicted victims who had fallen prey to the Corpse King, the old man cackling while the undead feasted upon the subjects beneath him. It was a stark reminder of the task Celdric had given me, and now that Sheara had been rescued, I had everything I needed in order to open the cursed tomb.

After arriving at the fortress, the goddess of healing had sought out rest in one of the drawing rooms. She must have grown tired of waiting, because she burst into the passageway, her hair windswept from the long ride and a traveling cloak warming her shoulders. She rushed forward, throwing herself against her brother's chest. His arms moved to embrace her as though acting on instinct, but they froze midair, his expression flitting from shock and relief to confusion and suspicion.

"I have missed you, dearest brother. The last few weeks have been harrowing. I did not know if I would ever see you again."

She peered up at him with wet eyelashes, her tears streaming down her face, and slowly, he raised his hand to wipe them away. "How?" he said, his voice mystified, as though he thought he might be in a dream. "I watched you die with my own eyes."

"It was a trick conjured forth by Celdric," she said, her voice cracking. "He trapped me, forcing me to be his prisoner." As she choked on her sob, her brother's expression darkened. "I cried myself to sleep every night, feeling so afraid and so alone. I thought he had left me there to rot, but then he came back, making me bleed for a bite of bread. I was so hungry, Ash, and pain burned at my skin day and night. I called out your name, but you never came. I was all alone."

The god of death looked like a blade had been plunged into his side only to have the wound salted a moment later. I took a step away from him as the temperature in the hallway dropped, turning my breath to mist in front of my face. "I will make him suffer a hundred time over," he vowed, "and when I'm finished with him, I will rip him apart with my bare hands."

Sheara sniffed as her crying began to fade. "He had help," she said, and then pointed a finger at me. "He is Celdric's vassal, a serpent of shadow. He helped the deceiver take me. He bound me in chains and forced himself upon me."

I stared at her in shock, bewildered by the accusation, but I didn't have time to think why she had cast it upon me like mud, because Ashearan was looking at me with murder in his eyes. I darted out of the way when he tried to grab me, knowing that it would only take one brush of his fingers to steal the life from my veins. He roared with fury, and as Sheara's lips curled into a sly smile, I realized that it wasn't her at all.

As the god of death turned his back on her to focus on killing me, she pulled out a hidden dagger and rammed it into his back. Ashearan's eyes grew wide with a mixture of pain and surprise as the person who he thought to be his sister yanked out the dagger and shoved it into him again and again in rapid succession. He spun around, clawing at her, but then he dropped to his knees as blood began to flow in golden rivers down his back.

"Celdric." He spat out the name like it was a curse, and the god of mischief grinned as he shed his disguise, his hair turning from sunshine yellow to brackish brown, his traveling cloak shimmering out of existence to reveal the dark linen shirt and trousers hidden beneath.

"My sincerest apologies, Ash, but I happen to like my limbs attached to the rest of my body," Celdric said. A pool of gleaming blood formed around Ashearan, the life quickly leaking out of him, but he was not dead yet. His power charged inside him, making the air vibrate as he readied a curse to drag Celdric down into a grave alongside him. Celdric raised his arms, and the darkness of the night rushed forward to crush the god of death. The curse burst out from Ashearan before the darkness reached him, and a lethal miasma flooded down both sides of the passageway. My shadow rushed up to form a shield and I enforced it with every ounce of my strength. When the curse collided with the darkness, I was thrown backward, crashing painfully to the ground at the far end of the corridor.

My shadow deflated, my power sapped dry against the poison of death. A devastation had been left in the wake of the curse, turning the wooden floors rotten and rusting the weapons that adorned the walls. Celdric was gone, likely having escaped through the shadows, leaving Ashearan to bleed out on the ground.

The real Sheara came running into the passage with Emrys following close behind her. Her expression fell when she found her brother dying on the floor. She hurried to his side. Golden ichor stained her dress as she knelt in the puddle of blood, grasping his face in her hands. His eyes rolled back into his head and he slipped unconscious. I wondered how much power it would take to bring a god back from the brink of death. It was probably a lot, because she pressed her lips to his as though attempting to breathe her life into his body, and the shell of her host withered, the corners of her eyes deepening with creases and her golden hair fading to silver.

Ashearan's eyes snapped back open, and he peered up at her with a dazed expression. "So it was true," he murmured. "You're alive."

She smiled as she squeezed his hand. "I am."

As I struggled to stand up, the rotting floor gave way beneath one of my boots, causing me to lose my balance. By the time I managed to wiggle my foot out of the hole, Emrys had made his way down the passage to crouch down next to me. "You okay?" he asked.

"I'm alive . . . for now, anyway." I observed Ashearan with caution, but he was no longer oozing with murderous rage, or if he was, at least it wasn't directed toward me. He wasn't the god I needed to be worried about. "Celdric has eyes and ears everywhere. He knew that Sheara had been freed from Ismadore and that this was our destination. He was waiting for us." My voice grew somber as I said, "He knows we helped free her, Rys. He knows we were the ones to expose his scheme. He's not a forgiving god. He will seek retribution for this."

Emrys exhaled a long breath as he raked his fingers through his hair. "Celdric is an entity of chaos. Even with my foresight, he's a difficult creature to predict. However, it's not in his nature to lash out in anger. He's clever, and cunning, and he enjoys his games a little too much. I doubt he will slit our throats in our sleep. It would be too quick and it would gain him nothing. We will need to tread with caution, but so will he. Death is a fearsome enemy to have."

Celdric might be wary of Ashearan's power, but I highly doubted that the god of death would agree to serve as a personal bodyguard and follow two mortals around for the rest of our lives. He would not protect us from Celdric's vengeance, but his wrath did serve to increase the value of a certain talisman locked away inside the Marcaida family crypts. Inside the tomb of the Corpse King was a necklace of teeth that would shield the wearer from the power of death. Celdric would want it now more than ever. I could use it to bargain with him. As though he already knew the turn my mind had taken, Emrys said, "You cannot give him the necklace, Koven. His vulnerability to the death curse can be used in our favor. Give him a shield and he will be an even more formidable opponent than he already is."

When I didn't reply, he gave me a pointed look. I heaved a sigh. "Fine," I relented. "I won't give it to him."

"Give me your word," he insisted. I arched an eyebrow at him, but his expression remained deadly serious. My throat constricted, making it difficult to speak, because while I had been taught that lies were a weapon to be wielded with the same ease and skill as a blade, I could not lie to him. My shoulders sagged in defeat.

"You have my word," I promised him, and he nodded, finally satisfied with my response. As I leaned back to rest against the wall, I started to consider the other option available to me. I had stolen chains made of pure Rasalan steel, forged with the strength to withstand the might of gods. I could turn them into weapons of my own so that when Celdric inevitably came for me, I would be ready for him.

CHAPTER 39

The last time I was inside the fortified city of Arlow, Cahal had made it very clear what he would do if I attempted to see Serenity again, so I decided it would be prudent to keep myself hidden. I watched from a nearby rooftop as she left the remedial tent to retire for the night. Dropping to the ground, I kept to the shadows while I followed her, wearing a cloak of darkness to help conceal me from prying eyes. However, when she disappeared into a tower with armed guards, I was forced to veer away. I was in the process of circling the building to look for another way in when Serenity stepped out onto one of the small balconies with an oil lamp in her hand. She watered the flower pots outside and picked a few leaves from a plant before returning to her room. Fate must have been smiling down upon me, because not only did I now know which balcony belonged to her, but it was also located next to a large ebony tree that grew alongside the tower.

I climbed up the tree, using it like a ladder and carefully testing my weight on the branches before shuffling closer to the balcony. I leaped the distance between the two, sailing over the banister to land in a silent crouch among the flowers. The evening was warm and Serenity had left the doors to the terrace open, a set of drapes the only thing separating me from the room. Parting the fabric, I stepped inside. She was sitting on the edge of her bed, having exchanged her healer's robes for a shapeless nightdress. The oil lamp burned on the bedside table. My lips curled into an amused smile when I noticed the glass jar in her lap, the scorpion from the mountains still trapped within it. She was in the middle of feeding it dead crickets when she finally noticed my presence and startled in fright. The jar tumbled out of her lap and hurtled to the ground. My shadow rushed forward to catch it, the dark tendrils gripping it like claws as it lifted the jar up and placed it safely on the table. The scorpion scuttled at the bottom of the glass, unsettled by the disturbance, but its legs couldn't get the traction needed in order to climb out.

"Koven," Serenity exclaimed, her eyes wide with surprise. She placed a hand over her heart and inhaled a steadying breath. "You scared me."

"Sorry," I said, moving toward her. However, when she flashed me a wary look, my boots came to a grinding halt. Cahal had told her about my brush with insanity—of course he had—and now she was probably terrified of me. Her sister had been a victim of madness, killed at the hands of the one she loved the most, and she wouldn't allow herself to meet the same fate. This conversation was going to happen eventually. If she already knew about my secret, then there was no point in delaying it any further. I tried to force the words out from where they were lodged in my throat, but my mouth had gone uncomfortably dry. I couldn't bring myself to do it, and I let the silence fester until she finally broke it.

"Cahal came to see me," she said, confirming my suspicions. She paused for a moment like she wasn't sure how to start this conversation, either. "He has never been flattering in the way he speaks about you, and I'm well aware that the two of you don't get along, but some of the things he said this time were . . . concerning." My heart grew heavy with dread. This spark between us had only just been lit and it was already about to be smothered. "Koven, I need you to tell me what happened. I've heard Cahal's side, and now I would like to hear yours. When we were at the sanctuary, you said that there were parts of you that I might not like. What did you mean when you said that?"

I should tell her.

I should tell her.

I should tell her.

You should, the voice agreed, making me instantly suspicious of the idea. If I told Serenity about the madness that lingered within me, it would ruin us. The voice wanted her gone. She was kind, and good, and compassionate. She was everything that madness despised, and she made me want to resist its pull. I didn't want to twist into some creature that she would be too scared to touch. That must be the reason the voice wanted her gone, because without her light, the darkness would be able to sink its teeth into me more easily. I needed her. She would help to keep me sane.

Serenity stared at me as she waited for an answer, her expression fluctuating between heartbreak and hope. "I'm terrified of hurting you again," I confessed, taking a slow step toward her and tracing a finger along the scar that trailed down her arm. "I have nightmares about it. I watch you die in my arms and I wake up with this fear that you will end up in a grave of my making."

When I looked into her eyes, it wasn't horror peering back at me. It was compassion. "That was an accident, Koven. You were in the middle of battling monsters, fighting for your life as well as mine. If you weren't there, I would have ended up dead. I know that you would never wish to hurt me." She was right. I wouldn't. I would sooner set myself ablaze and let the flames consume me until I was nothing more than ash. She deserved so much better than me. She deserved the truth. Even if it cost me everything.

"Gold is not the only thing that brings out my greed. You do as well." My fingers moved from her scar to her lips, and desire warmed my blood when they parted ever so slightly at my touch. "Like right now, all I can think about is how much I want to kiss you. I don't want to give you a glimpse into the darkest parts of my soul, because then I might never hold you in my arms again." I shifted closer until the heat of her body radiated against mine. "I want you, and when I want something, I take it. That is what it means to be a vassal of Celdric."

Her gaze roamed over my face, her breath mingling with mine, and I wondered if maybe the thing that existed between the two of us was not as fragile as I feared. Maybe it would not break and shatter the moment I allowed her to glimpse the parts of my heart that shuddered at the light. "You have told me of your fear and you have told me of your greed," she said, "but you have not yet told me what happened between you and Cahal."

My heart waged a war inside my chest, beating like a battle drum against my rib cage. Maybe the truth would serve to strengthen our bond, or maybe it would ruin it completely, and the fear of the latter wanted to override my better judgment. The honorable thing to do was to tell her the truth, and yet I couldn't bear to lose her. I wanted her. My sanity needed her. I was not a gallant knight from the tales of old; I was a vassal to the patron god of lies and thieves. If I held a diamond in my hand, it made no sense to let it slip through my fingers. I should keep it with me always, cherishing it every day instead of throwing it away.

"Cahal has a talent for getting under my skin. I want to bloody his nose every single time he opens his mouth," I admitted, knowing that the best lies were woven with pieces of the truth. "Emrys foresaw the fall of this city, and he ordered me to save it. So I did. The Kaltans had infiltrated the eastern gatehouse. It was a difficult battle, a bloody one, but I managed to stop them before they could allow the invading force to slip into the fortress and slaughter everyone inside. Cahal arrived at the gatehouse shortly after that."

I paused, waiting to see how she would react, but she remained quiet, intent on letting me finish the story. "We were both exhausted and there was still a battle raging on outside. The two of us struggle to get along in the best of times, and that was not the best of times. We exchanged words. I said things that I'm not proud of—things that only served to make the situation worse—and the two of us clashed. I tried to restrain him with chains of shadow, so that he would have the chance to calm down—you know what he can be like when he's angry—and that's when his men arrived and Brazial heaved open the gate."

Her expression was pensive, her brow furrowed in thought, and I could see that she wanted so desperately to believe this version of events. The one where I was the savior of the city rather than a madman reveling in violence as he splattered soldiers against stone walls. The one where Cahal and I merely had a disagreement that got blown out of proportion. Her heart was already on my side, but doubt was not a weed that was easily uprooted. This particular one was stubborn. It still needed one last tug before it would finally allow itself to be wrenched out. "I'm surprised that he even bothered mentioning it to you," I said mildly. "He and I are no strangers to quarreling, and this one didn't even last very long. It couldn't have been that bad. After all, we set it aside and took on Brazial together. Admittedly, we did not fare well. If Rin hadn't shown up when he did, we would both be dead, but it all worked out in the end."

Relief fell over her face like fresh rain, and the last traces of her uncertainty were washed away. "You're right; I do know what he is like when he gets angry." She shook her head as though chastising herself for ever allowing him to plant such insidious thoughts in her mind. "The way he was telling it, he made it seem like you were slipping into madness."

I let my lips curve into a smile, as though I found the accusation amusing, but I did not need to conjure up the awe I felt as my fingers trailed over the ridge of her cheekbone. I marveled at the skill the gods had displayed when carving out her form, her features so soft and delicate, her dark eyes framed by thick lashes. My gaze was reverent as it dropped to her mouth. "I must be slipping into madness. After all, I can't think of another way to describe the feeling I get when I'm around you."

She appeared startled for the second time that evening, an expression that looked all the more enticing when cast in the dim glow of the oil lamp. Desire darkened my heart, but this was a feeling that belonged to me alone. Madness had no claim to it. Shifting aside the sleeve of her nightdress, I laid a kiss upon her shoulder. "You are my morning sun," I whispered against her skin, enjoying the way her breathing quickened at my words. My lips traveled along the length of her shoulder, leaving a line of kisses in my wake as I slowly made my way toward her neck.

"My scorpion wrangler."

She tilted back her head, baring her throat. I was all too eager to accept her offering. As my teeth grazed against the soft flesh, she let out a gasp that made me impatient to push her back against the bed and find out what other sounds she could make.

"My poisons master."

I kissed her jawline before shifting my mouth closer to hers.

"My *corpos lillus*." My lips hovered an inch away from her own, eager for her kiss like a man that yearned for death, but I did not kiss her just yet. Instead, my fingers gripped the fabric of her nightdress, a silent question in my eyes. She lifted her arms up, allowing me to pull the dress over her head. I discarded the fabric a heartbeat later, the dress lying in a forgotten heap on the ground. I stared at her standing before me, beautiful and bare and soon to be mine. She arched onto her toes, brushing her lips against mine, claiming what was hers to take. My fingers raked through her hair as I deepened the kiss, tender and forceful at the same time. She let out a low moan and the last of my patience ran out.

I picked her up only to lower her onto the bed a moment later. She tugged off my shirt, adding it to the growing pile of clothes on the floor. She pulled my face back toward her, and as she enveloped me in another kiss, my shadow moved to yank off my boots. Her hands slid down my torso, falling prey to a greed of her own as her fingers roamed my collection of scars and the hard lines of muscle. Her hands slid lower only to pause when she touched one of my daggers. "That is not the blade I was looking for," she said, breaking away from the kiss with a laugh. Mirth tugged at the edges of my mouth while I removed my weapons and placed them on the bedside table next to the scorpion. The creature was no longer attempting to escape the confines of the glass jar. Instead, its pincers gripped the dead cricket as it enjoyed its meal.

"Why did you keep it?" I asked her. She sat up to look at the scorpion, a soft hum vibrating from the back of her throat as though in contemplation.

"I suppose I could say that the venom might prove to be useful in the future." Her eyes found mine and her lips curved into a small smile, revealing a tiny speck of darkness that dwelled within her heart. I wondered if that was what drew her to me in the same way that the dim light in mine was drawn to her. "But if I'm being honest, I just like having it around. It makes me feel a little dangerous."

The shadows in the room crept up the frame of the bed to untie the sashes that held back the chiffon drapes. They fluttered as they came undone, the shimmering fabric creating a world of our own, one crafted of silk sheets and promises of pleasure. I pushed her back against the bed, her hair splaying against the pillow, and my tongue flicked over the swell of one breast while my hand cupped the other. Her back arched at the sensation. My mouth trailed down her abdomen to find the sensitive spot between her legs. When she sucked in a sharp breath, I made a mental note to thank Faelan for the advice he had given me. The whimper that escaped her lips was almost as delicious as she was. Tendrils of shadow swept over her body as her pleasure became my pleasure. When she finally cried out, her fingers gripping the sheets, I emerged with a wicked grin on my face.

Shucking off my trousers, I positioned myself on top of her. She wore the robes of pleasure well, her chest rising and falling with heaving breaths, her eyes bright and her cheeks flushed. Her mouth slipped open as I sheathed myself inside her. Her body tensed against me, her fingernails digging grooves along my back, unaccustomed to the way she would stretch in order to make room for me. Then she relaxed, only to repeat the motion with the next thrust of my hips. I tried to walk the line between her pleasure and mine, my thrusts slow yet deep, my kisses as light as a feather, only to rake my teeth against her skin a moment later. Her body began to move in rhythm with my own as discomfort gave way to gratification, and as the need for release built up inside me, I gave in to my desire to increase the intensity of my strokes. Her moans mixed with mine as my heat spilled into her.

I gripped the headboard, breathless and slick with sweat, pleasure turning my blood to liquid fire. She stole one last kiss from me before I unsheathed myself. As I rolled onto my back, she shifted closer to me and rested her head atop my chest. I wrapped an arm around her, tracing invisible lines along her body while my heart slowly settled back down to a steady rhythm. However, as the desire ebbed away, its hunger sated, a trickle of guilt leaked in through the gap left in its wake. I didn't think the darkness lurking inside me had played any part in what had just happened. Yet it had grown quiet and still in a way that unnerved me as though it, too, had been sated. I tried to convince myself that it would be fine. I would be able to control it. I would fight the madness with my every waking breath. I would make her happy, and eventually, the lie that I'd told her tonight would fade into obscurity.

CHAPTER 40

Serenity slept soundly in my arms, her chest rising and falling in a steady rhythm. The night had fallen quiet, as though it was sleeping as well. Yet my eyes remained wide-open while I stared up at the ceiling, my fingers slowly running up and down the length of her scar. I searched my mind for the word to describe what I was feeling, so that I could understand why it stole my sleep from me. It took me a long time to figure out what it was. I was content, and that was not an emotion I trusted. Happiness was a fickle mistress, visiting whenever it pleased only to be gone in the morning, easily lured away at the beckoning of another. My eyes refused to close because deep down I was worried that this feeling wouldn't be here when they opened again.

The breeze snuck into the room from the open balcony, making the chiffon drapes around the bed frame flutter.

"I'm sad that I missed the show."

I froze at the sound of the voice, and just like that, my happiness disappeared, ripped away by the cold talons of fear.

Celdric sauntered toward the bed, his visage made hazy behind the sheen of the drapes. "I had a sinking suspicion that you were fond of this one. During the trials, when Ashearan summoned forth his undead army into the arena, you didn't hesitate to throw yourself into it. My vassals aren't known for their selfless acts of valor, which means that the reason you risked your life had to be because of her or the Blackwood boy. His personality leaves much to be desired, so I decided to hedge my bets."

Not wanting to wake up Serenity, I remained as still as a statue while his shadows slunk forward to part the drapes. His eyes were an inconspicuous shade of brown, choosing to be a ghost in the night instead of announcing his divinity with a glowing shade of gold. "I'm disappointed in you, Koven. I thought we had something special. You gave me your blood, still warm from your veins, and I gave you the reverend's head atop an altar. Clearly, it meant more to me than it did to you." He brandished a small pair of pliers like the ones bone-menders used when they needed to remove a festering tooth or a splintered piece of bone. My stomach gave an unpleasant twist at the sight of them. "I love betrayal and treachery, really, I do. The thing is, I have a reputation to uphold. I can't have people thinking I've gone soft and turned into a god of mercy, so someone needs to give penance. But because I like you so much, I will give you a choice. I came here for her, but I'm willing to leave with you instead. What will it be?"

It wasn't a choice. I carefully slid my arm out from beneath her head. I sucked in a sharp breath when she stirred in her sleep and only exhaled it after she fell still once more. Climbing out of the bed, I moved to grab my clothes, but Celdric stopped me with a hand to my chest. "Let's leave those there, shall we? It's been my experience that mortals are less likely to do something stupid when they're feeling particularly vulnerable. Besides, I rather like the view."

He let his gaze wander freely over my body, but the glint in his eyes was not born of lust. He was trying to make me uncomfortable, and I refused to give him the satisfaction. I wiped my face clean of any emotion as he called upon the darkness to drag me down into the shadow domain. The hardwood floor gave way to soft sand, and I found myself on the outskirts of the ruined city. The wild shadows of this place began to congregate around the god, flitting excitedly at his feet like faithful dogs upon the arrival of their master. The god smirked at me as though he already knew just how much he was going to enjoy this. "Kneel," he commanded.

We kneel to no one, the voice growled. However, my only choice was to obey. This was his domain, and I was but a vassal. I was unclothed and unarmed. The shadows that dwelled here would not heed my call, and if I tried to resist, I put Serenity in harm's way. I knelt, ignoring the wave of disgust that rolled out from the back of my mind as I did so. Celdric offered me the pliers and I accepted them with dread.

"You will give me two of your teeth," the god said, and opening my mouth wide, I inserted the pliers. My heart began to thunder in protest as the metal tongs gripped one of the molars. I tried to steady it. Unfortunately, fear was not a thing that could be easily bridled. I yanked on the tooth, but some of my hesitancy leaked into the action, and I only ended up pulling out half of it while the rest snagged on my gums. The pliers fell from my hands as blood pooled on my tongue. I hunched over with a groan, and when I spat the blood upon the ground, the shadows of this place rushed forward to lap it up like a cluster of puppies converging on a single bowl of milk.

Celdric squatted down next to me, and grabbing my chin, he forced me to look at him. His eyes had turned a gleaming shade of gold, sparkling with a dark and sadistic form of amusement as he gazed upon my pain. "The trick, Koven, is to be decisive," he said right before he shoved his fingers into my mouth and uprooted the rest of the tooth with a sharp tug.

Don't you dare scream, the voice snarled, practically strangling the cry of pain that threatened to escape my throat. The resulting sound that came out was a wounded gurgle. Celdric offered me the pliers again. With shaking hands, I returned the metal tongs to the back of my mouth and fastened them around another molar. I made sure to have a firm grip on it as I yanked out the tooth. This time the pain was enough to overwhelm the darker side of me, and the cry of agony finally tore free from my throat.

Pathetic.

Maybe I was, because when my gaze met Celdric's again, I imagined what it would be like to stick a thousand burning needles into those golden eyes. I caressed the thought like a lover, holding it close, cherishing it and all the pleasure that it brought me. But I never breathed life into the fantasy. Instead, pain raked its vicious claws along my jawline, and my blood seeped out onto the sand to feed the starving shadows.

Celdric admired the pair of teeth that rested in the palm of his hand. "I do recall asking you to steal a certain necklace for me. I'm going to need that. Every day that you fail to get it for me, I will come back for another tooth, and if I cannot find you, I'll collect it from that healer you are so fond of. Her smile won't be nearly as sweet once I get my hands on her." He paused to let the threat sink in. He needn't have bothered. I heard his message loud and clear. "I will get a necklace of teeth one way or another, Koven."

He turned away from me to head into the city of derelict buildings and broken streets. The shadows followed dutifully after him, leaving not a single drop of blood to darken the ground behind them. Although I had promised Emrys that I would not give the talisman to Celdric, I wouldn't be able to conjure up a plan to outwit and trap the god of mischief in the space of a single day. He would come back night after night until my skull could no longer grin, and if it wasn't me to suffer that fate then it would be Serenity, and I had also made a vow never to be the reason she got hurt again. My hand moved to cradle my aching jaw. I couldn't let this happen to her, and if I was being completely honest with myself, I didn't want to go through this again, either. Staggering to my feet, I headed for the gateway that was connected to the Marcaida Fortress.

I was grateful that the servants were all asleep when I emerged naked inside the fortress, my hand touching the canvas of a morbid painting on the wall. It depicted a widow, her face streaked black with tears in a display of grief. She was looking up at the crow feathers that rained down from the sky, the dark folds of her dress billowing around her as she knelt upon the ground, blood seeping out from the open wounds along her wrists. The corridor began to glow with the presence of firelight as someone haunted the halls. I didn't even get the chance to hide before Mei made an appearance, her hair undone and her body swaddled in an expensive silk robe decorated with black birds. My mind raced to come up with a plausible explanation for why I was standing unclothed in the middle of her home with blood dribbling down my chin. She came to stand next to me. However, instead of questioning my state of undress, she proceeded to admire the portrait.

"Grief has always been so becoming on Marcaida women," she mused. "I always thought I would make for a good widow. Alas, my little sister stole away my chance to be wed. I cannot be a widow if I am not first a wife."

Amari had been kind to spare the king that particular fate.

"Death did not take me with him. He did not ride for battle and blood. He rode instead for the Sacred City. His sister wants to sue for peace." Mei turned away from the painting to look at me with a wistful expression. "I'm not to be a widow, and I'm not to be Death's mistress. Fate smiles down on the rest of you, while abandoning me to this forsaken existence."

A creak sounded farther down the passageway, catching her attention, and she followed it as though chasing after a ghost. I quickly made my way down the rest of the corridor, carefully picking over the rotting floorboards that had yet to be replaced after the incident between Celdric and Ashearan. When I finally made it up the stairs and into the guest room that I was currently occupying, I breathed out a sigh of relief. I moved to fetch a spare set of clothes from the cupboard and froze when my gaze landed on Emrys, who was resting atop the bed. He hadn't taken off his shoes or crawled beneath the covers, looking as though he had come in here in search for me and ended up staying until he had fallen asleep.

I got changed as quietly as I could. Then, shrouding my steps in silence, I crept closer to the bed. I cast a wary look at Emrys before dropping into a crouch and prying open a loose floorboard. I winced as the wood creaked, but Emrys didn't so much as stir. Placing the plank aside, I fished into the supply satchel that was hidden inside and pulled out the piece of fabric that was stained with Sheara's blood. I carefully slid the plank back into place before sneaking back toward the door and closing it gently behind me on my way out.

The Marcaida family crypts were lit with flickering torches, clasped in the hands of the weeping statues that lined the walls. While I traveled through the tunnels, the wind wailed like screaming ghosts, but I couldn't find it in myself to conjure forth any more fear. I came to a stop in front of the tomb of the Corpse King. I studied the dead insects that littered the ground around it and then stared skeptically at the piece of cloth in my hand. It seemed like an awfully flimsy thing to withstand a death curse, but Emrys had said that Sheara's blood was the key needed to get inside. He had begged me that day with tears in his eyes not to open this tomb. I shoved aside the memory and the guilt that that came with it. This was needed for our survival, and he need not ever know.

I placed the gilded cloth over the stone slab and waited. Nothing happened. I didn't even know whether something needed to happen in order to break the curse. I had never broken one before. My hand reached for the tomb only to flinch away at the last second. It seemed unwise to gamble with my life without testing it first. Glancing around the crypt, my eyes landed on a spider that had made a home for itself between the wall and one of the weeping statues. My shadow snatched it from its web and deposited it on top of the cloth. The spider scuttled across it, only to twist and contort as soon as it touched the stone. It dropped dead to the ground, its legs curled up against its shriveled abdomen. The curse hadn't been broken. Maybe it was because the blood was dry and not fresh from the vein, or perhaps there simply wasn't enough of it. Fortunately, the cloth seemed safe enough to use as a shield. I should be fine so long as I didn't touch the stone. Steeling my nerves, I grasped the edge of the slab that was covered beneath the cloth and pushed it open. The rasp of stone echoed through the crypts as the tomb slowly inched open.

The scents of dust and decay wafted out to taint the air. Having been consumed by madness, the Corpse King hadn't been given the honor of an embalming. His body had been left to rot until it was nothing, so that he could never again be called upon by his kin. The skeleton inside had been hacked to pieces, its bones broken and shattered, the infamous necromancer having been butchered at the hands of his own children. That seemed to be the custom in the Marcaida family, favoring a quick and grisly end instead of a rotting existence in a cold cell. If those were my only two options, it would certainly be my preference as well.

There were other items sprinkled between the bones, unpolished family rings and the small skulls of birds. A necklace of teeth rested atop the skeleton's vertebrae. My shadow snuck in through the gap to retrieve the morbid piece of jewelry.

I slid the stone back into place before returning to the interior of the fortress and making my way toward the chapel. When I finally came to a stop in front of Celdric's altar, I could all too easily remember the sight of the reverend's head resting atop it like a sacrifice to a vengeful god. I would not be the next one to find my head separated from my neck, nor would I let my friends fall prey to Celdric's wrath in my stead. If he wanted the talisman, then he was going to have to give me something in return. I placed the threaded teeth atop the altar.

Celdric, I offer you this necklace of teeth, steeped as it is in sorrow and death. I ask that you spare my life and the lives of my friends in return. Accept this and let no harm come to us at your hands.

My request was vague, but sometimes that was the better option, allowing the bargain to cast its net wide rather than allowing a god to pick holes in the details. It was a gamble, but fate had seen fit to favor me thus far. I had faith that she would continue to do so.

I waited, staring at the offering, and when nothing happened, I began to grow nervous. Maybe Celdric was trekking through the shadow domain at this very moment, heading for the gateway that would bring him here so that he wouldn't have to bargain for anything. He could simply take the necklace and bring his wrath down on me anyway. I wasn't about to let him steal the one bargaining tool that I had. I would sooner throw it into the ocean than let him have it without gaining anything in return. I reached for the necklace, but then the shadows in the room shuddered to life and the darkness converged on the offering. When the shadows dissipated, the stone altar was empty. The bargain had been struck.

CHAPTER 41

I tugged on the cuffs of my dark coat. The fabric was heavier than what I was used to wearing, and it was more expensive, too. The edges were embroidered with silver thread, stitched with elegant designs of slithering snakes and blooming flowers. Although the outfit was intended as formal wear, I still managed to find places for my daggers to hide. Hopefully, I would have no use for them. The celebration that was being hosted by the royal palace was one of peace, the armistice between Kalta and Athearia now written in blood and sealed within stone. With Sheara having returned to her pantheon and Brazial having been taken from his, the conflict had come to a quick and decisive end, leaving the continent miraculously intact, and my bargain with Celdric had so far managed to prove worthwhile. He hadn't seen fit to grace me with his presence since.

I knocked on the door before entering Serenity's room, an amused smile curving at my lips when I found her fretting over her appearance in the mirror. I thought she might choose a garment with long sleeves to hide her scar, but her dress had no sleeves whatsoever, just a long piece of fabric that draped over one shoulder. The lilac suited her, the style simple and devoid of any embellishments, but she hardly needed it. She was beautiful just the way she was. She cast a glance over her shoulder at me. "Do you think it's terribly plain?" she asked, sounding worried as she ran her hands down her silhouette.

Walking across the room, I wrapped my arms around her torso and rested my chin on her shoulder as I studied her reflection in the mirror. After a moment of contemplation, I said, "Perhaps it is missing something."

"What?" she asked, her brow furrowing at her appearance.

"This."

I grazed my lips against her neck, and she inhaled sharply. The sound made me consider whether there were better things we could be doing with our time than dancing and feasting.

"And this."

I kissed her again, a little bit higher this time.

"And this."

I nipped playfully at her ear and chuckled when she let out a high-pitched squeal as though she found the sensation ticklish. Taking a step back, I tugged gently on the end of her braid, which lacked its usual flowers. She heaved a sigh, like she already knew what I was about to point out. "I didn't think the flowers would be formal enough for the occasion," she said.

"I had a feeling that this might happen." Digging into my pocket, I produced a small pouch woven from silk. I loosened the strings and tipped out the hairpins. While I hadn't managed to steal much of the dragon's hoard before the mountain claimed it, I had managed to get my hands on enough gold coins to buy two dozen hairpins crafted into the shape of aster flowers with petals made from amethyst. Her eyes widened at the sight of them.

"Oh, Koven, they're beautiful." She reached out to touch them, but then she pulled away, guilt creeping into her expression. "This is too much. I couldn't possibly—"

"You can," I said, pinning them into her braid, and the smile that stretched across her face was worth far more than gold. The voice grumbled at the back of my mind as though in disagreement, but it had already lost that particular argument with me when I was at the jeweler's.

Spinning around, Serenity arched onto her toes and planted a kiss on my cheek. "Thank you, Koven. I love them."

I offered her my arm. She hooked her own through it as I escorted her to the grand hall. The marble floors of the palace were softened by emerald carpets. The suits of armor that decorated the corridors set me on edge, because they looked too much like the ones that Scias used to stock the House of Tribulations, but I reminded myself that I was no longer at the Cenobium. In fact, the church had officially decreed that any student who had survived the harrowing experience on Spire had more than proved their strength and tenacity in the eyes of the gods. I had graduated, and with the help of Sheara's encouragement, the church had no choice but to give me the permission I needed to join any shadow court I wanted. My retainer's relic rested on my hip, its handle made of polished rosewood and its pommel shaped into the head of an eagle.

Music and chatter filtered out from the grand hall, growing even louder as the two of us joined the rest of the guests inside, some of whom had already taken to the dance floor. I stifled a laugh at the sight of Emrys stepping on his partner's toes. For all his strengths, he was a rather dismal dancer, but the young lady he was partnered with pretended not to notice. There were benefits to being born into one of the wealthiest families in the kingdom, yet Emrys didn't seem to care much for gold or romance. As soon as the song came to an end, he gave a quick but courteous bow of his head and made an attempt at a graceful exit. However, another girl was quick to corner him, and with an agonized expression, he allowed himself to be dragged onto the dance floor.

Serenity tightened her grip on my arm. "I've never liked these events much. I had to attend them after my sister announced her betrothal to Grayson Blackwood, but I always clung to the walls, yearning for the time they finally ended."

"We can go if you want," I said, and she blinked up at me as though she'd never thought that was an option.

"And do what?" she asked.

I flashed her a wicked grin. "Oh, I could think of a few things." She swatted a hand against my chest, scolding me for making such a comment in public, but I didn't miss the way her cheeks took on a rosy hue. "I was just thinking that the weather lends itself to a nice relaxing stroll along the coastline," I said innocently.

Her shoulder jostled into mine. "I don't need to be a truth-sayer to know that's *not* what you had in mind."

Servants flitted along the edges of the hall with silver trays bearing a diverse selection of wines and appetizers. Faelan snatched a drink for himself as he mingled with the guests, greeting the ladies and lords of the court with a welcoming smile. As I veered toward him, I caught the end of the wild story he was telling, for Rin Marcaida was not the only one rumored to have returned from the dead. The surviving students from the trials had carried news of the prince's demise back to the mainland. "And here he is!" Faelan declared, clapping me jovially on the shoulder. "Both my executioner and my savior, pulling off a trick worthy of the god of mischief himself."

The guests all turned to stare at me, enraptured by the tale. "And what was the trick with Rin Marcaida?" one of the ladies asked, and the rest of the audience fell silent in anticipation. Faelan and I exchanged a weighted look, neither of us certain on the best way to answer that question.

"If you want a good story, you should hear about the time when Faelan fell in love with his own reflection," I said in an attempt to divert the conversation. It worked. Their eyes sparkled with delight, laughter rippling through them. I ignored the glare that Faelan threw in my direction and gave him an encouraging pat on the back. "But I'm not gifted in the art of storytelling. I shall leave that in the prince's capable hands."

Before Faelan could find a way to spin that story into something a little less humiliating, the hall fell quiet as the king made an appearance. A golden circlet adorned his brow and an emerald cape flowed down his shoulders. His future bride walked beside him. Akira had finally cut the crow feathers from her hair, freeing herself from her grief. I didn't know if that was the reason for the smile on her face, or if it was because she would soon be wed. She already looked like a queen with her hair spun into a crown atop her head, wearing a dress of royal green instead of the black and crimson hues favored by her house. Her eyelashes and lips were painted gold, and when Faelan turned to see what had caught everyone's attention, he looked as though he might take up the custom of weaving crow feathers into his hair, grieving for his heart that had broken without ever having been held.

The minstrels started up a lively tune as Akira and the king took to the dance floor. I offered Serenity my hand, and she allowed me to sweep her into the middle of the hall as well. "It is a rather tempting thought to dip out early," she said, lowering her voice to a whisper. "But we should stay for a few dances and conversations first so our departure isn't construed as being uncouth."

I shifted into position, my one hand taking ahold of hers while my other pressed against her lower back, drawing her closer to me. "And what exactly did you have in mind after we managed to make our escape?" I said, my lips lifting into a teasing smile.

"A nice relaxing stroll along the coastline," she replied ironically. A low chuckle reverberated through my chest as my feet began to move with a practiced ease. After all, dancing was just a gentle reflection of combat. It focused on footwork, timing, and responding to the movements of the person in front of you. This activity just incorporated music instead of bloodshed. I tried to ignore the boredom that slowly crept its way out from the back of my mind. When the feeling only grew stronger, I decided to break away from the pattern of the other dancers. I lifted Serenity into the air, spinning her around before placing her back down on the floor, timing it just right so that we could fall back into rhythm with the rest of the couples. There had to be a granule of prophecy to her name, because as she beamed up at me, a calmness settled over my heart. The war had been stopped, Celdric had accepted the necklace in exchange for his apathy, and with Serenity next to me, the darkness shrank back to the recesses of my mind like the moon giving way to the sun.

As a pair of dancers twirled past me, I caught a glimpse of the woman's earrings. Two teeth dangled from her ears like a prized pair of pearls. She disappeared a heartbeat later, lost amid the revolving couples. My tongue snaked over my smooth gums, rolling between the empty gaps in my mouth where I was missing two of my molars. The peace inside my heart shattered like glass. I stumbled to a halt and Serenity's smile slipped away, her brows knitting together in confusion. My eyes frantically scanned the crowd for Celdric. If the god of mischief was here, then something was about to go horribly wrong.

With my feet rooted in place, the neighboring couple ended up colliding with me. They scowled at me before attempting to fall back into step along with the others on the dance floor. I moved through the line of spinning guests, the chorus of laughter and music overwhelming my ears, fracturing my concentration. Then the fiddles screeched into silence, and the dancers all came to an abrupt halt. Behind me, someone let out a shocked gasp. I pivoted, a dagger in hand, but it was not Celdric I saw. The king had collapsed, his eyes glassy as he stared up at the ceiling. The circlet had fallen from his brow to roll across the floor, wobbling on its rim until it finally toppled over, coming to a stop just in front of my boots.

Akira dropped to her knees next to her betrothed, her face horrified. She tried to shake him awake as though he were merely sleeping. As though this were a nightmare and it would all be over soon. The king did not stir. Tears poured from Akira's eyes, taking the gold paint on her eyelashes with them as they streaked down her cheeks, leaving gilded tracks in their wake. The sight of those golden tears dredged up a memory of Amari, her voice deceptively gentle while she threaded a bloodied piece of string between her fingers.

When fate meets fire and ash falls from the sky like rain. When light binds itself to the dark and the queen of sorrow weeps tears of gold. When the prophecy of old comes to pass and the fallen stars all burn to dust. Only then can the sun rise on the dawn of a new age.

There was a prophecy at play, one that had been woven by none other than the goddess of fate, and fate was cruel just as she was kind.

Serenity rushed over to the king's side, but as she laid her hands upon him, her expression grew mournful. There was no blood or gaping wound to suggest violence, nor any discolored skin or frothing mouth to point toward poison, yet there was no doubt in my heart that this had been a cold-blooded murder.

"Help him!" Akira demanded. "Heal him!"

"I'm sorry," Serenity replied softly. "I don't have the power to bring back the dead."

Akira shook her head, refusing to believe it. She took his face in her hands. "Come back to me," she told him, her voice stern, as though issuing him an order. "You have to come back to me." But she was not her brother. She could not whisper a corpse back to life. Her expression crumpled and she buried her face in his chest while she wept. Dread pooled in the pit of my stomach at the sound of her grief. Although Celdric had promised that he would let us live, he did not promise to let us live in peace. He would be an ever-present shadow on the wall, a wraith of ruin determined to haunt our every waking hour, and if there was something in our lives worth taking, he would make good on his title as the god of thieves.

Emrys shoved his way through the guests that had begun to crowd around the body. He came to a sudden stop when he caught sight of the king on the ground. "This isn't supposed to happen," he muttered, and fear flickered across his features to darken his eyes. It was the same expression he wore when he woke up from a nightmare only to find that the candle on his bedside had gone out and he was still trapped in the dark.

"What do we do?" I asked, but for the first time in his life, he didn't seem to have the answer.

ACKNOWLEDGMENTS

The process of writing and publishing a book is a daunting task! Fortunately, it's not a journey that an author undertakes alone. The simple truth of the matter is that *A Vassal of Shadow* would not have been possible without the support of so many incredible people.

To my family, who always believed in me, even during the times when I didn't believe in myself. To my mother, who is the strongest woman I know. Thank you for giving me the courage to put my work into the world. To my sister, for being an absolute girl-boss (and a functioning adult with a mortgage); your spare bedroom has been much appreciated over the years. Your little sister might be a vagrant, but now she's a vagrant with a published book.

To my friends, who have been an endless source of love and support throughout my writing journey. To Sarah, for teaching me that friendship is the purest form of love; I honestly don't know where I would be without you. Thank you for being my beta reader and encouraging me every step of the way. You are a ray of light in the dark (yes, I know that's cheesy. No, I don't care.) To Michelle, for having the strength to follow your dream and giving me the strength to follow mine in return. You are an inspiration! To Chance and Jason, for being relentless in your support and constant champions of my writing. This story would probably still be hiding in the depths of my hard drive if not for you. Thank you! Thank you! Thank you!

To the team at Podium Entertainment; there is a lot of hard work that goes into turning a manuscript into a finished and polished product; it has been an incredible opportunity to work with you. A special thank you to Brian for your endless patience. You saw the potential of what this story could be and you gave me the time I needed to do it justice.

To my developmental editor, Melissa. You are amazing! The first draft of this book is very different to the final version, and that's in no small part because of you. How you helped me refine this story into something cohesive and compelling is nothing short of mind-blowing. I feel so fortunate to have been given the opportunity to work with you.

Last but certainly not least, I would like to thank each and every person who took the time to read *A Vassal of Shadow.* Publishing this book is a dream come true, and I hope you enjoyed reading the story as much as I enjoyed writing it. I can't thank you enough for your support. It means the world to me. Here's to the next adventure!

ABOUT THE AUTHOR

J. C. Robins loves to read and write fantasy books brimming with magic, adventure, and dangerous quests. When she's not writing, she enjoys traveling to faraway lands in search of her own adventures. From the serene temples of Japan to the untamed wilds of Africa, her journeys fuel her passion for storytelling. Robins currently resides in the UK.